Praise for *Seven*

Penetrating and subtle, *Seven* deftly explores loyalty in changing times, what it means and what you give up to be a part of a community, a marriage, and friendships. Sharifa is a sympathetic everywoman; her relationships fully realized and deeply felt in this immersive, absorbing portrait.

— Eden Robinson, bestselling author of the Trickster trilogy

[*Seven's*] willingness to engage readers with this challenging, important subject matter is invaluable.

— *Booklist*

A brave and beautiful book.

— Judy Rebick, author of *Heroes in My Head*

Family secrets, loyalty, and betrayal lie at the heart of *Seven*. Delving into history can unearth deeper mysteries than one bargained for.

— Zarqa Nawaz, author of *Laughing All The Way to the Mosque*

A defiant and engrossing novel.

— Sarah Schulman, author of *Conflict is Not Abuse*

Doctor weaves sensitivity and hope into a gripping narrative. [*Seven* is] a soulfully-written book about a vexed cultural issue.

— Masooma Ranalvi, founder of WeSpeakOut.org

Praise for *All Inclusive*

An ambitious, thematically voracious novel on love and the wounds we didn't know we had.

— *Globe and Mail*

Her outstanding characterization and the depth of language establish the importance of Farzana Doctor's writing. In her startling and evocative description of the lives of people in the tourist industry, *All Inclusive* is more than just a title.

— Austin Clarke, Giller Prize–winning author of *The Polished Hoe*

Ambitious, original, mysterious, sensual, *All Inclusive* is all that — and a terrific read to boot.

— *Toronto Star*

A rare, somewhat whimsical but vibrantly coloured toucan in a nest of Canadian starlings … *All Inclusive* is not your traditional Can Lit (capital C, capital L), and thank god for it.

— *Plentitude*

All Inclusive is a page turner, and Doctor is a deliciously evocative writer.

— *Literary Review of Canada*

In the worlds that Farzana Doctor creates, ordinary people are wondrous and complicated, and all these things that divide us — countries, professions, sexualities, genders, races — are mere distractions from what truly matters. Her stories ring true enough to think our world could be that way too. One can only hope.

— *Daily Xtra*

By turns funny, moving, thoughtful, and erotic, *All Inclusive* is a powerful meditation on life, love, and loss. Farzana Doctor spins a passionate, page-turning tale about the sometimes invisible ties that bind. This is brilliant storytelling.

— Terry Fallis, author of *The Best Laid Plans*

Farzana Doctor's original, provocative new novel seduces (and challenges) readers on every page. *All Inclusive* is Doctor's best — and sexiest! — work yet.

— Angie Abdou, author of *The Bone Cage*

Doctor must be commended for her ability to render a disembodied "meandering whoosh" sympathetic.

— *Quill & Quire*

Praise for *Six Metres of Pavement*

Ismail Boxwala, an ultimately good man haunted by a horrible mistake, provides the focal point of Doctor's moving second novel in which she examines with crystalline clarity the plight of this gentle, middle-aged Indian immigrant living in Toronto.

— *Publishers Weekly*

The characters are refreshingly genuine … Doctor skillfully plays with concepts of motion, migration, and movement, both physical and emotional.

— *Globe and Mail*

If you're looking for believable characters, look no further than Farzana Doctor's fiction. She has a gift for reality-based situations and conveys anxiety and passion in a story that turns into a real page-turner.

— *NOW*

With a quiet, inward-looking analysis of Ismail's life, *Six Metres of Pavement* asks how mourning can make way for grief when it's cemented by guilt, and if memories can be defanged.

Simmering in the background is a remarkable portrait of immigrant Toronto.

— *This*

Novels don't often spring sudden tears from me. This story did it several times, and never with tawdry tugs at the heartstrings. The book cuts deep, to the core of love, universal need and our responsibility to others.

— *Xtra! Toronto*

It's enough to hope that Doctor would consider a sequel to this tender portrait of strangers finding community in each other. It would be worth the wait.

— *Lambda Literary Review*

I laughed and cried as I read *Six Metres of Pavement* and followed Ismail and Celia — endearing, brave, and foolish characters who have to live with the irreparable and irreversible. Farzana Doctor blends cross-cultural empathy with wisdom, and shows us paths to wholeness. Read this delightful, warm guide to remaking and choosing your family.

— Shauna Singh Baldwin, author of *What the Body Remembers*, *The Tiger Claw*, and *We Are Not in Pakistan*

A sensitively written story about the complexities of human relationships, with the added twist of the immigrant experience. A warmly felt portrait of an unusual but successful remaking of a family.

— *Sudbury Star*

SEVEN

SEVEN

FARZANA DOCTOR

DUNDURN
TORONTO

Publisher: Scott Fraser | Acquiring editor: Kathryn Lane | Editor: Shannon Whibbs
Cover designer: Sophie Paas-Lang
Cover image: istock.com/tunart
Printer: Marquis Book Printing Inc.

Library and Archives Canada Cataloguing in Publication

Title: Seven / Farzana Doctor.
Names: Doctor, Farzana, author.
Identifiers: Canadiana (print) 20190204478 | Canadiana (ebook) 20190204486 | ISBN 9781459746398 (softcover) | ISBN 9781459746404 (PDF) | ISBN 9781459746411 (EPUB)
Classification: LCC PS8607.O35 S48 2020 | DDC C813/.6—dc23

We acknowledge the support of the Canada Council for the Arts and the Ontario Arts Council for our publishing program. We also acknowledge the financial support of the Government of Ontario, through the Ontario Book Publishing Tax Credit and Ontario Creates, and the Government of Canada.

Care has been taken to trace the ownership of copyright material used in this book. The author and the publisher welcome any information enabling them to rectify any references or credits in subsequent editions.

The publisher is not responsible for websites or their content unless they are owned by the publisher.

Printed and bound in Canada.

VISIT US AT

 dundurn.com | @dundurnpress |  dundurnpress | dundurnpress

Dundurn
3 Church Street, Suite 500
Toronto, Ontario, Canada
M5E 1M2

For Nani

~ ONE ~

April 2016, Mumbai

I take a cautious sip. Tasnim Maasi pours half her cup into her saucer and sucks the tea down in one long, loud slurp. She pulls up her orna, which slid from her oiled hair to her shoulders, tucking the gauzy fabric around an ear to keep it in place.

It is going to happen today; this afternoon. Maasi's life is going to change irrevocably. Will she think that her favourite niece has turned traitor?

I cannot stop this moving train. What good will it do to announce the crash? After all, Maasi can't get off at the next stop. Instead I sit on the edge of my beloved aunt's couch, scalding tea burning my tongue.

Maasi appraises my full cup, raises her right eyebrow. I shake my head.

"Still too hot."

"You should do it like me." Her lips upturn into a mischievous smile as she empties the rest of her tea into her saucer, and a wisp of cardamom steam rises in front of her face. With a slight tremor, she lifts the saucer to her lips. "See?" she says proudly, as though chai drinking is a competition. She doesn't spill a single drop.

"All right." I tip my teacup to my saucer and chai dribbles onto her glass-topped coffee table. I pat the spill with a tissue. "Sorry."

"Anything wrong, Sharifa? You are quiet today."

I meet her gaze. Her eyes are a chestnut brown, and shinier than they used to be. These are my eyes, too, and the eyes of my mother, my cousin-sisters, and our daughters.

"Haa, Maasi. I'm sorry. I'm very sorry. There's something I need to tell you."

The doorbell tangs and, the coward I am, I am relieved. I inhale courage and wishfully think that I can be loyal to Maasi and my mother, my cousin-sisters, and our daughters all at the same time.

Later, when I share my day with my husband, Murtuza, he will ask me, "And what about you? What's being loyal to you?" I will not know the answer, won't even be able to make sense of the question.

Maasi rises, but I gesture for her to stay seated. Instead, I stand to unlatch the door.

August 2015, New York City

While I scan the sale racks, Zee bumps around the nearby plus-size section yelling, "Mom — this one!" every minute or so. I suppose little kids think all ladies' sizes are the same. I yell back, "Thanks, but no!" The two of us are probably driving the saleswoman crazy with our bellowing.

I show her a polka-dotted dress with cap sleeves, the sort of thing I might have worn in the classroom on a hot September day. Its asymmetrical hem is whimsical, yet age-appropriate. Most years, I've done this shopping while in countdown-to-Labour-Day mode, both anticipating and dreading my return to work at Morrison High School. But I gave my resignation two weeks ago, and the year stretches ahead like a flat and deserted highway.

Last year, when Murtuza and I first considered spending his academic sabbatical in India, I applied for a much-needed unpaid leave while he investigated Mumbai teaching gigs. The same week my request was declined, he received an opportunity to teach the graduate course he's been designing in his mind for years. Lenore, my vice-principal and mentor, suggested I quit, recover from my burnout, and work for her educational consulting business after Murtuza's sabbatical. So here we are — Zee and I — searching for a dress I can take on our trip to India.

"Pretty," Zee assesses, pushing a strand of her short hair behind her ear. Recently she's begun to have opinions about the clothing I set out for her each day. Last week she rejected half of my choices, so today I've encouraged her to make her own selections. She's wearing a yellow top with an emerald skirt and aquamarine socks, which doesn't look as bad as it sounds. Me, I've matched my beige blouse to a pair of brown shorts. My sandals are a shade in between.

I try on the dress, Zee's appraising eyes upon me. She cocks her head, her bangs falling into her face. "Mom, it fits, it looks good. But buy it in red, *not black*." Her tone is slightly mocking, like a makeover show host's. The sales clerk rushes to fetch one, taking orders from a girl just turned seven.

Later, on our way to the food court to share an order of Wong's lemon chicken, Zee stops me at Forever 21. I protest but change my mind when I notice one of my students, Farah, behind the register. She just graduated, and used to walk the hallways like a fashion model. A few months ago, Principal Pereira stopped to scold her for showing too much cleavage. I'd disagreed with the judgment but couldn't contradict Pereira. Farah reached into her backpack to layer a sweater over her blouse, but it was off again by the time she reached my classroom.

"Mom, look at these!" Zee points out a ten-dollar rack of frilly skirts. "Can I get one? You can get one, too, and we can match!" I call Farah over and she helps us find a size zero that fits loosely over Zee's straight hips. Not even their largest size, a fourteen, can pass over mine.

"I just bought a size twelve dress at JC Penney," I complain.

"Yeah, our sizes are super small. Sorry." Farah shrugs.

4

"You can still get yours, Zee. It's a good price."

"No," she pouts, "not if you can't wear a matching one."

"We'll look for something while we're in India," I console, glad that my daughter still wants to look like me, at least sometimes.

In the evening, Murtuza and I meet on the couch for the married person's evening ritual: TV. Along with a nightly bowl of microwave popcorn, we've been putting away two episodes of *The Mindy Project* after Zee is in bed. We guffaw and cringe in the same places; we are diasporic South Asian children of immigrants communing over the embarrassing life of a diasporic South Asian child of immigrants.

While the credits roll, Murtuza leans over, kisses my neck, and says, "Shall we turn it off now, or watch another episode?"

"Sure, Murti, we can turn it off," I say, sensing his preference. After all, it is Saturday and 9:00 p.m. I'd prefer to hit play, to be distracted by someone else's awkward world, but I appreciate my husband's good-natured and consistent initiative-taking. My friends and I talk about our lacklustre sex lives and waning libidos, and I feel like I'm the lucky one amongst us. At least we can say we are still doing it, rather than being in couples' therapy because we aren't. Or breaking up because we aren't. Or having extra-marital affairs because we aren't.

I'd never cheated in my life, neither on a test nor a time sheet. When my naturopath directed me to eliminate sugar, dairy, wheat, and caffeine last year to improve my immune system's functioning, I followed her instructions, to the letter, for sixty days.

How to make sense of the affair, then? It was just over four years ago, when Zee was three. Ian, a guy I once slept with, friend-requested me on Facebook. I recall experiencing a twinge of something, a flutter in my belly I could have interpreted as a prescient warning. I brushed away the sensation and thought, *Nah, it's just Facebook, and it's been ages since we last saw each other.* Plus, I'd heard from a friend in common that he'd moved to England. I thought we'd share a few likes, perhaps a little lurking. No problem.

At the time, I couldn't admit to myself that it was cheating. There were no secret liaisons in two-and-half-star motels we'd paid for in cash. No late-night phone calls. No sexy photos. Leave it to me to have an affair without ever really having an affair.

I layered on a thick foundation of denial until Murtuza found out. On a cool autumn evening, I returned home from Fresh Food Mart, lugging two heavy totes. When I saw his pained expression, I dropped the groceries, my fingers refusing to pretend that things were normal. Oranges rolled across the floor and I scrambled to collect them, glad for the small diversion of runaway citrus.

I'd left my computer on, my account open. Normally he wouldn't have used my laptop, but he'd forgotten his at his office and needed to order a book online. That's what he told me, anyway. I hope it was nothing more than that. I heard somewhere that eighty percent of betrayed spouses know when something is amiss and ambivalently search for evidence to the contrary. I don't like to think about Murtuza being a part of that statistical majority.

A part of me was self-righteous and indignant about the breach of privacy ("What were you doing snooping around on my Facebook account, anyway?"), but that fell flat when he looked at me beseechingly. "Why?" he asked, tears streaming down his cheeks. I wanted to dry his tears before they dripped off his chin onto the floor.

I sputtered a denial, "Nothing happened!"

He picked up my laptop and read aloud the latest message I'd sent to Ian. I went silent, and Murtuza continued reading, his voice growing louder, my indiscreet sentences to Ian booming and echoing off the kitchen tiles. I still said nothing, couldn't form words, imagined Murtuza leaving me, our marriage ending over something so stupid. I felt like a failure, to both my husband and daughter.

He stomped down to the basement, and I crept upstairs to check on three-year-old Zee, who was fast asleep despite all the yelling. I watched her breathe and wept for the end of my good life. Then I headed to the kitchen, unfriended Ian, and turned off the laptop. I considered padding down the stairs to talk to Murtuza, but I knew it would be pointless. His questions and thoughts and feelings would swarm around me like angry wasps and I'd be unable to do anything but bat them away.

Murtuza slept on the basement pullout for three days. Each time he emerged to look after Zee or make himself a snack, I attempted impromptu explanations, wishing I was more articulate, had rehearsed a few repentant lines. I've never been good at communicating my feelings when overwhelmed. He moved back to our bedroom but wouldn't talk to or touch me for another three days, despite my pleas and cajoling. Then, at last, on the seventh day, he threatened to end the marriage unless we saw a professional. He quoted facts and figures about infidelity and the importance of seeking immediate help. It was probably Murtuza who told me the statistic about cheated-on partners looking for clues.

Dr. Stanley met us together for the first session, during which Murtuza did most of the talking. I scanned the spacious office, which was mostly outfitted with Ikea furniture. Between nodding at Murtuza's statements of why we were there, I mentally listed:

Malm, Hemnes, Ektorp, Flöng, some of the items that fill our home. For years after we bought our bed, we referred to it as our Brimnes, our private joke. When had we stopped doing that?

During the following week's one-on-one session that she called an "assessment," Dr. Stanley wore her steel-grey hair in a single braid down her back, instead of loose, as she'd done during the couples' session. She recommended that I break off contact with Ian, and I pouted and told her I'd already completed that act of contrition. She might have misinterpreted my stiff embarrassment as lack of guilt because she leaned forward in her seat and spoke loudly, perhaps thinking that her increased volume would help me comprehend the gravity of my situation. She insisted that I commit to owning the cheating, and I imagined it was like an expensive, later regretted, purchase. I understood what she was getting at but couldn't help protesting, "But I didn't even kiss him! I didn't get to do anything! Nothing actually happened between us during those two months of messaging each other!" I was like a snot-nosed kid who'd been caught before tasting a shoplifted candy bar.

"Do you wish you had?" She puckered her lips and nodded, perhaps in an effort to look sympathetic. Had she ever cheated on the bald guy in the portrait on her desk? Maybe she understood my longing?

"Yes and no. I never wanted to hurt Murtuza." I didn't meet her gaze and instead focused on the hypnotic blue lines winding their way through her area rug. I wondered what its Ikea name might be. Then my hour was up.

Murtuza had his own individual session that week. I asked him how it went and he said, "Fine. You?" I said my session went fine, too.

A week later, Dr. Stanley began our session with a monologue mostly addressed to my side of the room. She suggested that I was seeking something lost, something left behind that wasn't literally Ian, but a part of myself that I'd once expressed with Ian. I didn't know what she was talking about, but my eyes welled up in response.

Murtuza took my hand, and his own eyes moistened, his black lashes made even prettier by his tears. I hated myself for hurting this man with pretty eyelashes. I hated myself for almost sabotaging my marriage to this man with pretty eyelashes.

"Shari, you were younger when you and he ... first met. You were childless, free. Now you have no time for yourself. You go to work, deal with teenagers all day, then come home and take care of a toddler, and after that you have to spend your evenings marking horrible essays. You don't see your friends like I do, even though I suggest it." He turned to Dr. Stanley and repeated, "I suggest it all the time. She never listens."

Then he exhaled, and as though remembering that he was trying to be patient, turned back to me. "You don't get away to conferences like I do. Maybe that's the part you've lost. Time for yourself."

The therapist nodded, crossed one slender pantsuited leg over the other. "You're on the right track, Murtuza. Sharifa, how do you feel about what Murtuza has just said?" My thoughts swirled too quickly in my head; it was too much for me to be on the spot like that. I nodded in agreement so that Murtuza wouldn't think I was being obstructive.

The next evening, Murtuza brought home a wall calendar and we began marking off slots with a green dry-erase pen. I signed up for a weekly hot yoga class. I had drinks with friends a couple of times a month. We instituted a Friday date night and asked my parents to babysit. I did feel better, I had to admit; the stresses of work and mommying a three-year-old mellowed.

A few months later, during our final session, Murtuza referred to the affair as my "tipple with infidelity," like it had been a delicate sip of sherry instead of the three hundred and forty-one messages he'd read over two desolate hours. I still don't know if he was being sarcastic, the way he is sometimes. I hope he was attempting gentleness, the beginning of forgiveness.

I wasn't tempted to chat with Ian anymore, but every so often I did miss our nightly correspondence, those messages tinged with innuendo, with the "what are you wearing?" and "I loved kissing you" and the "do you remember when we …" The little bit of cyber-naughty.

When I blocked him the night Murtuza discovered us, I didn't know that what I'd yearn for most was just that, the small exciting moment at the end of my day.

After ten minutes of teeth-brushing, flossing, and changing into my least boring nightie — the black cotton knee-length with the lace neckline, definitely not bought at Forever 21 — we are in bed.

"How are you?" he asks, his usual way of starting.

"Fine." I smile nervously, wondering if I am the least bit alluring. After nine years of marriage, I still don't have any moves. What if I were to say, "I'm on fire for you!" or the opposite: "I have a headache"?

He kisses me, the peppermint on his breath reminding me that our dentist appointments are next week.

His hands rove over my back and then under my nightdress. I copy his movements, feeling for the waistband of his boxers and the fine hairs on his slim buttocks. He rolls on top of me, sucks each of my breasts, always the left, next the right. I like it when he does that, and I breathe deeply, getting caught up in the moment. His mouth travels over my belly and lingers a few moments lower down. I think about the bottle of lube I recently bought and that I haven't yet overcome my shyness to tell Murtuza about.

"Ready?" he asks, cupping my right breast.

"Okay," I reply.

I try to relax. My friend Anita showed me her copy of a self-help book called *Mating in Captivity*, and I imagine that Murtuza and I are a pair of orangutans at the zoo. Then I feel weird for getting aroused by imagining we are orangutans at the zoo.

After a few minutes, Murtuza grunts and rolls off me, panting.

"Want to try the toy?" He purchased the vibrator years ago. He'd read an article about how, after having a baby, it was good to spice things up in the bedroom. We've tried it a few times, and while the sensation is pleasant, it is uncomfortable to have Murtuza apply the device to my vulva and wait expectantly for me to climax.

"No, I'm satisfied. That was good, Murti." I peck him on the cheek and get up to use the bathroom. When I return to bed, he lifts the covers and wraps his arms around me.

Early on, when Murtuza sporadically asked about my lack of orgasms, I reassured him that it was because we were still new. Then I said it was because I was pregnant, and then because I was a sleep-deprived new parent. And then he went out and brought home the vibrator and I finally admitted that I'd never had an orgasm, ever, not with anyone. This revelation soothed him somewhat, the problem clearly not about him but me. He's never said so, but I suspect that he's had much wilder sex with all the women he was with before me.

In my twenties, I read books about it. Attempted various positions. Insisted on oral sex. Spent a hundred dollars on toys. Now, I find it easier to accept things as they are, rather than perseverating on an unfixable problem. I can enjoy sex for what it is instead of looking for what's missing.

11

After my confession, he encouraged me to try again. "You're in your thirties now. Maybe it'll be different." Over the next couple of years I went along with his experiments: new books, new positions, new toys. I held a thin, golden thread of hope that maybe he was right and things could change.

Each effort was embarrassing, and the more we tried, the less I enjoyed myself, my bits the subject of his prodding and probing. "Look, I like it best when we do the regular stuff," I insisted.

And so here we are, post-coitus, sleepy. The sex was fine, and he is always considerate to check if I want more, and I always say no, happy enough to curl up with him afterward. I sniff his sweat, a mix of his deodorant and something else warm and musky, and fall asleep.

~) THREE (~

I'm on my way to meet Mom for a stroll through East River Park. After selling our Edison, New Jersey, house, and buying a Murray Hill condo last year, she's wanted to explore the city and go on excursions with me.

The bus is packed, its passengers a study of mobility and dislocation. If I could get everyone's attention, the way I used to do in my classroom, having to yell twice before they'd stop and listen, I'd do a hands-up exercise: put your hand up if you speak a language other than English at home? If you were born outside of the U.S.? If you are Muslim? Jewish? Hindu? Buddhist? Druze? A brown lady in a bright blue hijab sits in front of me, fanning herself with her *Vogue* magazine. An African American youth beside me slumps over his phone, his fingers typing furiously. He giggles, perhaps in response to a joke, and then glances self-consciously at me. I smile at him and turn my attention to the middle-aged white woman across the aisle surrounded by half a dozen plastic grocery bags. On this late August day, I smell sweat, floral dryer sheets, coconut oil, curry, and pizza.

Who are all these people? I never tire of this exercise.

I did attempt the hands-up activity in my classroom at the beginning of last year, during an introduction to the history of immigration.

"Isn't it amazing?" I asked them.

"So what, miss?" Maria, from El Salvador, queried. The rest stared back at me with trademark teenager demeanours: a combination of blank and sullen.

I told them it wasn't like this when my family arrived over thirty-five years ago. Toby, whose family originated from Ireland, screwed up his face and shot me a look that said, *Wow, you're old.*

While diversity is not exactly celebrated, things have changed. When we immigrated, we had to assimilate but just the right amount — my parents didn't want me to become too Western. I wasn't ever sure where the balance point was on that see-saw, but I followed their lead the best I could. We attended the masjid a few times a year. I figure-skated and snuck smokes and beers with my friends. I wore shalvaar kameez to social functions on the weekend and jeans to school.

I'm glad Zee has the opportunity to grow up with the kind of mix on this bus. Perhaps she won't wonder where she belongs (the U.S.? India? Nowhere?), the way I did, and sometimes still do.

I know that the upcoming trip to India will be complicated, as travelling to the "homeland" has always been. I'll breathe it in and cough it out. I'll feel grounded just in time to come home and be disoriented. It's not culture shock as people typically understand it, but its reverse: when I return to the States, the place I've lived almost my entire life, India will have made me a foreigner again. It will remind me of my outsider status, disrupt the forgetting, wake me up to the fact that the balancing act does require effort. For a time, I will be as self-conscious as the teenager beside me, trying to remember how to be invisible as I venture through the city.

——————◆——————

Mom meets me at the door in lavender and teal spandex. While she fills a water bottle, I wander into her solarium and peek at a watercolour-in-progess.

"Hey, this is good, Mom! You've really captured the sunset."

"Oh, it's just my homework for class this week." She pushes off the compliment.

She and Dad retired a few years back, both from high-level banking jobs, but it wasn't until after he died that she learned how to enjoy her non-working time. Before that, the two of them were aimless in retirement. They planned cruises and safaris but didn't take them. They puttered around their expansive home, cleaning and making small repairs. Twice a week they dropped off large plastic containers of the food Mom cooked but they couldn't consume. And then Dad collapsed while he was out in the garden, and she was in the shower. His heart stopped long before she could phone 911.

I drove to the house that day, missing the highway exit on the way there. I pulled open the screen door, half-surprised to not find Dad sitting at his spot at the kitchen table. A numb shock got us through the first few days.

A week after the funeral, she lamented, "I should have known."

"What do you mean?"

She palmed her face and sobbed. I put my hand on her shoulder, wishing I could contain the shudders moving through her. "His father died of cardiac arrest when he was in his late sixties. I should have forced him to go on that Alaska cruise we'd always meant to take. He'd say 'later.' Or 'soon.' I should have known there wasn't going to be much more time."

A month after that, she listed the Edison house and bought her East 38th Street condo.

Our stroll is turning into a power walk along the river. I pause, realizing I've been whinging about my upcoming trip for much of it.

"I guess this is a first world problem," I mutter proactively. My mother recently learned the phrase at the food bank where she volunteers and now peppers our conversations with it.

"Well, yes, sure. But I can see why you're nervous to go away for eight months! I would find it difficult to be in India for that long. Short visits — three to four weeks — are nice, but I've always been happy to get home. Back to my routines."

Mom, Dad, and I would travel every three years, for three weeks, our visits from mid-December to the first week of January. We were so regular that relatives could plan weddings around our vacations. My paternal grandfather died the day after Christmas the year I turned thirteen, and my cousins later joked that he'd scheduled his heart attack and subsequent demise so we could attend the burial.

"Yeah." I use the bottom of my T-shirt to wipe my brow. I'm winded, but my retiree mother looks fine.

"The only time we went longer was that first trip back, when you were small. We were there all of July and then you stayed in August. Remember? The weather was horrible! So we switched to winter visits after that."

"I do remember how hot it was! Didn't I get sick a lot that trip?" My skin prickles with the memory. I pause under an elm's canopy to cool myself.

"Yes, I think so." She gazes up at the green leaves above us. "But not at the beginning. I think you got a stomach bug toward the end of the trip, after we left."

I nod, the recollection seeming true, yet I don't really remember. I resume our walk, this time at a slower pace.

"Well, the university has been gracious to let Murtuza teach his course off their usual schedule — starting in September instead of July."

"They know non-locals can't cope with monsoons. The locals barely can manage it." She grimaces, perhaps remembering when she was one.

"You never want to live there again?" When I was a child, she and Dad had occasionally talked of retiring in India.

"Never. What would I do there?" She gestures at the river, as though to say, *I have all this*. I don't know what she means but sense not to ask.

"I'm going to be bored, aren't I?" When I first began planning the trip, it seemed a perfect transition from teaching to my consulting. However, I've grown accustomed to a manic eight-to-three-thirty schedule, followed by three hours of marking after dinner, ten months each year, for the past dozen years. Now that I've rested for six weeks and know I never have to go back, I wonder how I'll deal with eight months of downtime.

"You do like to be busy." She shoots me a knowing look. "Perhaps you can start the consulting work early, from Mumbai? It will give you some income while you're away, no?"

"We're all right financially." I remind her that we used my part of Dad's inheritance to pay down the mortgage, and she nods, looks away. I change the subject. "And Lenore says she won't need me for her new gig until April. It's a contract to review the state's home-schooling policies. For now, she just wants me to get familiar with them, which I've had to do, anyway, because I'll be homeschooling Zee in India."

"Won't that fill your days, then?"

"Sort of. From what I've read, it's much less effort with one child than a classroom. I'll give her projects and assignments, and supervise her through them."

"Well, what about you? Why not have your own project? Your MA was in history. You used to love research. I always wondered why you didn't do a PhD instead of becoming a teacher. Remember that thesis you wrote?" She's referring to my study of nineteenth-century Indian immigration to North America.

"Uh-huh." I bristle at her elitism. We'd argued when I'd applied to teacher's college. *You'll have so much more money and status as a professor*, she'd insisted.

"What I mean is that you could create your own research study while you are there." She backpedals, "You've always been curious about family history, no? Why not record it? I doubt anyone has."

Her suggestion gives me pause. I once considered doing an oral history with my grandparents, but I abandoned the idea after they passed.

"That could be a possibility." The idea makes my heart beat faster, and I realize that I'm two steps ahead of my mother. I slow my stride.

"And you know we have a patriarch — my father's grandfather, my great-grandfather." She looks at the cloudless sky, calculating, "Your great-great-grandfather. What was his name? Everyone talks about his legacy, how he went from poverty to creating charities and an educational fund for future generations. I applied to it for a loan for my education."

"Really?"

"Yes! His name was Abdoolally, I think. Self-taught man, didn't go to school. Had four wives."

"At the same time? A polygamist?"

"No!" She slaps my arm. "I think each one died and then he remarried as a widower. I'm not sure, but I think there was a rumour that he might have divorced one of them, too, which would have been highly unusual for his time. Ask your Tasnim Maasi. And your father's uncle, Abbas Kaaka, has begun keeping a family tree. Your dad's side is also somehow related to Abdoolally."

"Everyone in our family is somehow related to one another." I laugh and she does, too. My parents are second cousins. Murtuza and I figured out that we are fourth cousins, twice removed.

We pause to look out over the water, then backtrack. We are too breathless and hot for conversation, but my mind is moving lightning-quick as I plan the first few steps of my research project.

～ FOUR ～

January 1866, South Bombay

Eleven-year old Abdoolally huddled under the yellow glow of a streetlamp, his index finger pacing his laboured reading.

"The lion … lives … in the … jungle," he whispered. "His … ro … roar is … loud."

An elderly fruit-seller trudged by with an empty wooden cart pulled by a weary bullock. Just in time, Abdoolally wrapped his legs around the post to avoid a heavy hoof landing on his toe. A fly, one of the bullock's many winged passengers, hopped onto his hand and then onto the Hindi primary reader he had "borrowed" from Sunil, the nine-year-old boy of the family for whom he worked. He told his mother it was gift. Did she believe the lie?

Thinking of her, it seemed, could summon her. He looked up and saw her face framed in the window of the third-floor room they shared with another widow and her three young children. She fanned herself with her orna; despite the evening's cool, the day's heat lingered in the room. He waved to her and pleaded, "Five more minutes, Mummy."

She nodded, her lips a straight line, but he knew she was proud of him, knew they had left the village for a better life, and for now, their better life was just this, this one nicked book about a lion in a jungle that he struggled, word by word, to understand.

↶ FIVE ↷

I startle awake. Murtuza snores lightly beside me, his fist tucked under his chin.

I shut my eyes, retrieve and re-enter the strange dream I'd been inhabiting: I'm showing my cousin Fatema my bedroom closet in the old Edison house. It has a hidden door that opens to a passageway I've never had the courage to explore. But with Fatema there, I feel brave.

Before we can even approach the closet, we must clear a dozen heavy boxes that stand like cardboard sentinels before the main door. Then, after opening it, we need to yank away a forest of hangers that block the back of the closet and its concealed door. Each time we remove a hanger, another sprouts in its place, clothing magically reproducing. I grow tired and hopeless.

Fatema, in her bossy manner, nudges me out of the way and works at twice my pace until finally we can see the back of the closet. Without any hesitation, she swings open the secret door and crouches down to look inside.

"Do you want to go through first? Or should I?" I can't decide. She releases a long, frustrated sigh, her breath like a gust of wind clearing my mind.

I step forward.

I awake, shivering, my chest slick with sweat.

Murtuza stirs, roused by my distress. He reaches out an arm, its deadweight landing like a log across my bladder.

"You okay?" he slurs.

"Yes, just had a dream." I turn over and reverse into him, making myself the little spoon. He rests his cheekbone on my shoulder blade and exhales cool air onto my drying skin. I shift away so that our bony parts no longer meet and he cushions my spine with his cheek.

We match our breathing. I return to my childhood bedroom with its baby blue drapes and bedspread.

"You go first," I say to Fatema with certainty this time. She crawls into the hole. I watch the pink soles of her feet disappear, but I don't follow her.

"You coming?" she calls, in a voice that already sounds faraway.

--------------◆--------------

A gentle amber glow permeates the drapes, the first blush of morning. The clock tells me that two hours have passed since I drowsed off. Six twenty-four seems a reasonable time to surrender to wakefulness. I swing my legs out of bed and plod to the kitchen to put the coffee on.

At 7:30 a.m., or 5:00 p.m. Mumbai time, I send a message to my cousin Zainab, requesting her to help her mother, my Tasnim Maasi, turn on Skype. Maasi has lived alone since her husband passed a few years ago. Zainab and her husband were lucky to purchase a flat across the road from her soon after their marriage, an arrangement that benefited my cousin when her two kids were young. Lately, Maasi is the one who needs looking in on — not that she requires much — she is still active and has a servant to clean up, do laundry, and chop vegetables for her dinner.

I wonder if it's strange for my seventy-three-year-old aunt to be speaking to her niece halfway across the world via Skype. When I was a child, the land lines in India were notoriously unreliable, and long-distance calls expensive. When Maasi and Mom were children, most people didn't own telephones.

On good days, our irregular Skype calls morph into a group party with six or eight people gathered around our two computers, depending on who is home. After the first five minutes of fiddling with volume and acclimatizing to the oddness of seeing our own images in the left-hand box, it begins to feel almost normal to communicate this way, as though we are chatting across a wide coffee table rather than an ocean.

Zainab must be at work, because Nafeesa, her sixteen-year-old daughter, has been dispatched, and by 8:40 a.m., Maasi dials me.

"Nani, press this when you are finished," Nafeesa instructs her grandmother in Gujarati. Nafeesa looks ready for a party, her long lashes blacked with mascara, her mouth painted pink. She must have had to argue long and hard with her conservative parents to appear this glam.

"I know how to work it," Maasi grumps at Nafeesa. "I'm an old lady, but I know which button to press." Nafeesa apologizes, kisses her grandmother's cheek, then says a quick hello and goodbye to me before disappearing.

Maasi's English fluency developed after years of speaking to the gora tourists who frequented their Colaba clothing shop, which Zainab and her husband now manage.

My Gujarati comprehension is serviceable, but speaking full, grammatically correct sentences is a struggle. Like a child, I am perpetually in the present tense. We shift back and forth between languages. Maasi, and most of my Mumbai relatives, can do this with Hindi and Marathi, too.

"Sharifa, how are you?" Tasnim Maasi looks at me over her bifocals.

"Majama chun," I reply. She follows my lead and switches over.

"I'm looking forward to you coming. Soon, no? You've given Zainab all your details?"

"Haa. Us, too, can't wait." I make a mental note to look up "can't wait" in Gujarati. I give her updates about Murtuza and Zee, who have just left for the library and camp. She asks about our turtle, Tartala, whom she's never met in person but always inquires after. I move the laptop to his aquarium and she gushes when he pokes his leathery head out of his shell and stretches toward the screen. She marvels at how much he's grown since they last digitally visited. Tartala, as if in reply, wags his head left and right and then turns his tail toward the screen.

I feel her studying me as she adjusts her glasses again. Can she tell that I slept poorly last night?

"What would you like me to bring you from here?"

"We need nothing. Don't weigh down your luggage." Although Mumbaikers can purchase anything, and at a better price, it is still my habit to ask. Until I was a young adult, my family would fill an entire locked suitcase with chocolate, cosmetics, and Jell-O. I tell her about Mom's idea for an Indian research project, and she wobbles her head, like Tartala did, in affirmation.

"Has anyone done research into the family ancestry?" I continue. "On Abdoolally?" I ready my pen for any facts she might share.

"Oh, Abdoolally Rangwala." She smiles. "A great man. That would be very good research to do. I'll introduce you to people who work for his trust, but no, I don't think anyone is recording his life story." The businesswoman Maasi was, I know she'll complete some groundwork for me the next time she is out socializing.

"You know he willed most of his money to start charities for pregnant women and orphans? It was because every one of his wives died in childbirth." I scribble her words into my notebook.

"Mom thought he might have divorced one of them."

"No, no. She is mistaken, I think. I was told he was widowed three times."

Near the end of our call, there is a knock at Maasi's door and my cousin Zainab's face fills the screen. She came straight from work; she's still wearing her rida, a fancy one. It's our community's trademark hooded dress, a garment worn by devout women when out in public. I wear it begrudgingly and only at religious gatherings where it's mandatory.

"Like it?" She steps back from the computer to model. It's white with pink sparkly flowers dotted across the hem.

"Are those sequins?" I squint at the screen.

"A little flashy, no, Zainab?" Maasi mutters, but Zainab ignores the comment.

"Yeah!" She holds up a flower to the camera. "I got it for free, only — as a sample — from a wholesaler who wants us to carry some at the shop. I don't think we will, we mostly get tourists who want T-shirts and cheap skirts. But maybe we'll string him along for a bit so I can get a few more!" We all laugh at the joke. Her mother tells her about my history project.

"You should send out a questionnaire to the family," Zainab advises. "That way you can get some information in the next two weeks, before touching down here."

"Good idea." I write it in my notebook.

"I have to go and do namaaz," Maasi says, consulting her watch, confirming that it is prayer time. "I'll see who I can find who'll help you, Sharifa." We say goodbye and Zainab takes her chair in front of the computer.

"Have you heard of Survey Ape?" I smile at my cousin's mistake but don't correct her. Gratefulness wells up in me; I've always been able to trust in my resourceful family, and I'm certain this will be true for my sabbatical project.

Zee and I join Laura and Elena for a playdate at the park. Laura
and I found each other here five years ago, and while our then
two-year-old daughters tentatively navigated the sandbox, we
slipped into easy banter. She's a mompreneur who sells custom
T-shirts on Etsy and blogs about parenting. A year after we met,
she shifted her writing to marital communication, later separation, and after that, divorce and shared-custody arrangements.

This week's column is about dating as a single mom. She's
gone out with four men since her divorce a year back and tells me
about the latest.

"Research," she says, with mock nonchalance.

"Pretty good job you've got!" I quip.

We watch Zee and Elena on the swings, pumping their legs
to go higher. Six months ago, they would have been begging us to
push them, but now they boast self-reliance. I sigh with gladness
and disappointment. *One day, she won't need me at all*, I think.

"This guy I'm dating is really good, Shari."

"Good, how?"

Zee laughs when her swing hits its highest point. Her bottom briefly lifts an inch off the seat before the swing comes back down.

"Well, for one thing, he *lasts* a long time." She grins and waggles her eyebrows at me.

"Lasts?" I ask, distracted by Zee's high flying. She and Elena cackle, pump harder, then cackle some more. "Zee! Not so high!"

"Well, you know. In bed?" Laura rolls her eyes at my obtuseness.

"Really?"

"Minimum thirty minutes. Long enough for me to … you know … a few times." She looks away, breaking eye contact, and focuses on the kids. As though noticing them for the first time, she shouts, "Elena, take it easy. You guys are being unsafe!"

Zee and Elena let their legs go slack, and their swings begin to slow. I ponder Laura's words but can't think of a good follow-up question. Instead I say, "Wow, that's great. What's he like otherwise? Is he relationship material?"

"Look, they actually listened to us, for once," Laura gripes about the kids, but I know she's considering my question. She lists a few common interests and the things that annoy her.

While I half-listen, a question bubbles up: is my problem about *lasting*? If Murtuza could last even fifteen minutes, or half an hour, would it happen for me? I reflect on my earlier boyfriends, all of whom were energetic, youthful. They'd all tried. And just like Murtuza, there was that flicker of disappointment when they eventually gave up. Afterward, I'd have to try to be cheery and satisfied. I'd read somewhere that something like fifteen percent of women don't climax, and so I'd reassure them brightly, keeping my face open, unguileful: "Really, I get a contact high from you. All the feel-good chemicals you have, the endorphins, they come my way, just because I'm close to you." I so badly wanted to be okay with living in a society where one hundred percent believe in an end goal that fifteen percent of us don't experience.

Each partner grew progressively distant over time. In my head, I know they were poor matches, not meant to be, but my heart has always wondered if the sex had anything to do their serial demises. Did it weaken their confidence in our connection? Could it happen with Murtuza?

Laura is now talking about a different guy, someone new she hopes to see next week. I struggle to keep up. "What's his name?"

"Matthew. I found him on OkCupid. I'd like to see what it's like to date more than one person at a time. I've always been such a monogamist in the past."

I nod, asking myself, *In another life, would I want what Laura has?* Multiple orgasms and the thrill of novelty? My phone beeps; Murtuza has texted me three pink hearts.

"It sounds fun. Very different from the ordinariness of marriage."

"Yeah, it's good for now. I'm not ready for anything too committed. To tell you the truth, I don't know if I'll ever be ready again."

"One, two, three, go!" Zee and Elena scream in unison, as they leap off their swings-in-motion. I'm on my feet in an instant, my heart pounding. But their young legs are springs, nimbly absorbing the shock of their landings. They race to the jungle gym.

"Hooligans." Laura pats my arm.

"Yeah." I sit.

"So, you all ready for India?"

"Haven't even started packing, but we don't leave for another twelve days."

"Excited?"

"Actually, I wasn't all *that* excited, but now I am. I've decided to do an oral history project about my great-great-grandfather.

I'm going to interview as many elders as I can. I've always wanted to do something like this."

"Cool. So you're writing a book?"

"No, nothing that formal. I was thinking about a wiki or a blog or something. Maybe you can give me a tutorial when I get to that point."

We both look up when Elena cries out. She must have mis-stepped on her way down and fallen to the sand, but her wails sound more surprised than pained. Laura rushes over, brushes the sand off Elena's shorts. In a minute, Elena ascends the play structure to meet Zee at its apex.

The commotion passes and I text Murtuza back three purple hearts.

I check Facebook when we arrive home. A notification tells me that Zainab has invited me to the Rangwala Family Newsletter page. I join, scrolling through posts about an upcoming get-together. I click through a large unedited album of someone's wedding, but don't recognize anyone and then lurk on Zainab's page awhile, noticing that she's been on a self-help kick, sharing articles about "The 10 Things Happy People Do," "7 Ways to Love Yourself More," and other numbered lists that I don't open.

Zainab's moniker includes her maiden name so that her school friends will find her. She told me they wouldn't otherwise recognize her because she's no longer stylish and pretty. I don't see the frumpy middle-aged matron she views in the mirror; to me, she's still that girl who automatically won the role of princess in our childhood games of make-believe. In some ways, thirty years later, Fatema remains the prince. And me? I was usually left playing the lady-in-waiting.

Zainab, Fatema, and I are related through our parents — Zainab's mother, Fatema's father, and my mother — who are siblings. Nani dubbed us the Secret Cousins' Club for the way that we used to huddle, whispering our secrets to one another. We don't have any other girl cousins close in age, so it was just us.

Fatema was born in mid-May, Zainab in July, then me — trailing by a month — in August. It was as though our mothers had been on a synchronized procreation schedule never again replicated. I am the only "only" amongst the three of us; Fatema has an older sister and Zainab has two elder brothers, each three years apart.

When we were babies, Tasnim Maasi and Mom dropped Zainab and me off at Nani's for three hours every Monday, Wednesday, and Friday afternoon. Fatema was already there, because her family lived with Nani until Fatema was eight years old.

At the door, our mothers socialized for a few minutes and then all three rushed away to complete their shopping or errands. Mom told me that she nearly always returned home to nap.

I don't know how Nani coped with three of us still in diapers. Perhaps a servant helped. I cannot recall the earlier days, but I have snippets of memories from later. Nani would greet us in Gujarati with a jolly, "Welcome to the Secret Cousins' Club." There were sweets, and dollies, and lots of spots for hide-and-seek in that magical flat.

We spent our preschool years together, and after my family emigrated when I was four years old, we exchanged weekly blue airmail letters that often took a month to arrive, our questions, answers, and news shuffled and stale before reaching their destinations.

We let go of letter-writing when affordable long-distance telephone plans were introduced. Later we switched to email, then Skype and text. But we are busy, and so much of our communication is through Facebook, each of us peeking into one another's lives, liking and commenting. I sometimes wonder why we don't more regularly text the way we do with our nearby friends and family, especially now that it's all free. Maybe we're used to the geographical distance creating a barrier, have grown accustomed to being apart.

On social media, I'm the opposite of Zainab; while I use my birth surname in life, I've hidden behind Murtuza's on Facebook so that my students won't find me. The choice is sometimes disorienting; how can I be Mrs. Tyebji when I am Sharifa Bandukwala? Perhaps now that I'm no longer in the classroom, I might be able to return to my real name again. But then maybe not; Facebook is still a touchy subject for Murtuza and he might read more into it than I'd want.

Fatema took a good deal of cajoling to join Facebook, citing her growing reputation as a businesswoman. Of course, when she heard about it in 2006, she put her marketing people on it and her publishing house was one of the first in the world to advertise there, but she didn't create a personal account until 2010, as "Fat Ema." In the beginning, her posts reminded me of her teen self: interspecies love stories (the dog and the elephant, the donkey-cow pair) and jokes with a hint of political satire. But over the last couple of years, everything has centred on feminist issues.

Most recently, her energy has turned to reports about depressing things like female genital mutilation. I'd heard about it in the news, but before her posts I had no idea anyone practised it in India, let alone in our Dawoodi Bohra community. It seems borderline racist now, but I'd assumed it was an African thing; all the previous media stories I'd read focused on Egypt or Sudan or Kenya.

Today's article is a confessional, written anonymously by a woman who lives in Mumbai. I presume that her family hails from a small village. Hers is a horrible narrative about being taken, at age seven, to get "khatna" done, and only realizing it later, when she was in her thirties. "I'll never forget the pain, it was the worst I'd ever felt." I skim another paragraph, close the article, and click "like," a not-quite-appropriate reaction, under Fatema's post.

I turn off the computer and head to the basement laundry room to find our luggage. One by one, I haul three large suitcases up the narrow wooden steps and then up to the second floor.

"How does one pack for eight months away?" I ask Mom, over the phone.

"Lightly," she jokes, her way of letting me know that I'm taking the task too seriously.

"Right."

"But seriously, you'll be staying a few blocks from Zainab's and Tasnim's flats," she reasons. "You can take your dirty clothing there twice a week and a servant will launder everything for you. You'll buy anything else you need."

"We'll have our own washing machine."

"And a dryer?"

"I don't think so."

"You're going to have to hang your clothes on a line. We did that when we first came here, in the summer. When we had little money and needed to save electricity." Her tone is wistful, almost romantic.

We say goodbye and I head to Zee's bedroom. She needs a full school year's worth of second-grade curriculum and supplies. Once the workbooks and her pencil case are in her suitcase, she and I lay everything else on her single bed that she cannot live without for half a year: five everyday outfits, two special-occasion dresses, three pairs of shoes, a handful of favourite storybooks, and Ronald, her stuffed raccoon. The pile is much smaller than I'd imagined.

"That's all, Zee?"

"I think so." She's approaching this interruption to her routines with an attitude as casual as her grandmother's; the only reassurances she's needed are the promises that she will Skype weekly with Elena and rejoin her classmates in time for her late April birthday.

"Is there anything you want to put out of sight for when Su-Lin stays here?" She's the three-year-old daughter of the visiting academics who'll be renting our place and feeding our turtle.

"Like what?"

"I dunno, any toys or stuffies you don't want her to play with?"

She does a slow pirouette, scanning her room. "Nah. She'll feel more at home if all the toys are here, right? I'm getting too old for most of them, anyway."

Later, Murtuza and I continue packing. We're taking Mom's advice to carry one large suitcase each. We lay them out on the bed. His is navy blue and scuffed, and mine is pink and nearly new.

"We're a heterosexual stereotype, aren't we?" I shake my head.

"I'll trade you. I like pink." He tosses a pair of slacks in my bag. I refold them and place them in his suitcase.

"I'll keep mine. It has all these meshed compartments." I point out the bag's features, but I've already lost interest in my own argument.

"Do I need a suit?" Murtuza stares into the closet.

"Yeah. We'll probably be invited to a couple of weddings. And take a saya kurta in case it's an orthodox one. I'm taking my two ridas with me."

"Oh god," he groans, "we're going to have to go to a beard-wala event at some point." He frisbees a topi, the pillbox-style skullcap Bohra men wear, into his bag.

35

"Murti! You shouldn't say beardwala!" I wag my finger at him.

"Is topiwala or ridawala better?" He raises an eyebrow at me.

"Go ahead. Get it all out of your system now."

---◆---

I wouldn't have imagined I'd marry someone from our community; I'd heard too many stories from my Bohra girlfriends about men who started out as good boyfriends and transformed into fifties husbands after the wedding. Dinner on the table when I get home, keep the baby quiet, all that nonsense.

On our first date, Murtuza picked me up five minutes early in a car that smelled of pine. During our dinner at Mirchi, he scooped rice with his fingers while discussing the work of Audre Lorde and Zadie Smith. We shared our mixed-bag identities; we both grew up in towns near large cities — Edison, New Jersey, for me, and Brampton, near Toronto, for him — with liberal parents.

He can be absent-minded, the stereotype of a professor who, when engaged in his work, manages to tune out my calls. But he also is a rememberer of anniversaries, of my dislikes, of shopping lists. And when I was pregnant with Zee, he accompanied me to each prenatal class and read books on birth coaching. Because Zee was born the last week of April, when his academic duties were waning, he was the one to sacrifice sleep so I could catch up. I rarely changed a diaper. That sort of devotion, during the most tender period of Zee's life — and mine, too, as I learned to become a mother — sealed the deal for me; I truly knew he would be my partner for life.

Of course, we'd already been committed for two years by then, in a civil ceremony. Our choice not to also partake in a nikah disappointed my parents, who harboured secret and misplaced hopes for a sliver of traditional respectability. Murtuza rebuffed his parents' more persistent requests with "I thought you'd be happy that I married a nice Bohra girl!" And they were, for we'd both only dated white people before that.

Truthfully, I was ambivalent about the nikah — it takes exactly seventy seconds and approximately five hundred dollars — but Murtuza felt strongly about not including religion in our union. He's an agnostic, bordering on atheist, while I'm harder to label. I like a little tradition and membership in a community, even if I don't always follow its rules.

Our parents didn't press the point and paid for a reception under Mirchi's makeshift tents. It's still our favourite spot, but it's not the same these days, now that the place has grown popular among non-Indians and they have real plates and cutlery and ask if you'd like the food cooked mild, medium, or hot.

When I announced I was pregnant, both our mothers suggested that Alifiyah, Murtuza's sister, email the Syedna, the religious leader of the worldwide Dawoodi Bohra community, for a baby name. Mariam Fayji, my father's sister, did the same for my naming, only back then, before computers, she'd sought an in-person audience in Mumbai. Murtuza called the idea archaic, but I supported our mothers' wishes, arguing that the Syedna's suggestion wasn't binding. He acquiesced; I suspect his protest-response is a superficial one, while his Bohra training has the depth and strength of an old-growth tree's root system.

In the end Murtuza was vindicated. Normally, the Syedna offers a male and a female name, but Alifiyah forwarded us the email that offered a single, unusable name for Zee, or any child growing up in the West: Fakhruddin. Later, an ultrasound confirmed we were having a girl. "Who knows?" Murtuza had scoffed. "Maybe modern technology is wrong and the Big Guy is right. And it has a nice ring to it. Fakh-ru for short."

During the chhatti, the naming ceremony, Alifiyah whispered the surah into Zee's tiny ear:

Bismillaahir Rahmaanir Raheem
Alhamdu lillaahi Rabbil 'aalameen
Ar-Rahmaanir-Raheem
Maaliki Yawmid-Deen
Iyyaaka na'budu wa Iyyaaka nasta'een
Ihdinas-Siraatal-Mustaqeem
Siraatal-lazeena an'amta 'alaihim ghayril-magh-
doobi 'alaihim wa lad-daaalleen

Zee opened her eyes wide, as though her wise old soul knew Arabic and was finally hearing words she could comprehend.

"Arre waah! Zeenat is a very smart girl!" my mother gasped, which caused a collective murmur, like a gale through a stand of trees, to rustle through the room. I wondered about my daughter's future right then. Would good luck bless her? Would she be protected from danger, from society's ills, temptations, cruelties? When she was handed back to me, I held her tightly and uttered God's name. Murtuza heard me, met my gaze, and reached for my hand.

"Don't forget we'll be in Mumbai for Ashura. It might be difficult to avoid all the functions. You might need more than one saya kurta." I fold my new polka-dot red dress into my bag.

"Will we be allowed into those functions? I mean, they'll know we aren't even red card holders," he counters. He's referring to the now defunct system of cards that was used to regulate access to religious services, based on an assessment of a person's orthopraxy.

"It's a universal card now, Mom told me. I think she said it's called an ITS, or something like that. No more green, yellow, and red tiers."

"Oh, but you know that they're tracking everything and grading everyone: whether a man grows a beard or a woman wears a rida, whether they pay their dues, drink alcohol. It's Bohra Big Brother."

"Ha!" His sacrilegious talk tempts me. "If they had a card for sinners like you, what colour would it be?"

"Leopard-spotted, tiger-striped?" He laughs and I grab his arm and pull him into a hug. I love his quick wit, his ability to play with language. After a moment, he looks away, shyly.

"Shari, there's something I want to pack, but I'd like to talk with you first." His voice is a half whisper.

"What? What's wrong?" I sit on our bed.

"No, no. I just don't want Sleeping Beauty to wake up and overhear us." He gestures to Zee's room next door, then places a pleather case in my lap.

"Before you open it. I want to say that I'm looking forward to spending time with you in India.... And I thought this would be fun."

"Okay ..." The zipper's metal teeth unlock. I pull out a black blindfold and handcuffs.

"They're soft, made of leather," he says, taking them from my hands and pointing out the workmanship. There is a slight tremble in his voice. "Do you think you might like to try them?"

"I thought you hated *Fifty Shades*," I tease, deflecting my own discomfort. He discarded the book after the first twenty pages, claiming it had no literary merit. His face falls, and I drop the joke. "Sure, let's try it."

"Really?" He bounces a little on his feet, nervousness leaking out of him.

"Yeah, but listen, I don't need any bells and whistles." I grow tense, thinking that this is going to be like the vibrator shopping. "I think it'll be fun. For me. For us. If you don't mind?" He is tentative once more, his face soft, his gaze vulnerable.

"I don't mind, Murti." I rezip the case and place it in his bag. "Thanks for getting it." I look him in the eye and kiss him with my eyes open, watching as he closes his and relaxes into my embrace.

∽ SEVEN ℃

Bombay, 1870

"Abdoolally, sweep up this mess!" Hunaid, the herbalist's son, was only seventeen, two years older, but loved to act the boss. Abdoolally did as he was told, brooming the leaves and stems discarded after Dr. Chunara had compounded an herbal remedy for cough. He pushed the pile of green out the back door, where another boy, a poorer one, would sweep it elsewhere.

When he returned, Hunaid was helping a British officer in the shop. The short, broad man was squinting and making hand gestures, while Hunaid spoke to him in Hindi, pointing to the bottles and tins around him. Abdoolally had picked up a few English phrases from listening to the herbalist speak with the officers. In private, he mimicked their exotic words.

"Hullo. How you?" he attempted. The officer turned his green eyes to Abdoolally. They were bloodshot, with pink bags that clung like slugs underneath.

"Something for headaches, I need something for headaches," he said, pointing to his head.

"Chai banouoo?" Hunaid looked to Abdooally, speaking to him in Gujarati. He pointed to a packet of ginger.

"You make tea," Abdoolally said. "One cup water, one spoon this."

Just then, Dr. Chunara returned from his errands and took the packet from Abdoolally's hand. "What are the symptoms?"

The officer repeated his ailment, this time rubbing his temples to demonstrate his distress.

"Take the tea twice a day until the headaches pass."

The officer paid Dr. Chunara. When he'd left the store, the herbalist split the four coins, placing two into the register and two into Abdoolally's hand.

"You should follow his example, Hunaid! Learn some English so you can talk to the Angrez!" Dr. Chanara turned away from them both, returning to his work.

Hunaid glowered at Abdoolally, who reflexively rounded his shoulders and avoided the older boy's gaze. He busied himself with wiping the dust off the counter. Then he cleaned the large glass jars that held the loose herbs. Dr. Chunara glanced at him and nodded his approval.

Later, Abdoolally would hand over one of the precious coins to Hunaid, to maintain the peace.

～ EIGHT ～

I scrounge through kitchen drawers at 5:00 a.m. I'd been lying awake in bed, circular thoughts about whether or not to pack a flashlight making their eighth loop. Do power outages still happen in Mumbai? What about in the deluxe place Fatema has organized for us? I find a working flashlight, roll it in one of my T-shirts, and tuck it into my suitcase. We leave for India in six days.

I debate whether to crawl back into bed and realize I'm too awake for that. According to my mother's reports, I've always been a "fussy" sleeper, as though insomnia is much ado about nothing. I'm easy to rouse, and I usually need to use the toilet two or three times during the night. When I was a kid, my parents tried a number of strategies, including no liquid after eight o'clock at night, then seven, then six. But then I'd just wake up thirsty.

Zee is the opposite; from the beginning, she slumbered longer than other babies, and by the time she was two, she was quiet through the night. With puffy eyes and slack bodies, my friends would tell me how lucky I was to have a baby like Zee. I'd nod, knowing that yes, my life was easier than theirs, but that didn't mean I, too, wasn't sleep-deprived. I'd watch Zee sometimes, dead to the world, even when a phone rang or Murtuza and I squabbled. How I wished for that.

I grab naps when I can, push through with caffeine (before 3:00 p.m., obviously), use the middle-of-the-night wakefulness to get caught up on work. I imagine that during my year off I'll find a way to clear my sleep debt, that quicksand pit of accumulated time. It must be thousands of hours by now.

This morning, as I drink my first cup of coffee, my nerves are frayed, like wires chewed through by the mice I know live in our walls despite last year's pest-control call. I shake the thought, sip my coffee, watch the sun rise.

When I check my email a few minutes later, I see that my first Abdoolally survey has arrived.

Abbas Kaaka is my father's youngest paternal uncle. I sent him the survey link a few days ago, after Mom reminded me that he'd be a good source. He's well read, has travelled more than his contemporaries, and was a teacher, a career different from the men of his generation, most of whom were businessmen.

We're not close but I try to visit him at least once on each trip back. When I was doing my master's, we discussed my thesis topic, and he'd commented, "Did you include the *Komagata Maru* in your project?" He is my only relative, including my North American ones, who knows anything about this history.

He is on the board of the Rangwala Trust, a charitable organization that funds the hospitals and schools Abdoolally's inheritance built. Also, Abbas Kaaka knows something of our family's genealogy and has attempted an elaborate family tree, drawn on parchment paper affixed to his bedroom wall. By the time he began the project, his wife, Amtulla, had been dead a few years. She was a woman, from what I recall, who would not have tolerated the wallpaper of souls alive and dead decorating her home.

I click open his survey link and read his essay.

> Well, Abdoolally was quite the figure, not just for our family, who are his proud descendants, but for India as a nation. He was well known and respected by the British, as well as Indians. Of course I'm assuming you know of his numerous business pursuits, land holdings, and his charitable endeavours. I've attached a separate document for those. But what is most interesting is that he spurs on the imagination about how he arrived at such an impressive station in life!
>
> He had humble beginnings — and that is an understatement. He was an illiterate and penniless village boy arriving in the big city of Bombay. Can you imagine? He had attended no school at all. But he was ambitious, the sort of mind that manages to overcome all obstacles. When his businesses grew successful he purchased land, instinctively knowing which undesirable places would turn profitable. Come to think of it, he started out that way himself, undesirable, and then he became Abdoolally Seth.

I enter "Seth" into a search engine and learn it is a title that denotes greatness. Historically it was used to identify the wealthiest man in town. While I find this impressive, I'm not that interested in my great-great-grandfather's financial status. I reread Abbas Kaaka's words: "The sort of mind that manages to overcome all obstacles." My research question hasn't been well defined, but its edges are growing sharper, like a Polaroid image in the sun: I want to know more about my forefather's mind.

"I will miss you, my little Zeenat Zee Nut!" Mom squeezes Zee at Newark Airport.

"We'll see you in a few months," Murtuza says, and he and I hug her, A-frame-style around Zee, who still clings to Mom's leg. She has a ticket for a four-week visit in late March, returning home on the same flight with us. I lobbied her to come earlier, but she insisted that this first trip back without Dad would be challenging enough without extending it.

"We'll talk on Skype, right?" The thought of her being lonely while we are gone is like acid pooling in my belly. She nods and ushers us toward the security gate.

After we pass through, we have a two-hour wait. Murtuza gets his shoes polished and Zee and I drift toward Twelve Minute Manicure. Normally, this would have been part of my back-to-school routine. I ask Malina, the aesthetician, for coral pink, my usual. Zee scans the entire paint deck and picks up a red with sparkly shimmer through it.

"This one is nicer." She passes the bottle to me. Malina nods to Zee.

"Why not? I'm on vacation, right?"

Zee isn't interested in her nails but is captivated by the vibrating massage chair next to us. She giggles as its fingers poke their way up her bony spine. I watch the tickertape headlines marching across the bottom of a television on mute: "6,500 Syrians reach Austria, greeted by applause, food, and medical help. Jailed Kentucky county clerk Kim Davis says she will appeal contempt of court ruling for not issuing same-sex marriage licenses. GOP presidential candidate Donald Trump lashes out at conservative radio host."

"I still can't believe Trump is in the running." I shake my head at the screen.

"It's surreal," Malina says, and clips my cuticles.

Murtuza arrives, showing off his loafers' new sheen. He scoops up Zee, who is already bored with her mechanical massage, and takes her for a tour around the terminal.

In exactly twelve minutes, Malina finishes and tells me to wait for the lacquer to dry. I gaze out at the candy and cosmetic shops across the way, my fingers outstretched before me. A group of Bohras in traditional clothing pause at the electronics store next door, and I smile at a rida-clad woman who looks to be about my age. I wonder if we know each other, but she only smiles blandly before looking away.

I'm in stealth mode in my jeans, zip-up cardigan, and red nail polish, but perhaps they can guess from my facial features that I am of their clan. My father's best friend once insisted that he could pick a Bohra out of a crowd, since we are so closely knit and have similar features. That seems like a stretch, but a part of me wants to be acknowledged by these Bohras in the terminal.

What would it be like to walk through the world like this? While we have many family friends who don't wear Western clothing, Mom, Dad, and I nearly always did, except at all-Indian parties or religious gatherings. To be identified each and every day as Muslim, as foreign, as other, must be a burden. I notice that I'm not the only one looking at the Bohra group; others ogle, gazes curious, suspicious. Meanwhile, I mostly blend into the crowd.

Malina dismisses me with a friendly wave. I blow on my nails to be sure and join Murtuza and Zee, who are in the candy store, choosing a pack of gum.

An hour into the flight, Zee, who has been staring out the window into darkness, falls asleep, her head heavy in my lap. Murtuza slips his hand into mine. I like his grip; it's sure, dry, and warm. He isn't one for public displays of affection, but when there are opportunities like this — seated on a plane, in a movie's theatre, walking alone on the street — he'll reach for my hand.

I admire yesterday's haircut, spiky on the top, short on the sides. He still looks like the handsome man I met nine years ago, with his strong jaw and dimples. Like me, he's put on a few pounds, the extra weight making him more solid. He looks sideways at me, perhaps sensing my gaze.

"Glad we're going?" He asks.

"Yeah. It'll be a whole new experience for Zee, for us, for your work ... and now I have a research project."

"I'm glad you cooked that up for yourself. You know you never said — why this great-great-grandfather? I mean, him in particular?"

"Well, he's a significant patriarch, someone well known, so that's just practical — people will have records and stories. But I don't know, maybe he'll lead me to something more ..." I push aside a stray lock of hair that's fallen across Zee's face.

"Something more?"

"I dunno, maybe more understanding of the family, who we are ..."

"Who you are, maybe?" He squeezes my hand, and a warm pulse travels past my wrist, up my forearm.

"Maybe," I laugh self-consciously. "That would be a typical American endeavour, wouldn't it?"

"Hey, I'll be teaching post-colonial Canadian lit. From what I can tell, this self-searching thing might be a Canadian endeavour, too. At least for people like us."

"Right."

The lights go out and he allows our clasped hands to rest on his warm thigh. I take his cue and drop my head onto his shoulder.

I awake to blinding morning light. Zee has pulled up the shade.

"Sorry," she says, anticipating my annoyance. I snort, knowing she's done it on purpose.

"What time is it?" I ask, turning on my phone. It reads 12:06 a.m., which confuses me until I realize that its airplane mode ignores our new time zone, high above the Atlantic Ocean.

"I need to go to the bathroom."

"Okay." I swivel my knees left so she can walk past. A few hours earlier, I accompanied her and she told me that she'd go solo for future runs. She stumbles past Murtuza, using his thighs to balance herself, waking him in the process.

"She's going to the bathroom, it's morning," I apprise.

"Oh." He adjusts his pillow and is fast asleep within moments. I consider following Zee but my limbs are leaden. She returns after a few minutes, alarm in her eyes.

"I couldn't find you!" she whines. "I went the wrong way back and I couldn't find you!"

"That's all right. Here you are now." I take her elbow and pull her past Murtuza and back into her seat. "You know, I once travelled by myself from Bombay back home. Someone had to help me find my seat after going to the washroom, too."

"Really?" Curiosity distracts her from her distress.

"I was your age. My mom and dad — your nani and nana — and I went to India together, and then they had to return home before me. I stayed an extra month."

"By yourself?"

"No, I stayed with my nani, your nani's mother." She nods, as though remembering her. "My cousins Fatema and Zainab and I had sleepovers nearly every day I was there. But I did travel home all by myself, just that one time." The memory unspools as I talk to Zee.

"I was an unaccompanied minor." I pause to explain the words to her. "It was a big adventure, and everyone treated me very well, like I was a very special person. The stewardesses — they call them flight attendants now — were nice to me and brought my meals before everyone else. There were ground agents who carried my luggage; I got toys and crayons. It was great."

"Did you sit in first class?" She gestures to the front of the airplane. When we boarded, she asked me if the passengers there were famous people.

"No, just in regular coach like now. But it didn't matter. Back then, I was as small as you, and the seats felt huge."

"They probably were. They've only grown smaller over time. Everything cheapened," Murtuza grumbles, sitting erect and cracking his neck.

"Will I go back on my own, or will we all fly together?" Zee bites her bottom lip. "I could do it, you know."

"Of course you could. But you don't have to. We'll all come home together. Your nani, too, she'll be with us." Zee flicks her wrist, a dismissive gesture she's picked up from my mother, but I can tell she's relieved. A few minutes later, we smell overcooked eggs and spy the meal cart twenty feet ahead.

"Hmmph," Zee says, crossing her arms over her chest. "If I was an unaccompanied minor, I'd have my breakfast by now."

ᔐ NINE ᔑ

We arrive at Chhatrapati Shivaji Airport at three in the morning, the sky's darkness interrupted by the terminal's LED glare. The humid air is a homecoming, wafting petrichor, gasoline, and the tropical green that resists the pavement's incursion. The smell never changes.

Despite the early hour, the terminal is bustling, travellers and uniformed staff chattering, calling out, jostling. This, too, is how it's always been, only the building has modernized over the years, steel, glass, and marble replacing cement, the roof and walls stretching high and wide.

As we exit, two men, a porter and a driver, grab our luggage and elbows. Murtuza and I reject the taxi, acquiesce to the porter, and find our way to the Uber depot. We pass an uncrowded, roped-off area where locals text on their cellphones. I instinctively check to see if any of my relatives are there, even though we refused their pickup offers, given our pre-dawn landing. When I was a child, they'd have to stand behind a chain-link fence, an area that was tightly packed and poorly lit, scanning the parade of new arrivals. We'd listen for their cheers.

Five days pass in a blur of jet lag and making and receiving family visits. We had multiple invitations to live with others, but we didn't want to be underfoot in anyone's home for our extended stay.

Also, we resolved to have a separate bedroom for Zee, who has been sleeping on her own consistently this last year. We moved her into her own bed at two years old, but she often crept back into ours like a burglar. Halfway through first grade, peer pressure changed this, when she tearfully reported that her friend Melanie was calling her a sucky baby for not sleeping alone. I have no idea how that conversation began, but six-year-olds can be the meanest life coaches. And so Zee, chastised, vowed never to sleep in our bed again. I hugged her, congratulated her for being so grown-up, and secretly wanted to send judgy Melanie a brand-new Barbie.

The furnished Khar West flat Fatema secured for us is a change from our two-bedroom in Queens. The ten-storey building is called "Fortune Enclave," which made Murtuza and I giggle when we first read the signboard. Now we use the term whenever possible to refer to our flat, the way we once replaced "bed" with "Brimnes."

It's something out of a lifestyle magazine: marble countertops and floors, stainless-steel appliances, luxe linens. There is a large balcony, and from five storeys up, we can survey the neighbourhood streets. If we lean forward, there is a sliver-view of the ocean to our left. Two blocks away, in either direction, are trendy clothing stores and restaurants. The soundscape of honking horns and street hawkers is constant, only becoming intermittent at night.

Up this high, we see the tops of palm trees that make the air seem fresher, less dusty, than below.

We assume the affordable monthly rate Fatema quoted includes a subsidy from her, but she dismissed the idea, saying the flat belonged to a work associate who was doing her a favour. Fatema doesn't ever mention friends, only work associates.

When we are alone, I cover all the off-white sofas with bed-sheets to keep them pristine. We declined a servant, and so Fatema has instead arranged a weekly cleaning service.

Our first night there, Zee romped like a dog from room to room, exclaiming at their expansiveness. She was shocked to have her own bathroom, her face reshaping into a version of Munch's *The Scream*. Perhaps she was only being kooky, or maybe Melanie has a rule about this, too.

I was most impressed that Fatema's maid had stocked the fridge with two days' worth of meals for us. In addition, there is a spice dubba filled with cumin, coriander, turmeric, chili, and mustard seeds. When I found it, I breathed in their aromas, reminded of the time when Tasnim Maasi taught Zainab, Fatema, and me how to make our first vagaar, the fresh spice mix for curries. At Zee's age then, I'd watched, intrigued, as the seeds popped in the oil and the colours blended like paint on canvas. Zainab asked to stir and Maasi supervised her. Fatema grew bored and boasted, "I'm not going to cook when I grow up. I'm going to go to nice restaurants every day."

Tasnim Maasi retorted, "Well then, your husband will have to be a very rich man."

Without missing a beat, Fatema shook her head and countered, "No, no. I will be a very rich woman."

We'd all laughed, but I believed her.

Abbas Kaaka shares his more modest three-bedroom Bandra flat with his youngest son's family, as is the custom in India. We prefer our elders to not live alone, and parents tend to pass down property to their children. It's not always a peaceful situation; sometimes one generation doesn't appreciate the other's values and lifestyles. I've heard gossip that Abbas Kaaka spars with his son Tahir, mostly about drinking, and worse, about Tahir's insistence on keeping a bar at home.

"I think you last visited us many years ago? When Zee was a tiny baby? But now look! She is a little girl now." He takes Zee's hand and she shakes it with a solemn air, studying his face.

"I'm seven and a half, not that little." Zee crosses her arms over her chest.

"Oh, yes, quite true." He smiles and looks to me. "A bright girl."

"How old are you?"

"Zee, that's not a nice question." I place my hands on her small shoulders.

"No, no, she's quite right to ask. She volunteered her age, didn't she? Zeenat, I am eighty-seven. Can you believe it? Sometimes, you know, I cannot believe it myself. At times I feel like I'm still seven, or twenty-seven! It's very strange to get old." He shakes his head at his admission.

"Were you alive in the 1900s?" This is the same question Zee asked me about Murtuza's daadi.

"Oh yes! I was born in 1928." I take a moment to calculate: this is eight years after Abdoolally's death.

Kaaka's daughter-in-law, Khadija, brings out three glasses of fresh orange juice, glancing uneasily at the discreet liquor cabinet in the corner. Does she wonder if she's supposed to offer me vodka? Then she apologizes for the absence of the other family members; Tahir and their two sons are at work. Before she disappears to another room, Khadija makes me promise to return at another time for a meal with the family, a vow we both understand I'm not required to uphold.

"So how is the teaching going? Are you still enjoying it?" Kaaka asks.

"I'm a freelance consultant now. I just quit. I found the classroom too stressful. I lasted almost fifteen years."

"True about the stress. But I enjoyed the work a great deal. I did it for forty years!"

"Do you miss it?"

"A little, but not as much as I thought I would. I tutored privately after I retired, but then one day, calaas!" He claps his hands. "I realized I was finished with it. I didn't want to work anymore."

"I get it."

"But you … you're a long way from retirement."

I nod and smile. I don't want to think about work right now. I request to see the family tree and Kaaka guides us to his bedroom, a tidy widower's quarters. He tells me that Tahir and Khadija inherited the master bedroom after his wife died because they need the space and he doesn't. There is a double bed, a bookshelf, and pile of books on the table beside it. A metal almirah stands tall along one high wall, and across from it, the family tree. I gasp at how large and detailed it is, the handwriting tiny, to accommodate all the names.

"Here is Abdoolally, near the top. But just above him is his mother, Amtabai, and his father, Goolamally, who died when Abdoolally was a young boy. That's as far back in the record I could go." He clicks on a laser pointer and the red beam circles the crowning patriarch.

"You must have had to stand on a ladder to get him up there." The ceilings are about fourteen feet high.

"Tahir did those. My children were too afraid to allow me to climb up." I notice, for the first time, his stooped posture. A few strands of white hair criss-cross his balding pate. He circles more people with his red light. "Here are his four wives, and their descendants."

I stand on my toes to and scan the wives' names. "Sharifa!"

"Yes, you and his first wife share the same name. And see, your mother's father, your nana," he points two levels down, "is the grandchild of Abdoolally. Look, I'm here, I'm his grandchild, too; your nana and I were first cousins."

"So my daada and my nana are first cousins, too?" I imagine my two grandfathers growing up together.

"Yes, but their parents were only half siblings. See?" He points back to the top of the chart. "They had different mothers — Abdoolally's first wife and fourth wife."

I make notes in my book, digesting the confusing relationships.

Now the red light moves down to my level. "And there you are, Sharifa."

"Where am I? Where am I?" Zee dances on her toes, straining to view the chart.

"Oh, yes, Zeenat, you are related to this great man, too! But I still have to add you. I got a little behind on this project of late." I know that's code for his recent poor health; Tasnim Maasi told me that he grew depressed after he had a mild stoke last year.

He fishes a marker out of his bedside table's drawer and draws a careful line. He asks her birth year and prints Zeenat's name.

"Zeenat, you know something? You are part of the youngest generation of our family. You are the great-great-great-grand-child of Abdoolally!" He counts out the three "greats" on his fingers.

"Wow!" She smiles at Kaaka. I doubt she truly comprehends, but she is caught up in his enthusiasm. I scan their two faces, imagining what he looked like at her age, and what she will look like at his. Even with eighty years between them, I can pick out a family resemblance, as I often do with members from my clan: here are the same prominent noses, oval faces, small chins.

I ponder the top of the chart, aware that I am traversing a century and a half. No one who knew Abdoolally is still alive. We only have second-hand memories, family myths, and this grand wall chart to connect us all.

"I'm going to get all this down on the Geno Tree website so we have a permanent record of your chart," I tell Kaaka.

"That's wonderful. Use the modern technology, I say."

It is in my generation, close to the bottom of the wall, where the slanted lines of separation and divorce begin to appear on our tree. It's still a powerful taboo, and I sometimes wonder if it's one of the factors that kept Murtuza and I together four years ago; after that first terrible week of barely talking, our impulse, post-affair, was to seek help, and our second to remain cordial and respectful. Separation, while commonplace amongst our non-Bohra friends, is a still an abnormal rupture in our community.

The chart shows four marital breakdowns. I don't know the intimate worlds of these particular first and second cousins, but I've heard the rumours that circulated about Zareen in Columbus (her ex-husband was an alcoholic), Nabil in Toronto (his wife left him for a woman), Shabbir in Montreal (he and his wife just didn't get along), and Shireen in Paramus (her husband assaulted her).

I trace the solid line between me and Murtuza and say a silent, grateful Al-Humdulillah.

Is it a coincidence that these divorces are recent and amongst us diasporic kids rather than those in India? Dad used to opine that my peers have too many options. He lamented that we didn't hold the values needed to stay committed in times of stress, and that by selecting non-Bohra mates, our relationships would be vulnerable to increased conflict and stress. Even now, after his death, I want to argue that Zareen's drinking ex-husband is Bohra. As is Nabil's lesbian ex-wife.

I notice that Kaaka has neglected to record Dad's death with the standard genealogist's *X*. I take a deep breath, pick up the black marker, and scribe it myself. I know they will both appreciate the accuracy.

I step away from the tree, gazing back and forth to my laptop's screen to ensure I haven't missed anyone. Then I see it: a faint pair of lines crossing the link between Abdoolally and his third wife, Zehra.

---/-/---

I climb onto a chair to look more closely. So the rumour Mom told me was true! But why are the markings so noncommittal and almost unnoticeable? No children branch off from their names, their union a dead end.

In the living room, Kaaka and Zee sit reading, like long-time companions enjoying their quiet. *The New Yorker*, a gift I thought Kaaka might appreciate, is spread open on his lap, his lips moving slightly as he absorbs the text. Zee looks up from her second grade workbook, where she's filled in line after line of printing practice. I compliment her on her tidy letters.

"Are you done, Mom?"

I wipe her damp forehead with my sleeve and tell her to go sit directly under the ceiling fan; my girl isn't tolerating Mumbai's heat well. "Yes, I think so. Now I just have to get more people to fill in their missing branches."

"We do have a very large extended family. I was only really able to fit a certain number of people up there," Kaaka says, pointing to his bedroom.

"I have a question. Everyone tells me that Abdoolally's wives died in childbirth, but I see that he and his third wife, Zehra, divorced."

"Oh, yes, that's true. But we don't know anything about her or why they split."

"Really? It's a mystery?"

"Or just poor record-keeping. Also I suppose people don't like to speak ill of the dead ..." he says with slight smile.

"What do you think happened?"

"The cause would be similar to today's causes." He looks over to Zee, and I do, too. She draws in her notebook but is probably also listening intently. "Only the problem would have had to be quite extreme."

"One of them would have had to be very poorly behaved and the other one very unhappy."

"Correct." He carefully places a bookmark into his magazine before closing it.

Later that evening, I wonder about the divorce. Back then, people tolerated alcoholism, incompatibility, infidelity, and abuse rather than suffer the shame of divorce. Or at least women did.

I scribble a note in my book: *find Zehra.*

∽ TEN ∾

Bombay, 1877

He'd prayed for her, day after day. After completing namaaz he'd remain rooted to his musallah, sending his entreaties skyward.

"Please bring me a wife. Someone kind. Smart, loving … and oh, yes, beautiful."

Behind his supplication was not just a simple, romantic hope. There were practicalities; he knew he wasn't the most desirable groom. He'd saved and saved, and while he'd managed to purchase a simple one-bedroom flat for himself and his mother, he was still only an overseer at the printing press where he worked. And he'd heard from his friend Mohammed that many girls' families expected a large meher, a gift he and his mother would not be able to afford.

····----◆----····

"There's someone I think we should approach," Amta, his mother, advised him one morning. "The father is a pencilwala in the bazaar." She gulped back her tea and waited. Abdoolally nodded, remembering the humble shop he'd stopped at maybe twice. The man who worked there had a brusque manner.

"He and his wife are known to be devout. They have six daughters and two sons, and having gone through the costly marriage rituals now thrice, they may no longer be fussy for the fourth daughter." She raised her eyebrows.

"Who is she?" He set down his cup.

"Her name is Sharifa. She is fifteen already. She has a pleasant face. I'm told she cooks well."

"And the personality?" He bowed his head when he saw his mother's nostrils flare.

"Personality! Such modern ideas you have! You don't need to concern yourself with that. She is young. She will mould to your personality, no?" She stood, cleared the cups away, the conversation over.

That week, Amta's friend invited both her and Sharifa's mother for a gathering, orchestrating an informal visit. It was there that Sharifa's mother, understanding the nature of the occasion, made it clear that she and her husband would be happy with a small meher and even the parahmni, the wedding dress that the groom's family would supply, could be a less expensive gaghra choli.

And that was that. For the next three months, he and his mother scraped and borrowed what they could for the simple ceremony and feast. During the festivities, while he and Sharifa sat on a dais, he glanced at her shyly, her orna obscuring a full view. Did she have a pleasant face?

Later, after bathing, she came into the bedroom and sat on the bed beside him. He turned to her, taking in her round face, the dimples that revealed themselves with her nervous smile, her long-lashed dark brown eyes. Finally alone with his bride on his wedding night, a moment he'd imagined so many times over the previous months, he realized he had no idea what to do next.

He held her hands, the swirling orange mehndhi on her palms making him light-headed. But then she placed one hand on his cheek and looked directly into his eyes.

Her gaze steadied him.

∽ ELEVEN ᴄ

"The man had four wives?" Fatema clicks open a pistachio shell with her teeth, separating it from the nut with her tongue. I'm visiting her at her Worli flat, eager to share what I've learned so far.

"Yeah! We don't know much about them."

"No, we never do." She spits out the shell. "Men get all the attention, don't they? Welcome to India." She lounges on her sectional couch, stretched out like a queen. But royalty she's not; she's just home from a ten-hour workday. There are dark semi-circles under her eyes. I have similar ones, but not from overwork. Mumbai's noisy nights — filled with fitful honking and yelling — have kept me awake.

"I'll keep digging. By the way, men dominate history in the U.S., too. The women get erased."

"Not surprising," Fatema mutters, helping herself to another nut from the bowl. She gestures for me to do the same, but I shake my head. Pistachios are too much work.

"There's not all that much available about him, either, to tell you the truth. Very little online or in books. Plus everyone I've lined up to interview is too young to have ever met him. I'll be gathering memories of memories. How can they be accurate?"

"They might be, but probably not. Wait, let me guess, you've been told the old rags-to-riches story a dozen times now?" I nod and she chuckles. "Our family adores that trope. After all, most of us are businesspeople and have the same aspirations."

"It's your story, too."

"Not really. I had half the money from my father's business to start me off. Correction, my parents' business. All successful businessmen have quietly toiling women behind them. They look after their homes, their children," she said pointing to her chest, her eyes turning glassy.

"True." Fatema doesn't talk much about her parents; it's been a quarter of a decade since their fatal car accident, and their mention still upsets her.

"Anyway, what I mean is that Abdoolally's wives didn't get any credit for his success, just as my mother didn't for my father's business. His wives must have kept him fed, tidy, probably sane, too. Maybe they even advised him. I used to overhear my parents going over sticky situations with suppliers."

"Who helps you?" It's something I've always been curious about; Fatema is so solitary.

"I've had many helpers over the years. Business mentors from college." She bites into another pistachio shell. "But no wife! But that's fine, I have paid help." She smiles, referring to her driver, maid, and cook.

"They do keep you fed and tidy." I gesture to her well-pressed kurta and trousers, still fresh-looking despite the long day.

"And sane! What would I do without them? Maybe I am like Abdoolally myself. Guilty of taking all the credit when there are people —"

"Quietly toiling behind you?"

"Correct!"

"And is there anyone special in your life now?" I know to keep the question neutral; Fatema has had relationships with men and women over the years. From what I can tell, none of them have been long-term.

"No, no one right now. I enjoy being unattached."

"It has its advantages." I turn my gaze to Fatema's spotless six-star flat. I can't remember what it's like to not be attached to a husband and child.

<hr />

One of the relatives I've arranged to meet is Fareeda Kaaki, whom I visit the next day. She's my father's aunt, and Abbas Kaaka's widowed sister-in-law. When I was a girl, I used to admire her long hair and ruby-red lipstick; I think she was the only elder who wore makeup. Today she still has long hair, braided up and covered by a plain brown orna.

"Yes, there were four wives," she confirms as I reach for my notebook.

"But not all at the same time," I lead with the familiar joke.

"No, we are not a community that practises polygamy." She returns my smile. "But you know maybe some of the wives would be interested in more than one husband. Hah! What's that called, now?"

"Polyandry." I laugh along with my grand-aunt.

"Yes, pol-y-an-dree." She tries on the word.

"Really? You think Bohra women would like that?" I wonder what other scandalous talk she might allow to leak out.

"No, I'm being silly, only. Where did you say you live? Amrika?"

"Yes, New York."

"Oh, yes, that's correct. Now what was I saying?"

"Abdoolally had four wives."

"Back then hygiene and medical care was not good. This is why he wanted one of his charities to be a maternity home — to help women more safely give birth, to stop all the unnecessary deaths through childbearing." She gestures to her pelvis and I think about this tiny woman bearing six children. I wonder if she lost any of her babies in miscarriage, childbirth, or early childhood, as many of her generation did.

"True. But ... did you know? He and his third wife divorced."

"No, never heard that." She frowns and looks up at the ceiling for a long time.

"So you didn't hear about Zehra? You don't have any stories about her?" I stifle my disappointment. She shakes her head.

"So just the first two died in childbirth, then. That's bad enough."

Just then my body recalls the ache of Dad's loss and a grey sludge settles on my chest. Mom suffered much more, was depressed for weeks, refusing to leave the house or wear anything except tracksuits until she made the decision to pack up the house and sell it. Had Abdoolally suffered so when he'd lost his wives?

"I don't know how anyone would cope up with such a thing." Fareeda Kaaki shakes her head, as though mirroring my thoughts. "But he was a strong man, and he had his work. My mother used to say that he was a cool-minded person, not very emotional at all, or at least not the type to show anyone his sadness. Most of the men in the family are like that, really."

"I've never thought about that." Had I ever seen Dad cry?

"Did anyone tell you that his fourth wife was the widow of one of his workers?"

"No. Tell me about that."

"Oh, yes. She would have been a bad match for him, because he liked to read, was intelligent, educated, and she couldn't even read. But he must have respected her deceased husband quite a lot. Perhaps they were friends, I don't know. Anyway, he agreed to marry her because she was destitute. That was an admirable thing to do, a very Islamic thing to do. You know, he was known to be a kind man, someone who would ignore the authority of his position and sit to eat in the thaal with anyone. I just realized that you have the same name, correct? Sharifa." She pauses while I scribble down her thoughts.

"No, Sharifa was his first wife."

"Oh, that's right. I bet that was his truest love," she says, smiling.

"Why would you say that?"

"You have so many hopes and dreams when you are young.... They would have loved each other in the way that husbands and wives grew to love one another back then. There weren't any love marriages.... Did you have a love marriage, or an arranged one?"

"Love." I ponder what it might be like to start anew, four times, with a new partner, one who is barely known. To get into bed with them for the first time, only a short time after the previous one passed, and feel the heat of skin that is softer or rougher, less or more wrinkled. Unfamiliar skin. To learn new rhythms, demeanours, tones of voices. To start again, barely having mourned the last.

But didn't I do a version of this with the three boyfriends who spanned my twenties? I barely understood why they slipped away, and covered over my sadness with food binges and television. Then I started again.

Of course, for Abdoolally it was different. With the first two wives, he would have been anticipating the joy of a baby, but instead was delivered two beloveds' deaths. Would he have grown to fear pregnancy? Or sex? Would he have ever thought, *Not tonight, let us remain safe another night?* Did he ever think those wives' deaths were somehow his fault, that he'd seeded another loss? Then I write down this stray thought: *Perhaps all of that sadness poisoned his third marriage?*

"That's nice. Love." She pats my arm. There is a twinkle in her eye. "I barely knew my husband before we married. But he was a very good man. I think by the time we were together a few months, we were in love. He died six years ago. But I feel him with me everyday. That's how love is. They ... never really go. They never really leave you." There are tears in her eyes, and I expect her to shut down the memories, but instead she perks up.

"We went to Pune on our first anniversary. It was our first time going anywhere together, being completely alone. Because we lived with my in-laws. You know we didn't leave the bed for the entire weekend? We had a porter come and bring us food, even!"

I grin, delighted by this unexpected disclosure. My elder relatives rarely speak of personal matters, out of what I assume to be a sense of inflated privacy. Or perhaps it's that I've never asked the right questions.

She giggles, then dabs her eyes with her kerchief. "Now, what were you asking me?"

⟶ TWELVE ⟵

The following week, Zee and I visit Fatema at her company, the Bombay Press. I'm starting to get the hang of this homeschooling thing. The walk over, which requires keeping our eyes peeled for the sidewalk's disintegrating cement and sleeping dogs, is a half hour of health education. I've asked her to create a drawing from today's "school trip" to satisfy one visual arts unit.

"What do they make here?" Zee asks me. "Is it a factory?"

"Ask Maasi," I prod her. Earlier, I told Zee that Fatema and Zainab are like my sisters, and suggested she address them this way.

"Zee, I'm a publisher. This is a publishing house. We make books." She points to a glass shelf with dozens of recent releases in the lobby. "Do you like to read?"

"Yes," Zee says, almost inaudibly, clasping my hand.

"She's a little shy with you for some reason," I whisper to Fatema.

"Let me give you the grand tour, Zee. You will be our VIP today." She winks at Zee, who stares at her blankly.

"That means very important person," I inform Zee, whose eyes widen at the idea.

Fatema leads us down another hallway. She's expanded since we were here five years ago, taking over an additional floor and hiring more staff. As we pass employees' cubicles, there are choruses of "Good morning, Ma'am."

"I don't think I like being ma'amed," I say, and Fatema looks at me quizzically. She sends a young man away with an order for two chais and a Limca. A floor above, she introduces us to a group of editors who have small, windowed offices and call her by her first name.

The walls and furniture are white, kept spotless by the half-dozen people whose job it is to do so. The only smudges of colour are her authors' books, displayed in glass cases.

She leads us into her corner office, which is more modest than I had imagined. Inside, the furniture is not the standard-issue metal and glass that fills the rest of the building. I press my palm against her heavy wooden desk and she says, "It was my father's."

"It wasn't here the last time I visited."

"No, it was in storage. Got it out last year. Guess I'm feeling more sentimental these days. But let's not bore Zee with that talk."

I set Zee up with her sketch pad and pencil crayons.

"She's great," Fatema whispers. "Sometimes I regret not having a kid."

"Really?"

"It wouldn't have been practical. Work takes up nearly all my time. I mean, I wake up thinking about work and I go to sleep thinking about it."

"Like anxiety?"

"No, not like that, it's a creative pull. Work is my partner, my child. I'm excited to meet it each day, to get all the messes and challenges sorted. I don't like to be away too long."

"I'm lazier than you. I like my vacations," I joke.

"Sure, I like vacations, too. But work is my family. If my parents were alive today, I suppose I'd be obligated to be more involved with actual family."

I lift my eyebrows and she raises her palms in defence.

"Don't get me wrong, dear cousin-sister, I like spending time with you, always will. But I can do without the rest. Look, I even moved to Worli to create some distance between me and them. But then they had to build the bloody Bandra-Worli Sea Link," she says with a wry smile.

"It cut our travel time down to twenty-five minutes," I laugh.

"A modern miracle! But seriously, you know, even at my advanced age the family still ask me on a weekly basis when I'm going to get married?"

"A weekly basis. What a drag. Since we've been here, everyone has been asking when we're going to have a second child."

"Welcome to India. Each and every uncle and aunty wants to know why I am such an unnatural woman. Even my employees do, but of course they wouldn't dare ask the question. That's the best thing about being the boss. No one questions you."

After our drinks, she loads us down with a bag of books: an illustrated Premchand and a colouring book full of giraffes and camels for Zee, new fiction by an emerging Indian novelist for Murtuza, and for me a history of Bombay and a coffee table book about Gujarat. On the way home in the taxi, I wonder, *What would Abdoolally think?* It has been a daily pondering since I began learning about the man. The few interviews and online searches have revealed very little about his mindset.

I'm fairly certain he'd approve of Fatema, at least her output, profits, number of people employed. Would he care that she was unmarried and childless?

Had anyone ever asked him when he was going to have children? Were men, and especially rich men, exempt from such intrusions?

And when great-great-grandfather retired to bed each evening, was it work that was on *his* mind?

∼◡ THIRTEEN ◡∼

Bombay, 1883

Abdoolally sat on the floor, reading *Native Opinion*, the newsprint pages spread wide across his lap. The two older children, Raushan and Husein, were already in bed, while three-year-old Batool lounged in Sharifa's lap, suckling at her breast. Amta entered the room, making clicking noises with her tongue.

"Chaa. The child is too old for that now," she said sharply. Sharifa buttoned her blouse.

"It's for bedtime only. She can be hard to settle." She carried a dazed-looking Batool to the bedroom, flashing a weary look Abdoolally's way.

"Mummy, please don't be so critical. It hurts Sharifa's feelings. And she's good with the children," Abdoolally said in a low voice.

"She is only doing that to control pregnancy, son. She should be trying for another by now," Amta opined loudly, loud enough to be heard in the next room.

"That's not true. Didn't she get pregnant with Batool while nursing Husein? And Husein while nursing Raushan? And then she had that ... problem last year." He returned to his newspaper, not wanting to think about the child they lost through miscarriage. Just past the edges of the newsprint, he heard his mother's sigh.

He turned his attention back to a report about three lawyers who were starting a local political advocacy association. One of them, Badruddin Tyebji, had approached him after he took over the press last year. He'd felt flattered to be seen as an important businessman at age twenty-eight, and by such prominent men. He'd almost joined them, but wasn't sure he wanted to get involved with their petitions to the local government; to take a position against the British, who were his most significant customers, would be imprudent. In the end, he'd said it wasn't the best time for him with his business still growing. Perhaps he'd see how things went for them and consider membership later.

He folded the paper and said good night to his mother. In their bedroom, Sharifa was changing out of her gaghra into her nightgown. He bathed and joined her in bed. She looked at him, sullenness slackening her face.

"What's happened?" He asked, stroking her cheek.

"What she said is not true. I don't mind having another child … but …"

"But what?" He studied her face, fuller now than when they married six years earlier, but still girlish, pretty.

"It's only been recently that Batool got out of diapers, and all three sleep through the night … and well, it's been nice to have more energy lately … and you are so busy with work and …"

"You don't want more children?"

"Three is nice, no? Two girls and a boy. In my family, there were six girls, two boys, and it was a struggle for my parents. We're so much more comfortable. We have three bedrooms, ample space for all of us." She smiled, and he touched one of her dimples with his index finger. He loved how they transformed the topography of her face. All three children had inherited them.

"Yes, three is nice. I suppose times are changing. We can try to be careful, but there's no guarantee ..."

"I know, I know. We can try. And if we have more children, it will be a blessing, of course. The way I saw the last pregnancy until ..."

He kissed her forehead and held her to his chest. He stroked her long, soft hair until she fell asleep.

∽ FOURTEEN ᶜ

"What are you reading?" Murtuza looks over his text to mine. We're not used to this king-sized bed and the two-foot expanse between us. I lean over and hold out the cover of *Mullahs on the Mainframe*. It's an anthropological text, a book based on an American's PhD dissertation.

"Abbas Kaaka lent it to me."

"Hmm. Is it good?" He looks at the cover skeptically.

"It's decoded some of the religion for me. It's only been two days and I'm already on the last chapter." I've mostly understood the Bohra hierarchy of "Royals," with our apex leader whom we call the Syedna. However, even the most orthodox aunts and uncles haven't been able to offer explanations for our traditions besides a vague "that's just the way we do things" or "because Syedna says so."

"Like what?"

"Did you know that our imam, who descended from the Prophet, is believed to be in hiding, that it's a tradition that began way back when Bohras were being persecuted?"

"In hiding?"

"Yeah, to avoid being killed, he governs from afar through Syedna, his representative. It says here Bohras believe that the imam could be *anyone* amongst us, a shopkeeper or a wealthy land developer! Any of us might have bumped into him on the street, or had a conversation with him and not known his secret identity. He's undercover," I say dramatically.

"No way, that's what we believe?" He narrows his eyes.

"Yes." I'm amused that Murtuza has used the first-person plural. Perhaps Mumbai, the lap of our community, has rubbed off on him. But within moments, his expression shifts from disbelief to devilishness.

"Maybe I'm him," Murtuza jokes. I laugh along with him but uneasily, an irrational wave of sacrilegious fear rippling through me.

"It's funny, we all have photos of the Syedna, but he's not even our imam, but his rep, in reality." I shake my head.

Like most immigrant Bohra families, we had a framed photo of the Syedna on our Edison living room wall. As a teenager, I'd often felt his assessing gaze upon me when I sat on the couch, watching *Knot's Landing* or *The Bold and the Beautiful*. His picture was modestly sized, an eleven-by-seven, only slightly larger than our Sears family portrait and my annual school photos. When I brought home friends, they assumed he was an older relative. "Wow, your grandfather has a long beard!" my neighbour Sarah once exclaimed, and Mom and I only nodded. Perhaps we continue our imam's tradition of staying undercover, too.

"I noticed your mom didn't hang one when she moved into the condo."

"Huh, that's true. I wonder what she did with it."

"Goodwill?" He snorts at his own joke, and I giggle. We return to our reading. Within minutes, I finish the book. Then I scan the dozens of pages of glossary, notes, bibliography, and index, and study the handsome author's photo on the back flap. As I often like to do, a game since childhood, I close my eyes and flip the pages to random spot. It opens to pages fifty-six and fifty-seven. I read the heading "Circumcision," which describes the commonplace practice of male babies' foreskin removal shortly after birth, and a celebratory ceremony that takes place at age seven, the boys wearing a garland of flowers around their heads. I read further to the section about female circumcision.

> Female circumcision among the Bohras, as among some other Muslim denominations, is a matter of great controversy…. Sources within the community have given me wildly conflicting testimony: I have at various times been told the custom is absolutely forbidden, that it is occasionally carried out in secret, and that most Bohra girls are subjected to it.

I consider taking a photo of the confusing paragraph, and sending it to Fatema, but then change my mind. I'm not sure I want to discuss the topic with her.

I fan the book open to a section of black-and-white photos depicting typical dress in the 1960s, women in orna-gaghra, men in Western-looking suits. These resemble the snapshots from my parents' wedding album.

"Murti, look at these old photos." I hold the book up to him.

"I feel like I've seen identical ones of my family," he says.

"Just what I was thinking!"

"It's like they all used the same photographer, got the exact same angles. Even wore the same outfits! Look at those ties!"

"Interesting that until the eighties most men wore Western clothing. And the women didn't wear ridas. That's changed now."

"Syedna must have sent a memo," Murtuza deadpans.

"Sadly, I think that's sorta true. A correction against Westernization of the community."

I turn the page to a 1990s photo of a religious gathering, a sea of white topis and kurtas.

"There are no women," he says.

"No, look, here they are, right?" I point at the tiny figures in an upper gallery.

"Must keep them way up there, separate. Too much of a temptation to us boys, after all!" He kisses my cheek and opens his novel.

As I continue to study the photos, I think about how most people I meet have never heard of Bohras. It's odd because we are travellers; as a historically entrepreneurial clan, we ventured out of Gujarat, reaching across India and the oceans, seeking opportunity and larger markets. It's what Murtuza's and my parents did.

Abdoolally was one of the first of his generation to leave Dholka, their village. Abbas Kaaka believes it was his mother who felt that it was too small a place for him. Perhaps she saw something in his childhood that told her to pack him up and go to the city. Maybe he was one of those children, like Fatema, who boasted of becoming rich one day.

----------◆----------

A few days later, we return to Abbas Kaaka's to give back *Mullahs on the Mainframe* and borrow *The Bohras*. Zee stands in front of Kaaka's yellowing photo of the Syedna.

"Who's that? I keep seeing this guy." She points to the portrait.

"This is His Holiness, our spiritual leader," he informs her, and then, to me, he adds the correction, "actually, that is Syedna Mohammed Burhanuddin, who died last year. I haven't yet updated the photo to his son. Frankly, I don't like all the succession conflicts going on." He's referring to the fight between the deceased leader's son and half brother for leadership.

He looks pleased when he comes up with an apt metaphor for Zee. "He's sort of like your school's principal, but for our whole community. Actually, he's bigger than that. More like a school principal with rock-star status!" He chuckles.

Kaaka's description isn't an exaggeration. Mom and I visited the masjid many years ago when the previous Syedna was on tour through North America. I'd gawked as the elder men of the community rushed him as he entered the hall, each hoping for a touch, a few words, a blessing. Despite Syedna's bodyguards, younger men armed with whistles, a few groupies made it within inches of the leader and later emerged from the throng, elated. Others were not as successful and fell back, disappointed. These were usually dignified men — all of them married with kids, most of them doctors, engineers, accountants. I was glad that Dad wasn't part of the melee.

"Like Justin Bieber?" Zee asks.

"Not quite like Justin Bieber, Zee." I ponder how to make this make sense to her. "People like to have his portrait up to show respect, to keep him in their minds and hearts every day. Remember how we talked about the Pope? Your friend Katrina's family has a picture of him in their house?"

She nods. "But why don't we have a picture at our house? Aren't we Borda?"

I blush Bad Mother shame. "Bohra. Not Borda. Things are different in the U.S. This is done less over there, at least nowadays," I explain, mostly to Kaaka, my voice apologetic. Perhaps he knows I'm not telling the truth; most of Mom's old friends from the East Brunswick masjid display these devotional portraits in their homes.

"Here, you can take this one, Zeenat." Kaaka passes her a laminated, business-card-sized version of the new Syedna's image, which Zee takes eagerly. She studies it silently, holding it close to her face. I glance Kaaka's way in time to see him flinch as she stuffs it into the back pocket of her jean shorts.

"Wait, Zee, I'll keep that safe for you." I place it carefully within my notebook and slide both into my purse. As I often do, I wonder what Murtuza will say about this; his assessing voice has become an internal reference that sometimes makes me question my own, which I suppose is what happens when you've been married so long. Just yesterday, we'd argued about Zee's mithaq initiation ceremony. Neither of us had had any choice about our own mithaqs; to refuse was out of the question. I'd like to encourage Zee to consider it when she is older and able to make an informed decision. Murtuza scowled and shot down my middle-ground opinion with "I'll never encourage her to pledge her allegiance to a corrupt leader."

"Perhaps I'll get her a pen when I'm next at the masjid. Syedna will bless it and then she'll do well on her school tests." He looks at me tentatively, waiting for my approval.

"How does he bless it?" I ask.

"He blows on it." His lips purse into a slight smile.

"Why not?" I reply, while Zee watches us, her face bright with curiosity.

In the taxi back to our apartment, she asks how blowing on a pen will help her with math.

"I don't know, Zee. It's hard to explain. It's just what people believe. It's not logical."

"Do you believe it?"

"To be honest, Zee, I don't know. Do you believe it?"

She looks at me earnestly. "I'll have to meet Mr. Syedna first and have a conversation with him to know if he can do magic."

"That makes sense." But I know there will never be such a meeting. Religious leaders don't tolerate the wisdom or questions of seven-year-olds. I hug her close as we sway in the back seat of the taxi, weaving through Mumbai traffic.

꩜ FIFTEEN ꩜

"They are so long!" Zee purrs, caressing Nafeesa's red-painted nails with her stubby fingers. Zainab and I exchange a look of amusement; since they met three weeks ago, my daughter has been crushing on her sixteen-year-old cousin.

"Sharifa Aunty, can I paint her nails for her?"

"Oh, yes, oh, yes!" Zee squeals.

"Go for it."

I watch Zee's first manicure in progress, and consider how quickly things change; it was only a short time ago that I bored her with the identical activity at Newark Airport.

But then I recall that it was my cousin, Shaheen, also older by nine years, who enticed me in the same way. Her parents, somehow related to my father, emigrated a decade before us and lived an hour away. Our two families visited one another on special occasions. Not having an older sister, Shaheen filled a gap the way Nafeesa might be doing for Zee.

———◆———

Zainab and I sit on a couch by an open window, avoiding the polish's acrid, chemical smell.

"What are you going to do with this Abdoolally research?" Zainab's question feels like a challenge, although I'm not sure why.

"I don't know yet. Probably a wiki for the family, an electronic record."

"You should write a book. Do something important with all this effort." She slurps her tea just like her mother.

"I dunno, we'll see. My friend Laura suggested the same thing. It's been fascinating just to do the oral history. There is so much more I could collect and record beyond Abdoolally, if I allowed myself to broaden the questions. But maybe that's another project." The idea is like a firefly's spark. I tell Zainab about my visits with Abbas Kaaka and Fareeda Kaaki.

"You know she joked about how Bohra ladies might like to have more than one husband!"

"No! Not Fareeda Kaaki! She's getting more naughty with age, I think."

"She was fun. The only problem is that she wasn't alive during Abdoolally's time."

"If I know you, you're preoccupied with what you don't know, versus what you do." Years ago, Zainab labelled me an "overthinker" and advised me to do namaaz to stay "in the moment."

"You're probably right. I find myself wondering a lot about Abdoolally and his wives, what their relationships were like back then."

"Oh, things were very different back then. Marriage was an arrangement. A way to manage a home, a household. We expect different things today."

"Do you think Abdoolally was really attached to his wives, the way that Fareeda Kaaki was to her husband?"

"You mean romance?"

"Yeah. And did he suffer a lot when they died? Or when he and the third divorced? Or did he come to see love as something temporary, something he couldn't really count on?"

"What questions! You're really taken by all of this."

She reaches for her teacup, and during the pause I think, *Maybe love is better as an arrangement, for romance isn't something to be counted on.* I don't say this aloud, instead I intellectualize. "In our modern life, we worry less about death. Today it's infidelity, marital boredom, falling out of love."

"True. That's why we need faith. And family," she pronounces with conviction, patting my hand like a consoling elder, rather than a cousin born weeks before me.

"All right, little princess. All done!" Nafeesa announces, and Zee runs over to show off the pink dots at the ends of her fingers.

"Wonderful!" I examine her outstretched hands.

"Do yours in the same colour," Zee demands. Nafeesa passes me the polish remover so that I can rub away the chipping sparkly red from my airport manicure.

I interview three of my mother's older cousins, which turn into pleasant visits, each offering tea and snacks and exclamations over how tall Zee has grown. I hear nothing new, just the same depthless ideas about Abdoolally's ascension to wealth.

And everyone says all three wives died in childbirth. Rather than speak of such a misfortune, Wife Number Three's story was altered over time, her disappearance and demise turned into a common tragedy rather than an uncommon one. It was repeated over and over, like in a child's game of Broken Telephone.

I amuse myself by correcting them. The divorce, this bit of incongruous information, seems to confuse nearly everyone, and perhaps some of the spit-shine polish Abdoolally once had grows duller. I probably shouldn't do this to our family hero, but I want his anonymous third wife to be known as the outlier she was, even if no one can recall her name. I say it over and over to make them know her: Zehra, Zehra, Zehra.

———◆———

I return to Abbas Kaaka's to take a better photo of his wall; the family tree will be a good illustration for my blog's main page. I snap a few photos of just the wall and then one with Kaaka smiling in front of it, and finally one with him and Zee pointing to her newly scribed position on the tree.

"Do you know anyone who is a descendant of the second wife?" That part of the family tree is the sparsest, with only a single branch but no twigs. "I'd like to find someone who can fill that part in."

"I'll ask around. Funny how it's the first and fourth wives' families who are connected, but the line from the second wife got disconnected from us."

"Well, the family is huge. It's impossible to keep track of everyone."

"What else can I help you with today?" Abbas Kaaka asks eagerly and I wonder if he doesn't want us to leave yet. Maybe our visits are serving him as much as they are my research.

I scan my notebook, and pose the same question I've started asking others about how Abdoolally coped with losing his wives. As the words leave my mouth, regret follows in my next breath. A tear escapes from each of Kaaka's watery eyes and he pulls a cloth handkerchief from his crisply pressed trousers.

"I'm sorry," I say, "that was insensitive of me to ask you. It's only been two years since ..." I know better than to finish the sentence; he's just managed to dry his eyes. Zee steps forward and surprises me by taking Kaaka's hand.

"That's all right," he says, putting his handkerchief back into his pocket. "I'm known for the waterworks these days. People tolerate it from an old man. When I was a boy, we'd get a stern look for crying, for making a fuss about things."

"Yes" is all I manage to say.

"It's okay to be sad," Zee counsels, her tone solemn. She's quoting one of the books we read last year. "All feelings are important."

"You're quite correct, Zeenat." Kaaka laughs. Seeing him cheered up, Zee disentangles from our conversation and returns to the game she's been playing on my tablet.

And to me he says, "Grandfather must have grieved." I listen, and think, *Of course that's true. Why am I so silly? Why is this even a question for me?*

"I doubt it would have grown any more bearable with each subsequent loss. Maybe only worse. But he would have grieved privately, silently. He would have worked, got on with things."

"Work. The family mantra." I nod. We stay silent for a minute before he shifts gears.

"I think women have a much harder time. Widows have to sit in iddat, you know. They can't leave the house for over four months, there is no entertainment, no distraction. They are not supposed to look at the sky, even. My mother once said it was like torture for her."

"I think I read about that in the book you lent me. It's supposed to be a waiting period before the next marriage, to ensure the woman isn't pregnant?"

"Yes, that's the original purpose. But now we pressure old women, women no longer in their childbearing years, to do it. And with modern medicine, we don't require such an old-fashioned practice for younger women, even. Your mother didn't do the iddat for your father?"

"No. She's not that religious, I guess."

"Good." He blows his nose.

I nod, and I wait to see if he will say more. Instead, he leaves the room and returns with a notepad.

"I found the name of an archivist in Gujarat for you. She's the daughter of my colleague's cousin. Apparently very good." He rips out a page with a phone number and name: Meena Mistry.

"Thanks, I'll see what more I can dig up and then I'll give her a call."

"You know, you should ask your Khulsum Aunty these questions about Abdoolally; she might not have any historical information, but she might have a useful perspective."

⁓ SIXTEEN ⌒

Bombay, 1889

Abdoolally checked his pocket watch. As he'd done during the birth of his first three children, he cleared out of the flat to leave Sharifa alone with their mothers and the midwife. But why was it taking so long?

Just he and a peon remained at the printing press, all the others having gone for the night. He signalled to the boy and shrugged on his coat. Asghar jogged around the building, extinguishing the lamps. They stepped out into the warm night and Abdoolally turned the key in the large padlock. When the boy hesitated, he realized that he hadn't yet paid him his week's wages. He reached for a wad of rupees, and, with a note of whimsy — after all, he awaited the good news of his fourth born, another son, he hoped — he added a few more to the pile. Asghar bowed his head, a grateful smile on his face.

Abdoolally walked the three blocks home, still busy with shoppers and street hawkers. He considered the changes ahead. This new child, perhaps their last, was not planned like the others, a nine-year gap between them. He hoped Sharifa, who'd assured him she was pleased about the new arrival, wasn't secretly disappointed. The children had greeted the change with excitement, and the eldest, Raushan, especially looked forward to helping her mother.

He arrived at his building, but all was quiet. Something didn't feel right. He rushed up the two flights to his flat. At the door, his mother stood, silent tears streaming down her face. He pushed past her, into the bedroom, where Sharifa lay, pale, asleep, a bloodstain spreading across the white sheets of their bed. Sharifa's mother stared at her daughter, her eyes blank with shock.

The midwife glanced at him, averted her gaze, and shook her head.

He knelt by Sharifa's side, took her cool hand. He felt the midwife's warm palm on his back just before he collapsed.

∿ SEVENTEEN ℂ

My research has been like a scavenger hunt, taking me to distant relatives in every Mumbai neighbourhood. Kaaka's most recent clue sends me to Byculla. I arrive early, so I venture into the area's large vegetable market, a "must see" according to TripAdvisor. It's ten-thirty in the morning and bustling with vendors and customers haggling over produce. I slip on something green and slimy on the ground, but am righted by the hand of man passing with a cart of red chilis. I thank him, check that my purse is still closed — Zainab warned of pickpockets — and head deeper into the airplane hangar–like structure. There are rows and rows of wooden and metal tables filled with every kind of fruit and vegetable, more than I've ever seen in one place. After a round, I take photos of radishes and mosambis, and find my way out, cross the street and head to the coffee shop where Khulsum Aunty has agreed to meet me.

She is a great-granddaughter of Abdoolally, one of my father's cousins, and a social worker who counsels couples who have recently lost their children.

"This is interesting. We know what was passed down in terms of property and wealth, but you're posing emotional questions." She pushes a lock of grey hair off her forehead.

I nod, only just then realizing that that's what I've been doing. In the absence of a historical record, I'm investigating an emotional one. An unexpected quest for me, and probably futile.

"My grandfather once said that everyone was a little afraid of Abdoolally. It was because you'd never know if he liked, loved, or hated you because he had a stone face most of the time."

I scrawl *stone face* in my notes.

"I feel he passed that down — how could he not — he was revered in so many ways; those around would have wanted to emulate him. So this is part of his legacy, unfortunately," she continues.

"People say we are stoic, on both sides of the family. Murtuza describes me that way, too." I fidget in my seat.

"Yes. Love is understood, not shown." *Do I show it enough to him, to Zee?*

"But it's possible to unlearn that," I reply. "I read all kinds of parenting books while I was pregnant. And as a teacher I took a continuing education class on mental health. I hope I'm better off as a result."

"Yes, even my training helped. Talking and sharing is what we are taught in social work education."

"Exactly. That stone-face stuff is passé." I look to her but can tell her mind is elsewhere.

"You know, when my sister died of cancer last year, no one wanted to discuss it. We went through the religious rituals, but then everyone took their grief home. I imagine Abdoolally would have been like that. He would have taken half a day off work, people would have offered their condolences, then their salaams when the new wife came along. Forgetting. Moving on."

I nod, writing down these last two sentiments. I think about Mom, and how she hasn't shown any interest in marrying again, for which I'm glad.

"It's what most of my clients do; they try to have another baby to replace their deceased ones. Usually too quickly. And what happens? The new child inherits the grief."

"Like maybe a new marriage does?"

"Most likely. Feelings don't just evaporate into thin air."

We finish our teas, Khulsum Aunty returns to work, and I to the flat. I deposit our conversation into my blog folder, worrying that it is too tangential. I upload the photos from earlier in the week. While nearly everything I have is based on speculation, I am somewhat consoled by my new understanding of him, and all of us in the family. We forget, we move on. And now I am helping us to remember.

---------- ◆ ----------

"Was he a religious man?" I ask Fareeda Kaaki, who is happy to have me back for a visit. This time, her daughter, Shabnam, joins us. She volunteers on the board of Abdoolally's trust. The office is in south Mumbai, and Kaaka has suggested that I go there with her to take a photo for the blog.

"Of course he was," Fareeda Kaaki replies. The same query asked to three of my mother's cousins last week yielded two responses of "yes" and one "I don't know," but no details.

"In what ways?" I press. Fareeda Kaaki ponders my question, shifting her opinion. "Well, I do think he was religious but he was also a diplomat. He would have said something like, 'Don't keep the clergy too far or too close.' He was moderate. He respected them deeply, but maybe he wouldn't trust them one hundred percent, if you know what I mean?"

"No, can you elaborate?"

"He was an astute businessman. He wouldn't trust anyone one hundred percent. The same would have gone for the government. He would have been moderate with political matters, too, not too involved, but not too detached."

I capture every word, sensing the accuracy of her response.

Shabnam nods at her mother. "I just joined the Rangwala board a year ago and was tasked with cleaning up the files. I found a dossier that shows that he actually had a great deal of business dealings with the clergy. When they needed money, he loaned it. He sold them one of his profitable businesses, his first printing press, at a pittance, you know, so they would have a source of income, and room for lodgings." Shabnam shakes her head, and I want to ask her a follow-up question, but Fareeda Kaaki shoots her a glance, interrupts.

"Oh yes, he was a very generous man. Supporting the clergy was his duty." She presses her lips together, exhaling through her nose.

I make a note: *Follow up with Shabnam.*

"I'm not finding out anything that exciting," I lament to Mom over Skype later that week.

"What exactly are you searching for? A scandal?"

"No, not a scandal. Just something more substantial. But you know," I add, tired of my own complaining, "I do have a new angle to research."

"Oh, yes? What's that?"

"Did you know that he may have financially supported the clergy back then? Apparently, there are still unpaid IOUs made out from them."

"I didn't know that. Imagine. Today the Royals are very rich while so many Bohras live in poverty. I bet Abdoolally wouldn't like the disparity."

I sense a rant is about to begin, so I ready my pen.

"No, he wouldn't have liked that at all. He left a sizeable percentage of his estate to charity. His legacy helped many, but would he feel the next generations didn't do enough with it?"

I ask her to speak more slowly so I can record her words for the blog.

"All right, but don't quote me. Make this anonymous."

"Really? You can't express this openly?"

"I'd rather not."

The historical researcher part of me respects her wishes, but I'm frustrated with how few people have shared uncomfortable truths. I wish more people felt safe to talk. I tell her this.

"Last week, for example, Adam, Zainab's husband, said, 'I doubt that he was very pious. He was an incredibly busy guy, right?' Then Tasnim Maasi walked into the room and scolded him and said, 'Don't say negative thing about your elders, especially the dead ones.'"

"Oh, it must not be easy to be my sister's son-in-law!" Mom is enjoying the gossip. While I've not been the target of Maasi's critical edge, I know she and many others have been its bullseye.

"Then," I continue, "Adam rolled his eyes when Maasi wasn't looking. At first, I didn't understand his gesture, I mean, he wears the long beard and kurta of an orthodox Bohra man and is usually very solicitous with her. When she left the room again, he clarified, 'It's just that I understand. I do my best, but I know what it's like to run a business, especially one that doesn't cater to other Bohras. We can't just close down to pray if some tourist walks in and wants to buy a statue of the Gate of India.'" I laugh and Mom joins in.

"It sounded like an admission of guilt or a defence," she says, shaking her head. "Probably Tasnim admonishes them when they don't keep up with their prayers."

"I hope not," I say, wanting to temper this criticism. When I was younger, Tasnim Maasi encouraged me to pray. I remember leaning into her, her warm hands on mine as she showed me how to advance each tasbih bead.

We hang up soon after, and I flip back through my notes to find the one I wrote that day: *What was the Bohra spiritual leadership like back then? As policing as today?*

And now I add these ones: *Why is everyone so cautious? What would happen if people just spoke the truth?* Of course I do know the answer. Most Bohras have some critique of the religious leadership, which they whisper behind closed doors, to avoid the consequences of louder protest. And there are consequences.

We've all heard stories: decades ago reformers were punished with physical violence while others had their houses burned down. More recently, people talk about getting threatening housecalls and being refused marriage and funeral services. Social and business shunning. Parents are told not to associate with heretical children. These are cautionary tales, spread to guide the flock away from apostasy. And yet, in these shared stories, there is often an undercurrent of admiration, a hushed applause for the doomed protagonists. But most Bohras will never join the protesters; they want peace for their own families.

---------◆----------

I consult Fatema next; I need some straight talk. Or perhaps I just want confirmation of my biases? I meet her at her office, and she sends an assistant out for lunch. Five minutes later, a sweaty teenager arrives with two tiffins, the sort that wives might pack husbands. These came from a restaurant around the corner that specializes in "home food."

I mix the daal and rice and tell her about the unpaid IOUs that Shabnam reported to me.

"Shari, you must find out more. Can we collect on those IOUs from those corrupt devils?"

My cousin is unconcerned about shunning. Her parents are already buried and her sister is married, lives far away in Australia, and is similarly non-religious. And so, she can say out loud what I've been wondering and what Shabnam alluded to.

"What if it's partly his fault? This grand ancestor of ours might have planted the seed for their wealth! And what if that wealth brought the corruption and violence? The selfishness? The greed? A beautiful spiritual community turned into a cult?"

I shudder involuntarily at her strong language. Surely, we are not a cult. Sensing my disbelief, she puckers her lips and lists on her fingers the qualities of cults.

"One. Authoritarian leadership. We have that, right?"

I nod.

"Two. The belief in exclusive truth. In other words, we are the chosen ones, the *only* sect who will go to heaven. Well, not me. Maybe you." She smirks, stares me down, waiting for my response.

"Yeah, though who believes that?"

"Doesn't matter. It's what is preached."

"All right."

"Three. Discouraging independent thinking. No one is allowed to question or challenge or else you get number four. You can guess what that is?"

"Shunning."

"Correct." She glows with the pleasure of winning an argument. "Wait, we have one more."

"Uh-huh." I sense a bout of flamboyance about to emerge. And then, lifting her thumb, she says, "Five. Khatna."

I shake my head at Fatema, aware that she's been having a lark. "Okay, okay. We're not a cult. But almost, c'mon. And maybe our great-great-grandfather empowered the Royals."

"Well, I need to know more. Like exactly how much money he gave them. And perhaps he wasn't their only wealthy donor?" I counter, wanting to maintain a measure of objectivity.

"True. Most Bohras give their money and benefit business-wise. It's like that for every religious community."

"Right, so maybe this was a normal practice amongst the rich back then, too."

"Let me know what you find out. Then I'll get my lawyers on the IOU collection," she says, laughing with her mouth full of daal and rice.

Before I abandon my notebook for lunch, I write: *research the characteristics of cults.* When I look up, I notice her countenance has turned earnest.

"Hey, I meant to ask you something. Have you been seeing my posts about khatna these last couple of years?"

"Of course."

"What do you think of it?" She picks up a roti, scoops green beans, stuffs it all in her mouth.

"Well, I'm glad women are writing about it." The truth is that I barely skim the articles, my habit with topics pertaining to violence and abuse. Fatema regards me carefully, perhaps knowing I'm sensitive — during my tween and teen visits, I'd stop to give money to a little boy carrying a baby, and then grow flustered when I'd be surrounded by a flock of children with pointy fingers and outstretched hands. Fatema would have to say a few sharp words, clap her hands authoritatively, and extricate me from their throng. Then she'd tease me for being a "bleeding heart."

"You don't have to get involved if you don't want." Finished with her meal, she restacks the three metal dubbas, one atop the other.

"Involved?" I ask. Why would I get involved?

"Well ... activism isn't everyone's cup of tea."

"This is something that isn't so common, right? I mean, it's a traditional custom that is dying out?" I say, recalling the section on circumcision from *Mullahs on the Mainframe*.

"What? Why would you think that?" she retorts, with a tone I recognize. Once again I am the naive and spoiled American, not Indian enough. She lights her cigarette, inhales once, and then sets it in the ashtray, where it slowly burns like a toxic stick of incense.

The tiny muscles in her face shift, smoothen. *Stone-faced*, I think. *She does it, too.* She begins a lecture, her voice unemotional. This is Fatema shut down, disconnected, retreating from me. "Female genital mutilation is practised in India, mostly by the Dawoodi Bohras, our community."

I'm not finished my lunch but am no longer hungry.

In a monotone, Fatema reports what I'd already learned from a newspaper story she'd posted last year. "Bohras tend toward Type One or Four, as categorized by the World Health Organization," she recites, as though reading from a textbook. When I raise my eyebrows, she clarifies, "Type One is the removal of all or part of the clitoris, and with Bohras, most commonly the clitoral hood. Type Four is less defined — sometimes Bohras nick the clitoral hood — they call it 'just a nick,' as though it's nothing to cut such a sensitive part of the body." I focus on stacking my dubbas, latching them together. The bottom one is slightly warped, and I notice a small gap where the edges should meet.

"It makes some women have a lot of pain or aversion to sex, which is part of why it is done; the mythology is that it keeps girls from becoming promiscuous." Her expression is incongruous with her words; it's as though she is half-bored with the material. I wish I could only half-listen.

"Some girls remember it all and some block it out. It's traumatic ..."

"Look, Fatema, I should go," I interrupt her, and check my phone for the time. I'm curious why she's giving me this speech, but I'm afraid that asking will only prolong it.

"Okay, fine," she says, her voice cool. "I have a meeting soon anyway."

When I get home, Murtuza is browning meat and Zee is standing on a stool washing tomatoes. He has taken over the Mumbai kitchen, just as he did when we first moved in together, a year before we married. He rearranged the cupboards, restocked the spices. I cook, too, almost as much as he does, but somehow, the kitchen belongs to him.

"What are you two making?"

"Pasta sauce. I'm getting tired of Indian food every day."

"Oh god, me, too," I say.

"I used to tell my mother that when I was a kid. She'd make gora food every Sunday to appease me. Usually spaghetti bolognese."

"Funny."

"Is something wrong, Shari? You look ... stressed. Did something happen?"

"It's just been a long day, Murti. I need to take off my clothes, have a shower." I feel like my skin is coated in Mumbai's smog.

Under the shower's stream, I imagine its grey swirls rounding the drain.

∽ EIGHTEEN ∾

Bombay, 1890

The Khar residence, although more spacious and stately, was also quiet, too quiet. A floor separated his suite from his three children's bedrooms, and as he entered through the front door, he strained to hear their chatter. Perhaps they were playing carrom upstairs, for there were silences followed by periodic, high-pitched cheers.

His mother had advised him to buy the mansion, suitable for his growing family. He wanted to correct her, remind her that only last year his family had shrunk by one member, really two, but such talk only made Mummy cry, so he nodded, and shifted them there three months ago. She also said this place, with its Persian carpets, imported furniture, arching doorways, and stained glass, was appropriate for a man of his station, which also gave him pause. He had become successful in the past decade, yet when there were no visitors present, he preferred to sit on the floor rather than the padded chairs, the latter which he was sure contributed to his daily backaches.

He climbed the stairs and looked in on the game. His presence caused all three children to pause and stiffen like small prey animals.

He gestured for them to continue, and stood beside Batool, who said, "Take my turn, Papa." He shook his head and instead watched as she flicked the striker, driving a piece into a corner pocket. Batool cheered, while Husein pouted. Raushan, now fifteen and having decided she was too old for these games, commented from the sidelines, "Finally, Batool gets a point."

"Oh, come on, I beat you every time!" Batool retorted.

They turned to look at Abdoolally, expectantly.

"Well done," he said. They seemed to be waiting for more, but his mind had emptied, his mouth gone dry. When he looked at his children these days, all he could see were younger versions of Sharifa, and then a wave of sadness would wash over him. He'd learned that if he could turn away from it in time, it might not drown him.

"Did you eat dinner, Papa?" Raushan asked, frowning. She was a young woman now, the same age as her mother when she was engaged. When they were engaged. How hopeful he'd been back then, how full of happiness and love …

"Yes, I ate." And then he headed back to his quarters downstairs.

∽ NINETEEN ↄ

A few days later, after a morning of Zee's schoolwork and my reading, we take a nap together. We've been doing this a couple of times a week — working for a period, then looking into one another's watery eyes and mutually deciding to lie down. For me, it's about the noisy nights, while Zee is intolerant to the midday sun. She's learned how to crank up the air conditioning on her own but still, she often joins me in my big bed, starfishing on Murtuza's side.

As I slip into slumber, listening to my girl breathing beside me, a sensation of well-being settles over my skin like a silk sheet. I have the gift of a year off. I am married, have a wonderful daughter. I am happy.

Soon, I am playing fetch with a large dog, something like a Saint Bernard, only bigger. We are in the pristine Mumbai flat, and although I should be afraid of him breaking something, I'm not. When I toss the ball, he obediently, gracefully, catches it in his big maw. I test him, making the throws more challenging, a little to the left, a little to the right, a little too high. After a dozen or so of these, he grows bored of the game, midthrow, and flops down on the marble floor, drooling. My dreaming mind turns the flying ball, previously made of soft rubber, into a cannonball, and it crashes through the balcony's sliding door. The floor-to-ceiling pane cracks open, and a frigid winter gale rushes in. I awake, chilled from the frost's bite.

Zee is fast asleep. The AC is on high, blowing down on us.

I pull the blanket around me, close my eyes, and succumb to the dream again. I sense the dog is still in the room, but now I can't see him. From out of nowhere, he lunges, takes me down, and I am flat on my back, the wind knocked out of me.

Somehow, magically, I will my legs to kick, and their thrashing makes the dog disappear. But then, in the dark, a moist palm grabs first my right foot and then the left, a wrist bone clashing with my ankle. I can't see the face of the person who restrains me.

I open my eyes, blinking in the shaft of light coming in from under the blinds. With relief, I realize I am in our rented Khar apartment. I move my hands and feet, just because I can.

Zee snores lightly, covers thrown off. I examine the delicate skin of her wrists, her ankles, notice a new scratch on her foot. How'd she get that? I make a mental note to rub aloe on it when she wakes.

I stretch, swivel my hips, shake off the dream's torpid residue. I turn down the air conditioning and step out onto the terrace.

We are supposed to meet Tasnim Maasi this afternoon, to go see the Rangwala Building, the original home of the Queen's India Printing Press, one of Abdoolally's first businesses. I check Zee's curriculum, considering how to turn the excursion into a learning activity; it's our tangents that often make for the most interesting lessons. Today, we reviewed health material, which covered the basics about sex and gender and made cursory mention of people who don't fit into simple male or female categories. But Zee knows Lily, our neighbour who transitioned last year. I'd wondered if she'd have questions for Lily at the time, but she only wanted to know how long it takes for hair to grow from short to shoulder-length. Today, the brief reference to transgender people prompted Zee to ask me a deeper question: how did Lily know she was a girl? That sent us on a search that led us to a television interview with three Canadian children in the midst of gender transition. Home-schooling, an option at which I've always turned up my nose, is now making a great deal of sense.

---◆---

Two hours later, Tasnim Maasi and I bookend Zee in the back of a taxi. Maasi had suggested a rickshaw but the diesel fumes make both Zee and I cough. Plus, taxis can now be ordered through online apps, and drivers use GPS rather than what Murtuza dubbed "Indian Google," the practice of stopping three times for directions and using landmarks instead of addresses.

"Are we going to meet Abdool La Lee today?" Zee asks. It only now dawns on me that she's been imagining me researching someone alive, the way we'd earlier looked up Khalil, the fourteen-year-old transgender boy in the Canadian documentary.

Tasnim Maasi pinches Zee's cheek and explains that neither of us has met him, that he is an ancestor. I'd explained this weeks ago, but it must not have sunk in.

"Oh, you mean *dead*." Zee says this with the serenity of a meditation teacher. I stifle a laugh and Maasi murmurs the Al-Fateha.

"Yes, that's right, almost one hundred years ago," I clarify, and Zee watches Maasi mouthing the words to the end of the prayer. At the end, she kisses Zee's forehead. Zee wipes off the wet.

I gaze out at the road. Amidst the local storefronts are Western brands in bright LCD lettering: Nike, Puma, McDonald's, Tommy Hilfiger. There weren't as many five years ago, and I wonder if this strip will soon resemble an American outlet mall. When we pause at a red light, I spy a man on the sidewalk. I know he is Bohra from his white-and-gold topi, his long white kurta, and his grey beard that trails over his chest. He turns, his eyes meeting mine, and I swear he looks just like the sepia photo of Abdoolally that Abbas Kaaka showed me.

"Maasi, do you know that man?" I point in his direction. The taxi lurches forward. The light is still red, but our driver seizes the opportunity of a gap in traffic. We screech into the intersection, narrowly missing a collision with a rickshaw.

"Oh my god," I mutter, clutching Zee close to me. Maasi chastises the driver in Hindi and he shakes his head left and right, noncommittal, then speeds on. I turn, but the man is gone.

We get down on a busy thoroughfare under a flyover ramp. A nearby street sign tells me we are at Nagdevi Cross Lane. I snap a photo of the blue metal sign. We walk two blocks, because Maasi forgot the exact location and stopped the driver prematurely. It's a Muslim neighbourhood, and many of the businesses have signage with our telltale Bohra "wala" surname suffix. The buildings are older, shabby. Women with ridas like Maasi's pass us on the narrow footpath. I am not sure what we are going to find here.

"Just to see," Maasi informs. "It's interesting, no? This is where it all began." The doorman appraises us and half-heartedly steps aside because he has no real power over our entry. Besides, Maasi has already shot him a haughty look.

"That stare of yours could get us into the White House," I joke, taking Zee's hand.

"Who would want to get into the White House?" she retorts, causing me to sputter out unexpected laughter.

Inside it is cool. The building is a little worse for wear, the marble floors are yellowing and the golden paint peeling.

"It was once grand," Maasi laments. "I remember coming here as a child. It has not been well maintained. One day someone will tear it down, turn it into a high-rise. It's very sad, really."

"Yes," I echo, but I don't want to be too morose in front of Zee, so I don't pursue the topic. I take a dozen photos.

No one pays us much attention as we wander past windows with offices full of people in cubicles. On the fourth floor, I look out a window, wondering what it might have been like for Abdoolally. Would he have stood right here, scanning the horizon, seeing a different view from a century earlier? I superimpose photos I've found from his era: tree-lined, spacious streets, with horses and carriages and early versions of automobiles. Today, cars, motorcycles, and rickshaws jockey for road space. Diesel fumes permeate the air and most of the trees have disappeared.

We descend the stairs and circle around to the side of the building, where three small, ill-clad children sit in the meagre shade of a wilting tree. I shush Zee when she points at them. I know she can tell they are about her age, and senses the injustice in their different positions. They run up to us, chanting "paisa, paisa, paisa" in high-pitched voices. I take Zee's sweaty hand while Maasi rejects their entreaties with a fierce look and a reprimand.

"Why don't we give them something?" Zee asks. At home, I've allowed her to toss coins into the violin cases of street musicians, or the hats of panhandlers.

"Zeenat, if you give them even one rupee they will harass us all the way home," Maasi replies.

"I know it's hard to ignore them, Zee. But what Maasi is saying is true. The poverty here is so deep you can't fix it by giving out a few rupees. It's more complicated than that." My explanation feels too simple. Perhaps I can create a lesson out of this tomorrow.

The children start up their begging chants again, so we walk around to the front of the building. I stare up the four storeys, and to distract Zee, I point out the detailing on the Victorian window ledges. Maasi dabs her forehead with the edge of her rida.

"It must have been worth a bundle, even back then. I wonder why he gave his printing press to the clergy? There's a rumour that they weren't good businessmen so it didn't flourish after Abdoolally's time," I say, prodding Maasi for anything she might contribute.

"Well, they were spiritual leaders, not business leaders," she says. They are both now, I want to say.

"So did they sell it off later? Or do they still own it?"

"You know I have no idea. Perhaps they sold it. It seems to be all separate-separate offices now."

Murtuza is home when we return to the flat.

"Have a good day?" he asks, chopping onions and sniffling.

Zee tells him about our time with Maasi. She burbles about the old building and the doorman and the Limca she drank after.

"Learn anything new?" he asks me.

"Not exactly." I hesitate to tell him that it feels more like touring than research, and that I'm starting not to mind. He is focused on his teaching these days, his research more clear-cut; he's had his sabbatical goals defined for years. Me, I am meandering. I'm chasing a ghost, a projection of all our imaginations.

He finishes with the onions and pushes them into a hot pan. When he looks up at me again, he smiles.

"You look good. Despite the smog, you've got a tan from being here these last couple of months." I know that smile. He will make a move later tonight after Zee goes to sleep. I pat his back, wash my hands, and cut the four tomatoes he's laid out on the countertop.

Later, I bathe, recalling the afternoon's strange dream, but shake it off; I don't need to think about massive dogs right now. I turn my mind to Murtuza. I'm not full of anticipation the way he is. I wouldn't ever say this out loud; I know there isn't anything erotic about viewing wedded sex as good marriage maintenance. But it offers him a sense of security, something I've worked hard to achieve since the affair four years ago.

I give him a come-hither look, and that's all it takes. So easy and I just want it to be easy. He kisses me and I focus on the pleasant sensations, murmur encouragement so that he won't have anything to worry about.

I get distracted, my mind sending me to the mostly empty basement of the NYU Library.

My first boyfriend's angst about his lack of prowess had led me there. I found a book called *Learning to Orgasm* and hunched down in a corner with it, reading the first three chapters. The library was closing, and I didn't want to check it out, so I stashed it behind a desk and returned the next day to finish it. I followed the tips for many months: masturbate daily for ten minutes. Think of it as exercise, that you are building a muscle. Don't give up. Sometimes I thought I was getting close, but the feeling would peter out just as I welcomed it, like it has done with every partner I've had. Close but no cigar. Nick and I tried other things: we got drunk and had sex. We smoked pot and had sex.

Murtuza rolls on top of me, and Nick rolls away. My nice-smelling husband gazes into my eyes and I know that he has no idea that I've just time-travelled twenty years. He kisses me again.

In a minute he will offer to go down on me and I'll shake my head and ease him inside. He will sigh with gratitude and murmur that my body feels like home and I will be truly, sincerely glad. I will notice and breathe into the sensations like the book suggested, a pleasant, warm pressure. I will feel my heart bursting with love that what we are doing is loving. Healthy. Good. And when his body shudders and collapses onto mine, I will feel satisfied. And then I will hold him tightly, knowing that he is mine and I am his. And we will sleep.

But that is not what happens. He makes his oral sex gesture and I have no idea why, but I turn into a sack of wet sand, immobilized. He takes this lack of resistance as approval, and emits a thrilled "okay!" when I don't stop him. I push against the numbness, contract my thigh muscles, and feel a glimmer of something as his tongue laps at me. I tell myself to breathe into the sensations, but they are muted, as though coated in a fine anesthetic netting. My body is apathetic, leaden, and, wondering if I can move, I test out a bend in my knee. My pelvis rocks with this adjustment and Murtuza interprets this as encouragement. Still, there is little feeling, except for a new sadness, a blue warm rain. I realize that I am weeping, but it's silent and Murtuza doesn't hear or see it washing over me. Threatening to drown me.

I take a deep breath, manage to flap my arms to signal for him to stop. I clumsily turn onto my belly. I don't want him to see this odd despair. I wave my hand over my shoulder for him to come close.

From the way he grabs my hips, squeezing them too tightly in his excited fingers, I can sense his thrill. Once again I try to feel the sensations, and once again I can't. I continued my quiet crying, the pillow growing damp. Finally, the tears stop when his body spasms. While he breathes into my neck, I wipe my face dry with the sheet.

"Honey," he croons, "that was terrific!"

"Yeah," I murmur.

"It was nice to do something new, a new position," he laughs, giddy. "India is good for us."

"Yeah." My voice has the artificial brightness of an incandescent bulb despite the mucus that has thickened it. I am angry at myself for lying to Murtuza and also angry with him for not noticing. The irrationality of the moment muddles me and I am too tired to figure out how to handle it.

"Good night," he whispers. Then after a pause, he asks, "You okay?"

"Yes. Falling asleep. Good night." The easiest thing to do is close my eyes so no more tears will leak out. I roll over and he spoons me from behind and it takes me a few minutes of deep breathing to stop feeling like his touch will suffocate me.

∽ TWENTY ᶜ∼
Bombay, 1891

Abdoolally lay face down, Shaheeda sitting cross-legged beside him, kneading his muscles with her skinny fingers. Sharifa's hands had been so much stronger. In fact, everything about Sharifa had been more solid, substantial, including her mind. This Shaheeda was a wisp of a girl who had no thoughts of her own. When he asked her her opinion — in even the most mundane or domestic matters — she searched his face for the correct answer.

"Is it all right?" Shaheeda asked, perhaps sensing his displeasure.

"Try to push harder, no? I can barely feel anything," he grumbled. Maybe it wasn't fair to compare an eighteen-year old to his wife — his deceased wife — a woman who'd grown up with him, raised his children, supported him as his businesses thrived.

What would Sharifa think of the new girl? He imagined her amongst the guests at the festivities last month, her discerning eye on both him and his bride. She'd be glad he'd finally chosen a woman to take over her roles in the house and with the children, but he knew she'd find Shaheeda lacking, a poor substitute. And perhaps there would be something satisfying about that, the knowledge that their love was not easily replaced.

He rose abruptly, shaking her off him, sending her tumbling across the bed.

"Sorry." He shook his head. "I want to sleep."

He glimpsed her from the corner of his eye, righting herself, uncrossing her legs. She stood and slid her feet into her chappals.

"Of course, you are tired." He registered her clipped tone, for it was the first time he'd heard it. Previously, she'd only spoken to him in a melodic, little girl sort of way. But just now she'd sounded like his mother. He looked up at her, met her frustrated glance, her downturned mouth. He laughed, mirth rippling through his aching muscles, and at first she must have thought he was mocking her, for she took a step back and crossed her arms over her chest.

She was pretty, and those distinctive eyes of hers, brown with streaks of gold, shone in the dim room.

"I ... I don't know what is so funny.... Just, it feels good ... it's the first time I've laughed in a while." He giggled uncontrollably, trying to catch his breath.

He reached out his hand to her, his body thrumming with levity. After a moment, her angry glare softened, her face crinkling to match his. She took his hand.

It has been a rainy, muggy week, but this afternoon, the sky is clear and there is a breeze rustling the umbrella over our table. Fatema is between meetings, so I join her while Zee sits in one of Murtuza's classes, an English language arts lesson we concocted.

"You saw the petition against khatna I posted on Facebook?" Fatema asks. "It's a campaign to urge the Indian government to ban all forms of FGM, including khatna."

"I signed it. This issue is really important to you, isn't it?" What I really think, but don't say, is that it appears to be an obsession. I hope she won't lecture me like last time. Fatema gestures for a barista to bring us lattes. The cafe doesn't offer table service, but she is a regular and, well, it's Fatema.

"Yes, yes, it is."

"So, how come?"

"Last time when we spoke of it, you said you thought only the most *backward* people did it."

"I don't think I said 'backward.' I just meant, not in our family, I mean, no one I know has ever talked about it happening to them," I defend. The lattes arrive and I blow on my foam, take a sip. Fatema drinks down a quarter of hers in one long gulp.

"I don't know why I didn't correct you then, Shari. But you need to know that it's very common. People believe it is religiously correct." Her gaze is penetrating.

"Really?" I look down into my cup.

She inhales deeply on her cigarette, and her shoulders drop.

"You haven't given this much thought before?" she asks, kindly now.

"No, it was only your Facebook posts that made me aware. I'm glad that Australia case is happening. Do you think the perpetrators will be convicted?" It's big news for the Bohra community; two girls in Sydney told social workers about their khatna, and the local religious leader, the "khatna lady," and their mother were charged.

"I've heard through the grapevine that because it happened a couple of years ago, when they examined the girls there wasn't detectable physical scarring. That weakens the case."

"Is it possible it didn't happen then? If there isn't physical evidence?"

"No, in some cases there isn't obvious damage. I know many women who do have damage, but for others the cut was 'lighter' and healed up." She gazes at me, and I can tell she is holding something back. She pours a packet of sugar into her latte, only just realizing that it's too bitter.

"It's … it's happened to most of the girls in our family." She pulls on her cigarette and releases a long smoky sigh. Once again, she eyes me carefully, as though her words might break me.

"Oh no." My stomach drops. Fatema looks to her lap and I realize why she cares so much about this issue. "You? And Zainab, too?" I whisper. She nods, frowns. "Nani did that?"

She grinds her cigarette into the ashtray, and bites her bottom lip, hesitates. "Yes, and I'm sorry to say, your favourite aunt."

"Tasnim Maasi believes in khatna?" I ask, mouth agape. I can't imagine it. She's orthodox, but educated. She has email and Skype and a cellphone. Fatema watches me wordlessly for a moment.

"I can't say what she believes now, but yes, back then, she must have."

"I'm sorry that happened to you," is all I manage to say.

"Look, I have to get back to work. We'll talk about this some other time." Before I can respond, she's out of her chair. I watch her cross the street and notice that the ashtray is full of Fatema's brand, and my clothes reek of smoke.

On the walk back to the apartment, I sweat through my T-shirt despite it being cool for the end of October. When I arrive at the flat, Zee and Murtuza are still out. I check my watch, surprised I have been away for only an hour and a half.

In the evening, when Zee is in bed, my mouth is a spigot, Fatema's words gushing out in a single stream.

"I had no idea." Murtuza is dumbfounded. He's not on Facebook, one of those early adopters who rejected it once it grew popular.

"Yeah, me, neither," I say, the words strange on my tongue.

"Why haven't I ever heard about this before?" he asks, and I flinch, the way I do since the affair four years ago, when Murtuza finds out I've hidden something, usually something inconsequential. "Growing up, no one mentioned it to me. Not my sister, or mother."

"From what Fatema said, the orders come from the Syedna and his amils, but it's women who enforce it. The men are not involved."

"But isn't it strange that a father wouldn't know if it's happening to his own daughter? That's absurd." I follow his gaze down the hallway to Zee's bedroom.

"I guess I was lucky, growing up in the U.S. I still can't believe that Zainab's and Fatema's parents would allow it. They are modern people."

"Your mother never mentioned this to you?"

I shake my head. "I suppose it wasn't relevant. And Fatema says that no one talks about it after the fact. It's a bad memory, a secret. She said some girls block it out and so when they grow up and take their daughters for it, they don't even think it's a bad thing, just a normal rite of passage."

"A normal rite of passage ... do you ... do you think it could've happened to you? I mean, perhaps it might explain ..."

I stiffen, my instinctual response to this familiar *What is wrong with Shari sexually?* conversation. Only now, something different is happening. I hug my arms around my belly.

"Oh my god." Nausea creeps from the pit of my stomach. "I'd remember something like that, wouldn't I?"

"Unless you didn't. Right? Like Fatema said, some people forget." Murtuza is watching me intently, his dark eyelashes fluttering a panicky morse code.

"No. How could it be possible? My parents wouldn't have allowed that. They are in no way orthodox. Remember, they were red card holders," I say with a false laugh, a failed attempt at levity.

"Almost leopard-spotted!" He grins, joining in, half-heartedly. "You're probably right. But still, faith is an odd thing."

"No. I really can't imagine my mother permitting such a thing. Her beliefs are progressive." My voice is hard now. Our silly moment has passed.

"Okay."

"I'm pretty sure it didn't happen to me. No, I'm certain of it. I resent ... you thinking it's connected to ..." I don't finish my sentence.

"Okay. You know your parents best. And you know your body best." He takes my hand, the words, and his warm hand over mine, his apology. Normally these are enough to placate me, to allow easy forgiveness. But I can't receive them this evening. I am suddenly livid with Murtuza. Once again he's turned a conversation that has nothing to do with me into a line of investigation about my sexual issues. He's crossed this line too many times and I've had enough. I stomp off to bed before him, and pretend to sleep, remaining limp when he attempts to embrace me.

But something else lingers as I lie awake.

Could it be true? Could it have happened to me? I shift away from Murtuza, all the way across the king-sized expanse to the edge. No, my parents wouldn't have allowed it. Could they have been pressured? Aren't my genitals normal? No, it's ridiculous. It's impossible.

The next day, Fatema's words creep forward during quiet moments. I don't want to think about Nani and Maasi doing this to Fatema and Zainab. I consider calling my mother, but I'm not sure what to say. Should I ask her if it happened to her? Seek a definitive reassurance that it didn't happen to me? The idea of the conversation leaves me feeling flustered, foolish. I turn my focus back to Zee and my research, and resolve to push the issue away.

But I can't avoid Fatema forever. She made us dinner reservations at Hakkasan some time ago. As we arrive at the bustling restaurant, I'm glad for the buffer of my family.

"Hey, Cousin." Murtuza stands to greet Fatema, who has arrived just before us. He is relaxed with her, and I realize the khatna conversation doesn't seem to change how he sees Fatema.

"Hello, *First* Cousin," I say, hugging her with mock possessiveness.

"And you? Will you call me cousin or Maasi?" Fatema raises her eyebrows to Zee, who looks to me for an answer.

"Zee, remember what I told you? Fatema is like a sister to me, so she's kind of like your maasi."

"Hello, Maasi," Zee says, shaking Fatema's hand, as though being formally introduced for the first time. This performance is set up to make the adults laugh, and we do. "But why don't I call Alifiyah Fayji Maasi?" Zee then asks.

"Because Alifiyah is my sister and you call your father's sister fayji. And your mother's sister is your maasi," Murtuza explains. "Get it?"

Zee blinks at him.

"It's a little confusing. Each specific relationship having a different title." I stroke Zee's hair.

"Welcome to India. And then we have kaaka and kaaki and mama and mami, too. I think we would do well to drop all these titles and just call everyone by their first names." Fatema laughs. "So tell me, Murtuza, how's the flat working out for all of you? Is it to your liking?"

"Oh my god, Fatema. It's like a five-star hotel. Thanks again for arranging it for us," Murtuza says.

"It was easy. The owner lives abroad now and owed me a favour." She shrugs.

"Mom says our house seems like a shack now," Zee joins in.

"That is not true. You have a lovely older home. Your houses over there are quite different, that's all. You people like to preserve your very short history," she jokes.

"Is that why you stayed at the Park Hyatt during your last visit?" Murtuza teases. She'd declined our invitation, using the excuse that she'd be an inconvenient guest with all of her business meetings and late nights. But I read between the lines that she needed her privacy and room service. We saw her only a few times that week and she was vague about how she filled her schedule, when normally she loves to boast about lunches with famous authors and fancy awards dinners with industry colleagues.

I study the menu. "They have stir-fry beef tenderloin here?"

"Check the small print!" Murtuza smirks. "'Not real beef'!"

"It's buffalo. Somehow exempt from protection," Fatema informs us.

We order the buffalo, roasted duck udon, Ma-po tofu, Chilean sea bass, and a bowl of sweet corn soup for Zee. Murtuza fills Fatema in on the course he's been teaching on Canadian literature.

"Everyone expected it was going to be all Margarets." He laughs. "They're the only Canadian authors my students have heard of. And of course, I am including one Atwood and one Laurence short story, but the rest are people of colour and Indigenous authors like Vivek Shraya, Wayson Choy, Dionne Brand, Cherie Dimaline."

"Do those books get sold here?" I stir a drop of soy sauce into Zee's soup.

"Some, not all. We bought rights to a few Canadian authors this year."

"I photocopied excerpts for the less international works. I'll give you a list of them so you can scoop them up," he tells Fatema, who nods at the suggestion.

"Who is your favourite author, Zee?" Fatema inquires.

"Well, I don't have just one. I like lots of books."

"That's my girl. A big reader." Murtuza puffs up.

"Tell Maasi what you are reading now," I coach Zee. To Fatema I say, "She's already finished the Premchand you gave her."

"*Ramona the Pest*," Zee reports dutifully.

"Hey, I love Ramona!" Fatema tells her.

"*You* read it, too?"

"Yes! The whole series. Me, Maasi Fatema, and Maasi Zainab together. Remember I told you that many of those books are over forty years old?" I remind Zee. The conversation turns to Ramona

Quimby and her adventures, while waiters arrive and serve us from steaming dishes.

"Speaking of good characters, how is Abdoolally coming along?" Fatema pops a piece of duck into her mouth.

"Well ... slowly. I still know nothing about Zehra, the one he divorced." I glance at Zee, who has her nose in Ramona. "Finish your soup, Zee."

"Maybe he loved Zehra the most," Murtuza speculates, eyebrow cocked. "Maybe it burned so bright it was too hot to handle." He reaches under the table and squeezes my thigh. I've been cool with him since our conversation a few days back, and I know he is trying. It's irrational, but I don't feel like softening to him just yet. I cross my arms over my chest and lean away from him.

"Maybe she did something that broke his heart, or betrayed him," Fatema offers. I can tell she's picking up on our marital tiff and is trying to keep the conversation moving.

"That's assuming she was at fault for their marriage ending." I bristle. A part of me knows that I'm being tetchy, that I should just relax and enjoy this dinner. I gesture for the waiter. "Anyone want a glass of wine?"

We order a bottle for the table from one server, and within a minute a second server is pouring our glasses.

"Indian wines are really getting good." Murtuza sniffs his glass like a sommelier.

"Really good." I've had two big gulps and am beginning to feel agreeable.

"You know, about Zehra," Fatema says, "women didn't leave rich men in those days. I'm not saying it was her fault. But it had to be something pretty big."

"Religious differences? You hear about that sort of friction with Bohra couples sometimes," Murtuza ventures. He reaches for my hand, and this time I intertwine my fingers with his.

"I don't know, that seems like a modern problem," Fatema counters.

"Interesting, though. I wonder what the religious debates were back in 1900?" I feel my shoulders relax. I pull out my notebook and write the question there.

∽ TWENTY-TWO ⌒

Bombay, 1898

Abdoolally understood that miscarriages were common. Sharifa had had one and seemed to take the disappointment in stride, but then she'd already had three healthy children and was satisfied to have no more.

It was different for Shaheeda. So young, and yet she'd already had three, each one a heartbreak that left her grieving for weeks. Frankly, he didn't understand the depth of reaction, but he tried to offer her encouragement: next time, next time it will work out. Their British doctor, Dr. Fuller, reassured Shaheeda by telling her that miscarriages were God's way of ensuring that unhealthy babies would not be carried to term.

Their next time was different, and Shaheeda gave birth to their daughter, Rumana. A good pregnancy, an easy birth. The spell of bad luck, if you could call it luck, now broken.

Three years later, she was pregnant again. Perhaps, he thought, this next child, his fifth, would be a boy, a second son who would grow up to help Husein take over the business.

But this was not in Allah's plan.

Abdoolally asked the doctor, that tall white statue of a man: If pregnancy was natural, why was it so dangerous? Why did this have to happen a second time? Why did he have to lose another wife, another child this way? The doctor's watery gaze was gentle, but ultimately useless.

He took the question to his amil, the kindly older man he'd known most of his whole life. The cleric held his hand, a rare gesture, and the warm solid pressure of his touch calmed him. The amil preached faith in Allah's will, that it was Abdoolally's duty to accept a second wife's death from childbirth.

He could be dutiful, but not in the ways the amil suggested. He pledged that day that he wouldn't allow his daughters to die in such a manner. They would not be broken by birth.

He returned to his study and made a list of topics to take to the bookseller: miscarriage, childbirth, fertility. He would overcome his pain through knowledge.

He sauntered past his bookshelves, running his finger across the spines of his favourite volumes. He exhaled.

The children's Hindi reader, the first book he'd ever owned, caught his eye. He opened it, turned its now yellowed and worn pages, escaping to the jungle.

∾ TWENTY-THREE ᴄ∾

Perhaps it was the MSG. Or the wine. I lie awake, contemplating a nightmare.

I dreamt that I lived at the edge of a forest. While I stood on my deck, staring out at a green wall of trees, I thought I saw the outline of a lion, the kind that roars at you at the beginning of films: huge, majestic, commanding.

He didn't move, and so my dreaming mind assumed a trick of the eye, a rock and shrub formation coming to life in the dark.

And then his right jowl shifted slightly, and his gaze redirected, fixing on me. He was real. And waiting for me.

In an instant, my denial curdled into fear, and I rushed across the deck, slid open the screen door, and scrambled inside. By the time I'd slammed the glass door, he was an inch away, his hungry breath fogging the glass. I stared at his frightening muzzle, heart pounding. Haunting me for the next few moments was a confusing kind of warning: *apparitions can be real.*

In the morning I search for the dream's meaning online.

Lions symbolize strength and power and overcoming emotional difficulties, but if the lion is in attack mode there could be a self-destructive force, a challenge, or obstacle that must be faced.

My mind turns back to Fatema, to Zainab, to Maasi. To khatna. I close the page and the computer. I am not interested in self-destruction or challenges or obstacles. I am in India, on a long-awaited work break with my family. I want to sleep, to dream pleasant things, to vacation.

And yet I can't shake the nightmare. I tell Zainab about it when we meet in the afternoon. Her online Muslim dream site suggests a special diet to recover from an illness.

"No street food for you while you're in Mumbai," she teases, referring to my dual weaknesses for pani puri and stomach distress.

I laugh, welcoming Zainab's trademark lightness of being. Sometimes dreams are just dreams.

I watch her as she carries her laptop back to the bedroom. Like me and Fatema and all the women of the family, she is curvy, and growing rounder with age. As kids, we fit into one another's clothes and perhaps still could.

It's been a week since Fatema's confession about khatna and I haven't spoken to anyone about it except to argue with Murtuza. The words crowd in my throat, and I swallow them down. And anyway, how fair would it be to talk about something so potentially distressing to Zainab? Or maybe she doesn't see it this way? Could she believe in the practice, too?

Instead of broaching the subject, I chop vegetables alongside her as she prepares her family's meal. I share with her my anticipation to join my friend's consulting business in the spring.

"Al-Humdulillah! You've been talking about wanting a change for many years."

"Yes, she sort of suggested it two years ago, but I wasn't ready then. And then Dad died and …" I drift off.

"Losing someone really highlights what the important things are, no? We take happiness more seriously?"

I smile at her platitudes.

She tells me that the store is doing well, and she's decided to work part-time so that she can keep an eye on Nafeesa, who recently admitted that she is in love with a boy in the neighbourhood. Zainab and her husband, Adam, considered a prohibition on the relationship, but instead negotiated with the boy's parents to maintain a short leash.

"I don't want to react like my parents," Zainab admits. Maasi discovered she was flirting with a boy when she was seventeen, and severely limited her time outside of the house. The matrimony search, which had already begun, moved ahead with vigour and within six months, Zainab was engaged. I recall attending Zainab's wedding two years later, when I was twenty, feeling the ever-widening chasm of cultural difference between us. I was nowhere near ready for marriage.

"Why can't she be like Sharmeen? She never talks about boys." Sharmeen is her eldest, nineteen years old, studying at a Bohra college in Udaipur. "What if Nafeesa has sex? What if she gets pregnant?" She drops diced tomatoes into the daal.

"Well, she's sixteen. It's not like you can control her every move. Better to have open communication. When I was her age, I was sneaking around, lying to my parents. That's no better," I counsel. "You know, I told your mother about my first boyfriend right after he and I broke up. I didn't ever tell my mom. But your mother, who was so strict with you, kept my secret. Can you believe it?"

"I can. She is hard to understand that way. But then maybe she wasn't worried because you'd already broken up? If you were still together she might have told on you?"

"Maybe. What would you want me to do if your daughter shared a secret like that?"

"Oh Allah! Has Nafeesa told you something?"

"No, no! It was hypothetical! I swear."

"Things were much simpler when I was young." She shakes her head. "I had suitors, but it was very innocent. The most I ever did with them was hold hands, maybe a kiss on the cheek. I hear that girls these days do so much more."

"Which is why you have to talk to her. She needs information, about how not to get pregnant, about how to stay safe," I offer. My cousin's crumpling face tells me she's not prepared to have that conversation.

"I should have forced her to wear ridas like me. She's just a little too modern, too Western, I think," Zainab says. Then, with a mischievous curl of the lip, and a sideways glance at my sleeveless sundress, she says, "No offence." I wave away the insult before it can land.

Her phone chimes a reminder that it's time to pray, and she puts the lid on the pots and turns down the heat.

"I'll join you if that's okay?" I don't know from where this impulse arises; it's been many months since I last did namaaz. I follow her to her bedroom, and she unrolls two prayer mats with colourful floral designs. Hers is pink and purple, matching her rida. We both do waadu, the ritual ablutions, and I borrow a rida that matches my mat. As we stand side by side, speaking the prayers under our breath, bowing, prostrating, our knees cracking in harmony, I feel peace for the first time all week.

I envy Zainab. A nightmare leaves me questioning everything, searching for illusory meaning where there might be none. My cousin, on the other hand, can pass it off as a mild dietary warning. Where I have anxiety, she has prayer.

After, I carry home containers of kheema and daal for dinner. It's the same recipe we all follow, learned from the same woman, our nani, who would have learned it from her mother, who learned it from hers. Somehow, I can never quite get mine to taste as good.

ᴖ TWENTY-FOUR ᴐ

"You don't like Rooh Afza sharbat, Zeenat?" Tasnim Maasi serves us drinks on a silver tray. I take two polite sips before setting mine aside. Zee grimaces into the pink liquid.

"No, I don't think so."

"Have a taste at least." I know my cajoling won't work; once Zee's decided she doesn't want something, there's no point introducing it again for weeks.

Zee shakes her head, and looks up at me with doleful eyes. I push aside her bangs, which are growing too long.

"You know something, Zeenat? I don't know why we still drink this stuff." Maasi places all three unfinished glasses on the tray. "We have much better options these days!"

And then she lets out a rose-smelling belch, its timbre like a bullhorn's. Zee casts a glance my way, unsure how to interpret the odd behaviour. Since it's just after lunchtime, I don't have to labour to match Maasi's burp. The two of us break out into giggles, while Zee watches us, open-mouthed.

"Zeenat, do you have one for us?" There is a gleam in Maasi's eye, one she often reserved for me.

While I can occasionally goof around with Zee, playfulness doesn't come easily, probably because there are so many practicalities to attend to: did you wash your hands? Remember your lunch? Wipe from front to back? Maybe aunties, who are not mired by primary responsibility, are allowed to be kooky.

In fact, there has always been very little talk of morality or respectability between Maasi and I. When other biddies were encouraging marriage, Maasi only said, "If you'd like to meet someone, then fine, we can introduce you. But I've learned it's no good unless a person is ready and really wants it. It's a little like going on a diet," she added, winking at me as she bit into a butter cookie.

Maasi continues to egg Zee on, who gives it a good try, but doesn't manage to pass any gas. Maasi ambles out to her balcony and yells down to the man who runs the grocery stall across the lane.

"Ek batlee Limca!"

"Yes, Ma'am!" a man yells back.

Within a minute, we can hear the shopkeeper's son's chappals slapping down the hallway and dinging the doorbell. I run to the door and pass the boy fifty rupees. In the kitchen, I fill three glasses. As the fizz tickles my nose, I ponder the reality I've been pushing to the back of my mind: it was Tasnim Maasi and Nani who took Fatema and Zainab for khatna.

There must be more to the story. It's not that I think Fatema is lying, but I do wonder if she's got some of the details wrong, is misremembering. If Maasi was involved, perhaps she was pressured in some way, perhaps by her mother-in-law? Fatema said Nani was there, too, so maybe she was the culprit. But that's difficult to believe, as well; I only have positive memories of my grandmother. Yes, there must be more to the story.

I carry the Limca to Zee and Maasi, holding tight to the silver tray. My hands tremble, betraying my thoughts. Maasi passes a glass to Zee, who gulps it down in one go.

"That's much better, isn't it, Zeenat?" Maasi asks.

"We never drink this much soda at home. Too much sugar." I shake my head. "She's going to be hyper later."

"Well, when you are back home you can go back to your regular diet. But India is a place for Limca!" Maasi, too, downs her glass.

I shrug, give in. Zee comes through with a lemony burp and my favourite aunt claps her hands, cheering Zee's performance.

Zainab, freer these days with her part-time schedule, invites me back within a couple of days. I watch as she buzzes around her galley kitchen, preparing tea for us. Chicken curry bubbles on the stove, tonight's dinner. She gives it a stir, knocks the gravy off the spoon, and turns the flame down to low.

"Here, take this for Zee." She passes me a glass of orange juice and I check in on Zee. She's finished her math for the day. She was bummed that Nafeesa was at school, but appeased by the offer of a movie, and is already plugged into my laptop, headphones on, her focus on *Inside Out*'s opening scene. Zainab sets a tray with cups and a plate of cookies on the coffee table.

I tell her I'm planning a trip to Dholka, to learn more about Abdoolally.

"I've never been there. But people talk about it. Clean air, lots of space, beautiful old homes."

"My internet searches tell me it's kind of a dusty, crowded town. Maybe a century ago it was pastoral." But I, too, have grown up with our elders' nostalgic stories about the village.

We sip tea in silence, and I glance up to see Zainab looking at me.

"Still thinking about your lion dream?"

"No, I was thinking about Fatema, actually. Have you ... have you seen all the articles she's been posting? About the Australia case?" I know I am being circumspect, but speaking about khatna leaves me inarticulate. Zainab and I are used to getting personal, but this is different. This is a taboo even if no one has told us so.

"I'm surprised she is publicly posting about it, to tell you the truth. This is a private, religious matter. It's not something we discuss, at least not until the age when it is necessary." She holds her cup in midair, tea forgotten.

I nod, prepared to drop the subject, but then she continues, "She is making our community look bad."

"Yeah. While I don't question speaking out, I do wonder how this will get taken up by the mainstream." It's fine to make fun of Bohras amongst Bohras, but I don't want Facebookland to think we are monstrous. I imagine that Fatema would throw her hands up and say something like, "Khatna is monstrous!" and I would have to agree with that sentiment, too.

When I refocus my attention on Zainab, I see that she's turned pensive, as well.

"You know, I never even really talked to Mom about it, and Nani probably didn't talk to her." She fidgets in her chair, spills a little tea in her lap. I rush to pass her a tissue.

"Yes, it is out in the open now. The Australia case means that other communities will begin looking into it, begin prosecuting —"

"It's not fair that a mother will go to jail for something that is religiously required," she interrupts. "I mean, she was doing her duty as a parent, only. The goras will never understand our ways. Perhaps this Australia legal case is even a case of racism."

"Racism?"

"Yes, targeting our community. I mean, don't those Australians have enough problems of their own?" Zainab slices the air with her hands.

"Now you've lost me."

"Shouldn't they be fixing their own people rather than going after Bohras for something so minor?" Her voice has risen to a shrill bark. I glance Zee's way to make sure she is still immersed in her movie.

"But Zainab, it's not minor. It is a serious issue. Something that needs to stop." This much I feel sure about.

"Don't allow yourself to be brainwashed by all the media. It's just a tiny cut. It doesn't do any real harm. And it helps Bohra girls stay pure, loyal. Not too focused on sex." She shakes her head, agitation trembling through her neck.

"That isn't true, Zainab. You must know that. A cut down there can't stop infidelity. It's scientifically impossible," I say in a quiet voice, tamping down my shock at her words.

"Well, maybe that's true. I don't know. But something about it's worked for us for centuries. Look! No divorces in our community."

"I don't know, Zainab. I don't agree with you." I could mention Abdoolally's third wife, Zehra, but I don't want to argue. And perhaps Zainab is fatigued by the conversation, as well. She's slumped back in her chair, studying her hands.

"I can't even remember much about it." She stares off into space, and I try to fill the silence.

"Really, you don't remember it?"

"Well, only vaguely. I know I had it." She squints at the ceiling, as though the missing memory might have flown in like a lost parrot.

"Until recently I didn't realize that our family did it. I just assumed it was done among the less educated folk."

She shoots me a sharp look, and I immediately know that I've chosen my words poorly.

"Chaa. That's insulting!" The fight in her is back. "We've all had it done, and we are very educated. Why does tradition equal lack of education?"

"Sorry, I didn't mean ..." I trail off.

She nods, curtails her reaction. "Wait a minute, you didn't have it done?" Her tone is incredulous.

"No." I frown. "I guess because I was in New Jersey?"

"I think people do it there, too. Or they bring their girls here when the time comes. When Nafeesa was seven, there was a girl from Houston who was there with her nani."

"You took Nafeesa?" I remember back to when Nafeesa was as small as Zee. Just a little girl.

"Of course. Listen, even if you don't believe in it, there's no choice. Here if you want your daughter to be married in the community, it's required. The mother-in-law will often ask."

"They ask about a girl's genitals?"

"If not the girl directly, they will ask her mother. Your mother-in-law must have asked, no?"

"I doubt it." But I ponder the question. Murtuza's mother is somewhat traditional, but doesn't impose her beliefs on anyone. I glance Zee's way when she laughs out loud at the screen.

"I'm surprised. It's just a regular thing," Zainab counters.

"But little girls! It must be scary and painful for them. The articles I've read say that it's often done in unhygienic places and girls get infections." I know I'm not going to get anywhere in this debate, but I can't stop myself.

"You're making a big deal. It's not like that. How scary could it have been if I don't even remember? And the lady we took the girls to is very clean. Both Sharmeen and Nafeesa cried for a few minutes and that was that. We took them out for ice cream and they cheered up. Maybe in the past it was more unsafe, but like you said, we are an educated community."

"What are you talking about, Mom?" We both turn to see Zee's serious eyes upon us. Her right earbud is in, but the other dangles off her face. Perhaps she heard us mention Nafeesa.

"Oh, nothing important, Zee. Adult stuff. Watch your movie." Surprisingly, she complies. Usually, when Murtuza and I invoke the "adult stuff," she only grows more interested.

"I'll never get it done to her."

"And you won't have to. You won't be pressured. It's understood that you live a different life in the West." This is often how we've cooled down our tiffs, agreeing to disagree. She's the East, and I'm the West.

"So … it didn't have any impact on you at all? They say it can cause problems in the future," I ask in a low voice. Zainab looks away in embarrassment and I wonder if I've gone too far. She and I have had countless conversations about dating. She was my go-to cousin when it came to matters of youthful romance because, despite her parents' strict eyes on her, she had boyfriends all through her teen years. However, we've never talked directly about our sex lives, perhaps following an unwritten rule about marital privacy.

"No, none. Adam and I have always had a very good time together." Her faces spreads into a shy smile. "Even though it wasn't a love marriage … our chemistry was so good … from the beginning. I don't know about others, but I've never had any problems … in that department."

"May I ask you a more personal question?" I do a shoulder check to make sure Zee isn't listening.

Zainab shakes her head from side to side. It could mean *Yes* or *Maybe* or *We'll see*, but I push ahead anyway.

"So … orgasms?"

"Of course! Never a problem. Not at all! See khatna doesn't affect that! Anyway, don't they say that the brain is the biggest sexual organ?"

"Yeah." I tip my teacup to my lips but it's empty. "But then if that's true, why would khatna stop infidelity?"

As though she hasn't heard my question, she says, "All of that stuff in the media is an exaggeration. I really think it is." She stands up, clears the cups, and disappears into the kitchen.

∾ TWENTY-FIVE ℃

Bombay, 1899

A week after the nikah, he returned home late to find her in his library, so absorbed in a book that she didn't notice his entry. While he knew Zehra was literate — it was one of the praises his mother sung about her — he flinched when he saw her reading one of his books. If Sharifa or Shaheeda ever took one in their hands, it was to dust or admire them. Everyone obeyed his unspoken rule to not interfere with his library.

He watched her for many heartbeats before clearing his throat. She startled, clapped the book shut, *Elements of English Grammar.*

"I see you like to read?"

"Yes. I hope it's all right. I learned to read a little English when I was young, but I would like to improve, and to learn to speak the language, too." She stood, showed him the cover.

"You will not have any use for it. I speak English only with the Angrez, and only for business purposes."

"I thought that maybe ... I might help you. Even to entertain them when required." Her expression had shifted from embarrassment at being caught, to confidence, her gaze steady, her jaw set.

Her self-possession reminded him of Batool, recently married and now living in Poona. It hadn't escaped him that his new bride was only slightly older than his children. When he'd complained to his mother that Zehra was young enough to be his daughter, she'd chuckled and asked if he'd rather be married to an old maid.

"I think you will be busy enough with the household and Rumana."

"Quite the contrary." She straightened her spine. "Your servants take care of nearly everything for Rumana. I would like to put my education to good use. I'd like to be of help. With your business affairs."

He wasn't sure what to say. Of course, he was in favour of girls' education — he'd made sure his daughters knew how to read, write, and do basic maths. But this was to build their characters, ensure good marriages, and assist their domestic management. Exactly how did this girl think she could help him with business affairs? Her proposal was preposterous.

"I will have you take over Rumana's tutoring, then. Put the book back in its place and go check on her." He flicked his wrist, a gesture to end the conversation, and took his seat behind his large wooden desk. He heard the swish of her gaghra as she exited the room. When he turned, he saw that she'd taken the book with her.

∽ TWENTY-SIX ∾

I listen to Mumbai's night sounds. The city slows, but doesn't know stopping. Despite New York City's reputation, it's possible to hear little but the faraway rumble of a bus at 1:00 a.m. on our residential street. Here, horns beep and a chaiwala pushes his squeaky cart, calling out to a pair of passersby who might be thirsty. A crow caws, inspiring a dog to froth into a barking rage.

But it's not just the fracas thieving my sleep. I lie awake making sense of my conversation with Zainab, processing the fact that she doesn't remember much, and views khatna as a harmless tradition, while Fatema has the contrary experience and opinion. But, then, haven't they always played on opposite sides of the court, with me watching them pelt the ball back and forth?

I find myself siding with Fatema's activism while worrying that she's obsessed with it. And I understand Zainab's draw to tradition but can't believe that such a smart person knows so little about sexuality and anatomy.

I extricate myself from the bedsheets, step out onto the balcony, watch the men drinking chai. The tea seller moves along, ready to wake the next city block.

I know that faith and facts don't necessarily coexist.

I know that fidelity has nothing to do with intact genitals.

Does a lack of faith have anything to do with infidelity?

And then, within a heartbeat, I am back thinking about Ian.

While I didn't call it cheating, I sensed the inappropriateness of the secret. Grown women, married women, aren't supposed do that kind of thing.

As I've done many times before, I contemplate what allowed me to duck the rules of marriage to be intimate with another man. Perhaps it *was* a lack of traditional values, an interruption of my faith.

I like to imagine that my ethics kept Ian and I within the bounds of talk and fantasy, but that would be fooling myself. Had we not been caught, what might have happened? Would Murtuza have been as understanding if we'd gone a step further?

Other repetitive questions loop in the middle of the night: Why didn't I hide it better? Password-protect my computer? Log out of my Facebook account?

Did I feel entitled to misbehave, to walk a treacherous line?

What if Murtuza suddenly changes his mind and decides I'm no longer trustworthy?

Did he stay because Zee was so small? What about when she's grown?

In our last session with the therapist, I dared to ask, "Have you forgiven me?"

My heart ached when he shook his head, stared at his shoes. Finally he answered, "But I am willing to move past it."

I opened my mouth to protest — hadn't we been processing my mistake for months already? — but the therapist held up her palm.

"It might be too soon for forgiveness?" she asked.

"I think so. I'm not angry anymore. I sort of understand what Shari was going through emotionally, but I can't honestly say I forgive her yet. I don't trust her fully. But … I trust her enough to move forward and see if everything gets better … and then maybe I'll be able to forgive her and trust her completely. One day."

I remained quiet, knowing that my punishment was that we would have to carry on, move forward as he said, with this new, silent tension between us. One day, he might present me with his gift of forgiveness, but lurking within its box would be his inability to forget.

I have not forgotten, either. The therapist repeated a dozen times that online betrayal is betrayal. But here's the thing. Online sexy talk is not actual sex, for it's not actualized in the body. It means that I, too, have not mentally let it go, not one hundred percent. There will always be a question mark about the sex. It would have likely disappeared had I found out that sex is sex, nothing special. Nothing magical. But I don't *know* that, not in my body. It still holds the question. My body still wants an answer.

And so, as the men downstairs finish their tea and conversation, I allow the question mark to curl through my brain, re-imagining that one single night Ian and I had together. I don't permit myself this often, but tonight I don't feel like resisting.

It was over a decade ago, two weeks after Robert moved out, the beginning of Christmas vacation. I wasn't sad, the way I'd been after Jonathan four years earlier, or completely distraught like after my first boyfriend, Nick. No, with Robert I was only numb, weary, a three-time loser.

Joanna, a buddy from teacher's college, invited me to her colleague's house party. I chose it over a friend's birthday celebration, a gathering that I knew would be full of people who would overwhelm me with their sympathetic looks and *How are yous* and *I'm so sorrys.*

We arrived at 9:00 p.m., early for Manhattan gatherings, but the revelry was in full swing. I deposited my contribution of seven-dollar red wine on the kitchen counter, pushing aside four other empty seven-dollar bottles to make room. Ian came through just then, still wearing his parka, and I pointed down the hallway to the bedroom that served as the closet. A minute later, he scanned the beverage selection. Besides Joanna, who'd waded into the living room to greet the host, we seemed to be the only two sober people in attendance.

"'Tis the season," he smirked as we watched a group of four women down shots, laughing at nothing.

"I get it. Joanna told me most of these folks are teachers." Judging from the crowd, they were young ones like me, still completing our first "hell years" in the profession.

"Or social workers like me."

"Really, you?" With his shoulder-length dirty-blond hair and soul patch, he didn't resemble the earnest, buttoned-up types who visited my school.

"Yeah, I work at an addictions agency."

"Cheers." It was the kind of thing you say when you're feeling nothing and barely know the person with whom you're sharing conversation. At best, Ian and I were acquaintances with some friends in common. We clinked glasses even though we hadn't toasted anything.

I finished my first drink and refilled my glass and thought that maybe his chosen field made sense; he was a good listener, with penetrating eyes that made me feel like he actually cared.

Robert and I had grown distant and dismissive of each other in the past year, and I welcomed the attention.

"So, what else is new with you?" he asked. The only thing on my mind was Robert's desertion, but I didn't want to start crying under Ian's compassionate gaze. Instead, we commiserated about how badly we each needed a vacation. We didn't move from that corner of the kitchen all night. At 1:00 a.m., he bashfully asked if I might want to come back to his place. I didn't have anything else to do, and he was nice. The idea of my apartment, with half its furniture cleared out, was depressing. And I knew I wouldn't be able to sleep; insomnia had extended its woody roots since Robert's departure.

We padded through an inch of fresh snow in our midcalf boots, the air biting my cheeks. I was tipsy, but not drunk. Tipsy felt better than the numbness that had been occupying my body all week like a melancholic parasite.

We sat on his couch and he confessed that he'd been attracted to me for years but hadn't asked me out because I'd always been in a relationship when he was single, which he had been for the previous year.

"Well, I guess our timing worked out, now." For a moment, I wondered what I was doing in his bachelor apartment. There were milk crates for shelves and an Emma Goldman poster on the wall that made me guffaw: *If voting changed anything they'd make it illegal.*

He kissed me, and I mechanically reciprocated, assessing his lips to be plumper than Robert's, which I'd always found to be too thin. Ian ran his hands over my back and I mimicked his motions.

"You okay?" Perhaps he could sense that my mind was elsewhere.

"Yeah." I pressed into him. I told myself that I needed to do it, had to override my Robert grief so I could get over him. I buried my face in his neck and inhaled sour-milk sweat and a trace of cologne. What happened next surprised me. My skin began to tingle, like that time when at a cottage with friends, I'd jumped out of a hot tub and into a snowbank. An electric buzz travelled through me. My body woke up.

Ian pushed my sleeve up my arm and kissed the goose-pimpled skin there. He lifted my sweater to my belly, running his lips over my navel. He undressed me slowly, as though unwrapping a present in expensive paper. He exposed a few inches at a time, his teeth lightly scratching over me, his lips and tongue taking small tastes. Once I was in my underwear, he pulled off his jeans and T-shirt and covered me with his warm body. I rolled us over, took off my bra, and lowered my breasts to his face.

"You forgot a spot."

"Or two," he mumbled.

"Do you have any condoms?" I wasn't prepared; I'd been on the pill with Robert.

"Thank Jeezus I do!"

I wobbled off him when he reached down to the milk crate beside his lumpy futon, ripped open a shiny square, and asked, "Now okay?" I nodded.

He'd managed to unthaw me. I sensed my G spot for the first time, that elusive place about which I'd been reading for years. I squeezed his buttocks, guiding him in a rhythm that matched my rocking. It was like nothing I'd ever felt before or since. And then he groaned, and it was over. I glanced down to make sure the condom was still on for the ride.

"I'm sorry, I wish I could've lasted longer. Too much booze, I guess."

"It's okay, you did good." I patted his shoulder. I had come close, closer than I ever had. I still don't know why; we hadn't done anything that novel.

"We can keep going." He put his hand over my vulva, but I stopped him, probably out of habit. Now I wish I hadn't. I held his hand and told him I was tired. He asked me to stay the night and I did. In the morning, he made me instant coffee and a blueberry-flavoured toaster strudel. We agreed to get together after the holiday; he was leaving for Seattle to visit family the next day.

I went home to Edison for a low-key Christmas. My parents and I exchanged presents, put up a plastic tree, ate biryani, and didn't speak about the source of my glum mood.

My folks had a large dinner party on December twenty-eighth, all the guests Bohras. While we were setting the table for twelve, Mom glanced at me furtively.

"What?"

"Don't be angry with me." She confessed that she'd invited along the nephew of some family friends.

"Oh, come on, Mom! How could you? I just broke up with Robert!" Throughout my twenties, there had been a few sneak-attack setups like this, always with dull and dweeby men from the community. A pharmacist so nervous he couldn't make eye contact. An MBA who mansplained the need to keep the minimum wage low. A dentist with terrible breath.

"This guy sounds like a good match, though. Listen!" she said, her eyes pleading. "He's a PhD, an English professor at Rutgers! You like to read! And he's from Canada! He likes to cook! He is interesting!" She emphasized *interesting*, knowing my impressions of her previous matches. I crossed my arms over my chest.

I was about to argue that there was someone else I liked, someone I wanted to start dating. I might have listed: a social worker! With student furniture and anarchism! Toaster pastry!

I looked at Mom, saw the concern wrinkling her brow, and sighed. I nodded. After three unsuccessful relationships, maybe it was time to listen to my mother.

The guests arrived, and Murtuza and I were guided to sit across from each other. We made easy conversation, mostly about the books we were reading and the decline of public education. As he was leaving, he asked to meet for dinner two days later, away from the eager and watchful gazes of our families. A few days after that, we saw *Brokeback Mountain* and held hands while Jake and Heath kissed. He dropped me off in front of my apartment, and we necked a bit in the car. When I got in, there was a message from Ian on my answering machine; he was back from Seattle and wanted to know if I felt like coming over to his place. For a moment, I was tempted, but my lips still tingled from Murtuza's, so I deleted Ian's message. I called and got his voicemail the next day, and made excuses about not being ready to date anyone. I'd decided to give the nice Bohra boy a chance.

I let Ian go, and didn't think about him again until he friend-requested me many years later. To be clear, I don't want a relationship with Ian. Murtuza is my husband. But I do sometimes wish — in the way we wish for magical things that bear no consequences — for one more night with Ian.

Now, I return to bed, listen to Murtuza's soft breathing. I touch my labia, then deeper, entering the fantasy I permit myself when alone. It always begins with me passing through a revolving glass door, a whoosh of air-conditioning brushing against my warm body. It's somewhere near the airport, one of those large four-star chains that feel anonymous, yet respectable. We rendezvous at the bar and the other patrons might mistake us for travellers having a last drink before retiring for the evening. He looks different than when we first met, his hair short, and he's wearing a V-neck sweater over a shirt and stylish jeans. He thanks me for coming, tells me he's waiting a long time for this moment. My imagination skips us forward to when he passes me a key card, whispers the room number, his breath tickling the fine hairs in my ear. He leaves first. I follow three minutes later.

In the elevator I am alone with my thoughts. I am aware that I exist on a parallel plane to my real life. My heart races with the anticipation of Ian's touch, the reunion we've been awaiting for a decade. The elevator door opens on the eighteenth floor, and I step out.

There is a familiar pleasant awakening under my fingers.

I edge the plastic card into the lock and step inside. It's dark and I don't see him when he comes forward and pushes me against the wall, kissing me forcefully. I drop my purse, my body pinned by his. He pulls up my skirt and I am naked underneath. I wrap my leg around him and then he is inside me.

My body remembers, still, that night with him and within moments my G spot begins to thrum.

I fast forward and we are on the bed, still half-dressed, he on top of me and then behind me, my mind changing our positions in a frenetic search to find something to increase and intensify the sensations.

The faint hope, the one I don't like to admit having, whispers, *Maybe this time, maybe it's going to happen. Please.*

Still, my body won't co-operate, won't let go. I slow my movements, willing myself to calm my thoughts, in the hope it will help; I read somewhere that this is a good idea. But the slowing is like the volume dial turning everything down, both my mental noise and my body's excitement. I persevere, running the script over again from the moment I walked into the suite to the wall to the bed. And still, it doesn't happen. I rub my hand against my underwear's waistband, dry my fingers.

My mind quiets, and Murtuza's *Fifty Shades* pleather case drifts in. Since arriving in India, I've thought about it once or twice, but haven't mentioned it. Neither has he. Has he lost interest in it, or maybe he feels too shy?

Murtuza rouses, then rolls onto his back, a snuffly snore escaping. What would he think if he could watch the film reel I've just played? He knows most of me, but he'll never know this particular part, the woman whose mind drifts to places it probably shouldn't.

~⊙ TWENTY-SEVEN ᜡ

Murtuza has a two-week break in his teaching schedule and so I've planned a trip for the three of us to Goa. It's our first time to this state but I've always been curious; all my white American friends include Goa in their India itineraries and rave about it.

Despite having our own flat in Mumbai, this trip gives me a sense of truly being on our own as a family, the rest of the relatives blocked out. Knowing we are away, they don't send daily check-in text messages, their electronic buzz of concern and hospitality absent.

We stay at a resort that reminds me of a Costa Rican retreat I once visited. For the first few days, it's idyllic; we lie on the beach, eat our breakfasts and dinners at the same oceanview restaurant, and wander around town in between. It's a lazy, true holiday. The only non-spam email I receive is from Meena, the Ahmedabad archivist who Kaaka referred. She's offered to research Abdoolally for a good rate and so I send her all the information I have about him, and a list of specific questions about his wives. She suggests I give her a couple of months, which works for when I'd like to go to Dholka — her office is about an hour away from there.

Here we have a one-bedroom suite, with Zee on the living room pullout. It seemed large enough when we booked it, but is cramped by day four, and Murtuza and I bicker about stupid things.

On our fifth night, I check Facebook while he reads. I sense a shift in the room; he's behind me, helicoptering.

"Facebook hasn't changed since I left. Look how mundane it all is. Who cares about what Laura ate for lunch?"

"I read lots of interesting articles on my friends' feeds. And I don't mind knowing some of the day-to-day stuff. Look, Marla and Brian just got a puppy." I try to hide my annoyance that he is reading over my shoulder.

"Why do you bother with it so much? It's all just superficial nonsense."

"I dunno, everyone's on it. It's a way to stay in touch."

"It's performance art, not real life, Shari." He flops onto the couch and shoots me a challenging look.

I could continue the argument, tell him that a part of me is curious about what Fatema is posting these days, but we haven't talked about khatna since that tense conversation a couple of weeks back. I take a breath and stay quiet. Will he always, reflexively, glance over my shoulder to check what I'm reading? He picks up his novel and disappears behind it, which is a relief; I never know how to finish these quarrels.

When we fought as newlyweds, we'd keep talking, then yelling over one another until we'd both be too angry to resolve the conflict. I'd stomp away, slam doors, and then Murtuza would be angry that I'd abandoned him in the middle of a fight. Over the years, we've learned to sidestep, lower our voices, avoid the storm. For the next few days, we instinctively give each other more space and politeness. He lets me sleep in and makes breakfast. I take Zee for a walk so he can read. I swim while he builds sandcastles.

A few days later, we are out late and I have a craving for kulfi from a vendor on Baga Beach road. His five-by-five stall has the best badam-pista I'd ever tasted. At 11:00 p.m., we carry our kulfi sticks down to the beach. The restaurants and bars are closing at this hour, in compliance with a local law that disallows them from remaining open late during election season. Young people stream out of open doors, wobbly and boozy. I grasp Zee's hand, and Murtuza clasps her other one. A man stumbles past us and vomits against a stuccoed wall. Having reached the crowded beach, we turn back, sensing the unpredictability of the intoxicated throng around us.

"Wow," I say.

"This is weird, Shari. It's like people downed bottles just before last call."

"What's last call?" Zee asks. Neither of us respond and instead pick up our pace. Zee halts us in front of a puppy, curled in a ball on the pavement. At home, she's afraid of domestic dogs on leashes, but she coos over these sun-warmed and docile animals.

"Can I give him kulfi?" She still has a stick melting over her fingers.

"Yes," I say, "but don't get too close. Just put it in front of him." She holds the kulfi out and the dog savours it in a few rapid licks.

"Let's keep going," Murtuza says, looking at a group of twenty-something men singing their way toward us. "It's like zombie-land out here."

In front of us a group of girls walks unsteadily on high heels. A scooter zips past, narrowly missing them. They laugh at the near accident. At the main road, we flag a rickshaw back to our hotel. Later, Murtuza and I will describe this scene to amused friends and family as an innocent kulfi excursion that transformed into a vision of hell. It will be our co-constructed, exaggerated memory, and when we share it, over and over, we'll prod one another to add details, and finish each other's sentences.

—————— ✦ ——————

The Saturday after we return from Goa is my uncle and aunt's twenty-fifth anniversary party with forty of us crammed into a banquet hall's party room. Murtuza huddles in a corner, talking to three of my male cousins, the two of us sliding into an informal gender segregation that rarely happens in our New York social circles.

I chat with Sharmeen, who is home for a short break from college. She, like her mother, wears a fancy rida, while her younger sister, Nafeesa, is in a body-hugging kameez and skinny jeans.

"How's school?" Zainab told me that she's studying home science, popular among Sharmeen's friends.

"I'm enjoying it. But I think I want to go to study business courses next year. I'd like to work in the store."

"That's terrific, Sharmeen! Your parents might want to pass it along when they're ready to retire, like your nana and nani did."

"Plus, I think we could modernize it a little. Nafeesa wants to take fashion design, so perhaps we could sell more types of clothing, not just the tourist things."

We watch Zee running the perimeter of the room in a game of tag with two younger second cousins. During one of her loops, she slows, sidles into me, her face flushed. I pass her my water bottle and she empties it in three big gulps. Tasnim Maasi comes over and takes the opportunity to catch her for what Zee now calls a Wet Maasi Kiss.

"Well, Zee, soon you will be getting married yourself. Is there anyone here you'd like me to approach on your behalf? We can arrange your marriage today, this very day." Maasi spreads her arms wide, theatrically.

Zee looks at her quizzically. Then, after a long pause, she squeals, "Don't be silly, Maasi!"

She wiggles out of Maasi's grip and runs off with her new buddies.

"Our girls grow up quickly, don't they? One minute they're little girls and the next they are teenagers."

"Creepy," Fatema mutters under her breath, but loud enough for me to hear. I hadn't realized that she'd come to sit near us. "Keep an eye on her while you're here, Shari."

"What do you mean?" I whisper.

Just then Naima Mami and Huzefa Mama usher us to the next room, where all the furniture has been cleared away and five thaals, metal discs on short pedestals that fit eight people, are arranged on the floor.

"I'll explain later," Fatema murmurs. But I know what she's inferring, her warning unnerving me. It's ridiculous that I should guard Zee from Maasi. Still, I scan the room, my heart skipping a beat when at first I don't locate my daughter.

We find two empty spots beside Fatema at a thaal. I remind Zee how to tuck her feet under herself so she can sit comfortably and not sprawl into the next person's space.

A small bowl of salt is passed and I instruct her to place a pinch on her tongue.

"Eww. Why?" Zee winces at the taste.

"Who knows? It just a custom," Fatema answers.

"No, no, there is a reason," Tasnim Maasi counters, joining the thaal across from us. "It has to do with appreciating that salt is in the earth or somesuch thing."

"No, it's from an old belief that salt can cure us from diseases, I think." I try to recall what I read in *Mullahs on the Mainframe.*

153

"Like most of our customs, we don't really know why we do things anymore. We just continue them, on and on. Like sheep. Baaa," Fatema directs her animal noises at Zee, who cracks up.

"But this is a nice tradition, this eating together in the thaal, isn't it? We share one large plate," I say brightly, contesting my cousin's naysaying. And I mean it. It's one of my favourite Bohra rituals. "It's way more fun than eating at a table."

"True." Fatema nods. "And there are very important rules. Like see?" She builds a low wall of two standing samosas between her and Zee's spaces on the thaal. "This way your gravy won't spill into my section. We can eat together, but keep our separate territories, no?"

Zee studies Fatema's mock-serious face. Then, with a laugh, she pokes the samosa wall, causing its collapse. The rest of the ladies at the thaal giggle along with her.

"What are you teaching this girl? To play with her food?" Maasi chuckles.

"The best lesson a Bohra girl can learn: to question authority." Fatema takes a bite from one of the fallen samosas.

"Arré, let's eat, no?" Maasi shakes her head.

I watch these women, women I love, scooping rice with their right hands. We are skilled at making neewallas, bite-sized clumps inside thumbs, pointers, middle, and ring fingers, without dropping a single grain or letting the daal drip into our palms.

As I've done since I was a small child, I listen closely to the conversation. I miss the jokes in Guju sputtered out too quickly for me to follow, can't decode the subtext underlining dynamics too complex for a visitor. I look at Fatema, then across at Tasnim Maasi, and then back again, wondering what is going unspoken between them. Both sit stiffly, avoiding each other's gaze. Has their tension always been about khatna? Is that when it started?

My legs cramp, and my stomach churns despite the temptations of halwa, green chicken, ice cream, biryani, and kachumber. I hate that there's an unbridgeable distance between Maasi and Fatema. I suppose I've always perceived it, but I'd attributed it to lifestyle and religious differences. Now I know better.

It's not my issue and I don't want to get in the middle of it. And yet I know that Maasi, perhaps with good intentions, or not knowing any better, was somehow involved in stealing something precious from Fatema. And the hard set of my cousin's jaw, her unwillingness to look Maasi in the eye, belies the fact that she hasn't come to terms with the theft. Is Maasi even aware that she is being silently accused of a crime?

I listen to their silences and wish I could bring them together again.

∿ TWENTY-EIGHT ∾
Bombay, 1900

Despite the droughts and plague that had spread across India that year, the new century began with optimism for Abdoolally. He bought a second printing press in Dholka, and started the India Stationery Mart near Crawford Market. He and his family were lucky compared to most. But he'd learned over the years that sometimes luck didn't last.

When he arrived home one night after dark, Zehra met him at the door and said, "I think you should call for the doctor. Mummy seems very unwell." He rushed to his mother's bedside where his daughter Raushan stood, looking down at her grandmother with worry. Zehra must have called her over; she lived only two streets away with her husband and infant. So close in age, they related to one another as friends.

He pressed his hand to his mother's forehead. She was hot and unresponsive to his prodding.

"Could it be ...?" While the bubonic plague had claimed thousands of lives, it was mostly mill workers and those who lived in chawls who were most impacted. The family had relocated to

Dholka for a couple of months the previous year as a precaution, but had returned when the scare receded.

"Yes, we must call the doctor. Raushan, you go. You don't want to pass anything to your baby. Tell the servant to fetch Dr. Fuller."

"Yes." Raushan dashed down the stairs.

"What's happening, Mummy?" Five-year-old Rumana stumbled into the room, rubbing sleep from her eyes.

"Don't worry, baby, Daadi is just feeling a little sick but she'll be fine in the morning," Zehra cooed, pushing Rumana out of the sick room. "Let's go back to bed."

She lifted the skinny girl and carried her to her bedroom.

Abdoolally sat on Amta's bed and watched her sleep, as he had done many times before, back when they'd slept on the same mat in a small room they'd shared with another widow and her three children.

He whispered a prayer to Allah: *Please don't take her yet. Let this not be the fevers. Let her awake in the morning.*

I wish I hadn't clicked open the link Fatema shared today on her Facebook page. This one is by a woman named Insiyah, a citizen journalist writing about her khatna experience. I'm curious about this rising tide of women publishing their stories, their names, even their photos.

After the second paragraph, I pause; I'm not sure if I'm up for it today. Before I can decide, Mom rings me on Skype and I call Zee over from where she sits at the other end of the dining table, working on skip-counting puzzles.

"My Zee-nut!" Mom greets Zee.

"Nani!" Zee yells back.

"Where's Murtuza?"

"Sick in bed! Caught a cold. Hey, you're up late." It's almost midnight for her.

"Had too much caffeine this afternoon."

"Look, Nani!" Zee tells Mom all about how she just figured out that if there are four flowers in a bunch and there are three bunches, then there must be twelve flowers all together.

"Clever girl! Isn't this very advanced for second grade? That's multiplication," she informs me.

"I guess so, but they call it problem-solving at this level."

Zee shows her the full page of problems she's already completed, reviewing each one in detail. "You're doing so well, keeping up with your classmates," Mom praises Zee.

She updates us on her travel plans, and Zee loses interest in the adult talk and her math book and wanders out to the terrace.

I fill Mom in on the anniversary party, and she complains, "That brother of mine! He couldn't wait for me to arrive?"

"I guess they wanted to celebrate their anniversary on the actual date?" I tease her.

"I suppose," she concedes, pushing her lips into a pout.

Insiyah's article is still open behind Mom's face, and I recall the unease between Maasi and Fatema across the thaal. I want to tell her about it, to see what she thinks about khatna, but she interrupts my train of thought with her own news.

"So Brianna was crying in the hallway today." Mom shakes her head wearily.

"Really?"

"You know, this is her fourth breakup in five years! She just can't seem to find the right match."

"Oh no, poor thing."

Mom has mentioned Brianna, her thirty-year-old neighbour, to me on a few occasions, consulting with me about modern relationships, which is funny, because I mostly repeat what my friend Laura scribes on her blog.

Of course, Mom knows even less; she hasn't ever dated and probably never will. She and Dad were introduced when she was nineteen and he twenty-three. They were second cousins who knew each other vaguely prior to being set up, and their courtship consisted of two lunches, both chaperoned by an elder.

"Brianna told me that she met this last guy through a mobile telephone app. You swipe one way if you like the face, and swipe the other way if you think they are ugly! Can you believe it?" I laugh as she huffs with faux outrage.

While she tells me more about the intricacies of the dating app, my mind drifts to my last year in high school, when some of her Bohra friends suggested that it was time to commence my betrothal plans. Although we'd been in New Jersey for a decade and a half, the old notions persisted, at least among some in our extended family and friends. Mom was uneasy with their suggestion, but she encouraged me to meet a Bohra boy. "Not for marriage, you are too young for that, but just to meet, or only to be friends." While it sounded like she was resisting her friends' ideas, there was a glimmering hopefulness in her voice, an unspoken wish that I might desire some of what her more orthodox-minded friends' children wanted.

"Maybe later, Mom," I said, not wanting to disappoint. "I'm not really thinking about that kind of stuff right now. There are exams, and then starting college …" and she nodded, satisfied, or satisfied enough that I was a good girl on the correct path. The truth was that I'd been dating Nick since eleventh grade and we were "serious." We'd both been accepted to NYU and planned to live together in second year. My parents had no clue, believing me when I littered the house with lies about spending time at my friend Stephanie's house, or at the library, or the mall.

When Nick and I split in first semester, I travelled home for Christmas break, ten pounds lighter than at Thanksgiving. Mom congratulated me on my figure but questioned the dark circles under my eyes. I told her that I was tired from exams.

"Well, she stopped her crying and went home. I hoped it helped, a little."

"Brianna is lucky to have you." The screen freezes for a couple of seconds.

"Arré, bad connection! Oh, there, we're back again." She blinks a few times.

"You know, I wish I'd gone to you for support when I went through a breakup in college."

"What?" Her face falls, and I divulge the details of my high school dating. Inexplicable, delayed-reaction tears well up in my eyes.

"That boy who was on the debating team with you?" Her face screws up in concentration.

"I can't believe you remember." My wet eyes aren't for Nick, but my nineteen-year-old self who grieved alone.

"Why didn't you say anything?" She leans against her desk, cradles her face in her palm.

"I'd been keeping way too many secrets. I wouldn't have known where to start." I can't maintain eye contact, instead focus on my own video image.

"Oh, that's terrible. I'm sorry it was like that." She sighs.

"No, I'm sorry, too. I wish I'd told you. After the initial shock, we'd have been all right." I don't fully believe this, even now, old catastrophic teenage thoughts lingering: being grounded for months, prohibited from seeing my boyfriend, not being allowed to go to prom. Later, in college, I feared a loss of her trust and respect.

"I never encouraged you to talk about those kinds of things back then, did I?"

"You lived a very different life. How could you help me navigate dating and breakups? Have you even had a breakup in your life?" Then I back away from the screen a few inches, searching for the words that will correct the ones I just blurted.

"No." She looks away, too.

"It's like losing Dad," I say, filling in the silence that has just formed between us. "On a much smaller scale."

"Yes, I suppose I felt like that while talking to Brianna." She sniffs, reaches for a tissue.

And so we talk about Dad, about mourning, and then about how she is looking forward to joining us soon, getting out of the empty condo. I leave the subject of khatna for another day.

When I shut down Skype and close the screen, Insiyah's article loiters behind it. Scrolling down is like trudging through mud, and yet I do.

> I was taken to a strange place by a trusted older female relative, under false pretences, and then a scary, incomprehensible, and painful thing happened, after which I was given the cake I'd been promised earlier. I had been excited to go, I love cake. What child doesn't?

The particular components of these stories don't vary much, as though an entire community, generation after generation, is following the same terrible, unwritten script.

I push back my chair and go to the cupboard. I arrange a few chocolate chip cookies on a plate. I crunch one, the chocolate dissolving on my tongue. I close my eyes and think, *It's always the promise of sugar, the lure, the bait.*

Sugar and spice and everything nice ...

I open my eyes and look out to the terrace. Something feels wrong. Zee is no longer there. I call out to her and when she doesn't reply, I race outside. I scan the street below, my logic-brain shut down. When I run back inside, she emerges from the bathroom. I exhale.

"Whaaaat?" Zee, hand on hip, appraises me. I must look weird.

"I didn't know where you were."

"I had to pee."

"Did you finish math?" I check my watch, see that we still have another hour for home-schooling.

"A long time ago." She rolls her eyes. I walk away, breathe, sit at my computer.

"Okay. What's next? Health?" I open a file and consult our plan. I play a six-minute video on the tablet about the Food Guide Pyramid. A disembodied female voice describes protein, and Zee watches, reaching for the cookies.

The video ends. I grab pencil crayons and ask her to design a healthy lunch.

"A ham sandwich. That's protein and carbohydrates," she says. I'm impressed she remembers the words.

"What else would you put in the sandwich, for the other food groups?"

It's almost lunchtime, and so the lesson turns into an impromptu sandwich-building exercise. We have all the ingredients except the ham, of course. I cut the sandwich into two halves and explain that cheese doubles as dairy and protein.

"Why don't we have ham?" she asks.

"Well, Muslims don't eat pork. It's a religious belief."

"But why?"

Murtuza and I argued about this when we first moved in together. Except for trying a slice of pepperoni pizza as a teen, I haven't challenged the pork prohibition; it is a part of my identity. Murtuza, on the other hand, questioned everything, and finding no evidence that pork is unhealthy or "dirty," as I weakly contended, he ate it from time to time. We agreed to disagree, but I insisted that we not have pork in the house.

"Tell you what. That's a big question, with many answers. How about we leave it for tomorrow's class?" Perhaps I can weave it into geography or health somehow? She nods, satisfied to let the question drop. After we finish eating, I sit her down with her workbook, where she has to match up pictures of food — spaghetti, apples, meat — with their categories.

I return to my computer, close the Food Guide window. I also close Insiyah's article and am bounced back to Fatema's Facebook post. I hit "like" and then share the article in a private message to Mom, writing an ambivalent "thought you might find this interesting" caption above it.

I glance up to see Zee focused on her book, still absorbed by the nutrition material. She's curled up in her dining-room chair, all three-and-a-half feet of her taking up only a fraction of its seat. Everyone says she looks like me, but I see Murtuza in the shape of her lips, the spread of her nose. She brushes her hair out of her eyes.

"We really need to take you for a haircut."

"Is Tony here?" she asks with wide eyes. He's her regular hairdresser.

"No," I laugh. "We'll find someone nearby. You know, I went to a hairdresser here when I was your age. The owner made a big deal about an American kid coming to her salon and sent someone out to get us Thums Ups." I'd felt proud, then, to be from away, special.

"Can I have a Thums Up when I go?"

"Maybe. Finish your exercise."

She complies, and I try to recall the location of the salon, which was a short walk from Nani's. It was hot, and a standing fan was set to high, blowing the cut hair on the floor into a corner.

It's funny how I remember these random things. I hope Zee will remember much more of this trip, but perhaps it's normal for childhood memories to fade.

A blue double checkmark now sits beside the message I sent to Mom, indicating that she's seen the article. Will she read it? I assume that khatna happened to her. Will it raise her own terrible memories? Can she remember them sixty years later? Do I really want to know?

"Mom, I need your help with this next part." Zee is at my side, pointing to her workbook. We need to find an example of packaged food so we can read a label together. She grabs the box of cookies, still sitting on the counter, and together, we parse its nutritional value. Zee reads aloud the fats, cholesterol, and sugar content in a neutral tone.

"Mom, are these nutritious?" Her blank expression tells me the question is innocent.

"No. They have too much sugar."

"Sugar makes us hyper, right?"

"A little is fine. But yeah, too much sugar gets us hyper, and addicted."

"What's 'addicted'?"

"It's when we get used to having it and then we can't stop eating it." And then I think, *Or when it's offered, we are so excited we won't say no.* "Zee, I need to tell you something important."

"Okay."

"If someone ever asks you to do something when Mom or Dad are not around, make sure to ask us first, okay? They might say they are taking you for ice cream or cake. But you can't go for ice cream or cake unless Mom or Dad knows in advance, all right?"

"Even at birthday parties?" Her tone is disbelieving. I take a breath, try to be clearer.

"No. Mom and Dad will take you to the birthday party, so we will already know in advance. So that's okay. It's more if an adult wants to take you somewhere and they haven't asked Mom or Dad first."

"Nafeesa took me out for ice cream last week when I was at her place." Fatema's words, the warning to keep an eye on my daughter, bear down on me like an oncoming truck's headlights.

"She did?"

"I got chocolate mint. But it was different than in New York. It was very-very-very green." She yawns, her eyes glassy.

"And before the ice cream, did you go anywhere else?" My heart beats wildly, even though I know it's stupid to think that Nafeesa could hurt my daughter.

"No."

"Okay." I smile reassuringly, but I want to say *don't trust anyone, don't ever leave my sight*. But I can't say that. I don't want to scare Zee and I know I'm on the verge of doing so. My stomach roils, and a taste of cookies mixed with bile splashes up my throat. I swallow hard, swallowing it all back down.

We're settled into our Indian routine, as though it's normal for Murtuza to head off each day to the university and for me to stay home and teach Zee at the kitchen island. As I've done every visit to Mumbai, I wonder if I could live here, if I could be happy as an Indian transplanted to the U.S. transplanted back to India?

My phone's weather app still stores New York as a default option, and today the forecast is cloudy, twenty degrees Fahrenheit, with a chance of snow. I show Zee the screen, curious how she'll react.

"Imagine if it snowed right now here in India!" She takes my distraction as an opportunity to launch herself out of her chair and away from her workbook.

"That sure would shock everyone!"

"I could build a snowman on the balcony!" She slides open the glass door, recoils at the gust of warm air that rushes in, shoves it closed again.

"You could."

"Hey!" Her eyes glisten with new awareness.

"What?"

"I'm not gonna do that this year." Her shoulders slump.

"You're right. Not until next year. We're missing winter this year." I try to keep the cheer out of my voice; I'd prefer Zee not to inherit the winter-hate I learned from my parents.

"Awww." She pouts.

My phone tangs. It's Murtuza.

Need a break?

He's on his way back to the flat for lunch and offers to take Zee back to the library with him.

Yes. Find a book with pics of string instruments?

I'm thinking ahead to her music lesson, am stumped on how to teach it.

Yup. <3 <3

"Zee, change of plans. After lunch, Dad will help you at the library."

"The big library?" Her face shifts into a clownish version of excitement that might be sincere.

Murtuza arrives a few minutes later and I warm up leftover saag paneer and roti from last night's takeout dinner. The three of us eat, while Zee, still thinking about snow, explains that she will have to make twice as many snowmen next year to make up for this year's lack.

"You will," I say, and then Zee and I do a rough calculation of what that number might be: eighteen, or approximately three per month, doubled.

"Snowmen aside, being here is better than I thought it would be," Murtuza says, helping himself to more saag. "I mean, this is nice, isn't it? I teach in the morning, come home to a hot lunch with my two lovelies. The pace is leisurely compared to back home."

"I was thinking the same thing earlier. But then I remembered that you've only got one graduate course. I'm homeschooling Zee, not working all day. This is not a normal Mumbai life, Murti." I'm arguing more with myself; he's never wanted to live in India.

"True. But I do like this arrangement." He leans over and gives me a spinach-tasting kiss. Zee runs off to collect another book for her bag.

"I think it's been good for Zee, too. Have you noticed that she seems more grown-up and independent than before? She made her own toast this morning."

"Wow, and hey, I forgot to tell you — she told me she wanted to shower by herself today. She only needed me to turn on the water," Murtuza says.

"Hmm, that is new. Did you check to see if she actually used soap?"

"No, I guess I should have?"

Zee returns to the kitchen and I hug her goodbye, giving her a good sniff and nodding to Murtuza before he ushers her out the door.

Now that it's quiet in the flat, I consider transcribing my last Abdoolally interview, but dread the tedium. Instead I scroll through Facebook's newsfeed. I "like" Laura's most recent photos of Elena balancing high on a beam during her gymnastics class. An acquaintance from teacher's college is getting married, and her new profile picture is of two women's hands showing off sparkly rings. I type *congrats!* into the comment box below. I read through their other well wishes. I pause when I see that two comments above mine is one from Ian Boyko: "Wonderful news!"

I hover over his name, hesitating. Then I give in and click open his page. We are no longer friends, but his privacy settings are low and I can view his photo albums. There are many pictures of him posing with women, but I can't discern his relationship to them. Colleagues? Sisters? Lovers? His hair is shorter, the soul patch now grown into a full beard. My heart pounds. I force myself to close his page.

It's been four years since I strayed into his life. I feel like a daredevil who's just flown over a raging fire on my motorbike, exhilarated and relieved. He's still there and I'm still here.

I am still here. I have been allowed to remain here, despite Ian. I check the browser history. I manically visit ten other friends' pages to bury his. Not that I think Murtuza will go checking, but still, I have to hide him, just in case.

I send a message to Laura to see if she's still awake. We've chatted briefly while setting up our daughters' Skype calls, but the kids are always crowding us out. She replies by video-calling me.

"Hello!" She's propped up in bed, makeup off, her chestnut hair piled on top of her head in a lopsided ponytail.

"I thought you'd be asleep by now!"

"Nah, I was just reading. Well, reading Facebook." She laughs.

"Got a minute to talk about my blog? I'm trying to pick an easy platform."

She nods and tells me about two sites. I decide to go with the same one she uses so that she can coach me when I need help later. Then we switch over to more personal talk.

"So how's the dating going?"

"Remember how I told you how I was going to try to see more than one person at a time?" I nod to the screen. "Well, I've been seeing three. But … I sort of forgot to tell one of them that I was non-monogamous, and he got really mad at me. He accused me of cheating and then dumped me!"

"Oh, I'm sorry. Did you like him?"

"We had fun." She winces. "It mostly bugged me that he thought I was intentionally lying to him. I don't think people should assume anyone is monogamous while dating."

"True, not until you get serious. Though how would I know? I've only been a serial monogamist." While this is technically true, an inner critical voice reminds me otherwise.

"Yeah." She nods, pulling out her scrunchie to free her hair.

"Hey, Laura, weird question, but have you ever really cheated on someone?"

"Back in high school. I was young and messy. I was trying to break up with my first boyfriend but didn't know how." She squints at me through the screen. "Why do you ask? Did something happen with Murtuza?"

"No, not him. It was me." She raises her eyebrows. "It was … a few years ago." The story leaks out almost involuntarily, like air from an old tire. It's a relief to confess the indiscretion to Laura.

"Wow, was he upset?"

"Oh, yes." I tell her about couples' therapy while she nods empathetically. "We patched things up, thankfully."

"Why didn't you tell me before?"

"I'm not sure. I guess it's taken me a long time to feel less guilty about it? Thanks … for listening. I just suddenly needed to tell you. I don't know why."

"Anytime." She yawns and I take that as a cue to end the call.

"I'll see you Friday?" That's the girls' regular day.

"See you Friday."

I shut down Facebook and open my email, which I've neglected all day. There is a message from Fatema, sent at 3:00 a.m. It occurs to me that we were both awake at the same time, synchronized sleeplessness. There is a link to a password-protected film that she hopes I'll watch. A second email offers the forgotten password — FGM — and she instructs me not to share it with anyone. Why am I being bestowed this privilege?

Against my better judgment, I point my mouse to the link, and type the not-so-secret password. Words scroll across the screen: "A Pinch of Skin." A shiver races up my spine. I press pause, and turn off the air conditioning. Zee must have cranked it again.

Back at the kitchen island, I press play and perch on the high stool. I cross my legs, look down at my denim-covered thighs and wonder for a moment when they grew thick. When I was a girl, my mother used to pinch my knobby knees and sticklike legs and call me her foal. Now, these legs are strong.

I have to rewind the film, because I've missed the last minute or so, focused on my thighs and trying to remember the lyrics to that Nancy Sinatra song.

I start from the beginning again. A few women speak forcefully against khatna and I nod along. A couple of women say that it's a harmless ritual. They make me think of Zainab, and I pity them. There is just one lady who is vehement that the practice is *positive* for girls' sexuality. Her voice reminds me of Maasi's but of course I know that this woman, whose face is obscured by a cinematic smudge, is not my aunt. It's not Maasi's way to appear on a video like this.

I pause the film to get up to pee, and then again to make tea. I am sweating so I change into shorts, turn the air conditioning back on.

The credits roll and my heart races. I check the time. It's almost 2:00 p.m. I wish I could call Laura back. But it's not her I need to talk to: it's my mother. I need to finally ask her about all of this. Mom will already be in bed, fast asleep. But I call anyway.

She picks up on the fourth ring, her voice groggy.

"I'm so sorry for waking you. But …" I don't have an appropriate justification for shaking her out of her sleep. What am I doing?

She asks a half-dozen alarmed questions about our safety and in a calm and authoritative voice, the kind she needs when stressed, I reassure her that we are fine. "Can you go to your computer and turn on Skype?" I need to see her face. I wait two minutes, watching the clock, feeling childish for this drama. Then my computer rings, and she appears, hair tousled. She's brought her laptop to her bed.

"Did you see that article I sent you a couple of days ago?"

"Oh, yes, I read it today."

"I need to ask you about it."

She is quiet as I tell her everything I have learned about khatna. I give her details about the conversations I've had with Fatema and Zainab. I offer to send her the film link and she nods her assent.

"Is it possible that it happened … to me, too?" I finally get the question out, this question that for the last few weeks has been in my periphery, but from which I've been turning away, turning away.

"Oh, this is why you're upset."

I nod, chide myself for making this a big deal.

"Don't worry. We opposed it." She tells me that the family tried to put pressure on her when we visited India when I was seven. I relax into her assurances, but only for a moment.

"Who? Who put pressure on you?"

"Tasnim, your maasi. You know she has always been so much more old-fashioned than me. And she is only six years older!"

"You are so different," I agree, feeling a sliver of disloyalty to Maasi. I add, "But she's also so spunky, you know? It's hard to believe she believes in this stuff."

"Well, it's religion." Mom shrugs.

"Still."

"People think it's symbolic, not anything that would do any real harm."

"Yes, that's what Zainab thinks."

"I barely remember it happening to me, but the idea of it has always left a bad taste in my mouth … so when it came time to make that decision for you, I said no. We'd been living in Edison for three years already and we'd been exposed to different things, people, culture. Not only the Bohra culture anymore, although that was there, too. Ratna Aunty became my best friend. At the time it was a big deal to have a best friend who was Hindu!" She's fully awake now, back to her chatty self.

"So you said no. Then what?"

"Before we went to India, Tasnim called me saying she and my mother could make the arrangements for the three of you cousins. She thought it would be good if you did it together. I told Ratna, who was appalled, and her reaction got me thinking, really thinking about it. I remember her face when I explained it to her, saw how shocked she was, it was kind of like when you haven't given something much thought and then you see it clearly through someone else's eyes."

"So did you call Maasi back?" Impatience buzzes under my skin. I need to get to the end of the story.

"No. I knew I had to explain in person. She wouldn't understand, so I wanted to be delicate about it. You know, she was so bothered that I'd even cut my hair! I had that Dorothy Hamill cut back then and they didn't like it. She'd ask me things like, 'Are you doing your namaaz still,' and I brushed her off, telling her it was impossible to have an office job and pray at work." She rolls her eyes.

"So you told her in person?"

"Yes, I told her and my mother together." She flicks her wrist, indicating the completeness of her actions. "I said that your father and I didn't want it. She argued with me and said, 'Do you want her to turn out like Shaheen?' I couldn't believe it."

"What did she mean by that?" Shaheen, the older cousin I admired as a child, would have been eighteen at the time when Mom and Maasi had argued. She's married now, with two kids, and owns a thriving office-supply store in Detroit.

"She wore makeup and had a boyfriend. Somehow everyone in India heard the gossip! Her parents tried to rein her in, but she had a will of her own. Don't tell anyone — it was a secret — but just before we came to India that year, she had to have an abortion. Tasnim doesn't know that part of the story."

"Really?" Of course, no one would have shared this with me — I was a child — but it's strange to not have this information. What else don't I know about the family? It's like I'm peeling a boiled egg, only to find its yellow yolk soft and runny on the inside.

"Yes, it was the first time any of us had dealt with such a thing."

I nod, imagining Shaheen having to cope with her private drama while relatives spread rumours about her.

"Tasnim tried to persuade me with her ideas about Western influences and the need to control girls and all sorts of things I knew were nonsense, but at the time, you know I felt intimidated? She's always been a bossy older sister and sometimes I wondered if we should have followed more traditions."

I tense, hearing her contradict her earlier words.

I gaze into her eyes. She hesitates. I remain quiet.

"I know it's stupid, but later when you went through all those troubles in your twenties I wondered, *Was she correct?* But no. I never thought khatna was right."

"So, you stood up to your sister and your mother that summer, right?" I still feel fuzzy about the story.

"When we left you to stay that summer, I made Tasnim promise to respect our wishes and she agreed to not allow our mom, your nani, to take you for it."

"And you believe she did that?"

"Absolutely. She told me it was the parents' decision, that it was only her duty as an older sister to give me her perspective, but she wouldn't interfere beyond that."

Her eyes shine brightly, lovingly, from across the ocean, and I sense her certainty. And I also know how much she loves her sister, loved her mother, how hard it must have been for her to disagree with them.

I exhale deeply and it's as though I've been holding my breath for hours. I apologize again for the late call, and she waves it off. "It's okay, you were worried. And it's not like I have to go to work in the morning. I'm a retiree, remember?" She screws up her face, attempting to be goofy.

After we log off, I close Fatema's message, send it to my deleted items mailbox. It's all too much. The sadness of others is seeping into my skin. I've been perseverating on something that isn't mine.

∽ THIRTY-ONE ℃

Bombay, 1901

Zehra's quick mind and tongue resulted in many clashes, but also made her, well, interesting to Abdoolally. He began confiding in his new wife in the way he had done with Sharifa, and realized he'd missed doing so in the years he'd been with sweet but unworldly Shaheeda. With two more businesses now, there were so many more people to hire, to manage, to understand, and their pillow talk often turned to the pros and cons of promoting one person, firing another.

"You must make an appearance in Dholka, at least monthly, until you are sure your new overseer is reliable," she advised. "We can all go together, spend some time in the country air. Rumana can see her nani."

"You may be correct," he said impassively.

"I am correct! Why don't you ever listen to me? That overseer needs to understand he is being supervised!" Impatience rippled through her like an electric charge. It sparked its way across the bed to him. He had an urge to yell, to make her leave the bed, to just shut up for once.

But he was also tired and wanted peace, so he paused, breathed. "Okay, you are right, it's good advice." When her expression softened he added, "But you know, Rumana is lucky, she has two nanis and two nanas now that she has you." He squeezed her hand. While he didn't say it aloud, his mind trailed off to the recent subtraction of a daadi in his children's grandparent equation.

"Yes, my parents do dote on her. She is my baby now in almost every way. But they won't stop telling me they are waiting for a grandchild from me."

"We'll have one soon, I'm sure." But he wasn't sure. They'd been married already for a year and a half, and there were still no signs of pregnancy. He did hope it would happen soon, though, for he believed that it would mellow her, provide an outlet for her excess energies.

For the next few months, he, Zehra, and Rumana made monthly journeys to Dholka. While their purpose was business, for the first time in his life, Abdoolally experienced the trips as week-long holidays. They'd board the Bombay, Baroda and Central India Railway Company's evening train, bunking down in a sleeper car for the ten-hour journey, arriving in Ahmedabad at 6:00 a.m. There, they'd change to a middle gauge to Dholka, then eat breakfast while watching the passing sea of green from the train's window.

Once in Dholka, they took leisurely walks around Malav Lake and visited distant relatives who treated him like a king. He felt glad for the stability and wealth that had settled over his life.

What a shock it was, then, when the amil came to visit him upon his return from their latest visit, sharing the scandal that was now spreading through the community like a virus. What was worse was that Zehra didn't bother denying it, rather she launched into a long argument meant to sway him to her side. What gall! It was the first and only time he'd struck a woman, his hand whooshing through the air before he could stop himself.

The Syedna accepted his gift, his first printing press and the old building that housed it. He wouldn't miss it much — it held too many memories of those he'd lost. And it would have the effect of shutting down the rumours, restoring his position in the community.

And with Zehra, well … he'd have to move on, as he'd done before.

∽ THIRTY-TWO C∽

Fatema visits me at the apartment, the first time in the almost three and a half months we've been in Mumbai. I'm curious about what would make her pop over in the middle of the day, but she brushes off my question with a jovial, "What, I can't cut out early to see my favourite cousin?"

I raise an eyebrow at her.

"Well, I wanted to talk about that film I sent you."

"Oh, I see." We sit and I assume she's come to confide in me finally, to talk about the impact of khatna on her. Perhaps she wanted to be far from the office for this conversation.

"Murtuza and Zee are out today?"

"At the university. Would you like something to drink?"

"No, no." She fidgets in her seat. "So you watched the film."

"Yes."

"What did you think?"

"Well, it's a good film. Painful, though. I'm really sorry you had to go through that."

She watches me, and I keep talking to fill the space.

"I wonder, if Abdoolally were alive today, what he would think. I mean, maybe like most men, he'd be ignorant about it. But if he understood what was going on, that this is an edict from our religious leaders, would he still be their supporters? I mean, he must have cared for women, and children, advocating for maternity hospitals and education for girls. In his day, he must have been an outspoken person, just like you."

"Can we go out on the balcony?" She gestures to her cigarette pack.

As she unlatches the sliding door, I envision Abdoolally with us, as I have been doing lately. I know it's imagination, but I like him hovering near. It's good for my research.

Fatema sucks on a cigarette, the pale pink of her lipgloss staining its filter. I'm pretty sure Abdoolally wouldn't approve of the habit.

"They came fifteen years back. I was twenty-five and the business was beginning to take off. They wanted to know if I was looking for marriage, but really they wanted money." She blows a plume of smoke over her shoulder.

"Who came?"

"A few of Syedna's assistants. Henchmen. And henchwomen. Two of each."

"Really?" I'm not sure what she's getting at, but I allow her to take her time.

"They asked if I'd made my annual contribution. They asked why I hadn't been to functions in a long time. I was polite back then, Tasnim Fayji asked me to be. She didn't want trouble for the family. There were many marriages and burials yet to come."

"I can't believe you'd be polite, even if Tasnim Maasi asked," I joke.

"She pleaded with me, 'Couldn't you at least try to appease them?' I didn't want to, but I gave them money and they left me alone. Year after year. All those contributions I made would amount to a tidy sum now."

"The price you pay for being part of a community," I say. I imagine Abdoolally agreeing. Perhaps if he were younger, and Fatema were a man, they'd have made good colleagues, or perhaps friends. He hadn't had many confidants, according to Abbas Kaaka. I tell her all of this and she takes out her phone, makes a few calculations, cigarette dangling from her lips.

"The bastards," she says, showing me the figure on the screen. "This is how much I've paid over the years."

"In rupees? Still, wow."

"I don't agree with that idea of 'paying a price to belong to a community.' It made me feel like I was a hypocrite. If Abdoolally did it, then he was a hypocrite, too." She lights another cigarette and I watch the flash of the lighter's flame, the white tip turning orange with her first deep inhalation. She closes her eyes when the nicotine hits its mark, makes a slow and long exhalation.

"Agreed. But you felt pressured. Do you think Abdoolally did, too?"

"Maybe. As a businessman. You don't want to be shunned. That's mostly why I gave them money initially. My press was new. Now, I don't give a damn." She goes quiet.

"What are you thinking about, Fatema? I know there's something on your mind if you come to visit in the middle of the day."

"It's about the film."

"Tell me; I'm listening."

"You know, it killed my mother when she found out that they took me for khatna. Years before, she'd relented when people told her to get it done for my older sister, but when she saw how she cried, she refused to allow it for me. But they tricked her and ..."

"Tricked her?"

"Did it secretly. Without asking her."

"Oh." At least Maasi and Mom had the conversation. Perhaps Tasnim's mother, a sister-in-law, wasn't given that kind of consideration.

"Well ... it's just that you need to know who you're dealing with. I know you're close to Tasnim, but she is manipulative. Sneaky. You can't ever leave Zee alone with her."

"I'm so sorry it happened to you. And that she was responsible for it. I just don't know how to reconcile it all, you know? That version of Maasi, who hurt you, and the version that is my loving aunt."

Fatema stubs out her cigarette, flicks the butt into the air, and it falls down, down. Before I can respond, she says, "Look, I'd better get back to the office."

I watch her leave, a well of compassion rising. It must be so hard for her to talk about it. I don't know why — perhaps it is my empathy for my cousin — but when I go inside I rescue the short film from my computer's trash and play it a second time. The credits are rolling when I notice Zee standing behind me.

"When did you get home?" I pull myself from the film, wipe away the wet on my cheeks.

"A couple of minutes ago."

"Where's your dad?"

"We saw Maasi Fatema downstairs. They were talking, so I came up on my own."

"Oh."

"What was the movie about?"

"It's an adult matter, Zee. Not something you need to worry about." I close my laptop and look into her worried eyes. "I'll explain when you are older."

Her face grows wise and serious, her chin wrinkled. "But Mom, it made you upset. Your eyes are red. You've been crying."

"Oh Zee, it's okay. It's nothing."

"It's not good to keep feelings inside," she continues, parroting my own words back at me.

"You're so right." I pull her onto my lap. "This video is about some negative things that some adults do. With good intentions, or without thinking, sometimes parents do the wrong things. It made me cry to think about that."

"What did they do?"

"It's a religious thing. They did an unnecessary procedure that causes complications." I've intentionally used complex words and as a result, her eyes are big brown circles.

"Did they do it to you, Mom?"

"No, but to people I love."

"How can you show them that it's wrong, Mom?" Now she is repeating my advice for resolving conflicts with her friends. Her gaze is intense, and I meet it.

"You are such a good kid, you know that? You make me proud." I squeeze her until she wriggles out of my grip.

"Mom." She is relentless. How did I raise such a strong girl?

"Yes, you're right, Zee." And I think, especially since hearing Mom's reassurances, and knowing that I was protected, perhaps I should try to be a good ally to Fatema. Should I encourage her to talk more about it?

Satisfied, she wanders off.

I search the room, trying to feel Abdoolally's presence. But he is long gone.

The next few weeks blur. It's mid-January and I think I may have completed my Mumbai research, spoken to every relative I can find. I transcribe all my interviews. Next week I'll finish combing through the trust's archives. I read and reread Abdoolally's will, purchase a receipt signed by him from an antiquities dealer on eBay.

I've seen Fatema twice, wanting to hold a door open for her in case she wants to talk more about khatna, but she hasn't stepped through. I even told her about how my mother resisted it, which just seemed to make her sadder. For now, I'll leave it be.

Murtuza's birthday approaches. While he denies it, he enjoys a fuss: gifts, an overpriced meal, cake and candles. I walked Linking and Hill Roads until I found a shirt I think he'll like.

"Where would you like to go for dinner?" I ask.

"I'll let you know. Maybe we'll do something different this year."

"Tell me soon, so I can plan things."

"Actually, I've already planned things." He explains that he's arranged for Zee to go on a sleepover with Nafeesa, something Zee's been pleading with us to do for weeks. The two have bonded, big cousin-sister to little cousin-sister, and these days I'm wondering if we've done her a disservice by not having a second child.

"Okay. So do I make a reservation somewhere?" This is weird. Normally he wants me to sort all this.

"I'll let you know." He grins at his willful guile, and returns to his marking.

Three mornings later, when he opens his eyes, I wish him a happy birthday, and again ask him to choose a restaurant. Instead of replying, he jumps out of bed and rustles through his dresser drawer. He unzips the pleather case and dangles the blindfold from his index finger. I thought he'd long forgotten about it.

"How about we try this out tonight?"

"I was wondering when you were going to ask."

"I know, we've been here a long time already … I guess I've been a coward. But I was remembering that amazing time we had before the Goa trip, remember?… I dunno, I thought maybe we could try something new again." I think back to that strange night a couple of months ago, when the disconsolate mood took over, when Murtuza thought we were being wild. Since then, we've settled into our familiar weekly waltz. But perhaps Murtuza has been, all this time, trying to get his nerve up to try a new dance.

"Sure, if you'd like to. But can I ask you something?" He nods. "Why have you been so timid about this?" I sit cross-legged, hug myself.

"I really don't know." Murtuza comes to the bed, takes my hands, un-pretzels me. "I … I used to do it before, in the past, but for some reason I've felt uncomfortable to try it with you."

"Why?" Then, to take the pressure off him, I ramble, "It's not like this is completely brand-new for me. One of my old boy-friends sometimes liked to spank me; it's no big deal, it'll probably be fun."

"I know, I know. It's weird, how I'm not at all confident to get out of my comfort zone." He hesitates a moment and then says, "I think I associated this stuff with white people, white girl-friends. Not something you're supposed to do with a Bohra wife, the woman you love, the mother of your child. You know?" His laugh is high-pitched, nervous.

"Huh." I look him squarely in the face, viewing my husband from a new angle.

"Yeah, I don't get it, either." He scratches his nose.

"Well … I am a very good Bohra wife," I say, to lift the mood. He smiles and then frowns, becoming earnest again.

"We'll need a safe word, and you should tell me if there is anything you absolutely don't like."

"A safe word?"

"Yes, like red for stop." He further explains green and yellow, as though I am a new driver. I am tongue-tied all of a sudden, but nod my agreement.

The day passes as usual. Murtuza spends his morning at the university. Zee and I do a half day of addition and subtraction and reading, and later grab a taxi to Joggers' Park, an oasis in the middle of smoggy Mumbai. The sea breeze washes over us when we pass through the park's wall. Flowering shrubs ring various tracks where people saunter and speedwalk in shalvaar kameez, jeans, or running gear. A few folks actually jog. A group of elders stretch in the grassy centre.

We stand on a rock bridge that spreads over a pond with ducks, improvising a science lesson in which we identify trees and flowers, using a book Zee borrowed from the university library. The walk around the park is a unit of phys. ed.

At four-thirty, we head home and Zee presents Murtuza with his gifts: the shirt from me and a card she made by hand in "art" this week.

"Hurry, hurry, Daddy! Just rip the paper!" Zee orders, while Murtuza pretends to have difficulty with the task. Then Zee and I prepare the cake: she pokes ten candles into the icing, I light them, and carry the glowing cake out. I make them wait while I grab my phone to snap a photo of the two of them blowing out the flames. It's the lowest-key birthday I've ever experienced with Murtuza.

Nafeesa arrives exactly at six. While Zee runs to get her backpack, filled with god-knows-what for an overnight — she refused to show me, and I didn't have the energy to insist — I pull Nafeesa aside.

"Listen, I need to ask you something."

"Yah, all right, Aunty." She eyes me curiously. Does she know how hard it is for me to give up my child for the night?

"You know how there has been a lot of talk about khatna on social media lately?"

"Yeah, I signed the petition. Most of my friends did, too. Did you, Aunty?"

"Yes, me, too." I try hard not to fixate on the fact that she's been cut. I keep my eyes on her kohl-lined eyes. "If anyone talks about it in relation to Zee, you'll tell me, right?" My face grows hot.

"No one will do that, Maasi. Don't worry." I note that she shifts to Maasi, referring to me as her mother's sister. It's meant to be an attempt at closeness, but paradoxically it makes me trust her less.

"You won't ever leave her alone with anyone else, right?" It feels wrong to say it, but I remember Fatema's words and add, "Including your nani?"

"Of course."

I numbly watch her and Zee go out the door, down the corridor. They disappear, their laughter echoing from inside the elevator.

After once again checking to see if Murtuza wants to go out, I warm the previous day's daal, rice, and kheema, and watch the sunset from the kitchen window. After dinner, side by side at the sink, we wash the dishes. We take cups of herbal tea to the couches, carefully balancing them on our laps. He picks up a novel, *Aftertaste* by Namita Devidayal, and holds it in front of him, the cover, half of a woman's face, obscuring his. I'm wondering if he's changed his mind about the blindfold and cuffs tonight.

But it's his birthday, so I follow his lead, and read *The Bohras*, the book I borrowed from Abbas Kaaka. Twenty minutes and a chapter later, I sense Murtuza's eyes on me.

"I think we'll start now." He peers at me over his reading glasses, his gaze disarming. It's the way he looks at an arrogant colleague posing a three-minute-long question at an academic talk. It takes me a second to comprehend his intentions.

"Oh! Okay." A nervous giggle escapes. I study his face and detect a slight flaring of his nostrils, his mischief tell.

"Go to the bedroom. Change into the clothing I've laid out on the bed. Put on the blindfold. Securely, so you cannot see anything. Then wait." He dismisses me with a stern look and then returns to his book, appearing to read with rapt attention. I can't think of a witty retort, so I don't say anything. A part of me is intrigued, not wanting to interrupt his convincing roleplay, so I scurry away as I imagine I ought to.

On the bed is a black teddy. I finger the silk, recognizing the garment. Murtuza bought it for me as an anniversary gift three years ago, and I've worn it twice, maybe. When did he pack it?

I hear Murtuza moving about in the living room and so I discard my jeans and T-shirt in an inside-out pile on the floor and jump into the shower to wash away the day's sweat. I towel off, pull on the lingerie. It still fits, but is snug around the middle, and sticks to my lower back and belly, humid from the shower.

I slip the blindfold over my head, admiring its softness. It's convex-shaped so it doesn't press against my eyelids. A ring of light leaks in around its edges. I fumble with the pillows behind my back and lean against them. Then I wait.

I count to ten, then to one hundred. My armpits dampen, prickle. I count to one hundred again. I am about to get a peek at the outside world, when Murtuza clears his throat.

"Don't touch the blindfold."

"Okay, okay, I wasn't going to." I pretend I'm not startled.

"There will be no unnecessary talk. You will be silent except to use your safe word. When I ask you to speak, you will address me as Mr. Tyebji. Do you understand." It's not a question. I can almost believe this is not my Murti.

"Yes." I say this meekly, half for effect and half because it's how I feel.

"Yes, what?" This is definitely a question.

"Yes, Mr. Tyebji." I bite my lip to quell a giggle. For a moment, I wonder why "Doctor" or "Professor" isn't a part of his fantasy. When we first met, the titles were still new and he seemed amused when I used them in playful moments.

I tense and inhale sharply when he checks my blindfold; I thought he was across the room, not within reach. He adjusts the straps and the ring of light disappears to blackness. He opens and shuts a drawer. After a long pause, he places cuffs around my wrists. These, too, are made from supple leather, and fit like bracelets. When both are affixed, he gently pulls my arms over my head and I hear the metal links clinking together. I give them a gentle tug, confirming my confinement.

With hands around my hips, he pulls my body down the bed, and yanks away the pillows behind me so that I drop flat on my back like a rag doll. When he pulls my legs apart, I assume there will be more restraints, but there are none. I am a stretched-out X, untethered, exposed.

"Don't move an inch."

"Yes, Mr. Tyebji." Anyone watching might think we've done this before.

I have no idea what he does for the next few minutes; all I hear is indistinct movement from various spots around the room. Is he doing this to confuse me? Every so often he stops and I sense his eyes upon me. He unzips and zips something. Pants? No, the sound is wrong. The pleather case that held the cuffs and blind-fold? I try to remember if it held other items.

Then suddenly, he kisses me hard, pushing his tongue into my mouth. His lips are warm, insistent, and I am plunged into a tropical lake, pulled to its murky bottom. He doesn't let up until I'm gasping for air. It's the best kiss he's ever laid on me in nine years. Yes. The best.

"Do that again!" I exclaim, after I've caught my breath.

"No talking! Apologize for your mistake," he growls.

"I'm sorry." Then I remember. "Mr. Tyebji."

"Good. If you speak uninvited again, expect punishment." Without being able to see his face, I have no way of gauging whether or not he is serious. I have never heard Murtuza say "punishment" before, not even to Zee. I wonder, *Has he roleplayed this particular scene before? How does he know all the right things to say?* I'm amazed that he knows all the right things to say.

"Did you hear me?" His tone is gentler now, and while I know this is all a game, I'm relieved.

"Yes, Mr. Tyebji."

He kisses me again, in the same thrilling, asphyxiating way. I tense and curl my toes, fingers, all of me contained within that kiss. I want more, but he stops, his weight shifting off the bed. There is the sound of doors opening, closing. I can't tell if he is still in the room. Did he leave the flat? I listen carefully for his footfalls but he is light on his feet. I resume counting in time with my heartbeats. One, two, three, four, five, six, seven, eight, nine ...

And then he is on top of me, his whole body stretched over mine. While my chest and thighs and belly take most of his weight, it is my vulva that feels the pressure. Another kiss. He shifts his weight to give me a break, a chance to fill my lungs, and then leans into me again.

For a moment I wonder: is this his body? It's as though he's somehow reconfigured muscle and bone and skin to morph into someone else. Maybe it's not him and he's organized something else, something …? Is this my Murti? Just when I'm about to panic, call out for him, he says in a hoarse voice, "Do you remember your safe word?"

I exhale my relief, but the tiny hairs on my arms raise in alarm. *Why is he reminding me of the safe word? What does he have in mind?* Before I can reply, he commands, "Speak."

"Yes, Mr. Tyebji."

"What is it?" he demands. I describe the stoplight in intricate detail in a small voice that hardly sounds like my own.

"Good girl," he says, and I am immediately affirmed, proud, good. I laugh out loud with pleasure. And then something I don't expect: he slaps my left cheek. Not hard; it's not the sting of pain I feel. It's something else altogether. A rush of adrenalin. A pulse of joy.

"Why are you smiling? Is this a joke for you?"

"No, Mr. Tyebji. I'm sorry, I won't laugh again."

"You'd better not." He climbs off the bed, and I think I hear him stifling a laugh. Again, I hear a door opening and closing. My body hums with an arousal that is almost an ache. I want to protest, to call Murtuza back. Enough of this waiting! But instead I squirm on the bed, make myself more comfortable, bend my legs. I don't want to say the word *red*.

A minute later he says accusingly, "I see you've moved."

I immediately flatten my knees, return to my original position.

"Wider." I follow his instructions and he lifts the skirt of my lingerie up and around my waist. His face hovers over mine and his breath blows warmth over my forehead. He asks, "Are you going to be a good girl?"

I whisper these foreign words, "Yes, I'll be a good girl, Mr. Tyebji."

When he slides into me, I moan with gratitude. I don't want him to stop. I struggle against the handcuffs, wish I could grab him, pull him closer, tighter.

It occurs to me that usually I am waiting, patiently, for this part of sex to conclude, as though watching the clock for a school period to end. But not now. I want, I want, I want. I calculate that in nine years, in all of my life, this is the best it's ever been for me. I multiply the number of men times years, times frequency, numbers taking over my head. When I realize I'm doing this, I push away the thoughts, breathe deeply, and feel my nerve endings come alive again. And then Murtuza groans and goes slack. And then I am angry with him for stopping. And with myself for doing arithmetic, for mentally leaving, for wasting it.

All is quiet for a minute, and I wonder, *Are we done? Should I ask? What's going to happen next?*

The bed shifts, and I hear an electronic hum. The vibrator. He packed it. I'm about to say, no, that's okay, I'm fine, I'm happy, the way I always do, but I am constrained to my red, yellow, and green, none of which seem appropriate. I say nothing, and then the buzzing is inside me. I try to imagine the many branches of my clitoral tree. I try to imagine the vibrations as sounds waves reaching into its roots. I try. But I go numb.

"Yellow? No, red."

He stops, pulls up the blindfold. "You okay?"

I nod, and my breathing goes ragged. Then a whimper slides up my throat and I am crying. He rushes to release my wrists. He is shaking, clumsy with the metal links, Mr. Tyebji transforming back into Murtuza. Into Murti. Then he pulls me against his chest, strokes my hair.

"That was the best … you know … the best that it's ever been for me," I tell him through my sobs. And I mean it.

"Oh, I'm glad, I thought maybe I went too far." Against my cheek, his heart drums fear.

"No, it was good."

"Even that slap? That was all right?"

"Yes," I cough a laugh into my sobs. "Even that."

"So, why are you crying, then?" His eyes are attentive, gentle. He reaches for a tissue, dries my eyes, and we sit up, pull the covers close to our chests. I can't talk yet, so he does, explaining that he read somewhere that it's important to debrief. I nod, waiting for my head to clear.

"So you liked the handcuffs?"

"Yes."

"The blindfold?"

"Yes."

"My bossiness?"

"Yes, Murti, yes." This is not what I need to debrief about. I wait for him to review his checklist and then I place my hand on his chest.

"I was crying because it was the best. It was so exciting, and I felt so much. And I stopped myself. I realize I've always been stopping myself."

"Stopping yourself?" He nods, even though he's phrased it as a query. He's probably known all along.

"I go into my head, can't stay in my body. This was the best, the farthest I ever let it go. I let myself let go."

"Yes, you let me take control. You've never really let me before." He sucks in both his lips until his mouth almost disappears.

"I haven't? I guess that's true."

"No, it turns out I have to tie you up and not allow you to talk to get you to relinquish control." His brown eyes shine like a wild animal's in the bedroom's dim light.

"Can we try this again soon, Mr. Tyebji?" I ask, hugging him close and hiding my face in his neck.

"If you're a good girl," he replies. He pulls away, takes my hands, and kisses each finger.

∿ THIRTY-THREE ∾

The Rangwala Trust is in a building a few blocks away from the old Ahmedali Road building Abdoolally once owned.

The cramped office has a long, wooden boardroom-style table used for the trust's monthly meetings, and a dozen beaten-up filing cabinets. A ten-by-twelve reproduction of Abdoolally's photo is the lone decoration on the wall. The AC doesn't work. The ceiling fan's blades spin, lethargically stirring warm air. I'm glad I haven't brought Zee along.

While Shabnam, Fareeda Kaaki's daughter, emailed me some documents already — a copy of Abdoolally's will, and business ownership papers — this is the first time she's been available to let me into the office. She passes me two unpaid loan chits from 1901 and 1915, between Abdoolally and the Bohra clergy of the day. The latter was five years before he died. I'm not sure what Shabnam thinks I'll do with them, but she insists on going to the lawyer's office next door, where she is friendly with the Bohri office administrator, to make photocopies of the brittle paper.

Next, she shows me the original copy of his will. The paper is a frail as a dried leaf, the typed font crooked and fading in places. Shabnam stage-whispers in the dramatic style of a soap opera star, "You know, the will was contested! His children believed that he was leaving too much to charity and not enough to them. They got a higher sum in court." I take notes, and am glad when she tells me she has a few errands to run.

Alone now with all the yellowed paper and photos, I amuse myself inventing family scandals fit for *The Bold and Beautiful*: he didn't approve of his children's habits, their spouses, their work ethics. He was an astute businessman who managed large sums of money. Certainly the smaller-than-anticipated inheritances were no accident?

An hour later, Shabnam returns to lock up, and I text Fatema to see if she'll meet me at Café Coffee Day, near her office. We've only had a couple of quick visits since that day, more than a month ago, when she dropped by unexpectedly at the flat. I assume she won't be available now, but within thirty seconds she tells me she'll be free in thirty minutes.

At the café I scan the small groupings of easy chairs and tables occupied by couples and students reading books. Michael Franti's "The Sound of Sunshine" spills from wall-mounted speakers. I could be in a Manhattan café, except that here, all the patrons are Indians. Places like these weren't around a decade ago; they've been popping up and changing the face of Mumbai life with their expensive foreign drinks. I think of my old students for the first time in many weeks, knowing that if I were still teaching them, they'd be reading a chapter about the rise of globalization at this point in the year. I would have led a discussion of pros and cons, the latter list growing longer on the chalkboard. But right here, right now, I order a latte in English and know exactly what it will taste like. When the barista hands it to me, I see that she's spelled my full name correctly on the cup. I compliment her on the flower she's designed in the foam.

"Sorry?" she asks. I repeat myself.

"Ah! Okay. I didn't understand you at first. You look Indian. But you sound American." She says this matter-of-factly, but the comment grates on me.

I find a couch for Fatema and myself. She arrives and waves the server over. A minute later, her chai tea latte is delivered.

"It's funny that even in India, they call chai that ridiculous name."

"It's the only way they can sell it for ten times more than the chai-wala down the block. Capitalism," she says, with an approving tone. My students might have placed this assessment under the "cons."

Fatema tells me about purchasing the foreign rights of a novel written by an emerging American author. "It's very good. It's about a young woman who returns to Bangalore to look after her grandfather. Touching. In the process she learns about her history, culture, family secrets, all that. These sorts of books are quite popular among the younger generation here."

"I'll ask Murtuza if he's heard of her."

I fill her in on my day, show her the photocopied loan chits.

"What are you going to do with them?"

"I don't know. Maybe just upload them onto the blog?"

"Like I said before, too bad we cannot collect the debts today," she says, slapping the table, "with interest!"

"I thought Bohras don't approve of interest." I laugh, glad she's not being morose, the way she was the last time we talked about it.

"Correct. But some of us do." She blows on the chai.

"Well, the debts will never be collected. For now, they serve as proof of Abdoolally's generous and perhaps naive approach to the clergy." I tell her about the questions I have about his children's inheritances. "If only we could know the truth behind these financial decisions! Then we'd know more about his personality."

"I think you're more a biographer than a historian!" she teases. "You might be the only one in our family who wants to know these things."

"Maybe." I'm not sure how to take this. We sip our drinks, and then Fatema looks up at me.

"I'm more interested in the future, leaving a legacy.... You know we already have nearly eighty thousand signatures on our petition to make khatna illegal in India? In less than a few months!" She tells me a number of women in her committee have been going public about their own experiences of trauma and she is considering it, too.

"What would you say if you did go public?" I ask, bracing myself. I want to know, and don't, at the same time.

"I'd tell them about the unhygienic conditions, the lies we were told, the pain, the negative impact on sexuality," she says, her gaze dropping to the floor.

"You know, I never told you this, but I asked Zainab about her thoughts on the subject."

"Really? What did she tell you?"

I recount the conversation and Fatema sighs.

"Zainab has never learned to think for herself. She just follows whatever her mother and husband and Syedna say she should do." Fatema grows red in the face.

"Come on, that's not fair. Zainab is a smart person. She practically runs her father's business. It's so sad, the three of us used to have so much fun together, remember? I wish we could all hang out again."

"It's not her fault," Fatema says, taking a breath, slouching into the couch. "It's the religion. It's indoctrination. If the holy men say that khatna keeps women loyal, then it must be true. As

199

if it's women who need to be kept in line. What about the men? Perhaps we should cut off their cocks for good measure!"

"No one should cut off anything!" I wag my finger at her. "But you're right, that logic is stupid."

"And in the meantime, girls are getting infections, losing sexual pleasure."

"Zainab says it hasn't had any impact on her. Do you think that's true?"

"You asked her?"

"Yeah. She's happy 'in that department.'" I curl my fingers into air quotes to make Fatema laugh, but it doesn't have that effect. Then I feel bad for betraying Zainab's confidence.

"Well, lucky her. Not all of us have been so fortunate." Fatema shakes her head.

I wait for her to say more, but she doesn't. I sip my cooled latte, trying to compose careful words. The coffee lands in my stomach and curdles there.

"Do you want to tell me about how it's impacted you?"

"Maybe some other time." She checks her watch. "I have a meeting in half an hour. It's best I don't get too emotional."

"Of course. Anytime you want to talk," I say, half-relieved that she's once again closed the door.

"Thanks. Do you think I should go public?" She blinks uncertainly, an expression I rarely see.

"Will there be negative consequences, do you think?"

"Well, I've already distanced myself from the majority of the Bohra community. I'm already on the margins. It will be the close family — for example, people like Zainab — who will be angry with me."

"I'll help if I can. I can be a buffer," I say, unsure if I can fulfill this promise.

∼ THIRTY-FOUR ∽

Bombay, 1902

Abdoolally stood before his mother's grave. Hers was the first and only burial in the yard beside the modest Khar mosque he had built for her a decade earlier. He visited her weekly, offered prayers, but today, he wished for her counsel.

Would she have agreed with the amil's advice to divorce Zehra and send Rumana to her grandmother in Dholka? With no woman in the house, it seemed like the correct thing to do.

Mummy had liked Zehra, but had passed away a few months into their marriage. She hadn't witnessed their spats that became a daily occurrence. She wouldn't have predicted the near catastrophe that ended the union. But then, neither had he. Perhaps if he'd spent more time at home, been less occupied with work …

And now, since he'd given up one business to the clergy, he'd buried himself in his expanded India Stationery Mart to recover from the loss.

He stared at his mother's name, engraved into the stone in Arabic. The amil had instructed it be inscribed this way, but Abdoolally couldn't read Arabic. Hardly anyone could! Now he wondered why he hadn't argued with the amil and insisted on Gujarati.

"Did I do the correct thing about Zehra, Mummy?" The wind rustled the leaves of a nearby date palm, as though in response to his query. He looked up to watch them sway against the pink of the evening sky. He shook his head at his own sentimentality; he wasn't a man to look for signs from heaven.

In the year that had passed since he'd evicted Zehra, he'd questioned whether he'd failed to consider other options. Could he have avoided the divorce? Might the scandal have blown over? Had he reacted too rashly, allowed his emotions to guide his decisions?

Returning home, he retired to his library. He randomly pulled a book from the shelf, *Elements of English Grammar*, the text Zehra had read cover to cover. In their two years together, she had gained a decent fluency and had incorporated English into Rumana's education, as well. The book fell open to page ninety-five, an explanation of verb tenses.

The past perfect is used to refer to a time earlier than before a certain time.

He didn't like to dwell in the past, imperfect as it was.

He closed the book, slid it back into place on the shelf. Except for the shuffling feet of his servant, the house was silent. He'd seen his daughter Rumana only twice in the last twelve months. Perhaps it was time to look for another wife, and bring Rumana home.

∼ THIRTY-FIVE ∽

I'm planning a trip to our ancestral village, Dholka, at the end of February to learn more about my great-great-grandfather's origins. On the way back, I've scheduled a meeting with Meena, the archivist in Ahmedabad. I was going to take Zee with me, but her first question was whether there would be WiFi and air conditioning in the village and I didn't relish the idea of dealing with a bored and hot child. The people I really want to accompany me are Zainab and Fatema. But I know I'll have to convince them.

-------- ◆ --------

"It will be like old times, the three of us again," I cajole Fatema first.

"I don't know, Shari, that's three days away from office," she complains.

"What? We'll leave Saturday morning and return Monday night. That's technically one full day, isn't it?" I look at her, fluttering my lashes innocently, knowing full well that she works seven days a week.

"The three of us?" Zainab is more direct. "It sounds nice, but you know it's not like when we were kids. I'm not sure we'll get along."

"C'mon, we used to have such fun together. Remember," I reply, "it'll be the Secret Cousins' Club again!"

Zainab's face relaxes, and I know I have her. I put the date in my electronic calendar and email them both confirmations, naming our jaunt the SCC Reunion, hoping that will evoke enough nostalgia so they won't cancel.

On my family's first trip back to India, things were different than when we lived there. While I couldn't articulate it, I perceived that I'd become someone alien to Fatema and Zainab, no matter how much I tried to assimilate to their habits.

Seven-year-old Fatema called a formal opening to our SCC, modelling it after a Girl Scout ritual. She told us to cross our arms, right over left, and then link hands in a triangle. We then solemnly gazed into one another's eyes, and she said, "Let's begin," squeezing both our hands. Neither Zainab nor I were in Scouts, so we followed her lead.

Once we were properly convened, Fatema suggested we play carrom. I recognized the large wooden board and strikers but had long forgotten the rules. On subsequent days, they introduced me to Beh Thrun Panch, a card game that I lost, round after frustrating round. Later, I sat on the couch and watched the two of them speak Marathi to one another, a language they learned at school. I only understood every fifth word or so.

"What are you saying?" I demanded, my spidey-sense telling me that they were talking about me.

"You don't know Marathi?" Zainab asked, mouth open in surprise. She'd lost her two front teeth, and I mentally conjured insults I could use against her if later I needed them. Mine were already growing in.

"No, in Amrika, they only learn one language. My father said so. Here, we are smarter. We have English, Gujarati, Hindi, Marathi!" Fatema counted off the languages on her fingers.

"It's pronounced A-mer-ica."

Tasnim Maasi came to the balcony to check on us with a tray of Rooh Afza Sharbat. My two cousins gulped theirs down, but I left mine mostly undrunk.

"You don't like it anymore?" Fatema wiped her mouth with the back of her hand.

"What do you drink in A-mer-ica?" Zainab asked, a challenging glint in her eye.

I looked to Tasnim Maasi, hoping she would notice my discomfort and take my side.

"You don't want to be left out, do you?" she asked instead.

I shook my head and sipped the sickly sweet drink.

My Gujarati fluency withered and my cousins teased me when I flattened words with my New Jersey accent. Over time, my mother tongue became as awkward as the gangly teenager I was growing into.

Sometimes we debated about what was better in the U.S. versus India, all of us perhaps trying to regain our balance and figure out how the ground has shifted beneath our feet in the first place. Often I agreed with their Indo-centric perspectives about culture, fashion, and food, for I missed thinking like them, being like them. At each visit, I noticed that I'd changed a little more and irrevocably, my new home becoming more familiar than the old country. They, too, at ages ten and then thirteen, appeared to be growing apart from each other, but I didn't understand why. When we returned for Fatema's parents' funeral, it seemed like my two favourite cousins, at sixteen, had become polar opposites of each other. Zainab was preoccupied with boys, fashion, and her secret makeup stash. Fatema was focused on school and had a group of girlfriends who, like her, dressed androgynously. They hardly spoke to one another. I had to admit that the SCC was defunct.

⸻

Fatema wants us to fly, but I insist a train journey will be more scenic. My intuition tells me this trip must not be rushed. They both roll their eyes at the suggestion, but allow it with the provision that we take the luxury Mumbai Central–Ahmedabad Shatabdi Express.

We arrive at the station as the sun rises. Within minutes of being seated in the executive class car, our porter takes our meal orders. Fatema and Zainab choose the cheese omelette while I go for the upma vada with coconut chutney, an option unavailable on any North American train. Half-asleep, the three of us tuck in, but there is too much food for our just-awake bellies.

Like a disapproving aunty, our porter clucks at us when we gesture for him to clear our barely consumed meals. He brings us plastic teacups of steaming chai, and Fatema and Zainab pull out their phones, texting and messaging into the ether. Since the train began to roll, neither have interacted much with the other, except by joining in strained conversations I initiate. It's like I am the friend in common with two strangers.

How might I encourage them to talk? I remove my notebook from my purse, and review our itinerary, sneaking glances their way. We could be siblings, with our similar heights and bodies. Fine lines crouch at the corner of our eyes and none of us have begun dying our hair black, although we could; rogue white strands glint at our temples. Beyond that, we are as awkward as a scalene triangle.

My phone tells me that an hour and a half has passed, the grey cityscape outside the window becoming lush green. Murtuza has texted, saying that he's on his way with Zee to see his aunt who lives in Colaba, near the ocean. I showed her a YouTube video entitled *A Look at How Mumbai, Then Bombay City Was in 1920s*, and the waterfront monument looked remarkably the same as it does now, ninety-five years later. Even the grand Taj Hotel, which stands behind it, existed back then. Probably Mota Mota Nana looked out at the Arabian Sea, scanning the long horizon, the exact way Zee and Murtuza will today.

The porter rolls a beverage cart past us and I ask for water. Zainab and Fatema glance up long enough to reach for their glasses. I wish we could share a bottle of wine; it might loosen our limbs and tongues the way it does for my book club back home. No one gets drunk, but by the first half glass, the day's tensions fall away. We momentarily forget our jobs, spouses, and children and talk about the novel we've read. The book discussion is a prelude for more personal talk. That's when we remember our jobs, spouses, and children again, commiserating and laughing about reality. At August's meeting, we read *Americanah* by Chimamanda Ngozi Adichie, our conversation lingering on interpretations about the protagonist's love life. The discussion soon shifted to infidelity, most of the group weighing in harshly on the main character's lack of guilt for her indiscretions. I listened carefully, but kept quiet.

Wine is not an option this early in the morning. Anyway, Zainab doesn't drink, and even if she didn't mind, I wouldn't

partake; it would feel haram to imbibe in the presence of someone wearing a rida. I imagine Fatema feels the same way, but perhaps not; she might openly flout the rules just to provoke Zainab.

I study my two cousins, their gazes focused on tiny screens.
Then I pull a deck of cards from my purse.

"Beh Thrun Panch?" I don't wait for their agreement before I
deal the cards onto our shared table.

Fatema sighs loudly, making it clear that I am a giant pain
in her arse. "All right. One round. Then I have to get back to my
work emails."

"I haven't played this since the kids were small." Zainab collects her cards.

The clubs and diamonds and hearts and spades are magic,
evoking muscle memories of sitting cross-legged on Nani's living
room floor, our hands still too small to comfortably hold the
slippery cards. Before long, Fatema is trash-talking Zainab, who
spars like a champ. Then the two of them gang up, utilizing a
strategy that's always eluded me. I lose game after game. The
defeat is worth it. We play four rounds, and two hours and three
decades disappear.

Fatema's assistant has arranged a private car and driver, Muffadal,
to fetch us from Ahmedabad's train station and take us the forty-
five kilometres to Dholka. My map app says it should take us
seventy-two minutes, but I've learned that GPS doesn't accu-
rately estimate in a land where there is little adherence to traffic
regulations.

Muffadal prods the car through a traffic jam. I marvel at how
close our vehicle is to the motorcycle beside us. Its driver steers
his front tire into the two inches of space ahead of him while
his unhelmeted passenger perches sideways, preserving her sari's
pleats. Her body is slack, relaxed, one hand resting on his waist.

She wears flip-flops, one of them balancing off her left big toe. They lurch forward and are gone.

Muffadal beeps his horn into the wall of lorries and cars and a few minutes later we see the holdup's culprits: two cows meandering in the left lane. Everyone veers around them, giving them wider berths than they would another car.

"Bloody hell," Fatema grumbles.

"Last week Zee and I crossed a six-lane intersection with a heifer. We used her as our chaperone," I quip.

"You are a real Indian now!" Zainab laughs.

The traffic thins, and Muffadal honks with decreasing frequency. Zainab points out dozens of blue, purple, red, and yellow kites — children's hopes lodged in trees — remnants of the Makar Sankranti kite-flying festival that happened almost six weeks ago, in mid-January.

Finally, we exit the stop-and-start traffic and are on an open road. Along the way are gated communities with new houses, their stone walls keeping out the crumbling, smaller dwellings that border them. The landscape turns rural, and my eyes relax in a way that they cannot in Mumbai's crowds. Dotting the landscape are rice paddies, emerald marshes with drowned-looking plants. We pass an intricately carved and opulent Hindu temple with a ten-foot illustrated Gandhi poster overlooking it. It is surrounded by shanties.

"I wonder what great-great-grandfather have thought about the Mahatma's early political work? He was alive at that time."

"He'd be in favour of it," Zainab says. "Gandhi challenged the caste system, something we don't believe in as Muslims."

"And he would have supported Indian self-sufficiency and independence," Fatema adds.

"But one the other hand, he got a lot of his business from the British," I tell them.

A triple speed bump at a sign for Kashindra makes my pen jump. Conversation lulls for a stretch. Zainab naps, and while I can't see her in the front seat, I suspect Fatema is drowsing off, too. I gaze at a children's playground in the middle of nowhere, dry, high grass fencing it in. We overtake a scooter with a bungee-secured box filled with a pyramid of fried snacks. My stomach groans hunger and I unwrap a vada I saved from breakfast.

A sign announces Cadila and a sprawling pharmaceutical factory's campus where women in orange and red saris stand beside the highway, waiting for buses. Then more fields interrupted every few kilometres by small roadside dumps, gardens that grow a rainbow of plastic bags and bottles. We slow to allow a herd of donkeys to cross and I spy a man peeing by the side of a tree painted with wide reflective stripes. As we speed along, I wonder if Abdoolally made this trip to his home village, and what he might have seen along the way.

Muffadal announces the outskirts of Dholka. It looks like a smaller version of Ahmedabad — crowded, polluted. This is the newer side of a town that stretched out its long limbs from the original village.

We stop at a hotel booked through Fatema's travel agent, and she sniffs the air, as though smelling a foul odour emanating from the three-storey stone building. She mutters, "Minal said it was an original eighteenth-century mansion. Well, it was probably the only worthwhile place. But why couldn't we have stayed at my villa in Goa?"

Zainab laughs and casts a glance down the residential street. "Our ancestor wasn't born on a Goan beach, unfortunately."

I ignore them and pass a list of locations to Muffadal. "Can you take us to these places in the morning?"

He scans the list and flashes a gap-toothed grin. "You are visiting Abdoolally Seth's buildings."

"Yes, you know about him?"

"Yes, Ma'am. I am a relative of his." He straightens his spine, pushes back his shoulders, and I reflexively do the same.

The four of us throw out names, drawing our family tree, realizing that Muffadal is a descendant through Abdoolally's second wife, Shaheeda. This is the line Abbas Kaaka didn't know much about.

"Wow, you are what ..." I try to map the branch in my head, "our third cousin ... no, our fourth *half*-cousin, twice removed!" He's not just our driver. He is family.

"You lost me," Fatema says.

"So his second wife was from here, too?" Zainab asks.

"Yes. And her child, Rumana, was sent back here to be raised by her nani after her death. Later, Rumana married and moved to Ahmedabad. Some relatives live in Ahmedabad, a few in Bombay, and some of us settled back here," Muffadal explains.

"So interesting," I say, still making sense of the information.

"You must come for dinner while you are here." Zainab, Fatema, and I offer the standard response: yes, yes, let's see, perhaps tomorrow, if there's time.

"Isn't it odd that Rumana wouldn't have remained in Bombay after her mother died? Wasn't it normal for the new wife to take care of the previous wives' kids?" Zainab whispers to me as Muffadal waves and gets into his car.

"Who knows." I make a mental note to email the archivist to find out how old Rumana was when her mother died. Likely the other children, those mothered by Abdoolally's first wife, would have been grown up by then. "I don't know how long he waited before he married Zehra."

"That was the third wife, right? The divorced one?" Fatema leads the way into the hotel's lobby, which is a tiny front room off the refurbished mansion.

"Yes." The mystery of Zehra is like a mosquito bite that inflames when I scratch at it, growing warm, irritable. Impossible to ignore.

The hotel clerk is a middle-aged woman, perhaps a decade older than us. Her bindi is the same shade as her hot pink sari. She passes us ancient-looking metal keys for our suite.

We climb the wide staircase to the first landing. Our room is expansive, and its furnishings resemble museum pieces.

"Beautiful," Zainab murmurs.

"Not bad, better than it looked from outside." Fatema agrees. "This town really is small. Imagine what it was like a century ago." She looks out the velour-draped windows.

"Yes, that's the point, gals, to imagine it in Abdoolally's day." I look at the ornately carved doorways, the heavy wooden furniture, and sense we've come to right place.

◦ THIRTY-SIX ◦

It's early evening, and I listen to Fatema clicking on her laptop while I drift off. When I awake, an hour later, the sun is setting and Fatema is still typing. Zainab is standing on her mat, bending, prostrating, standing again, her movements brisk, businesslike.

I watch her, thinking about how Tasnim Maasi taught the three of us to pray when we were preschoolers, tut-tutting at the laxness her siblings were showing toward our religious upbringing. When she discerned that I'd forgotten the Arabic after three years away — my parents had become sporadic in their prayers and didn't enforce mine — she had Zainab school me again. Now, I watch Zainab mouthing the words, my mind following along: *subhanallah ... subhanallah ... subhanallah.*

I use the palatial, gilded washroom. When I return, Zainab's mat is folded and Fatema has stowed her computer.

"Ready for dinner?" Zainab asks. "The lady at the front desk says there are a few good Gujarati places nearby." We agree on one that is within a ten-minute walk.

The server brings us steaming thalis filled with eggplant cooked with fenugreek leaves, sweet and sour daal, okra curry, potato and tomato curry, rice, chapatis, dhokla, and kachumber. Later he exhibits a platter of burfi, squares in shades of green, orange, and brown. They are freshly made, creamy, and so much better than the facsimiles I buy from the shops in Edison or Manhattan's Curry Row. My pants are tight after the meal, but I have to admit they've been snug for a while. I tell myself I can return to my normal diet in three months, when I am back to the land of sub-standard thalis and burfi.

We walk to the hotel, at first going in the wrong direction. It's on a quiet street off the main one, and now that it's dark, the unfamiliar buildings are unrecognizable.

"There, we passed this house. Remember? You commented on its pink shutters earlier." Fatema points in their direction.

"And these puppies were here, too, unless they moved, or are a different litter." I look at three golden-haired dogs nestled into a single lump by the side of the road. I'd cooed over them on the way to the restaurant. Now their mother, teets hanging low, creeps closer, ready to protect her babies.

"Oh, good," Zainab says. "Yes, it must be down the road from here then. What time do we get up tomorrow?"

"Muffadal will arrive by ten, then take us on a tour of buildings funded by Abdoolally's trust." I list the sites we'll visit. "Then, he'll drive us back to Ahmedabad in late afternoon, and there may be time for a little sightseeing. In the morning, we'll meet with the archivist. Good?"

"Look what he created, what he started. Our community had such promise. Now it's gone to shit." Fatema kicks a stone and it skips along the road, coming to a stop in a pothole.

"Don't say that, Fatema. You are always so negative. It's not good for your health to spread negative energy." Zainab sighs.

"Come on. It's become so regressive over the last few decades. The religious leadership is more concerned with keeping people in line. And no offence, but ridas are a good example of that. They are a modern trend. It's all about making people conform."

"It's not that bad. Look how pretty these modern trends are. And isn't it nice to have something distinctive, special, to wear, to make our community unique?" She twirls, her skirt fanning out.

"And then those bloody ITS cards, to monitor everyone's movements," Fatema grumbles, clearly not amused by Zainab's fashion show.

"Well, we need to know who is allowed into gatherings, who has paid their dues," Zainab counters.

I watch them, fearful that our recent camaraderie is about to end.

"You mean who to shun or who not to shun?" Fatema retorts.

"Well, we have a tight community. We take care of each other. And a strong culture. Don't lose sight of that. And our cuisine!" Zainab continues to attempt to lighten the mood.

"We will never progress as a community while the leadership continues to control. They hold on too tight, and like sheep, the people follow."

"We are not sheep!" Zainab rebuts, her tone no longer conciliatory.

"Come on, you two —" I attempt.

"You are blind, Zainab. Just look at the khatna debates. We try to educate women and they parrot back that khatna is good for girls, that it is religiously required, that it helps to control women so they stay faithful to their husbands. It's utter garbage! They steal pleasure from girls, replace it with pain." She waves her hands, underlining each of her points.

215

"On the contrary, I have not had any pleasure stolen from me. Maybe if you got married, you would understand."

"I don't have to get married to know." Fatema looks at Zainab, incredulous, angry, her fists balling like a prizefighter's.

"I understand that it is different for each woman. Some are very badly affected, while others are not," I appease.

"And how about you, Shari? How did it affect you?"

I stare at Fatema, not comprehending. She inhales sharply, then looks startled by her own words.

"But it didn't happen to her. Did it?" Zainab looks puzzled.

"What? What are you saying?" My heart races.

Fatema pulls a cigarette out of her pack, lights it, and exhales smoke over her shoulder, but the breeze blows it in my face.

"Tell me! What do you mean 'how did it affect me'?" Her mocking words are headlamps shining bright into a dark forest. I begin to see the outlines of trees.

"Shari, don't get so upset. You're getting overwrought," Zainab counsels, alarm in her eyes.

"So … it happened to me, too?" I grasp the words as they tumble out. I feel Zainab's hand on shoulder, moist and warm, dampening my T-shirt. Fatema nods.

"I'm sorry. I'm so sorry. This is not how it should have come out." And now her hand is on my other shoulder. It is dry and cool. My two cousins stand like sentries beside me. All I can feel are their palms. Everything else is going numb. Disappearing.

"Tasnim and Nani took us to a woman's flat, someone we didn't know. This lady was old like a grandmother. There was a large carpet on the floor and the woman put down some sort of sheet over it. I wondered if we were going to be served a meal, but that didn't make any sense because we'd had lunch before leaving home." Fatema lights another cigarette, sits on the edge of the sidewalk. Zainab crouches beside her. I stand apart from them; can't bear to be too close.

"Zainab went first. Shari and I were taken to a bedroom off the living room where an older girl watched us … her name was Sherbanoo … who knows why I still remember her name, but I do — maybe she was the granddaughter of the cutter. Zainab seemed calm because she was the only one amongst us who appeared to know what was about to happen. I assumed that your mother must have let you in on the secret. Was that true?" Fatema interrupts her storytelling to gaze at Zainab.

"I think so. I think Mummy talked about it like it was something necessary? That it was about growing up, a rite of passage.

But, well, it's hazy. Although everything you're saying sounds familiar, but …" Zainab bites her lip, and her eyes well with tears. I look at her numbly, frozen in my ability to reach out to her. Was she beginning to remember? Would I?

Fatema resumes the story. "Sherbanoo gave us colouring books and crayons. It's funny, I recall us flipping through the pages of previously coloured-in animal outlines, probably the artwork of other stressed-out seven-year-olds. I refused to pick up a crayon, despite Sherbanoo's cajoling. You know, I had this feeling that we were being duped." Her assessment rings true; Fatema has always been the least naive of the three of us.

"After a short time, your mother brought you back," she looks at Zainab. "Then she took Shari next. I remember her saying to you," now she faces me, "'You don't want to be left out, do you?'"

Maasi's words feel like déjà vu. Fatema continues, "And then Zainab said, 'It didn't hurt much, it was just like getting a needle.' That calmed me, and so I believed I could handle it all fine. But then Shari came back, looking spooked, whining for her mother." She stubs out her cigarette and I shudder in the night breeze.

"You know, Shari, you moped and asked when you would go home, back to New Jersey, for many days after." She looks to me, and I wave her on.

"Well, it was my turn next, and like an idiot, I think I marched into the living room, almost proudly."

I can see her doing that. She was the tough one, the tomboy, the one who barely felt the scrapes and scratches that were perpetually on her elbows and hands.

"But when they told me to pull down my pants and underwear, I panicked and resisted. The women told me to calm down and then they …" She pauses, reaches into her pack for another cigarette.

"They held me down by my hands and feet. I kicked and screamed and writhed. I think I kicked the khatna lady in the chin." She lights her new smoke, inhales deeply. "I'll never forget it. It was the worst, piercing pain ever. I bled for three days. I wore my mother's sanitary pads, changing them, one after another. You two hardly bled, from what I could see, but we never talked about it, so I don't know for sure."

Fatema stops, the story finally over. I remember the part about missing my mother at the end of that trip, imagining I might die without her. I know Nani admonished me for crying, told me I had to be a big girl, that my mother wouldn't like it if she knew I'd been being such a baby. That much I know.

Now hours later, I lie awake, listening to the even breathing across the room and beside me. I can't tell whether my cousins are fast asleep or lost inside a similar maze of interior thoughts. I allow my hand to slide down my pelvis and rest over my underwear. A cut was made there thirty-three years ago, according to Fatema. It's odd to not remember and to know in my heart that her words are true. This story both belongs to me and does not.

My body, as though finally being given a missing puzzle piece, adjusts and repositions itself under my hand. But it is not an easy fit. My stomach, which loved our dinner, now roils. I have a terrible headache. I've popped three pills, and I wait in the darkness for the throbbing around my eyes to subside.

I have always loved my community, my Dawoodi Bohra community. It's the place I can return to, the place I belong, the one identity that is sure and strong. I've admired my family, and in particular, the women. But tonight I hate it. Hate them. I don't want any part of it anymore. I want to go home, get out of this awful village. I want my mother. I want my dead father. I want the Edison three-bedroom that's long been sold. I curl onto my side, press my temples.

I've defended my community. Like so many others, I've shrugged about the corrupt men who rule over the flock. I've tolerated them, and like so many of us, I haven't opposed them because they haven't before interfered with my life directly.

But now my community feels like nothing because, while the men might have made the rules, it is the women, women I've loved, who've enforced them.

This is why I have never had an orgasm. This is why.

In the dark I think, *Did my mother know and not tell me? Did my father? How can I continue to love my maasi now? Can I ever forgive her?*

I spring out of bed, grab my phone, and head out to the hallway, my stomach lurching with the sudden movement. The screen's blue light sends a shard of pain through my skull. I check the time — it's just past 1:00 a.m. — and call Murtuza.

"Honey?" His voice is groggy. Then there is alarm. "Are you okay?"

"Yes, I'm fine. Is Zee with you?" I lean against the wall, and then crumple to the floor.

"Sleeping. Why?"

"Since I've been gone, have you let her out of your sight? Did you leave her with any relatives?"

"No, we had lunch over at my aunt's, then we saw the Gate of India. Then we came home. We've been mostly at home since. What's this about?"

"Please. Please don't leave her with anyone while I am gone. Not Tasnim Maasi. Not any of your relatives, no one. Please, it's very important. She's seven. Murtuza. *Seven!*"

Fatema opens the door to our suite, shushes me, draws me in. Zainab switches on the light and I shield my eyes against the white glare.

"I'll explain it all later. But for now, you have to promise me. You have to protect her at all times. Do you understand?"

"Of course I will. I'm her father. But tell me, what happened? What's wrong?"

"Oh my god. She had that sleepover with Nafeesa. On your birthday." I shoot a look at Zainab. "Did anything happen to her?"

Zainab shakes her head emphatically from across the room.

"Shari! Talk to me! What's going on?" Murtuza shouts through the phone.

"They did it to me, Murti. They did it to me when I was seven." I sob, and gasp, and my thoughts muddle. Fatema takes the phone from me, and, in a low voice, explains my distress to Murtuza. I rush to the bathroom and throw up into the toilet, just in time. Zainab comes in, turns on the light.

"No, turn it off!" It goes dark again. The nausea has stopped, thankfully. I rinse my mouth at the sink and Zainab hands me a towel. She guides me back to bed and holds me close. I rest my head on her shoulder and smell the sharp tang of her sweat. She rocks me like one of her babies, smoothing my hair.

"It's over now, it happened a long time ago. It's over," Zainab coos.

"It's not. It's not over. My life, my sex life has been ruined by this!" I wail. She tells me to breathe. Holds me tighter. I stop crying, and slowly detach from her. I notice that Fatema is sitting beside me, her hand on my back.

"How are you?" She passes my phone to me. "I told him we'd look after you, but you should call him back. He's worried."

I nod and she dials for me. I move to the opposite side of the room, sit on a wingback chair. My head is still sore, but not like before.

"Shari? Are you all right? Should I come there?" Murtuza asks.

"No, it's better you stay there. I'm kind of a mess and don't want Zee to see me like this. Also, we have things to do tomorrow."

"You sure you still want to? Maybe you need some time to sort all this out."

"I think so. I don't know. I'll probably feel better in the morning."

"Okay, I'm here, Shari."

"Yes, I know. Murti. Remember what I said about Zee, okay?" He assures me he will, and then we say good night.

"How's your headache?" Fatema asks.

"Better. Sorry to wake you up like this." I cover my face to hide my embarrassment. I fear I am being overly dramatic.

"I wasn't sleeping, anyway." Fatema rubs her lower back.

"Me, neither," Zainab says. "You know, it's odd. Maybe I'm imagining it … but … I think I remember pieces now. At least those colouring books, the smell of the crayons … my mother smiling at me and telling me how … proud she was of me to be so brave and good. She … she told me I was the best one out of the three of us, that I did the best, made the least fuss. Like it was a contest. I remember wearing a pad that was very big and my mother told me I'd hardly bled because I'd been good … I remember the ice cream after."

Her eyes are wide, wondering, the memories a revelation.

"Because you'd been good." Fatema get up, shakes her head. "That bitch."

I wait for her to come back, to sit beside us again.

"Why can't I remember?"

"Some of the women in my activist group don't remember, either, but have been told by a relative that it happened. It's how the trauma works, apparently. It's mysterious. Some of us remember each and every graphic detail. Others have pieces, like Zainab. Sometimes I think it is better not to remember. Every time I think about it, it's here," she says, touching her forehead, "right here."

I nod, although I can't agree. At least she's got something to anchor her, even if it is something awful. Me? I am floating in an ocean of uncertainty.

"Shari, I am really sorry it came out this way. I wanted to tell you months ago, but when it seemed you didn't remember I wasn't sure ..."

"No. I'm glad you told me. It's better to know." I think that's true.

Exhausted, the three of us have run out of words. We turn off the lights but I stay awake for what feels like an eternity, listening to my cousins' light snores.

The sun rises, like any other day. Fatema is up first and orders room service, veg omelettes still steaming in their covered trays, chai, and the whitest bread. We are cautious with one another, overly polite, as we serve one another breakfast. I can only manage a few bites before pushing away my plate. Finally, Zainab breaks the silence.

"I really didn't know it was a bad thing." She stares into her tea. "I assumed it was harmless. Now, I don't know. I ..."

Neither Fatema nor I speak.

"Now I ... I don't know what to believe anymore. I guess I have to start thinking for myself." Zainab is wrestling with her faith, something neither easy nor familiar; a devout woman isn't supposed to question the rules. And even though she hasn't framed it as such, I can tell that she is laying the groundwork for an apology to Fatema.

"You know, you two are the only family I've ever spoken to about this," Fatema breaks in. "I've posted things on Facebook, I've been part of the activist group, but never have I talked to family. Why did we never talk before? We went through this nightmare together."

"Well, I completely blanked it out. So I couldn't talk about it."
I smile wanly. I am exhausted, on the edge of laughing inappropriately. I take a deep breath to contain my hysteria; I need to stay in this conversation.

"Me, too, but from what I am remembering, I think we were told never to talk about it, correct?" Zainab looks to Fatema.

"Yes, your mother warned both of us —" she gestures to Zainab and me "— to never talk to our parents about it, that it would cause trouble."

"Mom insisted it hadn't happened. She explicitly asked Tasnim Maasi and Nani to follow her wishes. Hah." Half a laugh escapes. I am being too glib. I wrap my arms around my body, try to still myself.

"My mother often thinks she knows best." Zainab shakes her head. Fatema nods, takes a big bite of her omelette, her appetite normal. She's the only one amongst us who seems better for last night's disclosure.

"Probably no one told your mother and so you returned home after things were all healed up anyway. But I did tell my mother," Fatema says.

Was I all healed up by the time I left? I can't remember any discomfort down there while on the plane, or when I met my parents at the airport. Or ever. As though in response, a pinprick of pain shoots through my vulva like a firework, exploding then disappearing. I hold my breath, but it doesn't return.

"My mother went over to your flat, with me in tow," she says, facing Zainab now. "She screamed bloody murder. She told your mother she would never speak to her or Daadi again. But of course she did. She had to. In those days we were living with Daadi. But it was never the same after that. We shifted flats a year later. Everything was so tense at home."

"So that's what happened," Zainab says, with a gasp. "I always wondered why there was a chill between our mothers."

"I'm surprised your mother didn't call mine," I say to Fatema. Our mothers *were* close, more sisterly than Maasi and Mom. When Fatema's parents died, Mom grieved a long time.

"I think she wanted to, but there was pressure to not make trouble, and then I guess time passed. All the unwritten rules daughters-in-law have to follow in order to get along." Fatema shakes her head.

"True, these joint families can be bloody difficult," Zainab agrees. I look at her with surprise; she's only ever spoken well of her in-laws.

There is a knock at the door, and a man in a faded uniform comes to retrieve our breakfast dishes. We pause our talk as he fills his tray. With a twinge of shame, I remember that half the floor must have overheard my outburst last night. I close the door behind him.

"One of my cousins married a non-Bohra. She took the mithaq, but still her mother-in-law insisted she get khatna before the nikah. Do you think it's easier as an adult?" Zainab asks, pursing her lips.

"Well, at least she would have been old enough to consent to it, and maybe to insist that it be done in a clinic. But still, why cut healthy tissue?" Fatema straightens her sheets and bedcover.

"I've always wondered why I feel kind of broken down there," I whisper. It's a question that had no proper context or answer before.

"Yes. It's likely the reason." Fatema continues to make her bed, tucking everything in neatly, even though we will be checking out later and a maid will strip off the sheets then. She punches the pillows to fluff them. "Fuck. Every time I try to be sexual, I remember why I'm broken down there. My nerve endings wake up and scream the reason."

And then I think, *And mine just won't quite wake up enough. It's like they are perpetually half-awake. Half-asleep.*

"I had no idea that could happen. I have been so lucky. I'm very sorry." Zainab slumps in her chair, stares at her feet.

"It's a good thing, Zainab. I'm always glad when I hear khatna survivors say it didn't harm their sex lives. I don't want anyone to go through this."

"Khatna survivors," I echo. "That's what this is called." The air is still for a moment, the silence difficult to bear. Fatema zips her bag, then comes to sit on the bed next to me.

"I went to a specialist the last time I was in New York City, that time I came to visit? I couldn't talk to you about it then. The doctor looked at my clitoris and told me that while the head is intact, there is nerve damage. She told me there is no good treatment right now, that I should see a sex therapist who can help me breathe through the pain when I have sex. Breathe through the pain! All I want to do is curse the religion when I feel that pain. Fucking Dawoodi Bohras! Fucking child-abusing holy leaders!" Fatema forms a steeple with her fingers and hides her face.

"Fatema ..." Zainab begins, and I shoot her a stern look of warning. This is not the time to encourage moderation in our language. I put my hand on Fatema's back, wait for her to breathe again.

"I'm glad you are telling us. It's good for us to talk about this." My words taste like artificial sweetener. I take my hand off Fatema's back.

"We will do more talking. We will do it together," Zainab says with a hale and hearty tone, rallying us. "All night long I have been thinking about this. Maybe we should talk honestly to Mummy about this."

Fatema and I exchange glances. I can't imagine how that conversation will go. With my favourite aunt, with whom I used to be able to share secrets. Will she defend herself, tell us that we are overreacting?

Perhaps she will say, *Bus apna ma che. This is how things are done, that this is just a part of our religion, our culture. We are Bohras and at thirteen we went through our mithaq during which we pledged allegiance to our holy leader, and we must do what he says. He says khatna is good for girls because it helps us to be naik, good and modest and faithful.*

I am suddenly too hot, all of these thoughts like kerosene flaring a fire. I move to the window to get some air. A cool breeze blows in. My body relaxes and my mind clears.

Or will Maasi apologize? Will she be sorry for the pain she's caused us? Will she have a reasonable explanation?

"Shari?" Fatema looks at me with worried and wet eyes, as does Zainab. I turn, and smile bravely, because for the moment, I can. With each of these two women by my side, I feel all right, at least for now.

∿ THIRTY-EIGHT ∾
Bombay, 1903

Abdoolally hadn't confessed it to anyone, but he didn't want to remarry. He'd been married three times, and look how those marriages had turned out — maybe he wasn't meant to be a husband again. Plus, he got along fine with his servants, and a new wife felt like a burden, a stranger he'd have to allow in, with whom he'd be required to share his bed and feelings. Inevitably she'd cry about something he'd done or not done (why did women have to cry so much?).

But there was Rumana to consider, and this improper arrangement in Dholka. She needed to return to the city, resume her normal life. Dholka was too small and too backward for a daughter of his.

It felt like a sign, then, when Asghar, his most trusted employee, a man he'd hired as a boy fifteen years earlier, died so suddenly. Abdoolally could complete a spiritual duty by marrying Maimuna, his widow, a woman so homely he barely remembered her face. He recalled her body, though, curvaceous, with wide hips, an ample bosom. She'd had one child already, four-year-old Shamoon, and would certainly bear him more. And with her, he'd insist on hospital births.

He'd sent for Rumana and her nani, Shehnaz, who arrived that afternoon. They were awaiting him in the parlour when he returned home early to prepare for the nikah. Rumana greeted him with a salaam, taking his hand and raising it first to the left side of her forehead, then to the right, then higher up. While he'd seen her twice a year since she'd moved north two years earlier, he noticed there was something different about the girl now.

"You've grown so much since I last saw you." She would be turning nine soon, but she already seemed to be a young woman.

"She's shot up a few inches this year," Shehnaz confirmed, pride in her voice.

"Papa, I want to stay in Dholka," the girl blurted, her cheeks reddening. "I like it better there. I feel more … comfortable there." Shehnaz raised her eyebrows and sighed, gestures that told him she'd meant for the conversation to begin differently.

"I would be happy to keep her in my care. She is wonderful company for me; otherwise I will be living all alone."

"You could both live with us instead, and now you'll have a little brother at home," Abdoolally said, redirecting.

Shehnaz shook her head, smiling at his offer. "She's made friends there, my neighbours have girls her age, and I hired a tutor as you asked so she could continue her studies. The air is fresher there, too, which is good for her lung problem …"

"I cough much less there, Papa."

"Already since we arrived she's been coughing so much." Just then Rumana broke into a coughing fit, her chest heaving and her cheeks pinking. "See? Bou khasee che."

They paused their arguments, and he shook his head.

"Please, Papa, let me stay there. I promise we will visit more often and I will continue to send you letters. I don't want to leave my friends, my nani." Her sentence ended with a wheeze and she looked at him with pleading eyes.

"It might be easier to start your life with your new wife this way, too. She will adjust more easily," Shehnaz continued their petition. Abdoolally recalled Shaheeda's and Zehra's early days in the house, and the way they, at first, behaved as temporary guests, especially when his children were present.

"All right." He shook his head. "But let us take this as a decision for now, and then assess if it still is suitable in a few months' time." Rumana's eyes danced as her smile widened.

Muffadal arrives at 10:00 a.m. On with the show; we've agreed to carry on with our planned itinerary.

"How did you all sleep?" he chirps, then knits his eyebrows at our tired expressions. We murmur, *not bad, fine, all right*. After a short drive, he parks beside a pair of nine-foot-high wooden doors in a long, concrete fence. We watch children meander through. They stop, crowding the narrow alleyway, and stare at us. Muffadal ignores them.

"This is the entrance to our Vohrawad." He explains that the old Bohra neighbourhood is two blocks long, and the side exit doors were once locked in times of danger. "It was in the early 1900s when there were outlaws who came on camels and robbed people. So the neighbourhood put in these locked gates."

"Camels? They came on camels?" Zainab cocks her head to the left. "And the Bohras couldn't fight them off?"

"Yes, that's what I was told. But they were criminals, probably threatening, violent."

"Bohras are not known for being good with conflict," I say with a straight face.

"Ha! Good one." Fatema guffaws.

Muffadal guides us through the gates and we stop at a school. The yard is made of interlocking bricks, several missing. I wonder how many children have skinned their knees here. There is a hand-painted sign written in red Gujarati script.

"Abdoolally Seth Vernacular School," Zainab translates for me.

"It was built shortly after his death. He bequeathed the money for it. They say he wasn't able to go to school when he was young. Nothing like this existed when he was young," Muffadal says. I know the story, have read documents at the trust that confirm it. But seeing the actual building — the bricks and mortar and children — is uplifting.

"Wow, our ancestor is responsible for this school." I then ask whether we might be able to go inside. He speaks to a man standing by the doors, the caretaker, who leads us through the building. We pass room after empty room.

Muffadal points out the middle and high schools, also both named for Abdoolally. He tells us that his own children attend school in these adjoining buildings. I would like a tour, but my cousins are not interested, so Muffadal and I go in alone. This building is almost identical to the primary building, except that the high school has a computer room, and Muffadal tells me his kids often complain that there isn't WiFi. "Imagine! Complaining about that!"

I nod, remembering that this was one of Zee's primary queries about Dholka.

We rejoin my cousins outside. They are absorbed in quiet conversation and startle when we approach them.

"What's happening?" I ask.

"All done?" Fatema asks in reply.

"It's dreary here. No wonder Abdoolally left this place," Zainab says under her breath so that Muffadal won't hear her. I can tell she is flagging; it's unlike her to speak this way.

Muffadal guides us into a maze of winding alleyways, past a block-long marketplace. There are two sweet stalls, and their sugary scents follow us, as do the curious gazes of dozens of Bohra people. We arrive at a simple, single-storey building he tells us is the masjid, its erection funded by Abdoolally's estate. I don't recall seeing those documents, but I might have missed them. Again, I ask if we can enter. "C'mon guys, I'll probably never come back to Dholka again. Probably you won't, either. Let's have a good look around."

"You don't have a dupatta," Zainab points out. She is the only one, with her rida, who is appropriately dressed for the mosque. I wish I'd thought to carry a scarf in my purse.

"You go in and have a look around and tell us what it's like." I peek in the door, but the contrast between the sunny sky and dark interior makes it difficult to see anything.

"I'll run and get two of my wife's dupattas. I'll be back in ten minutes." He rushes off while we protest.

"He didn't have to do that." I watch him disappear around a corner.

"And I am more than happy to pass. I don't enter mosques anymore. I'm done with religion."

"You don't miss it at all? I mean, the peace of mind it offers?" Zainab attempts. Fatema ignores the question and sits on the low wall in front of the mosque.

Across the street is another building, with small letters above the door that say, SETH ABDOOLALLY MEMORIAL HALL.

"Look, we can go check out that place while we wait for Muffadal." We climb the stairs and step into the cool of the concrete structure. Chairs line the perimeter, and through another doorway there is a kitchen.

"This must be where people come for meals after prayers." Zainab appraises the humble room.

"It's just like the hall where you got married," Fatema deadpans and Zainab tiredly lampoons a punch to her arm. It's not far from the truth. This might be a village, but until recently, the Bohra halls in the city were just as plain. We'd filled Zainab's reception space with floral garlands to disguise the disrepair.

A man emerges from the kitchen and Fatema explains our mission in Gujarati. He welcomes us and insists we sit while he brings us tea. By the time we've finished our cups we're less weary and Muffadal is back, wearing a gold embroidered topi, two dupattas slung over his forearm. I take them both, and hand one to Fatema.

"Just this once?" I cajole.

"I'm surprised they don't insist on ridas," she grumbles.

"No, no, it's empty right now, and they are not so strict, anyway," Muffadal counters.

Fatema looks at me dolefully, her eyes as sad as Zee's when she has to miss a birthday party. She wraps the cloth loosely, non-committally, around her head.

It's a simple mosque, nothing really special. The marble walls and floors offer cool and calm. The windows have intricate latticework, but otherwise there is little decoration. Zainab whispers a prayer and I am comforted by the dark, quiet space. I remember that I am part of a larger ummah, a faith, a clan. Despite its shortcomings, I still want to belong. Fatema stands motionless, then, with a slight head nod, she signals that she wants to go.

Out in the sunshine, Muffadal collects the dupattas and informs us that the mosque will be demolished soon because a two-storey structure is planned in its place. He points to the digging that has begun behind the building.

"There are rumours they found a tunnel linking Dholka to Ahmedabad," he whispers.

"All the way to Ahmedabad? Why?" I ask.

"It's thought to be a secret passage that Shia leaders could travel. Long ago, they were often at risk of assassination." We look around the back, the location of the alleged tunnel's opening, and are blocked by two stern-looking middle-aged Bohra men who stand guard.

On our way back to the car, Muffadal says in a low voice, "If the rumour is true, and the news goes public, the local authorities will delay the construction."

"Wow," Zainab says. "But this secret could have historical significance!"

"It's the way of our people, isn't it?" Fatema murmurs to me when Zainab walks ahead and is just out of hearing range. "To keep things hush-hush."

He drives us to Malav Lake, which is more like a large, artificial pond. Surrounding it is a carved stone wall with steps leading to the water. The remains of a squat building sit in the middle of the lake, attached to a beach by a long, wooden bridge. We pass a pillar with an inscription.

"Ah, a good story." Muffadal points to the words. "It says, 'If you want to see Justice, it's here.' Princess Minaldevi, who constructed this in the eleventh century, wanted to make the lake round, but there was a poor old woman who lived at the edge of it, and she refused to move. The princess, to show compassion, let the woman keep her hut, and so the lake isn't perfectly round. This story has become very famous in the state of Gujarat."

"Where was her hut?" Zainab asks.

"We're standing on it!" We cast our eyes down at the ten-foot block of cement under our feet, the divit in the princess's lake.

"The old woman's hut must have been pretty small," I say.

"Still, to defy a princess, not bad," Fatema says, nodding.

———◆———

We check out of the hotel and carry our overnight bags to the car. Muffadal takes them from our hands, placing each in the trunk carefully, as though tucking them in for the night. I take one last look at the historic hotel, the building rumoured to have been there since the early 1800s. Abdoolally would likely never have stepped foot in this place as a poor child, but after he bought his first businesses and lands, he might have been welcomed by its wealthy owners.

"You know, you should talk to my Banu Maasi. Shaheeda, Abdoolally's second wife, was her great-grandmother. She lives in Santacruz." Muffadal opens the back door for me. "Remind me, I'll give you her number when we stop."

"Thanks." I file the idea away, too tired to give it much thought.

We move from bumpy regional roads to the smoother asphalt of highways.

"Want to take in Ahmedabad's sights before I loop back to Dholka? There's Bhadra Fort, Sidi Saiyyed Mosque, Gandhi's Sabarmati Ashram." Muffadal makes eye contact with me in the rear-view mirror. Zainab and Fatema defer to me, but I know they are not the least bit interested. We are all too emotionally drained and sleep-deprived for tourism.

"Not this trip," I answer. Within minutes, Fatema and Zainab are asleep. I take out my notebook, record everything I can from last night's conversations. I forgot once and I won't forget a second time.

We pull up to Le Meridien, another of Fatema's choices, and once again, her treat. She laughs when we gawk at the lobby, which is more like an art gallery than a hotel, with its high, blue, illuminated ceiling and hanging geometric chandeliers.

"So fancy-pantsy!" Zainab marvels.

My stomach grumbles and I spot a restaurant off the lobby, where we eat overpriced Caesar salads and pizzas. At our lunch's conclusion, Fatema signs the cheque as though the numbers on the computer printout look normal to her.

"It's too much, let me pitch in," I insist.

"Naare naa!" She switches to Gujarati to make her protest more potent. We argue for a bit, both of us knowing she will win.

Our suite is eight floors up, with three bedrooms, three bathrooms, and a common living room.

"Wow, Fatema, I hope it wasn't expensive," I say.

"Not at all," she demurs. "The owner is one of my associates."

"Very nice!" Zainab pats the white comforter on her bed. "I'm going to do namaaz now." I check the time; it's already Asr prayers. Not for the first time, I admire the way Zainab's faith offers structure. I wash my face, look at my tired face in the mirror, and phone Murtuza. We check in quickly, skipping over last night's distress, and I tell him I need to talk to Zee. I called her when we first arrived in Dholka, an eternity ago.

"I miss you, Zee."

"When are you coming home, Mom?" There is a pout in her tone that makes me wish I could be beamed back, *Star Trek*–style, to the Khar flat. Even better, I want to teleport us all to our Manhattan home, away from every possible danger that lurks around every corner here in India. I steady myself, remember to make my voice neutral. I overshoot to chipper.

"Tomorrow night. Very soon, honey! I'll see you just before bedtime. What are you doing today?"

"We were in Colaba." She pronounces it clobber.

"Oh, to see Daddy's cousins again?"

"Different ones, and we went to the ocean. And then to Uncle's store. He gave me a T-shirt that says 'I love Mumbai.'"

"Oh, good," I say, reminding myself that she is loved and safe. "Let me talk to Daddy again."

"Don't worry, I've been with her all day. I won't leave her alone," he says preempting my question. I feel bad for not being able to trust him.

"I'm not worried." I heap more false cheer into my tone. "I just wanted to remind you about my arrival time tomorrow." I ramble on about how Fatema's driver will deliver me home. And then I tell him all about Le Meridien, and how posh it is. He seems to buy it.

"You'd better soak it all in. We've only got a short time to partake of your rich cousin's generosity," he says, with what sounds like a guilty chuckle. And it's true. It's already late February. Mom will arrive in three weeks and then we'll all go home together the third week of April. I groan, which only makes Murtuza laugh louder at his own joke. But really, I'm thinking about how Mom will be here soon and I'll have to tell her everything.

"Gosh, I need a nap." This is my first completely truthful statement. We say goodbye, and I stretch out on the most comfortable bed in the world.

With a rough shove to my shoulder, Fatema wakes me. I am about to complain, but see panic in her eyes. "Something's wrong with Zainab. I've rung for an ambulance." And then she's gone.

I clamber out of bed and follow her to the living room, where Zainab lies on the floor, a pillow propped under her head.

"I fainted only." Her voice is weak, and she's sweating in the air-conditioned suite.

"With chest pains!" Fatema objects.

"Chest pains?" I take her hand, which is damp.

"It's easing up."

"You were short of breath, too." Fatema looks to me, worried. "The ambulance should be here by now."

"Just try to steady your breathing," I tell them both, moving into crisis-management mode. I rinse a facecloth and press it against Zainab's forehead. She bats it away, sits up, and slowly rises to her feet.

A few minutes later, two men in uniform arrive. One has a handlebar moustache that I can't stop staring at. The men take Zainab's vitals while she insists that everyone is fussing unnecessarily. They ask her a dozen questions about her symptoms and she answers in uncooperative monosyllables. When she regains her strength, she says, "I'm forty! I was tired, only. A little overwrought."

"It might have been a panic attack," says Fancy Moustache, "but you should go to hospital for tests as soon as possible, just to make sure it wasn't a coronary event."

"It wasn't a panic attack! How could it be? I'm a very mindful person." Zainab shakes her head with a haughty air.

"Let's go tonight. We'll have the tests. Which private clinic is open right now?" Fatema ignores Zainab.

"Better to be safe than sorry," I coo at Zainab, stroking her hair.

Zainab refuses to go in the ambulance, but agrees for us to travel by taxi when Fatema tells her she has no choice about getting the tests done. "All this trouble for nothing!"

I help Zainab gather her purse and put on her rida while Fatema phones her assistant with instructions to call some VIP or another who will smooth our passage at the clinic.

An hour later, Zainab has had an EKG and chest X-ray, and we are waiting in the spotless and mostly empty clinic for her results. Her fingers worry her tasbih, each prayer bead a marker for her murmurings of "Astaghfirullah." *Forgive me.*

239

"What do you need forgiveness for?" Fatema mutters. I ask Zainab, a second time, if she wants me to text her husband and she shakes her head, continuing her prayers.

"Maybe all of this talk, you know, about khatna, has been hard on you." Fatema looks at us, guiltily.

"Astaghfirullah, Astaghfirullah, Astaghfirullah ..." Zainab ignores us.

"Zainab, are you okay? Talk to us." She doesn't answer. I look down the hallway, impatient for the doctor, who we all agree looks like a young Shabana Azmi, to return.

"It's time for maghrib prayers," Zainab says.

"You want to do them here?" Fatema is solicitous. "Maybe they have a prayer room somewhere. I can ask."

"No." Zainab grabs her phone, opens a compass app. "Just pass me a sheet from over there. That will be my mat." I spread the sheet across the small space, and stand beside her. I waggle my brows at Fatema, who sighs and, surprisingly, doesn't protest. She moves into the space beside me. I imagine it's been forever since she's done this, but, like riding a bicycle, Fatema's cellular memory takes over, and she synchronizes with us. When the young doctor appears, we are seated on the floor, just finished. I stand and hold out a hand to Zainab.

"You appear to be physically stable, Mrs. Motiwala. Your symptoms indicate a possible panic attack."

"But I've never had such a thing before. I'm not paagal!"

"You don't need to be mentally ill to have a panic attack," assures the doctor. "We can all be overwhelmed by stress from time to time. Did something happen recently to trigger this episode?"

Zainab shakes her head and Fatema and I nod. The doctor looks at us, half-amused, half-concerned.

When none of us offers anything further, the physician continues on with her recommendations, which for tonight include a good meal, rest, relaxation.

"I will take care of that," Fatema says, picking up her phone, calling someone who will call another someone who will arrange something for all of us.

We return to the suite, and ten minutes later a room-service attendant brings us dinner: daal, rice, kheema, raita, kachumber. Home food, comfort food. We dig in, even Zainab, who at first shakes her head, insisting she has no appetite. Each dish tastes as though it could have been cooked by a relative. How did the hotel's chef manage to get it right?

Fatema chews and says, mouth full, "I told them to cook the Dawoodi Bohra recipe. Who knows? Maybe one of our cousins works in the kitchen."

We rise early, all of us sluggish even though we reported pleasant sleeps in our big white beds. I pack my shoulder bag and text Murtuza to buy a bottle of wine for my arrival tonight. I need a break from my thoughts. Also, I know he'll have many questions, and they'll be easier to answer with a glass in hand.

After breakfast, I encourage Zainab to stay at the hotel, to rest until checkout time, and meet us at the station. She will have none of it.

"I'm healthy. Last night was something out of the ordinary only," she asserts.

Our appointment is at nine-thirty and what should be a short ride is taking us thirty stop-and-start minutes. I check my phone every few minutes, fretting we'll be late and wishing I hadn't scheduled everything so tightly. Our train is at eleven-fifteen, and my one hour with Meena is diminishing minute by minute.

We approach a fender-bender, the cause of our delay, the two drivers in the middle of a roadside shouting match. We finally pass them and arrive at Meena's home office on a side street just off the congested Mirzapur Road. I rush up the stairs, taking two at a time, while Zainab and Fatema follow a few steps behind. Meena greets us at the door wearing jeans and a green T-shirt, and looks like she might be about around our age, judging from the few grey hairs sprouting from her part-line. She wears bright red lipstick, cat's-eye glasses, and shakes our hands vigorously, waving away our apologies about tardiness and bad traffic. She guides us toward her living room and seats us on a long, blue leather couch and grabs a folder from her glass-topped desk.

I notice she is not wearing a wedding band. There is no sign of any children in this immaculate house, but then middle-class Indian homes often look this way, hired help maintaining their dustless, toyless appearance.

"All right, we'll get straight to it since we don't have much time." She sits across from us and spreads open the manila file on the coffee table. "This is your copy. I'm so glad you called me two days ago. I hadn't thought to search Rumana, Abdoolally's child from his second marriage, in Dholka's records and after I did, I was able to fill out a few more details."

After meeting Muffadal, I'd texted her information about his lineage.

"Great," I say.

"So … I've compiled archival information on as many family members as I could find, but because you asked me to focus in on Zehra, here's what I've pieced together." She pauses, takes a deep breath, and so do I. "Zehra was married to Abdoolally for two years, and then they divorced. He didn't marry his next wife, Maimuna, until about two years after."

"So that's probably when Rumana would have gone to live with her grandmother in Dholka, then?" I recall what Muffadal told us.

"I can't say, but it would be logical if no one else was around to look after her. Abdoolally's other kids would have been grown up and his mother was deceased by then," Meena adds, tapping her pen on the table.

"I still want to know what caused the divorce," Fatema says.

"Archival records don't tell us that, but we do know what happened next for Zehra. And this is where things get interesting." Meena smiles at Fatema. "There is a record of her remarrying a Dawood Slatewala about five months later, in Dholka."

"That's pretty fast!" Fatema says.

"Dholka? Was Zehra from there?" Zainab asks.

"No, Zehra was born in Bombay." Meena points at a page to help us follow along. "Her father was a wealthy businessman there. He had a jute factory."

"Why would a city girl want to go to a village to remarry?" Zainab wonders.

"I don't know. We only know that Dawood was not a wealthy man, but he lived in Dholka and worked for Zehra's father, distributing jute in Gujarat." Meena turns a page to show us his documentation.

"So let me get this straight ..." My mind is swimming. "Now both Rumana and Zehra are living in Dholka at the same time? The old part of town we saw is pretty small, especially the Bohra area ..."

"Yes! From the records, they were neighbours, a few houses between them," Meena confirms. "It is interesting that Zehra's father would have arranged this marriage. It would have been quite a step down, status-wise."

"Maybe Zehra and Dawood were lovers all along!" Fatema laughs.

"But how would she even have met him if he lived in Dholka and she was in Bombay?" Zainab asks.

"Maybe she just didn't have many options as a divorced woman?" I ask.

"I have something more to show you." Meena seems to be enjoying this slow unspooling.

"Zehra had two children with Dawood — one, Nabil, died in infancy. The other, Rasheeda, died when she was twenty. Zehra outlived her husband by ten years. She had no heir and left her entire inheritance to Rumana."

"Wow!" Fatema's eyes are wide like a child's at storytime. "So she and Rumana stayed close."

"Probably. I can't tell you for certain, but this act does suggest a certain sentimentality, or a desire to look after Rumana, who by the way, would have been well set herself. As a child of Abdoolally, she received an inheritance from him, too, according to his will."

"A desire to look after Rumana," I repeat.

"That's all I've got about your mysterious Zehra. The rest of what's in the file is more of what you already know, but read it through — perhaps I clarified a few details here and there about him and his other three wives."

"We need to get going," Zainab says, checking the time. "Our train leaves in half an hour."

We board the train minutes before it departs the station. We haven't spoken much since leaving Meena's, all of us digesting the new information.

Fatema breaks the silence. "I'm still trying to figure out why Zehra would marry a guy in Dholka."

"And only five months after her divorce," Zainab adds.

"My money is on an affair!" Fatema says. I shake my head.

"Whatever happened between Abdoolally and Zehra … and Dawood, what's really clear to me is that Zehra loved Rumana," I say. "That relationship endured."

"Huh. So the real story here is not about the divorce, but about a stepmother and stepdaughter staying together despite a divorce." Fatema slaps her knee.

"You like that, don't you?" Zainab laughs.

"It's the more feminist story. The story of the women in the family." Fatema raises her eyebrows. It's a reach, but I nod, wanting it to be true. Still, I can't help dropping into the reality that Zehra was probably evicted for something she did, or that she was perceived to have done, and then she was forced to reconstruct her life later. In a way, her life journey, and Abdoolally's, forked, causing her to travel to the tiny village from which he'd originated.

After our meals, I close my eyes. I'm much too tired to think, to talk, to play cards. I'm not alone; my cousins have retreated behind their electronic devices. As I drift off, I remember that just two days earlier we were on a different track, taking a train in the opposite direction. I was hoping for a cousin-sisters reunion, a tourism-slash-research jaunt to Dholka and Ahmedabad. I didn't count on learning about my khatna. I place my hand in my lap, feeling it grow warm where it meets an old hurt. There is still so much to process about that, but for now I let it go, allow the train's rhythm to lull me. I open my eyes only to notice as we slow and pass through Anand, Vadodara, Bharuch, Surat, Vapi, Borivali. Finally, we reach Mumbai.

∿ FORTY-ONE ↺

Bombay, 1905

Only eight hours after he'd deposited her at Dr. Fuller's clinic, a special arrangement he'd insisted on, the teenaged peon came knocking on his door shouting excitedly, "Baby is born! Baby is born!"

"Shamoon, come! We're going to see your mother and the baby," Abdoolally yelled upstairs. He asked the boy, "Tell me. Is everything okay?"

"I think so," the boy replied.

Abdoolally and six-year-old Shamoon entered Maimuna's room. He exhaled relief when he saw her sitting up in the bed, holding the swaddled baby in her lap. Maimuna's mother beamed at them.

"You are fine?" he asked, inspecting her face. She looked pale, and there were dark rings under her eyes.

"She is just tired. Which is normal," Maimuna's mother answered.

"Look, look at the baby. She is fine, too." Maimuna held the bundle out to him. "Take her."

He hesitated. He hadn't held a baby since Rumana was born, more than a decade ago. He placed one hand under the tiny head, the other under the legs, and clutched the bundle close to his chest. Then he lowered himself, his ageing knees aching on his descent, to Shamoon's height. The baby opened her eyes, looked at them with drowsy curiosity. Shamoon touched her shoulder gingerly, as though petting a skittish cat.

"She's so fragile," Abdoolally murmured.

"No, she's not. She is a healthy baby girl. And I am healthy, too. You musn't worry," Maimuna said firmly. "We are blessed."

"Al-Humdulillah," Abdoolally whispered. He passed the baby back to her. "I've made plans for you to stay here overnight. Just to be safe. We'll come to pick you up in the morning, if Dr. Fuller says that all is well."

"Yes, dear," Maimuna conceded. She'd already argued about this the previous week — this whole clinic thing was unusual. She should have been at her mother's home, or at the very least at theirs. But she'd surrendered to her husband's anxieties.

Abdoolally and Shamoon stepped outside, onto the street.

"I finally have a sister!" Shamoon exclaimed. "What will she be named?"

"We have to go to the Syedna still. We'd planned to go next week, only she came early. But you know, you already have three sisters, and one brother," Abdoolally corrected.

"But I'm not related to them."

Abdoolally looked at the little boy who was so forthright in his speech. Normally, he would have disapproved of the backtalk, but tonight his mood was bouyant.

"Yes, that is true, but so it is true that they are your siblings. And you and I are technically not related, and yet I am your father, just as your first father was your father." He clapped the boy's back. "Life sometimes gives us riddles, no?"

248

Shamoon frowned as he gathered and sorted all these facts like carrom pieces arranged asymmetrically in the middle of a board. He nodded thoughtfully, and reached up to hold the older man's hand as they made the trip home.

∽ FORTY-TWO ᖴ

Fatema's regular driver meets us at Mumbai Central Station.

"What's his name?" I whisper to her, while he loads our bags into the trunk. I feel guilty for not having asked before and consider, that like Muffadal, he, too, might be a distant cousin. She makes the introductions, a bemused look on her face.

"Thanks, Varun." I shake his hand.

"Most welcome, Ma'am."

He navigates through the crammed streets. When we arrive at Zainab's building, Fatema and I get out to offer a limp hug, and I watch her wearily climb the chipped front steps. Zainab was subdued on the ride home. Perhaps she is contemplating the rewritten story Fatema has given us about our childhoods. I wonder if she'll process this with anybody tonight — her daughters, or husband — or will she be alone with her thoughts? I look across the street, three floors up, and scan Maasi's dark balcony. Then I turn my gaze back to Zainab. Fatema observes my worried expression.

"She will be fine. She is strong."

I nod, knowing she's right, but I also know some part of me feels lost right now. I can't identify it, but it tingles like a foot that's fallen asleep. I'm guessing Zainab feels the same way.

I text Murtuza to tell him I'm nearby. After five minutes of heavy braking and swerving, we reach Fortune Enclave. Fatema squeezes my arm and whispers, "I'll telephone tomorrow." Varun passes me my bag. When I turn to face the lobby, Murtuza and Zee are standing at the door. Zee runs out in her nightie, and throws her arms around my hips. I lean down and hold tight to my scrawny seven-year old, breathing in her just-washed and still damp baby-shampoo-scented hair.

We read ten, fifteen, then twenty-two ("just a few more, Mom!") pages of *Ramona the Brave* before I convince Zee it is time to sleep. When I emerge into the living room, Murtuza has two glasses of Sula Shiraz poured. I take a big gulp and lean into him. He puts his arm around me and I rest my head on his shoulder.

"I missed you. More than Zee did, even, if that's possible," he whispers.

"Me, too. What a weekend. I never expected all this." I drink more wine, feel its warmth descending, defrosting. I recount Meena's discoveries about Rumana and Zehra.

"I can't imagine sending Zee to live with your mother if you died." He shivers, and I pat his chest.

"I'm not dying."

"So, no more details about the divorce?"

"Only confirmation of dates. But I'll wager he divorced her and not the other way around."

"Right." Murtuza refills my empty glass.

"I hope that whatever she did back then to inspire his anger was worth it."

"You mean, like a love affair or something?" His tone is light, as though he is enjoying the intrigue of it all, but I can feel his neck and shoulders tensing.

"It might have been that. Maybe she was in love with Dawood Slatewala all along and was having an affair ... but I hope not." I realize I've chosen my words well, because Murtuza's shoulders drop.

"You might never find out."

"Maybe." I stare into my glass, get lost in the deep red. Red like blood, like life, like rage. I put down my glass.

"Shari?"

"Yeah?" I realize I'd drifted away.

"Do you want to talk about khatna?"

"Not yet. I just ... can't." Although I'm not sure. The wine is making my body both light and strong. It makes me brave, solid. But I say, "I've got to let it sit for a little while."

"Okay, whatever you need." His eyes are dark, his gaze penetrating. I kiss him, and I can tell he is at first surprised, but then he follows my lead, kisses me back.

"Kiss me hard, like before." He does, and I'm turned on, transported, just like I was then, Murtuza becoming the fierce presence I need him to be.

After a couple of minutes, he asks, "Would you like to?" in that considerate and kind way he usually does, and the spell is broken. But I don't know how to tell him that the spell is broken. The good wife in me nods; after all, I've been away for a few days, and it's been over a week since we had sex. I empty my glass, take a quick shower, change into a cotton nightie, and wait for him.

It goes the usual way, it's nice, and I am half-numb. Only now, I can perceive the numbness, the pane of glass between me and everything. And now I know why it's there. But it doesn't help, this knowing. Actually, it ruins everything because I have no idea how to shatter it. It was easier to be clueless.

He climaxes, and I don't, and instead of telling him that I'm satisfied, I curl up in a ball and sob. I can't stop it and I don't want to. I haven't ever cried during sex except these past few months in India and it feels pathetic. India has turned me into a crybaby. I'll never be able to have normal sex again. I might never be able to have sex without crying again.

Murtuza tries to comfort me, to uncurl me and hold me, but I only grow smaller, tighter. I feel his hand rubbing my back. I hear his self-recriminations: *I am so sorry, honey. I shouldn't have suggested this. I'm sorry. We shouldn't have had sex tonight. I was so insensitive. I'm sorry.* I hear him, but can't respond, can't help him.

I lose myself in the sobbing, don't know how long it goes on or why it stops. When I open my eyes, the bedside lamp is turned on, blindingly bright. My pillow is wet.

"Did I do something to upset you?" He looks so scared, his face taut, his eyes bulging.

"No. No, it wasn't you. It was me." I reach out my hand, let him hold it.

"You? What do you mean?"

"I was just so sad. I started to think, to realize …" How to put it into words?

"What?"

"Khatna did this to me. When we have sex. Maybe every time I've had sex. With anyone. I've been only …" I trail off, searching for words.

"Only?" His voice is soft.

"Only half there. Protected from something that could happen. That's why I hold myself back …" I feel as confused as he looks. He scooches closer, takes my other hand tentatively.

253

"It'll be okay, we'll get through this. Together. Don't worry," he says, solemnly. My eyes fill with tears again, but this time I don't pull away. I'm too tired to pull away.

∽ FORTY-THREE ᥫ

A dog barks, setting off a chorus of other canine yelps and yaps. It's 4:08 a.m. I think I fell asleep shortly after ten. Six hours, not bad. I pad to the bathroom, then to the kitchen, and switch on the coffee pot. There's a faint ache around my temples, residue from last night's red wine and tears.

I open Meena's file to the section about Abdoolally's marriages. Much of what she documented I already knew, but she has filled in missing dates and ages from archival records. The facts are the steel girders of my project, strong and firm.

He married Sharifa in 1877, when he was twenty-two and she sixteen. They had three children, each a year apart, Raushan, Husein, Batool; girl, boy, girl. They were eleven, ten, and nine when she died in childbirth, at age twenty-eight, she and her barely born perishing together. When I first heard about the poor state of maternal health during that period, I was shocked; while I laboured for fourteen terrible hours with Zee, I never imagined I could die that way. Now, having heard this story repeated often,

I've become inured to how these young mothers were so easily lost, expendable.

The nine-year gap between Sharifa's second last and last pregnancy leaves me curious; was it an accident? Maybe there had been several miscarriages in between, but there are no records for such commonplace tragedies. Meena included an annotation that Abdoolally and Sharifa were not related, and their marriage most likely arranged. *But could it have been love, too?* I wonder. Had they exchanged longing glances when they saw one another in the street or at community gatherings? Or perhaps I'm painting them too innocently; they might have been covert lovers, boyfriend and girlfriend. I shake my head at my own romanticism. Probably not.

I ponder our names. From what I can tell, I am the first Sharifa in our family's tree in a century and a half, the name slipping away, almost forgotten, like she was. Mom and Dad told me Syedna chose Sharifa, but today I like imagining this ancestor as my namesake.

He waited two years before marrying eighteen-year-old Shaheeda, a prolonged mourning period, according to Meena's speculation. The children, in their tweens, would have been looked after by servants and Abdoolally's mother. He was twice Shaheeda's age, and she barely five years older than her eldest stepchild. Was she like a big sister to them? Or does one assume the required authority and maturity of a mother, the way an actor steps into a role?

Three years pass and Rumana is born. Again, there is no mention of miscarriages before her, but I would assume there must have been; teenagers are fertile, after all.

Shaheeda leaves Rumana motherless at age four, dying in childbirth like her predecessor. She was only twenty-five. Rumana's stepsiblings are adults: Raushan twenty, Husein nineteen, and

Batool eighteen. Meena included a ledger from the printing house from that year which includes Husein's signature, evidence that he was working for his father. Raushan would have been married a couple of years by then and Batool just married.

Abdoolally waits three months, a paltry grieving interval, and marries wife number three, Zehra, the twenty-two-year-old daughter of a fellow wealthy businessman. She's a little old, almost past her wedding-expiration date for the time. Why the nuptial delay: illness? A previous engagement that didn't come to fruition? Education? A bad reputation of some sort? Despite Abdoolally being forty-four, he would have been a great catch with his wealth, and only one small child in tow.

And how did he look upon this new, young fiancée? Already married and widowed twice, he sought her so soon after Shaheeda's demise. Was it a practical process, like purchasing a new home? Or was he selective? One would think that you get better at choosing a mate, the more experience you have, right? You begin to create mental lists of preferences, like the ones my friends and I kept. We assessed new boyfriends, comparing the qualities revered and hated in the previous relationships. We hoped for just the right combination of sexual passion and intellectual and emotional stimulation. We longed for every need to be met.

When they first sat down for chai, did Abdoolally and Zehra talk about books, politics, ideas, the way Murtuza and I did? And had they already known one another for years? I'm assuming that Zehra would have been a contemporary of Abdoolally's children, perhaps friends with his daughters.

I pause, remind myself not to use my modern lens to view these ancestors, whose norms were vastly different.

My friend Laura comes to mind. I received a notification that she sent a message yesterday, but I haven't yet opened it. I read it now.

Hey! More relationship drama to report! I just ended things with the two guys I was dating. One was annoying and the other was cheating on his wife! It made me think about our last conversation, and how glad I am that you confided in me. I'm here for you, girl, whenever you need to talk.

Funny, I'm not all that bothered about these last two guys. Have I become jaded? Well, I just reactivated my OkCupid profile and am having dinner with someone tonight ...

I miss you and our jungle gym talks! Ding me when you're online again.

In some ways, I feel so far away from that city, that life. I am on the opposite end of the globe, literally and figuratively, right now. I return to the file.

Almost two years later, Zehra and Abdoolally divorce. It's 1901, the beginning of a new century. They have no children of their own. Rumana is sent to live with her maternal grandmother in Dholka sometime after.

I read over the paragraphs about Zehra's life in Dholka, which Meena already shared. Then I read them again, mentally searching for traces of what's missing in their stories.

Two years later, at age forty-eight, he marries his fourth wife, Maimuna, the only one to outlast him. She was the destitute widow of his employee and two and half decades his junior. She had a son with her previous husband and then two daughters and a son with Abdoolally. She lived to be ninety-nine, dying in 1980, and I imagine her longevity as a sort of compensation for the first two wives' early demises. Zehra, too, lived to be an old woman, dying when she was ninety-two.

He died in 1920, at age sixty-five.

I finger the smooth cardboard of the file and then close it. This is all I have: my family's bio-data and a hundred questions.

Knowing I won't be able to sleep, I Skype Laura. She waves and croons a hello while wiping her hands on a towel; she's been washing her dinner dishes. I glance over at our sink, see that Murtuza has carefully arranged yesterday's wineglasses on the drying rack. When did he wash them?

"So good to see you again!" Laura asks me about my research and Mumbai's food, and I offer anecdotes.

"So, tell me about the date you had — was it last night?" I try to remember the hour at which she messaged me and then calculate the time difference.

"Yeah, oh, a total flop. He talked about himself through the entire dinner and then mansplained — to me! — blogging," she laments.

"Oh, no!" I laugh.

"I asked him if he'd ever written a blog, and guess what?"

"Never. But he knew everything and wanted to teach it all to you, anyway?"

"Exactly." She guffaws. "Hey, what time is it there? Are you calling me in the middle of the night?" I nod and tell her it's 5:00 a.m. She gives me a sad face. "What's going on? Do you want to talk some more about that whole situation?" She's alluding to the affair.

"No, it's about something else, something bigger ..." Somehow it feels easier to tell her the hard things this way, the computer screen a confessional. I consider my words; my head is so full that I don't know how to parse the important information properly. Instead, I blurt, "Laura, I've never had an orgasm."

She sits back in her chair, and considers what I've said for a moment.

"Never?... With no one?... Not even alone?"

I shake my head three times.

"Gosh. I had no idea."

"Well, I never said anything." I shrug, like it's not a big deal.

"And here I've been going on and on about my sex life this last year. On and on." She twirls a lock of hair around her finger.

"That's okay, I like hearing about it." That's mostly true.

"Well, lots of women don't have orgasms, right? It's normal, right?"

"I used to tell myself that. Now, well, I'm realizing that the reason might be something ... abnormal." I rest my chin on my hands, stare at my image in the left-hand corner.

"What do you mean, abnormal?"

"I ... I can't get into that right now. It's all kind of fresh. Stuff I've learned since being here." I watch her watching me.

"Is it serious? Do you need to see a doctor?"

I did see a doctor once, when Zee was a toddler. I'd developed a strange skin condition "down there." It itched. It embarrassed me. My family doctor sent me to a gynecologist to check it out.

"Probably a mild form of lichen sclerosus," the specialist tut-tutted as she stared into my vulva. "Doesn't look good, though it's common and treatable." My mind shifted to underwater plants, growing and spreading under my delicate skin.

I had to return two weeks later for a biopsy. They required one-eighth of an inch of tissue from three places and I told myself not to mope about it. It was tiny, almost nothing. But then I added it all up to three-eights of an inch, and thought, *That's almost half an inch.*

After applying the freezing, the doctor picked up her a medical instrument, something that resembled a tiny hole-punch. The intern, who had been studying the whole process with unblinking eyes, flinched when the doctor began. I shut my eyes, counted my breaths, told myself to relax while the doctor did the procedure, and the intern murmured ridiculous words: *Very good! That's it! Almost done now!*

Before the appointment, I'd read everything I could find on the internet about a vulvar biopsy. Some women said it felt like a mosquito bite after the freezing wore off, but they must be delusional. It was more like a cigarette burn, though I'm only speculating on what that would feel like.

"Oops," the doctor said, and I opened my eyes to see she and the intern crouched on the floor, as though searching for a contact lens.

"What happened?" I craned my neck.

"Sorry, we dropped one of the samples, I think. But it's okay, two will be enough." I would think about that the next day, when all three lesions burned under a stream of hot urine.

The doctor gave up the search and once again faced my vulva and I allowed my head to drop onto the papered table.

"While you're down there," I asked, my voice squeaking, "there's something I want you to check out. It's kind of ... personal." She didn't reply, so I took her silence as permission to continue. Who knew when I'd have another opportunity or the gumption?

"So. I've never had an orgasm. And I've tried. Lots of things. So, I'm wondering ... is there anything ... that physically doesn't look right?" I specified the physical because I wanted her to know I wasn't stupid, that I understood orgasms are ninety percent, or something like that, psychological.

"Well," she spoke slowly, "there are many reasons women are anorgasmic, most of them not physical, but on a purely physical

261

level, I can tell you that you've got some architecture loss, probably caused by the lichen." I visualized crumbling buildings, falling walls.

"Oh, and, there's a very thin scar on your hood, maybe also from the lichen? But listen, none of that should stop a woman from orgasming … the clitoris is mostly under the surface, and multi-branched." I imagined a forest's canopy, but the view didn't relax me.

She asked about penetrative sex versus toys and other embarrassing queries that I barely remember now. She paused to find out whether I had any other questions, and I shook my head, rustling the table's paper cover.

"Okay, all done!" she said brightly, as though we hadn't just had that awkward conversation, me lying on my back, legs in stirrups. She handed me a sanitary pad, one of those bulky ones from 1985, and then she and her tense intern exited the room. Before I left, I scanned the floor for the one-eighth-inch part of me, wishing I could have it back.

"It's not like that. Not a medical problem," I tell Laura. I feel foolish for opening up this conversation and then shutting it so abruptly. "Listen, I'll tell you more in person. When I'm back."

"Okay. You sure you don't want to talk about it now?"

"Yeah. Sorry to lay this on you. But I feel better somehow. To have told you half the story."

"Well, I'm glad. You'll tell me the other half sometime, right?" Her eyebrows scrunch together.

We confirm that we'll see one another again in a few days, when we organize our daughters' virtual visit, and then we end the call.

I step out onto the balcony, look down at the street below, where the day is well underway. The fruit seller is receiving a delivery of mosambi, their chartreuse skins bright from five storeys up. Two women in crisp saris rush across the sidewalk, beginning commutes to office jobs.

I recall that after the gynecologist appointment, I recounted the bare minimum to Murtuza, comparing the experience to a dental visit, the worst part being the freezing. He cringed. Now I think about Zainab's seven-year-old description of "getting a needle" after her khatna, how similar it all sounds.

I sank into a funk soon after the appointment. I went through the motions, teaching all day and picking Zee up from daycare, but I was kind of checked out, letting Murtuza take over with Zee while I went to bed early. I told him I was fighting a cold.

The deep blue mood lasted weeks, lightening gradually, me a boat, rowing myself back to shore. Back then, I couldn't understand why I was so sad.

But now, I think maybe it was the act itself, the cutting, that triggered it.

I dutifully applied ointment and the infection cleared. Ian messaged me. Then I forgot all about the gynecologist. Well, not forgot, just stored it away on a mental shelf.

I imagine the khatna in a small metal lockbox, higher up on the same shelf, so high that none of my ladders can reach it.

The sliding glass door swooshes open and Murtuza joins me on the balcony.

"Are you okay?" He rubs his eyes. "It's early."

"Yeah, just couldn't sleep. I Skyped with Laura."

"How is she?"

"Good."

"Did you talk to her about everything that's been going on?" He puts his arm across my waist.

"Well, a little. Not that much. It's just a lot to tell."

"It's important to talk about the khatna, Shari … when you're ready." I appreciate the last part; he knows I can't be rushed.

"You know what I was thinking about just now?" I remind him about the biopsy.

"Oh yeah, didn't they lose the specimen?" He nods, remembering.

"In hindsight, it was difficult to do all that alone. I think it made me sad. If I had to do it again, I'd probably ask you to come along." I leave it there, can't quite hold all the other threads I've been weaving in my mind, at least not securely enough to tie off the ends.

"I'd probably want to." He smiles uncertainly.

"You'd probably crack jokes while squeezing my hand too hard, like you did when Zee was born," *Soon*, I think. *I'll tell him what all this means. Soon.*

∽ FORTY-FOUR ℃

Dholka, 1911

Abdoolally left Bombay Central Station in the evening, and arrived in Dholka the following noon hour, weary from the journey. He was fifty-six, no longer a young man.

Normally it was Rumana who travelled south, but she'd recently fallen ill and cancelled her trip to Bombay. He'd use the visit as an opportunity to check on his printing press, ensure that his manager's reports were accurate.

Rumana greeted him at the door. When she rose after finishing the salaam, he realized they were almost the same height now. She was seventeen and he hoped she'd stopped growing, for if she were too tall it would be hard to find her a husband.

"You look so much like your mother these days," he said. A gauzy silver orna draped over her long black hair and looped over a blue blouse that cut low across her small cleavage.

"Really?" she asked, smiling. He nodded, but then he wasn't quite sure. It had been a dozen years since Shaheeda's death and he could barely mentally call up her face anymore. He studied

Rumana's features and Zehra's confident demeanour came to his mind instead. He brushed the thought away.

"Are you feeling better now?" He looked into her unusual topaz eyes and then recalled, *Yes. Those are Shaheeda's eyes.*

"Yes, much. I'm still a little weak, but if you'd waited, I could have come to Bombay in a few days, to not waste so much of your time, Papa."

"I do think the air here is better for you. Bombay is getting so congested."

The next day, he visited his printing press, and found everything in tip-top shape, as though someone had warned the staff of his arrival. Of course, Dholka was a small town, and he was a big man, so word must have travelled to the manager. He inspected the large room and its monster-like metal machines, all of which were clean — too clean — for the middle of a business day. On his walk back through the main street of town, he stopped in at a local sweet shop and bought a pound of burfi for Rumana and Shehnaz. He paused outside the hosiery store beside it, and looked in its windows, admiring the men's kurtas on display. Just as he was about to move on, a woman stepped out of the store, carrying a large parcel. He made room for her, and they locked eyes. No. It couldn't be! Zehra?

Her initial look of shock turned to something that resembled a flickering warmth.

"Hello, Abdoolally, khem cho? How have you been all these years?"

He nodded to her, but his mouth was dry, wordless. What was she doing in Dholka?

"Did you buy those for Rumana?" Zehra pointed to his box of burfi. The sun glinted off her wedding ring. He'd heard she'd remarried, but didn't listen to the details when his daughter, Raushan, had shared the gossip years ago. He hadn't wanted to know.

"Yes," he stammered. "What are you doing here? Visiting someone?"

"Oh no. I live here. I've been here for the last ten years." Her lips lifted into a sad smile. Then, gesturing with her chin to his box, she said, "She'll like those. They are her favourite sweets."

∽ FORTY-FIVE ∾

I carry two lattes to the patio table Zainab has scored for us, after hovering close to a pair of young men who'd long finished their coffees. It's been a week since we last saw one another, a week since Dholka.

"Wow, Mumbai hipsters are just like Manhattan hipsters," I say, watching the guys depart.

"I don't like that hairstyle." She's referring to the guy with the bun perched atop his head.

"Well, sometimes good things come when men mess with gender rules." I'm echoing Laura's opinion; she'd scolded me when I'd similarly mocked a man-bun.

"Look at this." Zainab leans over our table and points to her phone. On the screen is the Facebook page for Fatema's activist group.

"You joined?" I sip from my bowl. The froth leaves a faint moustache before I lick it away.

"Well, yes. Just checking it out, only. I wanted to see what they are discussing." I, too, joined the group, about a month ago, but after the first few glances I stopped lurking. I just can't handle reading any more articles about khatna, and worse, I don't want to read the bitter backlash comments that litter the page. It's enough that I know my own story now; I don't want to be an activist about something so personal.

"I've been talking with my friends, you know, quietly. We've been told by our amil to keep away from this group."

"Really? I can't believe elderly clerics have Facebook profiles!"

"Don't be silly. They use Facebook, Twitter, and all the apps to communicate with the community. They are very modern, high-tech. They are monitoring these groups."

"I had no idea."

"Some of my friends, you know the ladies in my menege group? They won't join but some want to talk. So I have been telling them that I am just realizing it can do more damage than good." She brushes away a tear.

"Oh, Zainab." Has she been suffering this week? I've been meaning to check in with her, but didn't get around to it.

"You know, a few months ago, Nafeesa came to me and questioned me about khatna — she'd signed a petition against it. She told me she was angry I took her. I didn't listen to her, thought she was overreacting, being suggestible to things she was reading. And then ... last week ... just after getting home from Dholka ... I started thinking about it. About how Sharmeen had bled a lot. And how Nafeesa cried after ... oh, Allah! I did that to them!" More tears come, and her face turns pink.

"Zainab, you didn't know. You were just doing what you'd been told was right."

"I didn't question anything. I should have. Why didn't I? I used to be so much more daring when I was young. But somehow that all changed after I got married. Astaghfirullah."

"Oh, Zainab ..." The weight of her regret is palpable.

"I've spent the week reading, and talking to people. Maybe I can help others understand. I feel … I feel that now I need to make up for my ignorance." She reaches for her hankie.

"That's good," I tell her, squeezing her shoulder. "You might have an impact. Maybe more of an impact than petitions and social media. You might change their minds through conversation. But … but take your time. You're still sorting this all out yourself, aren't you?"

She shakes her head, brushes away my suggestion.

"But what if Sharmeen or Nafeesa have problems like Fatema or you? Because I have always had no issues," her voice hushes, and she tucks a loose lock of hair into her rida. "I never thought it would harm them."

"They might. Or they might not. You should talk to them so that they will understand what's going on with their bodies." I run my fingers over the smooth ceramic bowl. What if I'd learned about this when I was Nafeesa's or Sharmeen's age? What if I hadn't had to read all those books, guessed at the problem? If I'd sorted it out early on, maybe I could have turned things around. My chest tightens at the idea that it's too late now, that sex will always be a problem. My head begins to fog and I shake away the fear. I can't think about it now. I gulp my latte.

Zainab scrolls down the page and reads aloud. I try to listen, but I'm distracted by a fruit seller passing on the sidewalk, sing-songing about papayas for sale.

"The East Brunswick, New Jersey, jamaat — that's your jamaat, correct? It has issued a letter telling their congregants they must follow the law of the land and not perform khatna in the United States. They must also not take their daughters to another country to have khatna done. And look, there are other letters posted, from England, from Australia, from Canada, and five others from the U.S."

"All of this in reaction to the legal case in Australia."

"Yes."

"I wonder if Mom has seen this yet? She's no longer active with the jamaat, so maybe not." I scan the screen.

"Maasi Nisrin arrives soon, no?" she asks, referring to my mother.

"In a couple of weeks." Actually, in thirteen days.

"Have you talked with her yet about …?" She doesn't finish her sentence. Neither do I.

"I'm waiting to talk in person."

"She's going to be upset with my mother." Her eyebrows rise, turning the statement into a question. She is aware of the degree to which her mother betrayed my mother. And then I think, *We three girls have been keeping quiet for over three decades, unknowingly protecting that sister relationship.*

"Did your mom think the secret would be watertight forever?" I mutter.

"I doubt she thought that far ahead. Oh, boy, they are going to have a fight."

I nod, but I cannot process that yet. I point to Zainab's screen. "This is good news, right? People will follow these instructions?" I want to be hopeful.

"Well, the comments I'm reading say that these letters might only be for show, a way to avoid legal trouble like what happened at the Sydney jamaat."

"I think people will follow the local laws." But what do I know? The last time I was at the East Brunswick jamaat was for my father's prayers and burial.

"Insh'allah," Zainab says, nodding. "I mean, at least for those on the fence, or those who don't want to be in any kind of trouble."

"Or maybe they might become more secretive?"

"Possible. But how much more secretive can Bohras be about this?" She rolls her eyes. I meet her mischievous gaze and snort at the ridiculousness and truth of her statement.

"I know! We were tricked by your mom and Nani. They tricked my mom and Fatema's parents. And probably their mother was tricked by someone. It's all so cloak and dagger." Then I shudder, when the blade's imagery comes to mind.

Fatema arrives, full of energetic apologies and excuses about a teleconference that ran long. We catch her up on our conversation, and Zainab shows Fatema her smartphone.

"Yes, we're still waiting for another couple dozen letters from jamaats all over Canada, the U.S., and Europe. And of course, Saifee Mahal, but that one's a bigger fight." She points behind her, in the direction of the Syedna's residence, a few kilometres away.

"Do you think that will ever happen?" I glance at the road, spot an old man ambling on the footpath that edges the café's patio. He is stooped, has a long beard, and wears the typical topi and white kurta of an orthodox Bohra man. Zainab and Fatema look his way, too. I want to say that he looks like Abdoolally, but I refrain; they will tease me for seeing a ghost. Since beginning this research, I have been imagining seeing our great-great-grandfather everywhere. Then it comes to me: here in Mumbai, there are many Abdoolallys in our midst. Many of the senior orthodox men here resemble him at least a little, having held on tightly, or reverted to, the ways of the previous century, as though their long beards, topis, and kurtas will protect them from modernity's ills. I imagine Abdoolally would have found this strategy disconcerting. Or would he?

"Is that your Zoeb Mama?" Zainab asks, referring to Fatema's maternal uncle.

"I don't think so." Fatema squints in his direction. The barista brings her drink and she takes a sip without thanking him.

I turn to watch the old Bohra man again.

"It is your Zoeb Mama!" Zainab waves at him and he makes his way over.

"Arré! Why did you have to do that?" Fatema grumbles at Zainab. She stands to greet her slowly approaching uncle. She takes his hand and goes through the motions of a salaam. He gracefully pulls away in mock embarrassment of her deference. Next, Zainab and he repeat the performance. Then they introduce me; he is from Fatema's mother's side, a line I don't know that well.

"Oh, the last time I saw you, it was many years back. I think you were a teenager." He takes my hand in both of his.

"Chalo, come sit, Mamaji, have some tea with us." Fatema pulls a chair from a neighbouring table.

"Na, na, Dayam is waiting at home for these." He points to a bag of onions. "She'll be wondering where I've gone."

"Give her my salaams," Fatema says.

"I just wanted to tell you, Fatema, we've heard about the social work you've been doing, the educational efforts around the females issues. And Dayam and I support it. It's time for things to change, to progress. Anyway, come by sometime for lunch; we haven't seen you in a long time. All of you come," he says, looking to me and Zainab.

"Thanks, Mamaji. I will," Fatema replies. Zainab and I nod, too, and say goodbye.

Fatema watches him head down the sidewalk, then drops into her chair.

"Did he mean —" I ask.

"Yes. 'Females issues' is code for khatna," Fatema murmurs.

"Wow." Zainab turns to watch the old man disappear around the corner.

Zainab and I order a second latte from our chair this time, benefiting from Fatema's status.

"Listen, you two, I have been thinking." Fatema glances side to side, leans in, and lowers her voice. "Those jamaat letters are bullshit. Won't accomplish anything. Even that conviction in Australia will be appealed. We have to do something here in India, to shake things up. The problem is that FGM hasn't been banned here."

"Won't your group's petition accomplish that? Make it illegal?"

The server arrives with our drinks.

"Maybe, but that will take a long time. We still need tens of thousands more signatures, then we have to present it to the ministers, then they will go through their whole process, which can take eons. And they will need as much popular support as possible. Our members have been publishing articles and so on, but we need to do something now. Something dramatic, to get more attention."

"Like what?" Zainab's eyes are bright. The conversation is having an opposite effect on me. I gulp back my latte, hoping to counteract the drowsiness.

"We need to name the cutters. The problem is that none of our members have been able to access this information, or don't want to share it if it implicates their families. Some are also very tied into the community and prefer to not get too controversial. We've tried a number of avenues."

"You really think that will have an impact? Going public with their names?" I challenge.

"People in our community hate public embarrassment. They might avoid that particular cutter or the cutter might stop." She looks less sure of herself now. "Well, it can't hurt to expose them, anyway. They deserve it."

"Fewer cutters could mean fewer khatnas, maybe? And since it's legal here they won't go to jail, right? Just embarrassment? That's good," Zainab says.

"Do you know her name? The woman who did us? I assume she's dead by now," Fatema asks Zainab.

"She died last year. Her name was Munira Aunty. Mom and I took my girls to her when they were small," Zainab says, the pink returning to her face. "She was very old."

"Munira Aunty," I repeat, the small hairs at the back of my neck standing tall. Perspiration prickles my armpits.

"You know her, Shari?" Zainab asks.

"No, I don't think so. Her name sounds familiar, somehow." I search my brain, but there is only a feeling, a glimmer of recognition.

"I wonder who took her place. Would she have an apprentice? Do they work like that?" Fatema pushes on.

"Probably. Mom will know. But she might not tell me, now. I broached the subject yesterday and told her I support your group's efforts. We had a disagreement."

"You did?" I turn to her, shocked. I'm awake now. "What did she say?"

"I raised it in a sort of current events kind of way. I didn't talk about us. I couldn't … discuss it like that. It's still very … emotional for me." She lifts her cup, takes a drink. Her cup rattles on the way down.

"Maybe you shouldn't have too much coffee, Zainab." I pat her back.

"Good for you! I'm proud of you for speaking your mind to her!" Fatema praises, raising her cup into the air.

"It makes sense you're emotional about it. So am I." My voice wavers.

"I think if I ask her about the new cutter, she will be suspicious. She knows I'm spending more time with Fatema these days. And there would be no reason for me to need to know: my daughters are well past that age and it will be years before they would take their daughters. Not that I will encourage them," she says, her words speeding up. She takes in a shallow breath, then another. "I will actively discourage them; I feel so responsible."

"Okay, okay, just breathe. Everything is okay," I counsel. Zainab starts to pant, beads of sweat now on her forehead. Fatema jumps up, asks the server to bring water to the table. A pitcher and three glasses arrive.

"I'm so hot," Zainab whispers.

"Can I take this off?" Fatema asks, untying the collar strings of Zainab's rida.

"Okay." Fatema pulls off the hood, and I lift the rida up and over Zainab's head. The action reminds me of undressing Zee late at night, limp as a rag doll. Under the garment, Zainab wears a hot pink T-shirt with the word COOL in bejewelled lettering. I can't help myself; I sputter into giggles. Then Fatema sees it, too, and laughs. Zainab looks down at her chest, catches the joke, and smiles through her ragged exhalations.

"My kids ... gave it to me ... on my last birthday. Because ... I am so ... cool." We sit quietly for a few minutes, waiting for her to fully recover.

Finally, she stops sweating, and pulls the top of her rida back on.

"I just had an idea about how to get the information." Zainab loops her hood strings tightly, makes a knot.

"Zainab ... please, stay calm." I don't want us to trigger another panic.

"How?" Fatema asks.

Zainab sips water and shares her brainwave: she thinks I should be the one to ask Tasnim Maasi. I will say that I've been watching the controversy unfold, that I know what it's like to grow up in the West, with all of its loose values, and that, although I'm not certain it will help, I'd like to offer Zee khatna, just in case it might assist her. Her words are ludicrous, nonsensical.

"You'll tell my mom that she is the perfect age, it's almost like it's meant to be. And because it is prohibited in the United States, you will do it in Mumbai before you leave." I stare at Zainab, dumbfounded, as she continues.

"And then you ask her, 'Can you tell me who to go to, someone who is clean, maybe even someone who is a doctor? Because I'd prefer hygienic conditions in a clinical environment.'"

"Perfect!" Fatema nearly yells. I want to laugh, but they are both being earnest.

"She'll never believe me. 'Loose values'? C'mon, she'll be suspicious right away."

"Maybe not. You know it plays right into her thinking. She might be relieved that you've crossed over to her perspective," Fatema muses.

"She's always had a soft spot for you. That might make her ignore any suspicions she could have. I mean, when other people were talking bad about you, she always defended you," Zainab says.

"People talked badly about me? What'd they say?" I'm not sure why it matters, but it does.

"Oh, just things about when you were dating goras when you were in your twenties. She always said that you were a good girl and capable of making good judgments. Imagine! I only was caught smiling at a boy, and she married me off so quick." In that moment, a confusing knot of thoughts tighten.

I love my maasi.

But how can I love her after what she did to me?

My cousins stare at me, awaiting a reply. I focus.

"And when she finds out that I'm lying to her?"

"She'll never have to know. You just get the information, give it to me, and that's it." Fatema snaps her fingers.

I think, *Maybe it could be that simple. I would simply be an information-gatherer.*

"Yes." Zainab nods. "Let's do that, but instead, I'll take part of the blame. You can say you told me the cutter's name, and I told Fatema."

"I don't know," I say, latte bile rising in my throat. "What if she asks to go along? Or what if she takes it as permission, and just takes Zee to the doctor without me?"

"Actually, you could make that work in your favour," Fatema says, pointing at me. "You will invite her to come along, you will even say that she is a stand-in nani for Zee, since your mom won't support it. But in the end, you won't show up for the appointment, you will say you've changed your mind, perhaps we'll say that Murtuza found out and disagreed."

"And we won't ever allow her to be alone with Zee, not ever, so there is no way she could take her without you knowing," Zainab reassures.

"And then my group will take the doctor's name to the media."

"I don't know. I have to talk to Murtuza about this."

"Yes, of course, he has to be in agreement," Zainab says.

I know he feels helpless about khatna, especially because I haven't truly opened up to him. I've been treating him as though he isn't a part of this at all.

"I don't know if I'll be able to pull this off convincingly in person. I'm not much of an actor," I say.

"We can script it, rehearse it," Fatema says.

"Or here's another idea. Mom is on email. You can say that you don't want to talk about this in person, because the two of you are rarely alone, and you want to keep this secret. You can be more convincing over email," Zainab adds.

Maasi has invited me over twice last week, and I've delayed our visit, made excuses. A part of me never wants to see her again.

"I'm supposed to go over there tomorrow with Zee."

"Perfect. Go have a regular visit with her. Then, in the evening, send the email."

"Wait, is she on Facebook? Does she follow the debate there? Would she know that I'm a member of that group?" I point to Zainab's phone.

"No, Facebook is too much for Mummy. But just to be sure, let's both leave the group." I watch her swipe her phone open, squint into the screen, and make the changes. I log on to the café's free WiFi and do the same.

"Before I forget, Muffadal — the driver who took us to Dholka? — he called and gave my assistant his maasi's number. For you." She passes me a piece of paper that says Banu +919833620880.

"I'd forgotten all about her." I absent-mindedly slip the number into my notebook.

Later, going home in a taxi, I reflect on the "plan" and wonder whether Fatema and Zainab crafted it in advance. I feel as though I've lost Beh Thrun Panch three times in a row. I replay the conversation, shake the thought away.

After Zee is in bed, I share my cousins' idea with Murtuza.

"Let's do pros and cons." He rips a piece of paper from a legal pad and readies himself to take notes on a bisected piece of paper. I pat his arm.

"All right. Pros: help the cause."

"Which might be empowering for you?"

I nod and he scribbles.

"Cons: she may find out and be angry, even if they take the blame."

"Anything else?"

I shake my head, can't think of anything. He points out the longer pro side.

"But it's deceitful, right?"

"Think of it as our tiny contribution to ending this practice," he says. I register him saying "our." I place my hand on his thigh and feel its solidness.

"I think I've been making it more complicated. Like we're ganging up on Maasi or something?" I venture, trying to make sense of the emotional soup splashing in my mind.

"It's not like she doesn't deserve to be confronted." He pulls away, looks at me closely.

"Maybe, but I don't want to do that. I am not ready for that. I can't do that." I hear my voice growing shrill, my body overheating. "It wasn't all her fault."

"What do you mean? She intentionally disrespected your parents' instructions. Imagine if someone did that to us, to Zee?" His voice has risen, too, both of us too loud to hear each other.

"Don't pressure me!" I stand, take a few steps away, shake my head. We both go silent for a minute.

"Sorry. I don't mean to pressure you," Murtuza finally says.

"I know, Murti…. Listen, I know it doesn't make any sense. It's just that I can't really get my head around the idea that she wanted to harm me. She grew up in this culture, right? She would have truly believed that she was doing the right thing. If anyone is to blame, it's her mother, her grandmother, her great-grandmother," I say, waving my arm farther back with each generation. "It's probably Abdoolally's fault! Or his mother's fault!"

For a second, a hot wind blows through my brain and I can't think.

"Okay, okay." Murtuza stands, takes both of my hands in his, looks me in the eye. "I get what you are saying."

He guides me back to the couch.

"It's so … confusing. I know she's to blame, but I don't … want to hold her … solely responsible, you know? And she's my favourite aunt, the one who treated me the best … it's all really mixed up for me."

"You don't have to blame her. Keep it simple. We'll just get the information about the cutter. Or maybe we don't have to do anything at all. It's up to us to decide, right?" Once again, I hear his use of first-person plural.

"You'd like to do this? You want to be a part of this, too?"

"Yeah." He nods, exhaling in that way that tells me his patience is wearing thin. "Khatna affects me too, right? It harmed you, but it impacts us, our relationship. It would feel good to actually be able to do something about all of this, take some kind of direct action. I think men should be more involved."

"Right." I pat his arm. "They should. You should."

I watch him go to kitchen, open the fridge, and pour glasses of water. I follow him, open a bottle of wine, and carry two glasses, by their stems, to the living room. Then I fetch my laptop from the kitchen.

"Why don't we begin a draft now?" I say.

"You think?"

"Well, I'm going to see her tomorrow." I open my inbox and then my email. I reach for my wine; my mind is as blank as the screen.

"You want me to start?"

I nod and pass him the laptop. I listen to the clicking of the keyboard, the staccato, irregular beats of his thoughts spilling out. I read over his shoulder.

> Dear Tasnim Maasi,
> As I've grown older, I find myself connecting more to our traditions. I've been thinking lately that I might like to have khatna done for my daughter before we leave. You see, I'd like her to have a strong sense of her culture, and it's sometimes difficult to do that in the West. An initiatory rite like this would be good. I under-stand that it can be done by a doctor these days, which makes it a safe procedure. Can

you refer me to a doctor for this? Please keep
this confidential.

"That sounds good." Of course, it sounds heinous because it's khatna. But also, this is the first time I'll be lying to my aunt; I never had to, not like I did with my parents.

"Anything to add?" Murtuza asks, drawing me back to our task.

"Start a new paragraph at 'I understand.' Oh, and simplify the language there." I point to "initiatory rite."

"I guess 'barbaric rite' won't work?" he mutters. "How's 'traditional cultural practice'?"

"Too academic. Just say 'tradition.'"

"Let's add that this is urgent?"

"Good idea, I want this to be over and done with before Mom arrives." I don't want to pile on to what's already going to be a hair-raising showdown between my mother and Maasi.

"What should the subject line be?"

"How about 'Important question about Zee'? No wait, just use her first initial. I don't want her name attached to this," I venture. He nods, types it in, then turns to me.

"You all right?" He studies my face. Do I look weird? I relax my jaw.

"Yes." I reread the email, and lean over him to save it in the draft folder. *There is still time*, I tell myself. I won't send this until tomorrow. "I'm sure."

I expect our visit with Maasi to be strange, but it isn't. Zee sidles up to her, just as I would have done as a child, allowing Maasi to kiss her cheek and feed her a biscuit. After a time, Zee asks to play games on my tablet.

We make chai in the kitchen and I carry the two cups to Maasi's sitting room. With a slight tremble, she pours half of her tea into a saucer and lets the masala steam escape. She lifts the saucer to her lips and slurps, the loudest slurp she can possibly make, and looks Zee's way. The mischief distracts Zee from her angry birds, and Maasi slurp-slurp-slurps again, making Zee laugh out loud; now that she knows Maasi's games, she no longer hesitates to enjoy them. I follow her lead, pouring and drinking from my saucer, but I can't seem to amplify my sips, because my heart isn't in it.

I put down my saucer, and watch the two of them. These antics are reserved for Zee alone, as they once were for me; Zainab told me, with a measure of envy, that Maasi is as strict with her kids as she was with her. What internal rule makes her the serious matriarch with her direct bloodline, but the clown with us?

Maasi's already wrinkled face is crinkled with mirth. I can imagine her thirty-three years younger, my special maasi, eyes twinkling just for me. I try to picture her taking me, Fatema, and Zainab to the cutter's apartment.

I don't have these details — Fatema didn't offer them — but I visualize a three-storey rundown building, like the ones in this old Bandra neighbourhood. We pull open a heavy door, crowd into a manual lift, the kind that buzzes until you've properly closed the rusting metal grates, and are jolted up. Then down a short hallway. The three of us might have jostled to ring a doorbell in a childish competition for joy. A woman we don't recognize comes to the door and we are ushered in quickly, the adults speaking in hushed tones. Something doesn't feel right; Maasi looks tense and wafts a piquant sweat. *What's this place?* Fatema might have asked aloud, the question that I, too, would have been thinking.

The flat is dark, heavy curtains veiling the windows. We pass a living room. Its furniture is shabby, the upholstery faded where lethargic bodies rested, the wood stain of table legs worn where restless toes rubbed. I don't think these are details Fatema related. Could they be memory?

I imagine-remember Maasi pulling the old woman, Munira Aunty, aside. I know her name now. Or have I always known her name?

We three kids might have picked up on the adults' agitation, wondered about our detour from our Kwality ice-cream-procuring excursion. And yet, we trusted that the elders would eventually take us there. As they did.

"Want more chai?" Maasi asks. I take our cups to the kitchen. I light the gas stove, wait for the chai to reheat. Munira Aunty's kitchen might have looked just like this one, only smaller, and dimmer. I picture paint peeling from mildewed walls. As a child, whenever I pointed out details like this, signs of neglect or damage in people's homes, my mother would shush me and later educate: *Not everyone is as fortunate as we are.*

I refill our cups, and carry them to the living room. Zee is now seated next to Maasi, explaining how her game works.

"Let me try." Maasi takes the tablet and follows Zee's instructions.

"Now! Press here! No, here!" she says, and Maasi's bigger and less nimble fingers fumble.

I smile at them, but again, my mind is carried away — am I getting carried away? — to Munira Aunty's living room. From there, we were prodded forward by the older girl, the cutter's grandchild, Sherbanoo, to a bedroom, a space just past the decrepit kitchen. My mind draws a mental map of the flat for me.

The medium-sized bedroom is much like Abbas Kaaka's high-ceilinged widower's room. Instead of the family tree, there is a crack reaching wispy fingers up the wall, and spiderwebs dangle listlessly from the ceiling. I know this last description must be false, for unlike North American homes, I've never seen an Indian flat with cobwebs; there are always women available to sweep them away.

Fatema's information fills in the scene now, and I see myself perched at the edge of a twin-sized bed with Fatema, Zainab, and Sherbanoo. But my brain takes over, creating dialogue. *Don't be afraid*, Sherbanoo might have said, and when Maasi collected Zainab, she might have told us, *Be good girls*, and then shut the door.

What standard are you in? Sherbanoo may have asked us, as we waited, listening to the sounds of muffled cries coming from two rooms away. I may have replied, *We don't call them standards. We call them grades in the U.S. I'm going into second grade.* Fatema, the one more likely to ask questions, might have demanded, *What are they doing?* And the older girl might have said, *I'm in standard six.* The cries from the living room might have stopped then, and we may have all listened to the silence before Sherbanoo non-answered Fatema's query with *See, it's nothing. Very fast. Nothing to worry about at all.* She might have blocked the door when Fatema stood to open it. And then Zainab was brought in, a strange calm in her eyes as she obediently followed the script she had been given: *It was easy, like going to the doctor and getting a needle.*

And then it would have been my turn.

"Yes, you won!" Zee squeals, interrupting my imagined-memory, my non-memory, or hyper-imagination. Why was it all so vivid in my mind? I pull a notebook from my purse and scribble it all down before it blows away like a pile of dried leaves in a windstorm.

I breathe, listen to Zee tell the aunt I love the most to play again. I watch my girl's face soften with pleasure as my aunt's gentle hands stroke it.

Then I remember that I have a mission. I stuff my notebook away.

"Okay, okay, enough. You play now," Maasi tells Zee and we return to drinking chai, this time sans slurping. I must look normal, present, ordinary, because she asks me to tell her about the trip to Ahmedabad.

I've gone over this with Murtuza. I must wait. On the way out the door, I will mention to her that there is something sensitive I want to talk with her about, but I don't want to do it with Zee present, so I will send her an email tonight. I must stick to the script.

I open my phone, flip through a few dozen photos of buildings, offering the bare bones of the trip, scraping away the meat of the story. I scrape it all away. Maasi takes in my visual storytelling with polite interest.

"You know I've only been there once myself. A long time ago. Not much seems to have changed."

I check the time, tell Maasi we should get a move on. I pack our things, and tell Zee to run ahead and press the lift button. At the door, I muster an earnest look, manage to blurt, "I'm going to send you an email about something important." My eyes tear up a little, but that isn't part of the plan. Zee yells that the elevator has arrived, and I rush away.

∿ FORTY-SEVEN Cᴖ

Bombay, 1911

Maimuna waited for his reply. He only glowered at her.

"Did something happen in Dholka to upset you?" She repeated her question.

He counted the years: ten since the divorce, ten since he'd seen her. He'd barely thought about Zehra over the decade. So much had happened. His printing press and stationery business had grown. He'd bought and sold land. He'd married Maimuna eight years ago, and they'd had two daughters. She was pregnant again. Ten years had passed.

So why had the brief interaction with Zehra bothered him so? He'd been unable to sleep properly since, and it felt like a rock had settled in his stomach. His mind continually roved back to their conversation, the way she seemed to look right through him. An old melancholy, the kind he'd felt after Sharifa's passing, settled upon him. But why? He hadn't loved Zehra that way, and after her foolishness, it was a straightforward decision to divorce her. Yet none of this felt the least bit straightforward.

"Did you know that Zehra moved to Dholka?" he snapped, his question an accusation.

"Zehra? Zehra Slatewala? The one you …" She didn't finish her sentence. They hadn't ever talked about Zehra, or, for that matter, Shaheeda or Sharifa. He hadn't permitted it. But of course she knew of all of them, had even met Zehra when she was married to Asghar. Everyone knew. While her parents were pleased for her marriage to Abdoolally, given his affluence and her widowhood, her nani had wondered aloud if Abdoolally's string of bad marital luck would somehow infect her, too.

"Yes. Of course, that Zehra! Who else would I be talking about? Did you know that she lives close to Rumana?"

"I heard that, yes." She took a step back from him, placed a hand over her belly, as if shielding it from his raised voice.

"Why didn't you tell me?" he demanded.

"It was none of my business." Maimuna looked down at her round stomach and then said softly, "And … it was bad enough that Rumana lost her first mother. Wasn't it good luck that she could grow up knowing her second mother?"

"But she's the wrong kind of influence for my daughter!" he growled. "You know what she did!"

"Yes, but that was all taken care of, no? Rumana is a good girl. So whatever her influences, she has turned out fine. You don't need to worry." She patted his back where his spine had begun to curve.

"Bring me chai." He dismissed her. He wanted to be alone. He was a man of great leadership, wealth, and intelligence. But in that moment, he knew he'd been a fool.

⁓ FORTY-EIGHT ⌒

The next morning, Maasi's reply arrives.

> I am glad that you are taking matters into your
> own hands. It's a mother's decision and her
> duty to remove the haraam ki boti.

A rough translation of the last three words: *sinful flesh.* The
hood of the clitoris, the focus of a woman's evil.

> Not to worry, things have changed lately, and
> while most people still do it the traditional way,
> I know khatna can be performed at the Shifa
> Hospital.

This is one of the hospitals dedicated to the care of the Bohra
community. "Traditional way" means shabby flats and old ladies
and fear.

> I've been told they use an anaesthetic cream.
> The whole thing from start to finish will take
> less than twenty minutes. Most of it is waiting
> for the freezing to kick in. Then the doctor will
> come in, do a tiny cut that Zee won't even feel,
> and she'll be sent home with an antiseptic
> cream. It's very safe, modern, and easy.

How does she know these details?

I think back to my vulvar biopsy, which sounds remarkably similar to what she describes. I applied a pain-dulling cream twenty minutes in advance, then the doctor injected freezing, the most painful part of the procedure, in the three biopsy locations. Then I waited there, alone, in the examining room, waiting to go all the way numb.

She ends off with:

> I can make the appointment with Dr. Rubina
> Master myself and come along with you.
> When shall we book it?

I call Murtuza into the room, and point to the computer. He reads over my shoulder.

"Congratulations, we have what we need." His gaze is glued to the screen. Perhaps he's reading it a second time, absorbing it all.

"She makes it sound so routine. Clinical," I say, dully.

"Like a trip to the dentist."

I wonder if it's just coincidence or if he recalls that this is how I described the biopsy.

"She must really believe that this is good for Zee." I lower my voice and look over at my daughter, who sits in the living room, her face scrunched up as she carefully colours in a map of India. It's a geography morning.

"I guess." He, too, turns his gaze to Zee.

"Do you think it's less traumatic when people do it this way? I mean, this way there are no infections, pain, or wrong cuts," I whisper. I'm not sure what I'm getting at.

"Well, we don't know the incidence of infections. But this is certainly a wrong cut," he says quietly. He touches my shoulder. "Right?"

"Right. Yes. I just mean the traumatic part is no longer there. You know? It would be less scary, and maybe less of a surprise and not a lie? If a child is told that she is going to a clinic to have a procedure done?"

"Maybe. But there would still be the long-term risks. Scarring. Nerve damage, sexual issues."

"But what I'm saying is that maybe the *biggest* consequences arise from pain, from the scariness of it all. From the lie." My voice grows louder as we circle around. He shushes me, gestures to Zee, who is still focused on her work. She doesn't like colouring outside of the lines. I take a deep breath.

"I don't understand what you're saying. Do you find the medical procedure acceptable?" He's using his professor tone now.

"No! No, it's still bad. I … I don't know. We put baby boys through medical circumcisions all the time, in the name of religion. Hardly anyone complains about that."

"Some people complain about it. One day people might look back and realize it's archaic, too. And I don't think you can compare foreskin removal to cutting the clitoral hood, which is far more delicate, Sharifa." He only ever uses my full name when he lectures. I glare at him angrily, and then rub my eyes, my face, my jaw. Everything feels taut. I hear him exhale, then feel him pat my back, then stroke my hair. I push his hand away.

He attempts. "Tell me what's upsetting you, Shari."

"I just ... wonder ... I mean, what made *me* so messed up? Was it a bad cut? Was it the fear? Would this have been a neutral thing if it had been viewed the way male circumcision is? If it wasn't a secret, if it was done by a doctor?"

"Maybe. I mean, I was circumcised, as were all the men I know. It's no secret, it's a rite of passage that is widely accepted. I don't feel any shame or discomfort connected to it. Male circumcision isn't about controlling sexuality. It's purported to be about cleanliness, which might be dubious, too —"

He's about to say more but I interrupt. "But not all khatna survivors are messed up. Zainab is just fine." But then I remember her recent panic attacks.

"Khatna is also a grave betrayal of trust. That's the basis of trauma. You and your mother trusted your aunt and Nani to do the best for you and then instead they did something harmful, something that shattered your trust." He blinks, looks up, as though trying to remember something.

"Oh, god. You've been reading." He doesn't usually speak in psychological jargon.

"I have been reading ... a little." He flashes me a self-conscious smile.

I stand, stretch, make myself breathe. Zee looks at me, curiously, and I am glad for her distraction.

"How's it going?"

"Almost finished."

"Okay, finish up then and then we'll do something else."

I look to Murtuza. He wrings his hands. I consider his words. I'll never know if it was a bad cut or the fear. But he's right, what I do know is that I trusted them, and they did something harmful for all the wrong reasons.

This clarity is something, at least.

"Want me to draft a reply?"

I nod and he slides the computer onto his lap and begins to tap.

I go over to Zee, compliment her on her work. She points out all the states in India, and explains her colour choices.

"Are we done school yet today?" she asks, and I check the time. Technically, she should continue geography for another half hour. There's a video about Mumbai's flora and fauna I could get her to watch while Murtuza and I finish the email to Maasi. It's not part of the curriculum, but it might be interesting. I find it on the tablet and plug in her headphones, noting that we have seven minutes and forty seconds.

I return to Murtuza, who has finished. He reads aloud:

> Dear Maasi,
> Thanks for all of this information. I'm afraid I cannot do the khatna after all. I spoke with Murtuza about it last night. Maybe I shouldn't have, but it's hard for me to keep secrets from him. He is very against it — I was actually very surprised he was so upset about it. I don't think he will change his mind. And I can't make a decision about Zee without his agreement.
> See you soon,
> Shari

"Change the 'see you soon' to 'love,'" I instruct, and he makes the edit.

"Do we send it?"

"Yes, and blind copy it to Fatema. And Zainab." He accidentally adds them on the cc line, then catches his error.

"Crap. We're not very good at being spies, are we?" A laugh sputters out like a hiccup. He stares at the screen, double-checking everything.

"Wait, does it make sense that you decided to talk to me about it? I mean, will she wonder why you'd do that?" His eyes dart left and right. His question alarms me; I try to think, but my mind is crowded, a storage space cluttered with useless objects.

"What other reason can we give for why I'd back out so fast?"

"What if you said that I borrowed your laptop, and then saw the subject line of the email thread, and then got curious, you know, because it has to do with Zee."

"Okay …"

"And then I was angry and confronted you about it? It adds more tension this way." He waves his arms in a creative flourish. I wait for the penny to drop, for his hands to still.

"Well, we know that scenario is realistic, anyhow." I stare at the gold band on his ring finger and, as I've done many times before, thank god that we made it through the affair.

"Huh, yeah." There is a slight smile on his face that grows wider. Not a grin, exactly, for that would be asking too much, but still. It's the first time in many years that we've even touched the subject of the affair.

"All right, change the second sentence to say all of that instead." I watch the gold band bounce with each keyboard strike. When he's finished, he reads the new lines aloud to me. *I left my laptop open and Murtuza read our emails. He was very angry that I would plan something like this without his knowledge and he is very much against khatna — he sees it as harmful. We had a big fight. I can't go ahead or keep secrets from him.*

"It does sound more dramatic. And believable."

I reread it, imagining Maasi digesting it, her lips turning downward, her eyebrows hunching into a frown.

"I think it works."

"Want to sleep on it, and send it tomorrow?"

"Send it. I want this over and done with."

The email leaves me nauseous all day, and I obsessively check my messages, waiting for a reply. Eventually, my phone rings, and Maasi's name fills the screen.

"Hello?"

"Hello, Sharifa. Can you talk? Is Murtuza there?"

"No, he's out with Zee."

"I've been thinking about the problem," she says, her voice melodic, reasonable-sounding. "Another way to do it is for you and Zee to stay behind, to change your flights, and then we can do it after Murtuza is back in America."

I freeze. Was she the one to suggest to my parents that I stay behind in India? Was that a khatna scheme? No, no. My mom and dad and I all talked it over before the trip, and in the end it was my decision. I'd wanted to spend an extra month with my cousins.

"Hmm," I say, waiting for my head to clear. "I don't know, Maasi, I'd feel bad about doing something so dishonest. He'd never forgive me if he found out." My mind spools backward again. Does she even remember *her* duplicity?

"Fathers these days are different than in the past, so involved." Her tone sounds mocking.

"Yes. And even if I didn't say anything, Zee probably would. She's a little chatterbox," I say, not recognizing my own words. When have I ever described my expressive child in this way?

"It's true. They are very close." Again, there is something bitter in her tone. "Did you know he'd be against it?"

"We've never discussed it. It makes sense in hindsight. He tends to lean toward being against the religion, while I'm more in the middle. I like many of our traditions." I force my voice to remain neutral. "But what Murtuza says also makes sense."

"So, you agree with your husband?"

"Well, I can see both sides now. I believe this should be something Zee consents to when she is old enough to do so. As an adult. Anyway, I don't want any more arguments with my husband," I say with an amateur actor's sigh, hoping she will back off.

"I think you've been spending too much time with Fatema. As has Zainab." My heart jumps with the mention of my cousins. Does Maasi suspect the ruse?

"It's not that. I just realize, after talking more with Murtuza, that it's more complicated. I hadn't given it enough thought before. For now, I've decided against it. Sorry for wasting your time."

"All right. Okay, do what you think is best. Ultimately, it's up to the parents to make the decision." Her tone is conciliatory, almost sweet now. She is supportive Maasi again, non-judgmental Maasi.

After we hang up, her words play on my mind. Did she use the same words when reassuring my mother that I would remain safe?

Seeking distraction, I turn back to my Abdoolally research. When I open my notebook, Banu +919833620880 falls out. I dial the number and she picks up on the third ring.

"Hallo?" Her voice is so much like Tasnim Maasi's.

"Banu Aunty?"

"Yes. Who's calling?" I introduce myself and explain my research.

"Ah, yes, Muffadal told me you might phone me. Come over and meet me. But listen, I'm going to visit my daughter in Delhi tomorrow. It will have to wait until I return. I'd love to tell you all about my daadi. I was very close to her." We set up a meeting for when she is back.

∿ FORTY-NINE ∾

"I listened to a podcast today. A radio documentary," Murtuza takes my hand. "About khatna."

"Oh, yes?" I say evenly, but inside, I am a porcupine curling into a spiky ball. Our undercover operation ended five days ago, and I want to be done with this issue. But I know Murtuza. He is an academic. He likes to learn new things from books and podcasts and films. He then enjoys synthesizing that information, pondering and theorizing, and then disseminating new theoretical knowledge. I don't want him to do that with my experience.

"It was from a survivor who was talking about the impact it had on her sex life ... and her process of reclaiming her sexuality." He says this last part brightly, presenting me with a half-full glass.

"Okay." I pull my hand away, cross my arms over my chest.

"Do you want to hear more?" I nod yes, but the rest of my tightly wound body signals "no." He looks at me skeptically, so I nod again. I do appreciate the question, the effort at collaboration. I unlock my arms, fake a more open posture, push through.

"Okay, I made some notes." He rushes over to the dining-room table, and grabs his yellow steno pad. I watch him from the couch. Years ago, during our couples' therapy, I learned that I had the habit of withdrawing from his caring approaches. The awareness mortified me, and in moments like these, when all I want to do is pretend that Murtuza does not exist, I force myself to meet his eager gaze.

"She said a trauma therapist told her that she had to approach sex differently. That it didn't have to be all or nothing, you know, no assumptions about where it was going to go. That she could stop and start wherever she needed, whenever she felt uncomfortable." He takes a breath, and his words speed up, all of them escaping in one long ramble. "That she had to voice if she didn't like something or wanted something different, instead of pretending it was okay. The therapist said this is the path to healing, for the survivor to learn how to be in control of her own body."

"Hmmm." It hadn't occurred to me that there was a path to healing. Why?

"She — the survivor I mean — said that she had to find a partner she could trust, to have sex like it was her first time, as if she and her partner were exploring it all like something new, something co-created."

"I can't even imagine that."

"For example, we might start kissing, and then if you feel bad, you could say, thanks, that's all I want to do right now. Or we might be in the middle of, you know, intercourse? And you could do that. Or you might say I don't like how this or that feels." His eyes look strange to me, his eyebrows stretched high. This man, this sweet man.

"That creates healing?"

"I guess the idea is that when you get to feel more in control, you prove to yourself that you have the control, whereas the khatna would have taught you the opposite. The woman in the documentary said this process made her feel more present during sex, because it undid the message the trauma gave her."

"One terrible day when I was seven would teach me I have no control? I dunno, Murtuza, I feel like I do know how to say no. It's not like we do anything I don't actually like." I try to bat away his arguments, but then it dawns on me, that if I'm not completely there, how would I know? Do I feel in control of my body? Maybe I do, and I don't, at the same time.

"It's really up to you. It is your body." His eyes are soft.

"You wouldn't be disappointed? If I said, 'Thanks, that's all I want'? Like, in the middle of things?"

"Maybe a little bit in the moment. But in the documentary she said it was how she figured out some new boundaries. So it might be strange at first, but it could help. And I'd be really happy if that happened for you."

"What if it doesn't, and instead all we get is a lot of inter-rupted sex? Then neither of us will be having any fun. At least with the status quo you get to have fun." As soon as the words are out, I hear their wrongness.

"What? Is that how you think of me? As someone who wants to use you for fun?" He shoots me a weird look; he is disgusted.

"No. No. It's just … with the status quo, we could coast along, just be normal. Or normalish." I sigh. I don't know what I'm trying to say.

"It's no fun for me knowing that you're not feeling good," he says quietly. "We need to change this now that we're aware of what's wrong."

"Right. That makes sense." It doesn't really, but Murtuza seems sure.

"And this stopping and starting might be a temporary thing," he says, recovering, checking his notes. "The idea is that after a while, you eventually stop having a traumatic response to intimacy."

"I'm having a traumatic response to intimacy?"

"I think? On some level. Maybe not consciously."

"You got all that from one podcast?"

"Well, no. After the podcast, I did some reading. Well, more reading." He averts his gaze, smiles at the floor.

"You did research. Like, full on." I match his smile.

"It's how I feel safe." He blinks and looks away. I consider his words. He's been feeling unsafe. How did I not know?

"Give me a little time to take all of this in?"

"Of course, Shari."

"And maybe send me one of the articles you read? But only one? And the most practical of the bunch?" I hold up my finger to make my point. "Something short."

"No problem. I saved them all."

---------◆---------

A few days later, I allow myself to open the article. He's also sent the link to the podcast, but I don't listen to that; his summary is enough for now.

The instructions are just like he said: *the survivor* (I flinch at the word) *must tune into her body and notice the sensations that arise during intimate touch* (something about this makes me flinch, too, but I don't reread the sentence to identify what). The article labels what's been happening to me as dissociation and *is a normal thing experienced by a large percentage of trauma victims* (another flinchy word).

Dissociation is the skill of being there, and not there, at the same time.

It helps to block out pain, or difficult emotions.

Children are particularly good at learning this skill.
It may indicate there is repressed memory of trauma.
I pause here. I am amnesic about khatna. Fatema is not.
Zainab has patchy memories, ones that interweave with Fatema's.
I know there is nothing easy about remembering. Still, I envy
them. My own memories — if they even are memories — are as
flimsy as tissue paper.

And now I have this manual on sexual healing. Marvin Gaye
croons to me for a minute, and I let him.

I read on.

Many women have never learned to say "no" to sexual partners
because instead they learn to use sex to please their partners more than
themselves. I flip through mental images of past lovers, considering whether this assertion might be true. I don't want to linger
there, so I continue.

Early trauma increases this inability to say "no," this lack of con-
trol. Instead, they, or we — I'm working hard to locate myself
within the text — learn to dissociate.

Once again, my mind drifts back to my previous boyfriends.
I've never been coerced into anything. I was always an active
participant, probably more active, more adventurous that I am
now with my husband. But when I squeeze my eyelids shut, I
know there was a familiar half-here, half-thereness about sex
with them, too.

Sometimes this was helped along by booze. A few times
pot. Sometimes I daydreamed, made lists, focused on the wrong
things. That's what I thought, then, anyway, about my straying
mind and body. But really, according to this theory, I was, I am, a
woman seeking a necessary escape hatch. I am a blinkered horse.

I look up from my reading to see Zee's eyes on me.

"Okay?" she asks. I've missed whatever she's been explaining to me. I hope it was a brief question, rather than a report

or soliloquy. Probably a question; she's been working on math this morning.

"Sorry, Zee. I was concentrating on something else. Tell me again?"

"I want to put this up on the door now, before Nani comes." She holds a piece of paper ripped from her spiral-bound book. It says WELCOME NANI! So she wasn't working on math all this time.

"That's beautiful. How did you know to spell *welcome*?" I look more closely. There is a rainbow below the words, a sun shining above.

"That was last week's spelling, remember?" She rolls her eyes, puts her hands on her hips, the pantomime of a teenager.

I nod, pretending to remember the lesson. I find a roll of tape in the kitchen drawer.

"Which door?"

"Mom! I told you earlier: it has to be on the front door so that it's the first thing she sees in the apartment!" She waves her arms in wide circles. I have frustrated her.

"Right. That's a great idea." I follow her to the foyer, and help her affix the sign so that it hangs straight.

"Perfect." Zee steps back to assess her work.

"Nani will love it." I check my watch. She won't arrive for six hours. Yesterday, I made up the second twin bed in Zee's room. I still have to begin dinner preparations, and confirm her flight status.

"Come, Zee, let me show you something fun." I open a new tab over the dissociation article. I show Zee where to type in Mom's flight number on the airline site and then a map pops up on the screen.

"That's her airplane?" Zee's mouth gapes and her eyes widen. She is seven again.

"Well, kind of. An image of where her plane is now. Looks like it's over Lebanon."

"Over Lebanon," she repeats the words three times, in slow motion, as though in a trance. I point out other countries near the flight path: Syria, Iraq, Jordan, Palestine, Saudi Arabia, Iran, Pakistan, countries the school curriculum hasn't touched. She's mesmerized by the live map, the blinking light that represents Mom's plane.

"Look! It moved!" She leans forward, makes a smudge on the screen with her finger. Just then, Murtuza gets in, joins us in front of the laptop.

"What are you two doing?" he asks.

"Watching Nani's plane!" Zee squeals.

"Geography," I whisper. The sexual healing article is open behind the airline site, and Murtuza runs his finger over its tab, the corners of his mouth crinkling into a smile. I nod, a sensation of melancholy covering me like a crocheted blanket.

"It moved again," Zee squeals, confusing my sadness, shoving it away. I refocus on the flashing light.

~ FIFTY ~

When I get up to pee, the living room light is on.

"Ah, you are awake, too?" Mom asks. It feels normal to have her with us, even after all this time apart.

She is on the overstimulated side of jet lag, and me, well, I'm experiencing my normal insomniac edge. I check the clock; it's 1:00 a.m. I assess whether my bladder will hold a cup of herbal tea through the night. I put on the kettle and make us both a cup of chamomile.

"I had a plan to pay back my sleep debt, but it hasn't worked out so well," I say, wanly.

"For as long I can remember you were like this. Up and down, up and down all night long." She shakes her head.

"Yeah, I know. I'm so glad Zee doesn't have this problem."

"Early on, you were just like Zee. I think the sleep problems commenced after you started school. Your teacher noticed, that pregnant one?"

"Mrs. Fields." Second grade, the teacher whose belly grew all year until she left us in March.

"You still remember her name! Yes, her. We were all concerned that your school performance had dropped that year."

I sip my tea, stay quiet, waiting to see what else she'll share. She reminds me that my B average became a full-on emergency to them. They hired a tutor. And somehow, I caught up even though I still wasn't sleeping normally.

"Yes, it was right after you came back from India, come to think of it. At first we thought it was jet lag. And then you sleep-walked. Thank god that stopped. We'd find you standing up, asleep, in the middle of the hallway." I don't reply; I've heard the story many times. My nightly wanderings perplexed and alarmed my parents, who worried I'd disappear out the front door and deep into the suburbs. As a precaution, they affixed bells to all the doorknobs.

"Do you remember when the sleepwalking would get worse?" I ask, knowing the answer.

"Every couple of years, I think," she says, her eyes squeezed shut in concentration. "It was always connected to time changes. Jet lag."

"Coming home from India."

Great, another khatna consequence.

"Yes, that's right, come to think of it. You always had trouble adjusting. It's odd, though, that it would trigger sleepwalking." She yawns. "Do you think it might happen when you go back?"

"Maybe." *Tomorrow*, I think. *Tomorrow I'll tell her why India makes sleep impossible.*

The chamomile did its work and I am somewhat rested for a change. It's eight-thirty and I'm supervising Zee's toast-making. The toaster pops and she stands on tippy toes to retrieve four slices, which she places, one by one, on a plate. Murtuza and I compliment her on her butter- and jam-spreading skills, which are so meticulous that by the time we each get our slices, the bread has long cooled.

"When we go home, I'll teach you how to pack your own lunchbox," Murtuza tells her.

"Maybe next year. One thing at a time," she says sagely, accumulating crumbs on her chin.

Mom is asleep, so I suggest that we do the morning math lesson in our pajamas to avoid waking her.

After half an hour, there is stirring, and then Mom emerges into the hallway.

"Nani! Do you want toast? I can make it for you. I learned how. I've been making my own breakfast for a long time now!"

"All right, sounds good." Her voice is gravelly. "I need a cup of tea first."

I plug in the kettle and think about the conversation we will have later. Maybe we'll go out to lunch. Or perhaps we'll stay here. Would a public place be better?

"How did you sleep, Mom?" Murtuza asks.

"Like a log. But I'm foggy. It's bedtime in New York right now."

"It took me a week to adjust," he tells her, taking the dirty plates to the dishwasher. As he passes, his arm brushes mine and I startle.

"You all right?" He knows I'm in knots about talking to Mom.

"Can you mind Zee for a couple of hours around lunchtime?" My heart is pounding, my body leaping ahead in time. It's already told my mother everything, is frightened of the words I've already uttered, the terrible reaction she's already had.

"Of course. Or I can drop her at Zainab's, and come back and be with you, or a mix of both, if you want." I am overwhelmed by the options.

"I don't know, Murti, I don't know." I busy myself with pouring hot water over a teabag, then mixing in a teaspoon and a quarter of sugar. I squeeze out the bag.

"Okay, tell me when you know." He passes me the full fat milk, purchased for Mom's arrival.

Three hours later, Mom is showered, dressed, and more alert than I'd expect on her first day in India. Murtuza and Zee have cleared out, the pretext a burning research need for a paper he wants to complete. He will give us some time alone, then drop Zee off to see Nafeesa, and check in with me.

"What would you like to eat?" I ask Mom.

"I'm craving pani puri. I haven't had it in so long!"

"Street food on your first day? I dunno, Mom, you don't worry you'll get sick?"

"No, no. Last time we came, we went to a restaurant, very clean, that has good pani puri. Your dad said it tasted better than the street, even." Her wide smile pinches at the mention of my father.

"Okay. Let's go." We gather our purses, rush out the door, attempt to outrun our memories of him.

Mom insists on a rickshaw, and directs the driver in Hindi, her jet-lagged brain and tongue reaching for language she hasn't used since her last visit. He nods and hits the accelerator and we are off. I worry that I will lose my nerve, so I yell over the rick's motor and into her ear, "Mom, there's something important I want to talk about at the restaurant." *There*, I think, *I can't avoid it now.*

"Something important? What?"

"Not here, it's too noisy. At the restaurant."

"Okay," she shouts back. If she's disconcerted, I can't tell; she's occupied with scanning the street. "Not much has changed since we were here last. I'm surprised. It always seems like a new country each time we return. Oh, look, there's your father's tailor. He's got a new sign."

Back home, she had gradually stopped talking about herself in the first-person plural, emerging into her singular experience. Her talk of her New York life is completely devoid of Dad. But now, he is with us, a passenger on our ride.

At the restaurant, I point to a corner booth, far from the other patrons. We look over the laminated menus.

"Oh, yes, here they are! One order pani puri, one order bhel puri, one order dhai puri?" she asks excitedly, and I nod. She is a kid in an adult version of a Bandra candy shop.

"So you have some news?" she asks, after the waiter takes our order and returns with two bottles of water.

"Maybe we should eat first?" I don't want to ruin her much-anticipated meal.

"Tell me." She purses her lips, unconsciously mimicking my expression. "Is something wrong? What's happened?"

"No, everything's okay. But … remember when we had that conversation about khatna a while back?" I'd felt an off-kilter relief after that talk. Khatna was something that might have been my cousins' experience, but not mine. I was still the American child, the protected child.

"Yes, I recall. I've been hearing so much about it these days. The activists here are doing good work."

"You know Fatema is very involved in that group?"

"I'm not surprised. She has always been so strong. Maybe in your lifetimes things will change for the better in our community."

The waiter arrives with our first plate of puffed, deep-fried puris filled with potatoes, onions, coriander, and chili-infused liquid. Mom picks one up, passes it to me. I stuff it into my mouth in one bite, the volcano of spices erupting on my tongue.

"Oh god, this is good." She wipes her lips with her napkin.

"Really good," I agree, allowing the food to be a satisfying diversion.

The waiter drops off two iterations of the same dish, one yogurt-filled and the last a sweet and crushed-up version we eat with a spoon. For now, I'm happy to feast, and not talk. We crunch our way through the three plates.

"So what about khatna do you need to talk with me about?" She's skilled at picking up dangling threads.

"There is something you don't know, something no one ever told you." I cover my mouth and burp up the puris, my stomach reacting to my words.

"Go on." She cocks a perfectly shaped left eyebrow.

"After you and Dad left, Maasi and Nani … they took Zainab and Fatema and … me … to the khatna lady." I look up at her, register the shock in her eyes.

"No. I told Tasnim I didn't want that for you."

"She did it anyway."

"Are you sure?"

"Yes."

"Why didn't you ever tell me?"

"I don't know why I didn't say anything right after … I think they told us not to? But then with time, I guess I forgot." As I try to explain, I am confused.

"Forgot?" She looks skeptical, and I tell her Zainab remembers little, that it was Fatema who told us the story.

"Then maybe it isn't true. Fatema was just a little girl. Perhaps she doesn't remember correctly. It was a long time ago. Maybe you weren't there, but she imagined you were there." She is shaking her head and waving her hands. I breathe deeply, will her to stay still.

"She remembers it vividly. She told me I was there." I try to keep my voice slow and quiet. I need to be calm, but I am anything but. The pani puri rumbles in my stomach, and I again burp its reflux.

"Then maybe you were there, but it didn't actually happen to you. Maybe they just took you along. You wouldn't forget such a thing." Her eyes are narrowed, her brows furrowed, the picture of someone grasping for something slipping away from her. For a split second I think, *Maybe. Maybe this makes sense. Maybe I was only there, but it didn't happen to me.* My stomach lurches.

"No, people do forget. Apparently, it's a common thing to forget." I strain to recall the words in the article Murtuza sent me. Now I wish he were here. He could parrot it all back, authoritatively, and Mom would listen, believe him.

"I don't know what to think." She piles the three plates, one on top of the other, a small wobbly tower.

"It happened," I whisper, massaging my belly. My brain is full of all the arguments and counterarguments that have been forming in my head since I found out, all the details and clues that I've been collecting for the last twenty years: the sexual issues, insomnia, the gynecologist experience, the online affair (can I blame the affair on khatna, too?).

I want to lay all of this out for her, convince her to believe me, convince myself to believe myself. I hold my belly, hoping to control the spasms moving in unpredictable upward waves. Mom doesn't seem to notice.

"No. My sister promised me. I told her she couldn't take you and she promised not to take you. She promised." Her eyes are focused somewhere behind me.

I rush out of the booth, look left and right in search of the bathroom, and scurry to the back of the restaurant. I make it to a Dettol-smelling toilet, just in time. I expel everything, the lunch and all the details and clues, all the arguments and counterarguments, everything. I am emptied out, relief rippling through my body. When I flush and turn around, Mom is there, waiting for me. She presses a wet paper towel to my flushed face.

I close my eyes and let her dab my forehead and cheeks. Then she clutches at me, holds me while I whimper and sob into her shoulder.

"It happened. It really happened."

"Okay, okay." Her neck smells of Oil of Olay, the moisturizer she's worn since I was born. I inhale and think little-girl thoughts: *Don't tell. It was nothing. I want my mom.*

~⊙ FIFTY-ONE ⊙~

Bombay. 1915

Abdoolally stood outside of the Cathedral and John Connon School. He gazed up at the impressive four-storey structure with its arching windows and spacious balconies. He imagined what it would be like to be a young man taking classes in such a grand institution. *Yes, he* thought, *this is the place for my grandson.*

And so he sat down on the front step.

"Tell Reverend Savage that I will not leave until he comes to his senses," he instructed the doorman.

Only five minutes earlier, he'd been inside the headmaster's office. His request had been simple: he wanted to enroll Raushan's son, Gulamhussein, into the prestigious school.

"But Abdoolally Seth, I'm sure you must be aware, this is a British school." Reverend Savage had looked over his specs at Abdoolally, appearing perplexed.

"Yes, I am aware."

"And while I'm sure your grandson is very intelligent —"

"You think he's not as intelligent as a British student?" Abdoolally had glowered at the headmaster.

"Well, no. This is not about relative intelligence. It's just that this school is for British students only. It's our policy."

"Is it not time for you to change this policy, this anti-Indian policy? Times are changing. India is changing. Do you not want to be seen as a modern school? My grandson will be a fine addition as your first-ever Indian student."

"I'm sorry, it's just not possible. If we admit your grandson, then who knows how many other Indians will come forward with the same request?"

"And what would be the problem with that? I noticed that your upper balconies need some maintenance. I'm sure you'd benefit from the fees we Indians will pay."

"My decision is final." Reverend Savage had stood, and opened his office door for Abdoolally, who with a sigh, had raised himself up and walked out, his posture erect.

But now, he crossed one leg over the other, and enjoyed the fine January day. He tilted his chin to the sunshine, and closed his eyes. A minute later, the doorman brought him a chair and a cup of steaming chai.

Abdoolally knew he wouldn't be sitting long. While he'd been a respected member of the community for years, since the war started, he's been held in particularly high esteem by the local leaders, especially the British, because he held one of the few licences to import paper from Europe during these times of scarcity. In other words, he held the key to a precious resource. If the headmaster didn't know that already, he would know it soon. Yes, today would be day to change history, a day to do something useful.

Within thirty minutes of his sit-in, the headmaster was at the front door, apologizing and inviting Abdoolally inside.

∾ FIFTY-TWO ∾

When we return to the flat, Murtuza is there waiting. He takes one look at our washed-out complexions and follows me into the bathroom where I brush my teeth and splash cold water on my face.

"Are you okay?"

"Yes. Maybe. I don't know, Murti."

Mom shoos him into the living room and I sit on the bed, numb. Murtuza's voice sounds terse, but I can't make out what he's saying to her. Many minutes pass. She comes into the room, tucks me in, closes the drapes, and then steps away from the bed.

"No, please stay." My voice is weirdly high-pitched, like Zee's when she whines.

"You don't want to sleep?"

"Do you believe me?" She climbs onto the bed and plumps a pillow behind her back. I rest my head on her lap.

"Yes," she whispers. I open my eyes to the room's semi-darkness, take a deep breath. I orient myself to the reality that I am forty, in India with my sixty-seven-year-old mother. I have a husband in the next room. I have a daughter who will return in a couple of hours.

"You know, I only remember little bits about my own khatna ..." Sorrow dampens her voice.

"Yeah?" I turn my head to look up at her chin.

"Well, everyone in those days had to get it done. It was mandatory for my generation."

"I read that it happened to nearly everyone in my generation, too. Eighty-five percent or something."

"With each generation, maybe there will be a fifteen percent decrease. Hopefully more." But there is no optimism in her tone. Her belly contracts with her heavy exhalation.

"Do you know how it affected you?" I sit up, so that we are shoulder to shoulder now.

"Well, I don't know, really. But I think ... maybe it made things less pleasurable for me, you know, in an intimate way. It's why I didn't want them to do it to you."

"Me, too ... it had that impact on me, too." I lean my shoulder into hers. Her arm is warm, solid.

"Is it very ... important? I mean, all the ladies' magazines would say so, but aren't there more important things in a marriage?"

I shift my body away from her wrestle with denial. I don't want to be jostled by it. "Of course there are more important things," I snap. "But that's not the point."

"I suppose I don't like to think about it." She switches on the bedside lamp.

We sit in the golden light together, wordless. Perhaps she, too, has no idea how to steer this conversation. It feels like minutes before I break the silence.

"Why?" I force out the question that's been caged in my throat for weeks. "Why did you trust them?"

"I'm asking myself the same question." She turns away, swings her legs off the bed and rests her face in her palms. I look at her bent back and regret the accusation in my question.

"I really believed that I could trust them. You know, until you've had a child, they treat you like you are one. After I had you, they began to see me as more of an equal. Then we went away to the U.S., and they seemed impressed with me, how I carried myself, how I was my own person.... But then again, they didn't appreciate all the changes they saw in me. I don't know. I ... I just assumed that they would respect my wishes." She turns around and faces me. Her eyes are vacant, her cheeks slack.

"But that was stupid. Why would they? My mother and sister always thought they knew what was best for me. I should never have left you alone with them." Her eyes fill with tears.

I see her in a way I haven't before, as the younger sister, perhaps the least respected member of the family.

"No. But ... you didn't know, I guess." My absolution is weak.

"I was naive. I am so very angry with them. I will have to talk to my sister about this. I am going to have it out with her." Her face is hard now, her tears angry.

"No." I shake my head.

"I have to give her a piece of my mind —"

"No."

"What do you mean, 'no'? She has to answer to me." She points to her chest.

"She has to answer to me. And Fatema. And Zainab. This is a conversation for us to have with her," I say.

"I'm supposed to see her tomorrow. How will I do that without bringing this up?"

"I don't know. You'll have to figure it out. We've all waited a long time for this. We need to do it our way." I don't tell her that I haven't a clue what that means.

"Listen, there's something else you need to know, in case she raises it, though I doubt she will." I share the plan to trick her into giving us information about one of the local cutter-doctors.

"Oh my god, Shari! She's going to find a way to get it done, and then expect you to be grateful to her. She's going to take Zee herself, so that Murtuza cannot blame you!" Mom's eyes bug out of her head.

"No, we won't let that happen." I shake my head against the possibility.

"You must never, I mean never, leave Zee alone with that woman!"

While I already knew this, its meaning lands, really lands. I cannot trust my favourite Maasi to not harm my child.

"I know, Mom. I know how to protect my own daughter." A moment after I say it, I realize I was too caustic. But I don't apologize, don't want to. I lift back the covers, get out of bed.

When Murtuza brings Zee home, Mom observes, "That's a big bandage on your knee!"

"Apparently she fell on the street. It's just a scratch." Murtuza explains.

"Tasnim Maasi got me the bandage," Zee reports.

"Zee, did Nafeesa take you to visit Tasnim Maasi?" I ask her.

"She had to go someplace so Tasnim Maasi took me shopping with her. Then we went back to Nafeesa's place after."

"Wait, Nafeesa didn't tell me that. She left you with Tasnim Maasi?" Murtuza asks Zee.

"Where did the two of you go?" I demand. A wave of nausea returns. I imagine my aunt taking Zee to the hospital, for the fake appointment I pretended to want.

We all stare at Zee for a minute, and her face crinkles into worry.

"We went to buy vegetables and I fell down and then we went to visit her friend and that's where we got the bandage. Then … we had ice cream and then we saw Nafeesa again," she sputters, in response to our interrogation.

The mention of ice cream makes my heart pound but I take a long, deep breath, not wanting to scare Zee.

"Which friend did you visit?" I make my voice sweeter, to calm Zee.

"It was a lady who lives close to where I fell down. Tasnim Maasi took me there to wash my knee and put on the bandage."

"Do you know her name?" Murtuza asks. Zee shakes her head.

While Mom distracts Zee, Murtuza and I head into the bedroom to call Nafeesa, putting her on speaker. At first she denies leaving Zee with her nani, then says she had a class, and when we press her further, she admits that she went to see her boyfriend, and asked Tasnim to take her for an hour.

"Please don't tell my parents."

"Nafeesa, you can never ever leave her alone with your nani, do you understand? We can't trust you if you ever do that."

"Yes, of course," she says, alarm in her voice. "But I saw her going shopping. And Zee loves the fruit market. So I thought it would be fine. It was less than an hour. Did something happen?"

"No, it's probably fine," Murtuza concedes.

"Promise us, or else we can't allow you to see our daughter again." My voice is hard.

"I promise."

Murtuza hangs up and I collapse on the bed.

"Oh my god. While we've been so focused on ourselves, something really awful could have happened."

"But it didn't, right? It was just a scrape. Zee seems fine." Murtuza rubs my back. I catch my breath.

"Wait, I have one more thing I have to ask her." I go to the living room to find Zee. Murtuza follows me.

"Honey, did you go pee when you came home?"

"Just now she did," Mom replies.

"Is everything all right down there? Did the pee sting at all? Was there any blood?"

Zee shakes her head, a look of confusion and fear on her face.

"I'm overreacting, aren't I?" I whisper to Murtuza.

"I think so," Murtuza agrees.

The next day, most of the family gathers at Zainab's place. Mom and Maasi greet each other in their usual way, and Maasi is oblivious to the fury rippling under her sister's semi-pleasant surface. As rehearsed, Murtuza is aloof with Maasi, acting the role of the offended husband, one he performs well. Zainab and I exchange tense and knowing looks. When Fatema arrives, Maasi sniffs and directs a disapproving glare at Zainab, the gathering's hostess. Zainab's husband and daughters are there, too, warm and awkward toward Fatema; they don't socialize often.

I pull Zee close to me, and throughout the lunch, I am the sort of helicopter parent I usually disdain. I notice that Murtuza, too, maintains a vigilant gaze.

I complain about the heat, tell him I'm going out to the terrace. Fatema steps out a minute later. I look over my shoulder, notice Maasi's glance following her. I point to the sunset. "Let's pretend we're admiring the view. She's watching us."

"You're funny," Fatema teases, and looks east, away from me. "She doesn't suspect, only thinks I'm a bad influence, as she's always believed."

"I hate all this scheming. I'm glad it's over."

"I forwarded the email to my group."

"You removed my info, right? And Maasi's?"

"Of course." She points at a building, participating in my pantomine. "You told your mother what happened? She was a bit teary when she said hello to me."

"Yup. She knows everything. She's angry with Maasi, guilty she allowed it to happen. I think I'm mad at Mom, too, which I know is messed up."

"Correct, it's that royal bitch in there you should be angry with." She lights a cigarette. I haven't smoked since eleventh grade, behind the school's gym, but I take it from her hand, inhale deeply, hold the smoke a moment, and pass it back to her. The tobacco scratches my throat, and I cough. She laughs at me. The nicotine hurries to my brain.

"I hope Zee didn't see me do that."

"You were so quick I almost didn't see you," Fatema jokes.

"Oh, the breeze is nice out here, isn't it?" Zainab crosses the terrace to join us.

"Just lovely," Fatema says, loudly and with too much gaiety. Her levity is infectious and for a moment we pretend we are lunching ladies, enjoying Mumbai's weather.

"So what happens next? With the doctor?" Zainab asks, breaking the spell.

"We're going to picket her hospital. Alert the medical association. Call the media. Make it a big deal. Maybe three weeks from now."

"We should go back inside," I say, peering over my shoulder.

"Official ending of the SCC meeting." Fatema stubs out her cigarette and tosses it over the side of the terrace.

While in the shower the next morning, a glimmer of a memory arrives, a tentative visitor.

"Behave well for us," Mom whispered, tears in her eyes, the day she and Dad left for the airport. They'd used up their long-saved-for three-week holiday. I still had a month of school vacation.

Six months earlier, they'd asked me if I wanted to stay the extra month, and of course I was excited, thinking only about mornings with Nani and nightly slumber parties with my cousins. The reality of my parents' absence only dawned on me when their four suitcases and two carry-ons queued in the front hallway.

"I will," I said solemnly, my eyes becoming wet, too. I didn't want to cry. After all, I was a big girl. I was brave, and was going to travel home all by myself.

On the trip from New York to India, they'd prepared me; our journey was one long lesson in international travel. They pointed out all the things they believed I'd need to understand for the way back: the conveyor belt on which I placed my duffle bag for inspection, the uniformed guards, the meanings of airport signage: male and female figures that depicted bathrooms, the knife and fork that meant food, the capped man who was a customs officer. They described the plastic envelope I'd wear around my neck with my identification and boarding passes. Mom had even demonstrated how to use the soap dispensers in the airplane, which were different from those at school.

"Listen to your nani and nana, all your uncles and aunties," my father joined in. "They are your parents for the next month." Did his voice crack when he said that? Was it difficult for him to leave me behind?

"I know, Dad." Did I roll my eyes the way Zee does when she thinks I'm getting too emotional?

I shut off the water and wrap a towel around me, then grab a pen and my notebook, jotting down the unspooling memory.

I didn't miss my parents for the first while. Mornings — when Zainab and Fatema were at school — were boring and I awaited, with anticipation, their return at two o'clock. Later in the month was different. A curtain of misery pulled down over me. Homesickness settled in my belly, in almost daily bouts of diarrhea that Maasi blamed on the servant, who once let me drink from the regular water bottle instead of the special boiled one. I wanted to cry but waited until the lights were turned off at night. Fatema or Zainab heard me in the dark and tattled. I asked for my mother every day, and at some point, my nani admonished me to stop, that I was ruining my final week of vacation with such foolishness. Ashamed, I complied. I was a good girl.

Now I know that khatna made me a homesick girl, made me cry for my mother, made me want to go home.

While I had already begun to assimilate into an American child in the three years prior, khatna reinforced this unconscious, destabilizing process.

Khatna warned me that India was a place from which to flee.

I pause. No, that's not quite right, for khatna happens in Australia and the U.S. and every country where Bohras call home.

Khatna warns girls that no place is safe.

I continue writing.

Finally, it was time to leave. At the door, with my suitcase, my cousins cried, but I didn't. They promised to send me letters once a week and I reciprocated the promise. But my heart was no longer in it.

I rub the cool skin over my heart.

When I boarded the plane, the Indian flight attendant in charge of me cooed about how cute and pretty I was. She reminded me of perfumed and lipsticked Fareeda Kaaki. She brought me a plastic bag with the airline's pin, crayons, a colouring book and teddy bear, the same things I'd been gifted on the London to Bombay leg. I considered asking about the promised extra toys and chocolate, but felt shy to press the call button, even though Pretty Kaaki-Stewardess said I could. Trays of food arrived and were cleared away.

At Heathrow, a young white woman took me by the elbow, all business, and deposited me in a room with a dozen other children. Every so often an adult would enter the room to deposit a child or two. Then another adult would enter to make a withdrawal. I knew the removed children were catching flights, but still, it was discomfiting when they left.

It was a sterile lounge, fashioned into a daycare by adults legally responsible for children. There were busted toys on the floor, one of them the same lock-block garage I had at

home, except missing all the little cars. There
were metal benches, white walls. I recall a faint
sour odour; perhaps someone had puked days
earlier and they hadn't been able to get it out of
the industrial carpet.

I reflexively cover my nose to block the illusory smell of
vomit.

Some of the kids played with the sad toys. One
girl, about my age, cried in the corner, and a
uniformed lady attempted a shushing. When
the lady returned to her position behind her
desk, I went over. Her name was May. I remember because I asked, "Like the month?" and
she nodded. Or maybe it was April, or June, I
don't know. She was en route to Vancouver and
pointed to the large wall clock and told me she
had only a couple of hours before her flight. I
realized then that no one had told me how long
I had to wait. I wasn't sure if I should ask the
woman behind the desk; she resembled Mrs.
Cook, my first-grade teacher who, every day, at
two o'clock, lined up half the classroom for over
an over-the-knee spank.

After some time, two uniformed women
served us fried chicken fingers. May offered me
hers and I ate her share. A tall man came for her
after that, and we shook greasy hands, knowing
we'd never meet again.

A cheerful older lady with brown curly
hair later arrived for me, and we left the room,

stepping into a windowed corridor. It was sunny outside and I wondered if it would be sunny in New Jersey. The airline lady asked me all kinds of questions about where I'd been as she guided me through Heathrow, her warm hand on the back of my neck, to my gate.

On the London to JFK leg, the seat beside me was empty.

I put down my pen and leave the notebook open in case more arrives.

Zee strides into my bedroom while I dress, her expression pouty.

"What's wrong?" I close the clasp on my bra, then stroke a line of deodorant across my pits.

"Nani won't let me make her toast." She sniffs and tears fall. She pushes her face into my lap and her little body shakes as she sobs.

"Oh, honey." I pull her up to sit on my lap. "Maybe she doesn't want breakfast right now?"

"No …" She huffs as she inhales, "She said … she said … the toaster was too dangerous for me, that I could get tercuted."

"Tercuted?" I wipe her wet face.

"Electrocuted, I said." Mom peeks into the bedroom. "She was poking the toast with a butter knife."

"I was trying to get it out," Zee whines, her tears subsiding. She leans into me, her body heavy.

"Was it stuck? They didn't pop out on their own?"

"I was checking them."

"Beta, you can't do that when the power is on. You could get an electric shock!" Mom explains, sitting next to Zee on the bed.

"Your nani is right, Zee. She was just watching out for you." Mom smiles gratefully. I meet her gaze.

"What's an electric shock?" Zee asks, her curiosity overpowering her upset. She slides off my lap and I pull on a sundress.

"Aha! This morning's lesson! We can fit that into science, maybe. Probably."

They return to the kitchen to eat their breakfast, while I rub moisturizer on my face.

I close the notebook, thinking about children and adults, and their conflicting needs.

∼ FIFTY-THREE ∽

With Mom here, our routines shift to shopping and visiting relatives we've thus far neglected. We return to the flat each evening tired, which is fine with me — less time to think, to wade through the murky feelings and memories that invade my stiller moments.

Instead they creep into my sleep.

This morning, at five o'clock, my brain registers the sound of car honks. I press my eyes closed and I am at a busy clinic, about to have some sort of medical procedure. Two women in light green gowns and masks beckon me from the crowded waiting area into a large, white examination room. It has a table pushed to one side. I can see shimmers of our reflections in the immaculately clean floor tiles.

One of the women picks up a folded plastic tablecloth and shakes it open. It has the faux-embroidered pattern of my mother's round safra from back home. She spreads it on the floor, and the other masked clinician helps her to smooth its edges. They stand beside the table and gesture for me to come over.

I skirt the edges of the safra — a safra is used for communal floor eating, and not meant to be walked over — but the women shake their heads, and point down at it. My clammy feet stick on the new-smelling plastic. When I step into its middle, one whispers, using her voice for the first time, that I should lie down. I'm nervous, yet oddly acquiescent. I arrange myself so that I am properly centred, arms and legs crossed to not take up too much room.

The other woman's bushy eyebrows turn into angry exclamation marks. She directs me to remove my pants. They are yoga-spandex-tight, and I struggle with them from my prone position. I think, *Shouldn't I have done this while standing?* I writhe like a fish on land, pulling the fabric down, inch by inch, until finally they are off. The other woman shakes her head impatiently, indicating that I should have removed my underwear, too. With dream logic I think, *Of course, how dumb am I?* With almost the same difficulty as the pants, I pull them off.

The two clinicians have now moved to the corner, engaged in their preparations. I wish they'd cover the lower half of my body with a sheet, but I know better than to disturb them. They look identical, camouflaged in their scrubs, except one has bigger hips and breasts.

I am glad to at least be wearing a T-shirt. I look down at my chest, read the slogan emblazoned across my breasts: RAMONA THE PEST! I smile, because I've always wondered where that T-shirt ended up. I thought I'd lost it. Then I think, *Zee would like a matching one.* I'll have to find her its twin.

The slimmer one bears down on me, holding a large pair of shiny silver scissors. She jabs me with them lightning-quick.

"See? It's nothing." The larger one's tone is sweet, and for the first time in my dream, I have an urge to flee.

I awake again, my pulse so strong it could shake the bed. I reach down, feel for my underwear. It's there, and it's dry. I chide myself: my imagination is in overdrive. But something about the nightmare feels real. My vulva stings from the clinician's jab, or it thinks it does. My clitoris is awake and aching. I rest my hand there.

Murtuza snores softly next to me. Each time I close my eyes, try to sleep again, I see the glint of the scissors. Each time I say to myself, *No, no, it's just overthinking, this is not a memory*, the throbbing intensifies. I breathe deeply, visualizing my breath going as low as my vulva, as the sexual self-help article suggested. It helps. I reassure myself, *I must be dreaming about things I've read online*, and the sting returns, the clinician's jab is like new, as though my vulva is angry with my denial.

In the half-haze of sleep, I attempt something different.

I inhale, all the way down. I think, *This is real, this happened, it hurt. I remember.* Something unclenches, so I continue, *This is real, this happened, it hurt, I remember.* I do this five more times. Once again, the pain releases its grip, little by little, with each iteration.

Next I try another set of words: *I am remembering. This happened to me.* My heart slows. I repeat the words, whispering them, the words outside of me now. Again and again I say them, susurations becoming sighs, then murmurs.

Murtuza opens his eyes, turns to me, reaches over, asks, "Are you okay, did you have a bad dream?"

I manage to say, "I just remembered something in my dream."

"Tell me what you saw," he says, reaching for me.

I recount the women, the masks, the scissors. The T-shirt. "I used to have that T-shirt. I think I wore it that day." Then I continue the mantra: *It's real, I remember, it happened.*

He rocks me, answering each of my calls with his response: *Yes, I'm so sorry.*

We do this until a dappling of light spreads itself under the drapes, and I fall asleep.

The next morning, I enter a scene of domesticity: grandmother/ mother/mother-in-law is at the stove, making chai the old-fashioned way, loose leaves, milk, and spices in a pot. Granddaughter/ daughter stands on a stool beside her, apprenticing. Son-in-law/ father/husband washes dishes at the sink. Daughter/mother/ wife has been absent, and the clock says 10:20 a.m.

"Did you sleep well?" Murtuza asks, drying his hands. He switches on the coffee maker and it awakes with a hiss and drizzle.

"I think so." Our glances linger a moment. Mine is self-conscious, grateful. His is cautious, gentle.

"Nani said we should go to Elephanta Caves for my geography lesson!" Zee rushes at us.

"I can go with her if you need to rest today," Mom says. I wonder what Murtuza has said to her. Or perhaps she is reading the upset in my puffy eyes.

"No, Mom has to come."

"I'd love to go. It'll be good to get out. I haven't been there in years."

"Me, too." Murtuza says, latching on to my fake enthusiasm, an unspoken mutual project. "We went when I was around your age, Zee. There are monkeys there that steal your food. One grabbed a cola can out of my hand when I wasn't looking."

"Monkeys drink soda?" Her eyes light up.

I tune out the story, one I've heard many times, and Mom interrupts the coffee maker's drip to pour me a half cup. I scan the kitchen again. We do look like a normal family on a vacation in India. We do.

"Murtuza told me you had a rough night." Her inquiring look tells me she doesn't know the details. I tell her I'm fine, add milk to my cup, take a sip. She looks away but can't hide her hurt. I've been keeping her at arm's length for the past few days. She mirrors my posture, one hand on her hip.

"Actually ... I had a nightmare. I'm starting to remember things about back then," I say, keeping my voice low.

"About the khatna?" she whispers.

"Yeah. It's like my mind has been delivering little bits of information. Some of it feels quite literal, and the rest, well, sort of comes in code."

"Are you all right?" Her face tightens. I expect that some part of her wants to tell me not to take it all so seriously, that it was a long time ago. She asks, "Do you want to tell me about any of it?"

I shrug and she takes my arm and leads us into the living room and we sit on adjacent couches.

"It's tiring. But also ... helpful, kind of. It sort of makes things make more sense. It's like my brain is working on a puzzle, and now I have more of the pieces," I grapple with words, none of them a very good fit. "They're painful pieces, though. I think I just need to sit with it all, let it settle, before I can talk about it."

She nods. "Well, that is how you sort things out."

"Oh yeah?" I say, just to keep her talking, so that I don't have to.

"Since you were a child. You share only after you've figured it all out. Remember when you were trying to decide which college to go to? You came to us with your pro and con list already completed! Then you gave us a lecture about why you thought NYU was the best option. You just needed our validation, not help with the actual decision-making process. You handled that all internally." She smiles, lost in thought. I don't remember doing all that.

"Murtuza complains about it all the time. That I spring decisions on him."

"Probably because he doesn't feel part of the process." She taps my knee, emphasizing the point. "And you know, you have to do things your way. But ... I wish I could be a part of it, too. I wasn't there back when ... when you needed me, and I wish there was something I could do to help now."

I look up and see that Murtuza and Zee are no longer in the kitchen. I hear their faint chatter in her bedroom. I exhale, sip my coffee. I have a good daughter, a good husband, and, sitting before me, a good mother. She looks at me expectantly.

"It's kind of like when I became a teacher. Suddenly, I had this new identity. I could tell people, 'I am a teacher' and it felt half true and half not. For a while, it was like I was wearing someone else's uniform." I focus my gaze out the window, searching for the right words. She nods, waits.

"Khatna feels sort of like that to me, half true and half not. It's like it happened to someone else and to me at the same time. It's surreal. The memories, or the dreams or the images or whatever they are, feel true, and they also feel like fiction." A brown seagull sits on the balcony's ledge. It stops and stares at me before it lifts its wings and takes flight.

"You know, I felt like that after your father died. It was a shock. When people referred to me as a widow, I didn't know what they meant." Her eyes well up. "I wasn't ready for the new role then. I'm still not."

The gull is back, as though returning to fetch something forgotten. Then it alights again.

I reach over and take her hand, her tears allowing me to draw near to her. I focus on her pain, easier to touch than my own. She places her other hand on top of mine. I wonder if I should put down my cup, free my hand, add to the pile.

"This is life," she says, shaking her head and then sitting up tall, "we are always having to accept new realities, often before we're ready. Only ... it's harder when you are a child."

"And then we're sometimes forced to act, to figure out what to do, before we're ready." I gently pull my hand away.

"What do you mean?"

"I wish I hadn't gone along with Fatema's and Zainab's request to trick Maasi into giving us the khatna doctor's information. The timing wasn't right for me. I'm still uneasy about it. I wish I'd said no. But it's already done." The words, just-formed thoughts, drift through the air between us, like a few errant snowflakes, the beginning of a blizzard, if I allow them.

"I've been thinking, too. I'm wondering how to deal with this. And I know," she says, holding up her hand in response to my look of impatience, "that you and the girls don't want me to talk to Tasnim. That's fine. But I need to find some way to address this, eventually. Maybe after we go home. Maybe on my next visit here. I'm not sure. But I need to tell her what's on *my* mind."

"Maybe we can do it together, in a while." More snowflakes fall and I wonder, *Are these new ideas or delayed ones? Have I always wanted this?* I imagine her and I, side by side, confronting Maasi. I'm not sure it feels quite right, but the notion makes Mom smile, so I let it be. She squeezes my hand.

"What is Fatema's group going to do with that information?"

"They're planning a demonstration at the hospital. They'll publicly shame the doctor. Force the medical association to take a stand against her. Make it a big media event. They want to scare other doctors who are doing khatna."

"That's good. But —" she bites her bottom lip "— won't that mean that everyone will just go to the non-medical cutters? That's worse, isn't it?"

"Maybe. She says this is part of a larger campaign to get the Indian government on side to ban the practice." I recount Fatema's strategy. "I hope it doesn't backfire."

"Are you going to the demonstration?" Mom asks. This time I imagine all of us: Zainab, Fatema, me, and Mom standing in front of the hospital with placards, shouting. The last time I did anything like that was back in university, when the women's centre protested funding cuts. I nervously stood in the background with my handmade sign while my friends created a ruckus. Since then, I've signed petitions, but I avoid rallies. Murtuza sometimes attends them with his academic friends, but it's not my thing.

"I don't think so. Are you?"

"Is it dangerous, do you think?" She furrows her brow.

Murtuza and Zee emerge from the bedroom. She's wearing a lavender skirt with a light pink top, likely a suggestion from Murtuza, who favours complementary shades.

"What's dangerous?" Zee asks us.

"Still talking about the monkeys?" Murtuza asks, when Mom and I hesitate.

"Yes, that's right, that's what I was asking," Mom lies.

"Why don't we look it up, Zee?" I scoop her into my lap.

"Another science class?" she asks dolefully.

"Okay, okay. We'll just go see for ourselves, shall we? Experiential education only today."

∼ FIFTY-FOUR ᴄ
Bombay, 1919

Abdoolally sat in his friend Mirza's law office. Lately, he hadn't been feeling his best, had almost constant fatigue that his doctor said was expected for a man in his midsixties. It was the third time he and Mirza had met to redraft his will.

"Wouldn't it be simpler if I were a poor man?" he said to Mirza with a sigh.

"Perhaps. But you are not. And you have important decisions to make."

"I've made them. Here are my changes." He read from a hand-written page. "One third must go to charity, one third to pay for future generations' education, and the rest divided amongst my heirs."

"Abdoolally, the bulk of your estate will go to strangers?"

"Not strangers, exactly. See?" He pointed to his notes. "The main charities are the maternity hospital and the school for Dholka children. And as I said, the one third for education is for all my relations yet to come. I want them to spread out that money, so that no parent will ever have to tell their children they cannot afford education."

"This is an unconventional way to do things. It might upset your family."

"So be it." Shouldn't his children be grateful? All had had childhoods vastly different than his own. He had provided well for them, ensured their comfort, stability, and most of all, educations. But Mirza might be right. There were eight of them, from three wives, the eldest forty-one and the youngest eight years old. A few he knew better than others, geography and time the distance between them. But there was nothing to do about that now. In recent years he'd tried to make up for his early absences by spending more time with his younger children and his grandchildren. He'd done his best. Who could fault him?

"As you wish. I will have it typed up for you to sign next week," Mirza said.

～ FIFTY-FIVE ～

Fatema's name flashes on my phone's screen. I move to pick it up, but a faint buzzing in my head, a warning, stops the impulse. I press decline and she doesn't leave a message. She calls again two minutes later. I walk away from the phone.

Earlier today, one of her comrades emailed me to ask if I'd like to contribute to their blog. I could pen an anonymous piece about my thoughts on khatna, she suggested. They need more first-person narratives, more women to be vocal about the issue. I understand the sentiment, but deleted the missive without replying. I don't want to be involved. Why do I have to be involved?

My cell dings a minute later, indicating a waiting text message.

We have a problem with the email. Can you call me?

I check the time. Murtuza, Mom, and Zee ventured out ten minutes ago, their mission to buy mangos for tonight's dessert. The fruit stall is only a few blocks away and they'll be back soon, my solitude's brevity a comfort.

I open the list of recent calls, tap Fatema's name. It rings just once.

"Sorry, I was in the bathroom when you called."

"No problem. All fine on your end?" I sense she doesn't want an answer, would prefer to rush forward to her problem. I have an urge to dally.

"It's hard to believe we just have another two weeks left here. The time has passed so quickly. I've grown accustomed to life in Mumbai. It's going to be strange to return to New York." This would have been true last month, but no longer. I've begun to pack, am counting down the days.

She edges into my meandering. "Sure, right. Listen, there's something I need to tell you. I sent the email, with all the identifying information removed, to one of my contacts at *The Post*. He says his editor can't use it."

"Why not?" I ask dully. I barely care.

"He says that without the full source details — meaning the 'to' and 'from' information — he can't verify that it's real. He can't use it in a story."

"Well, then, he can just write about the doctor, right?"

"He says he can't say that a source verified her as a cutter unless he has the source's name. He says he can keep the source anonymous in the newspaper story, but he himself has to know who the source is."

"Which means?" Her repetition of the word *source* irritates me.

"I have to tell him it was an email between you and Maasi. But, listen, Shari —"

"No way."

"I trust this guy. He's an experienced journo. He just has to see your names. But he won't reveal your names. Won't print them."

"And if I don't agree?"

"Well, that's fine. He'll still cover the demonstration, but he won't be able to say he has a source that verifies the information. He said the very best-case scenario is if you make the appointment, and audio-record the interaction with her."

"That's crazy! No! I won't do that."

"I know, Shari, don't worry. We will try to find someone else who will do that with her or another cutter. I know that the email itself was a lot to ask." Her tone is sincere, but why do I feel like she is working up to sell me something?

"Yes, yes, it was. It's all I can do."

"So, let's not waste your efforts. Let him see the original email, with his assurance that he won't reveal your names." There it is. She presented me with the much scarier option to make this one seem simple. I discern the manipulation, so why do I feel swayed?

"And you're sure you can trust this guy?" I rub my temples.

"Yeah, he's interviewed members of our group and has always used pseudonyms when asked. He's decent."

I listen to her breathing for a moment, prolong her waiting.

"All right, Fatema. I hope you're right."

We hang up and the flat feels like April in New York, cool, damp, dull. I turn off the air conditioning and open the sliding glass doors, allowing a hot wind to blow in. I stare down five storeys at the road below, people and cars in miniature, scurrying busyness. The outdoor thermometer reads thirty-six degrees centigrade, and gradually, my chilled skin begins to roast in the blistering sunshine. I picture Fatema's journalist friend. Why didn't I ask his name? After all, he'll have mine. One more person will know that I've been subjected to this practice. And one more person will guess that Maasi is implicated, and will judge her. He will know our names without ever having met us, without knowing who we are as people.

Without knowing that there is love between me and her, between niece and aunt, victim and —

What's the correct word?

I can change my mind. I can say no.

I rush back inside, pulling the glass door roughly, and it bounces as it closes. I pull the latch. Just as I'm about to phone Fatema, Zee bursts into the flat, wearing green, red, and purple, a multi-hued flag waving in my direction. She holds a mango up to my nose, demanding I smell it: ripe, sweet, alive. Mom and Murtuza saunter in behind. I leave behind my phone, and we cut open the fruit, and its orange flesh forms a slippery pile on a plate we place in the fridge for later. On the balcony, we each suck on a goatla, the hairy stone, cleaning them with our teeth and tongues, mango juice dripping off our hands and chins.

───────◆───────

Murtuza is completing his teaching and marking duties and Zee is technically ahead of her schoolmates' lesson plan, although we'll have to see how she fares when she returns to the classroom. While I didn't cheat on the reading, writing, and arithmetic, all other subjects involved impromptu trips, talks with family members, and tangential online searches. More than once, I've needed to remind myself that it's only second grade, and we've probably done all right.

And me? I've almost finished editing the Abdoolally blog. I uploaded all the documents I copied from the trust, as well as everything that Meena found. I wrote a factual description of his life, including what I know about his wives and a few of his children. I documented my interviews with Mumbai family and the trips to Dholka and Ahmedabad. It's all very neutral. The "great man" story remains.

But there is still one piece I haven't written: my own impressions and questions about who he really was. I'm mulling that over. I still need to meet with Banu Aunty, and see if she has anything to add. I'm hoping for a little more description about Shaheeda, and perhaps Rumana, too.

As the work recedes, we've been shifting from being almost-Indians to foreigners on vacation. It's like changing our wardrobe; all this time we've been donning false but familiar garments, ones that smell and look Indian, and it's time to fold and store them away, and wear our usual outfits in preparation for the journey home. I find myself opening my eyes wide like I did the first week here: I notice the jostle of a city bus, study the slumped postures of office women on their way home from work. I'm curious about their husbands and children. When I am caught looking, I know my gaze is too open, that I give myself away as a foreigner.

"We still have two bottles of red left," Murtuza says, passing me a glass. Both Zee and Mom have gone to bed early after a hot afternoon tromping around the Kanheri Caves.

"Can't take them home, right?" I clink my glass to his.

"Just over a week left. I'm surprised to say I'm a little sad to leave. I thought I'd be tired of India by now, in a rush to go back. I know you're ready to go."

"The suitcases are mostly packed," I say.

"I get it. This trip has mostly been professional for me, with personal on the side. For you it's all been personal, even the historical research. It's a lot to deal with." He stretches his arm across the back of the couch to pull me close.

"Not what I imagined. But it's all good, right? Growth?" I raise my glass in false cheer.

"To growth." Glass strikes glass. We sip in silence. He nuzzles the side of my head, and I relax into his touch. Then I realize it's Saturday night. I wait for it.

"I was thinking. Would you like to try out the stuff in that article I sent you?"

"What article?" Of course I know what he's talking about, but I'm buying myself time, otherwise my answer would be a flat-out "no." Honestly, until he just reminded me, I'd half-forgotten about it.

"The one you read just before your mom arrived? That sex one? Where we pause as we go? You pay attention to when you are uncomfortable?" He continues listing descriptors until I admit that I recognize the article in question.

"Oh, Murti, that sounds like a lot of work." I pull away from him, realize the movement is too abrupt, adjust so I'm not so far away.

"It doesn't have to be. It could be fun. Play." He waves his fingers like a magician's, the same gesture he uses when trying to convince Zee to eat a new vegetable.

"All right." I sigh. The article did make sense to me, I just hadn't planned to talk about it, or act on it, so soon.

"Don't look so glum about getting naked with me." His face falls for a millisecond, but then he dons a goofy smile.

"No, no. It's not about you. It's … about me. Dealing with all this."

"I know, I know. But remember you get to stop it at any point, right? It might be five minutes if that's all you can handle. Just five minutes." Once again, his expression is bright, but I bristle. I don't like the insinuation that I might not be able to *handle* this.

"We'll try it for ten minutes." I rise from the couch, remove my clothes in the bedroom, and briskly shower. I'm about to choose my black cotton nightie but remember the lacy teddy Murtuza surprised me with on his birthday. It dawns on me that it's been weeks since we had sex, right after I found out about the khatna. How many Saturdays have passed? Four? No, five. I slip on the lingerie and feel its silky slide down the length of my back. If we're going to do this work, I think, we might as well do it right.

He looks at me tentatively, and says, "Ready?" I hunch my shoulders when he places his hands on them and says, "Just relax, it'll be okay." I feel the press of his palm and the resistance in my muscles. A soft fog drifts across my brain.

"It's happening already." My voice is a silverfish, ready to disappear with a metallic flash.

"Oh. We should pause, then."

I say nothing.

"The article said to pause, breathe, acknowledge what's happening, and wait until your body says go again."

I pause. I breathe. "But why did it happen so fast?" I whine. I am too fully aware of how damaged I am. It was better before, better not to know.

"Breathe." He inhales and I mimic him. After a few breaths, I nod to him.

"I think I know what happened, maybe. You asked me if I was ready. You always say that. I hate that. *Ready?* Like we're going for a bloody hike or something." There is a vehemence in my voice I don't expect. I want to punish my husband for this single, innocuous word.

"Okay. So that word bothered you."

"It made me tense. And then you tried to massage my shoulders and that made it worse."

"Wow," he says, pulling away, looking thoughtful. "Do I always do that? Maybe I notice you being nervous and then don't know why, and then I think I can help relax you. But that's perhaps been the incorrect thing." He is steady, intellectual, which only makes things worse.

"What does your fucking article say we should do now?" I spit. He darts me a scared look. We are both already in over our heads and we haven't even started.

"Let's breathe again, okay? Just pause and process this?" He takes my hand, and after cursing at him ("All this fucking breathing!") I allow myself to feel his warm fingers. After a minute of inhalations and exhalations, I am less pissed off.

Another realization: he didn't ask me if I was ready when he blindfolded me. When he was rough and in charge, it wasn't like this, not until the end, when he resumed gentleness.

Which just feels fucked up.

I tell him this, and he nods excitedly, ideas popping with each head bob.

"Yes, that must be it! Something about the gentle approach feels scary to you." He looks at me like we are scientists who have just stumbled upon a major discovery. I go with it. My anger has petered out, and his statement is an opening through which I can place one foot.

"Untrustworthy. Something about the gentle approach feels like I can't trust you. Isn't that insane? I'm insane."

"What feels untrustworthy?"

I breathe for another minute, at his prodding, and then it comes to me.

"It's sort of like I have to watch out, to be on alert, and wait for things to go badly." The lock box on the towering shelf unlatches, snaps open, and spills words. And then shuts again. I stare up at the ceiling, waiting for more to fall.

"Huh. Gentle means 'be vigilant.'" He looks stumped now. I know he's itching to do an article search on this, is listing keywords in his mind. But I don't want to talk anymore. I'll need to juggle these new ideas on my own, toss them high, catch them, drop them. By myself.

My body says "go" and I get out of bed, double-check that the door is locked. I grab the pleather case, and throw it to him. He lifts his right arm, catches it, his reflexes catlike.

Just as the time before, I am titillated and amused by Murtuza's play at dominance. Turned on. One who is quick to assimilate new information, he incorporates the sex-therapy article's ideas, ordering me to check in with him, to pause, to practise our safe word. I comply, calling it a few times when I don't need to, or at least when I don't think it's needed, just because he's told me to.

But then I do it on my own, without his prodding. Yellow and red let me pause, catch up to myself. We wait.

We wait until I say green. We wait until I am here, and nowhere else. The frickin' therapy article was right. Could it be right?

I listen for his breathing and know he is watching me carefully. How does he feel about me being in charge? I randomly call "green" and within a minute, "red," just to see what will happen.

"Good girl," he says each time. Then he uncuffs my hands, but leaves the blindfold on. I say "green."

When he enters me, he growls in my ear, "Use your safe word."

"Red." I feel him slip out, realize this sensation is new. We have never parked in the middle of this road before. I feel my vulva tingle, wanting. I say, "Green." In total, we repeat this process five more times. I know, because I'm counting. Twice it occurs to me that I've spaced out a little bit, my mind travelling to sounds outside our flat, or to random thoughts about laundry, the contents of my suitcase. I only realize it when Murtuza barks, "Safe word." These times I've gone away without knowing, the safe word not even an option. I wonder, *Why did I leave? Is it normal to leave? Doesn't everyone get distracted?*

After the fifth pause, my body shifts into a more relaxed place. It reminds me of that time when, years ago, in university, I took a toke of a passing joint at a party, my mind lifting, my body going light yet remaining solid. Remaining there.

I tilt my pelvis, meet his. Our bodies rock together in a synchronized rhythm. All I can feel is that single part of me, as though a hot spotlight has focused there, leaving the rest in darkness. I push against him harder.

"Tell me what you want," he says in his stern Mr. Tyebji voice.

"More," I gasp, the word surprising me. He pulls out. I want to kill him. But then, then his fingers — how many? — are inside me, pressing, groping. He's never done this before. I've never allowed him.

"Do you need your safe word?"

"Green, green, green!" I yell.

And then, and then, it happens. My body releases, gushes, jolts into alertness. I career down a toboggan hill, faster, faster, faster, losing control, about to crash, and then my sleigh transforms into a tube and I am inside a waterslide, warm, and land with a splash. I open my eyes, and I am still underwater. It's not what I expected. Not how it's described in books. It's anticlimactic, even if it's a climax. It's not magical, but more like years of tension disappeared, like my body has just said, *Stop it, stop worrying about this thing you've been worrying about, stop it now.*

Well, perhaps that is climactic.

Limp, I pull the blindfold off, and clutch him to me.

Twenty minutes later, we are under our blanket, flat on our backs. Murtuza wants to debrief, but I say, "Red. We'll theorize tomorrow, Murti."

"But that was … very special. I'm so curious about why that worked, and … so fast. The article said that the pausing technique could take quite some time. That we would need many months of healing."

"Red. Red. Red. Screw the healing," I pause so he'll hear my unintended pun. "Yes, it was special, but can we just let it be for now? I don't want to overthink." I do suspect that this will take many months, that this was odd beginner's luck, that it won't happen again so easily. But I don't want to ruin the moment.

"Okay, okay." He nods, then turns on his side to face me.

"So, your first time?"

"Yes."

"Ever? Like not even with …" We lay there for a moment, tension skipping through his silence.

"With …?" After a second, I grasp that he's asking about Ian. "Oh. No. Never. Not with anyone. Just you. Only you."

"Okay …" He smiles, closes his eyes, his long-awaited question answered. One I didn't know he'd been waiting to ask. How could he have imagined it happening with Ian? I study his placid face, glad his mind has settled.

I listen to his breathing grow more rhythmic. In the quiet, my mind clicks though multiple thoughts at once. I turn to him.

"Hey, are you asleep?" He rouses, shakes his head no, his stubbly chin scraping my shoulder. "I was thinking. Do you want to go to the demonstration the day after tomorrow?"

"Yeah, I do." He shifts away to look at me. "But I thought you didn't?"

"Well, I'm not going to wave any placards or anything. But I want to go, at least to see what it's like. I'll just be a bystander."

"Should we take Zee or ask your mom or Zainab to mind her?"

"They'll want to go, too. We'll take her along. Hey! Maybe it'll fit into a health lesson."

"Haha."

"I just think maybe I'll want to be there. Fatema told me it's the first time anyone has held a protest like this. At a cutter's office," I say, my throat going dry.

"Yeah, I'm game." He sounds groggy. I shift onto my right side so that he can curl around me. He drops off first, but it's not long before I follow him.

⌇ FIFTY-SIX ⌇

When I look up directions for Banu Aunty's Santacruz flat the next morning, I realize it's only a twenty-minute walk from Fortune Enclave. So close, and yet none of my relatives knew to direct me to her. From the outside, it's a once grand and now flagging mansion with spacious balconies. The staircase up to the third floor has Spanish tiles in blue and green hues, matching the transoms' Victorian stained glass. She greets me at her door, wearing a floral-patterned shalvaar kameez and pink plastic flip-flops. Her hair is completely white and when she smiles, her eyes sparkle a shade of topaz. I stare, perhaps a little too long, at her striking face. No one has described Shaheeda's appearance, but now I imagine I am seeing her beauty passed down four generations. I haven't seen these eyes in anyone else in our family.

Banu leads me into a grand, antique-furniture-filled formal drawing room. She mentions that her brothers' families take up the first and second floors and that she raised her three children here, one of whom lives in Delhi, and the other two in Canada.

"The place is much too big for me now, but I don't feel lonely with all the nieces and nephews and their kids coming and going all the time."

A servant brings tea, and then she looks at me expectantly.

"My research is mostly about Abdoolally, but few people know much about his wives, and I've heard very little about Shaheeda, your great-grandmother." I tell her what I know of Rumana's migration to Dholka after Abdoolally and Zehra's divorce.

"Well, as you know, my daadi — Rumana — her mother died when she was young, so she didn't get to know her. She was close to her second mother, Zehrabai. She didn't keep close ties with her father's side of the family so I don't have much personal information about Abdoolally." She taps her forehead as though to trigger her memory. I ready my pen, waiting to hear about his wives.

"What can you tell me about Zehra?" I prod.

"I met her many times, on special occasions at my daadi's house. She died in the sixties, I think, when I was in my early twenties. My daadi doted on Zehrabai the way a daughter would. I recall she was a strong woman. She always asked me how I was doing in school, encouraged me to study." She goes on to tell me that she is a retired accountant.

"I'm curious about why Abdoolally and she divorced."

"Oh, I know that story. My daadi told me everything about that. For one thing, they had a very big age gap, and he was always working. This would not have been an issue for most women, but Zehrabai, educated and modern by that era's standards, was not happy to be left alone all the time, so there was a great deal of tension between them."

"Interesting."

"And there was more, the straw that broke the camel's back, as they say." She gazes at me, as though reading my face. Then she appraises my polka-dotted sundress in a way that makes me squirm.

"More?" I cross my right leg over my left.

"Are you aware of the current controversy about khatna?"

"Of course." I hold my breath.

"What do you think of it?" The amber in her eyes grows duller, darker. Do I tell her the truth or aim for something neutral? What if our opinions differ and she doesn't want to tell me more about Zehra and Rumana?

"Honestly? I think it's a terrible, outdated practice," I say, exhaling.

"I agree," she says. "As did Zehrabai."

"Go on. Please."

"Apparently Zehrabai had a very bad experience herself, and so when it was time to take my daadi for it, she bribed the khatna lady to not make the cut, but to falsely confirm that it was done. The lady agreed, took the bribe, but then went to the Syedna's wife and told her the whole story, perhaps hoping to gain something — business or status, I don't know. The Syedna's wife spread the word about it — the community was still very small then — and eventually it got back to Abdoolally, who by then was very embarrassed by his wife stepping out of line."

"Oh my gosh." I've stopped taking notes now, struggling to absorb her story.

"My daadi said it was not good for him or his business to be seen to be lax with his wife on this. Like today, but maybe even more so, people were very much in one another's business, personal and work. So he divorced her."

"They divorced because Zehra faked Rumana's khatna," I murmur, letting this information sink in.

"Yes. That and they fought constantly, too."

"And why did Rumana get sent to her grandmother in Dholka?"

"I believe this was meant to be temporary. But my daadi had asthma — pretty bad, as I recall, so this might have been a reason.

Dholka still had clean air back then. Shame that the air quality has declined. Just like everywhere else in India." She shakes her head.

"And then Zehra moved to Dholka after the divorce, so they stayed in touch. Do you know how that happened? Why she remarried someone in Dholka?"

"I don't know. Oh! But I can tell you that she and her husband Dawood were good together. He died when I was a teenager, but they seemed very happy as an old couple."

"So … did Rumana end up having the khatna done?"

"Oh, yes, she was taken back to that same lady who had taken Zehrabai's bribe and it was done." She claps her hands twice, as though shaking away crumbs.

"That's too bad." My stomach drops. Zehra lost her battle. I ask Banu to pause so that I can record her words.

"But the story doesn't end there." She waits for me to stop scribbling and then continues, her voice mischievous. "When my daadi — Rumana — heard the full story of what happened, she was just married. My daada — her husband — was a very good man, very sensitive, very respectful of women. He made sure that my father and my aunts were well educated."

"And?" I say, sensing a digression.

"So they knew the local cutter in Ahmedabad, where they lived at the time. Ummul was a friend of my daada's family, probably a distant relative, too. One day, she got very ill, and needed surgery for something, but she was a poor woman and a widow. My daadi and daada paid her hospital bills and even took her into their home for her convalescence. She was so grateful to them, and especially to my daadi, who cared for her, that she asked how she could repay the kindness. My daadi told her that she wanted her to stop doing khatna."

"Rumana asked her to stop doing khatna?" I capture the words in my notebook.

"Yes. Now this lady Ummul said she couldn't do that, because how was she going to make a living? Doing khatna supplemented her family's income. So daadi had a better idea. She asked her to be the person people could go to if they wanted to have a false khatna, the kind Zehra had tried for her. She asked Ummul to promise to do pretend khatnas for anyone who asked for a "special khatna." My daadi secretly sent her a good number of women who wanted to have this done and paid her a supplement each time she did one."

"How many do you think wanted this?"

"Well, at least one in ten of the khatnas she did was this 'special khatna.' And she probably did fifty, sixty khatnas in total each year. And she had a nurse train her on how to sterilize her implements so that the real khatnas she did were at least safer."

"Wow, that's impressive."

Banu meets my gaze and cocks her head. "You really think so?"

"Yes, I'm really glad to hear of this underground resistance. Do you know if there are many cutters today doing pretend khatnas?" And then, following a hunch, I add, "My cousin, Fatema, is one of the lead organizers trying to change the laws here."

"That's your first cousin?" I nod and then explain our relationship through Abdoolally's fourth wife. I list names of all the relatives in common.

"Sorry, I don't know those people. I've heard some of their names and maybe met a couple of them, but as I said, my daadi didn't mix much with the Rangwala side."

"It's a large family," I admit.

"Okay, then, before I go on, you must promise to keep this to yourself. You can't even share it with that cousin of yours."

"Wait, can I share what you've told me so far?"

"You can write about Zehra and how she tried to stop khatna for Rumana. And you can say that Rumana didn't allow it for the girls in her family. That's all. You must not say anything about Ummul, or else you could cause trouble."

"I promise," I whisper, placing a hand over my heart.

"Well, Ummul made her daughter her apprentice. Her name was Bilkis. Now Bilkis continued her mother's 'special khatna' practice, out of respect and loyalty for my daadi. And her daughter, Saleha, has done the same thing. I pay her salary. She lives in Bandra, close to here."

"How does no one find out? Don't the kids end up talking about how their khatna didn't have pain or bleeding?"

"She tells everyone that she uses a numbing ointment that stops the pain and bleeding." She laughs. "Petroleum jelly."

"Petroleum jelly? No one sees though the deception?"

"No. Saleha smears the genitals with a tissue coated in the jelly. Then she mimes the act with a scalpel, a sleight of hand, and tells the girls to close their eyes. She pinches them near the area. So if the girls are asked, they will say something happened to them. But there is almost no pain, no bleeding, no khatna!" Her face splits open into a devilish grin. I laugh again.

"Now, if people ask her to do a real khatna, then Saleha has to make a light nick." I cringe at this description, knowing there is no such thing. Banu continues, "But not on the clitoral hood, where it's supposed to be, but above, on the labia, in order to avoid any damage to the clitoris. There's very little bleeding."

"Really?"

"This is part of the problem, you know. The true cutters say they are cutting the hood, that it's harmless, but all the tissue there is just too delicate and small on a seven-year-old. Imagine how small! They end up doing damage, even if they intend not to. Same thing with the doctors."

My clitoris burns with her graphic description. At the same time, a part of me is embarrassed to be having a conversation about genital anatomy with this older aunty. But mostly I'm in awe of Ummul's and Bilkis's and Saleha's subterfuge.

"I can't believe no one has caught on." I shake my head.

"Saleha is very busy through word-of-mouth referrals. She is getting older, so I've got to talk to her about getting an apprentice. She doesn't have any daughters to pass all this down to."

"This is brilliant. Did you know there is a protest happening tomorrow, a protest against a doctor who does cutting? Would you like to join us?"

"Oh no. That's not for me. I have to make my contribution in my own way." She winks at me.

"Fair enough."

"And remember, you can't tell anyone, and I mean anyone, what I've said." I make my promise a second time. In the taxi home, I write in my notebook: *I found Zehra. I found Rumana.*

∿ FIFTY-SEVEN C∿

Bombay, 1920

I, ABDOOLALLY AHMEDALLY KUTBUDDIN RANGWALA, Bombay, Dawoodi Bohra Shia Mahomedan Inhabitant DECLARE this to be a FOURTH CODICOL to my last WILL which WILL bears the date the 30th day of April 1920.

2. WHEREAS by Clause 6 of my said WILL, I HAVE DIRECTED that my Executor Mr. Mirza Mohamed Khan shall have the power to sell my property situated at Ghogha Street, and shall invest the net sale proceeds to establish and maintain a maternity hospital in my native village of DHOLKA and after his death such person or persons as may be the Trustee or Trustees of my said WILL shall have the power to maintain the hospital buildings and services as they see fit, as are authorized by Section 20 of the INDIAN TRUSTS ACT, 1882.

IN WITNESS WHERE, I have hereunto set my hand this 24th day of October 1920.

SIGNED by the above named

ABDOOLALLY AHMEDALLY KUTBUDDIN RANGWALA

as a FOURTH CODICIL to his last WILL dated the 30th day of April 1920 in the joint presence of myself and us who at his request and in such joint presence

KUTBUDDIN DHOLKAWALLA

have hereunto subscribed our names as witness....

Sd. JEHANGIR ALAMJI KHAN, Solicitor, Bombay.

Sd. ALI MOHAMED NASHIRWANJI

∽つ FIFTY-EIGHT Cᔆ

We arrive at our designated meeting spot, a Charni Road coffee shop three minutes away from the Shifa Hospital. Fatema introduces us to four of her friends, but the names gallop by before I can catch a single one. One of Fatema's comrades, a young woman who appears to be in her twenties, explains that we will be gathering at the steps of the hospital with our placards.

"Try to make lots of noise. The press will be there." She surveys our sparse group. "After that, Aleesha will begin speaking." She gestures with her thumb to one of the women we first met, the only one amongst us wearing jeans and a T-shirt. Fatema had instructed us to "look Bohra," which is funny because Bohras wear all styles of attire, but we comply and Mom and I don our ridas for the occasion, and Murtuza wears a kurta and topi. Zee, wanting to be included in our dressup, wears a shalvaar kameez. Before leaving the house, we modelled our outfits for one another, Murtuza joking that this is the best use of his religious garb, clothing that hasn't left the closet since our arrival in Mumbai. Me, I like the feeling of protection the rida offers; only my face can be seen, and I plan to wear sunglasses when the media's cameras roll.

"Before and after the speakers, we will picket outside, as long as we can stay, and hand out leaflets," the younger woman continues, holding up a piece of paper folded in half. The cover reads, STOP KHATNA!

"We are not going inside?" Murtuza asks.

"No. They have security. And once they see us, they will barricade the door."

"What is a picket?" Zee asks.

"It's a kind of show. We're trying to educate people," Murtuza says, and Zee nods.

A few minutes later, a dozen more women and three men gather, and once again there are quick-quick introductions. The young woman repeats her instructions. More questions are asked and then a brief hush falls over the newest arrivals. How many of them have attended a protest before? What brought that aunty here? That uncle? That orthodox-looking young couple? I assume most of us are Bohra from the familiar names. And that all the women have been cut.

Zainab arrives with Nafeesa. "Wah! Look at you, Murtuza! So handsome!"

"Thank you." He feigns bashfulness and tips his topi in her direction.

"And you!" She points at me. "When did you buy this rida? In 1999?" Her rida is of the newest style with fine beadwork around the collar. Mine is a simple white poly-blend with a faint rippling of pink through it.

"That's a pretty close guess." Mom smirks. "I must have bought this for you a decade or more ago. Yet it still looks new, barely worn."

"Yeah, yeah. Maybe you can give me one of your stylish hand-me-downs," I say to Zainab.

"Gladly!" Zainab says, and asks Nafeesa to take a photo of Mom, me, and her.

I pull Nafeesa aside and remind her that Zee is her responsibility today, and that she must take Zee for a walk the moment I give her my signal.

"Don't let her out of your sight, understand?" I use my most aunty-ish voice. "No going off to see boyfriends and leaving her!"

"Yes, Maasi. I'm so sorry for last time." She blushes red and I regret being so heavy-handed. She goes to collect Zee, who is distracted by Nafeesa's latest manicure — red and blue alternating nails. All Zee knows is that we are here to protest a bad doctor, and that's all I want her to know.

Fatema touches my elbow. The group has begun to trickle out of the coffee shop.

"So glad you all came. It means a lot."

"To me, too," I say. "So, is all okay with your journalist friend?"

"Yes, he assured me. He'll say that he has a verified source. That's all. Adnand should be here soon."

"Good." Sweat prickles where my rida's hood meets my neck. I undo the drawstring and reach my hand back to wipe the damp away.

On the footpath, our group, now about twenty strong, merges into the flow of pedestrians before reconstituting in front of the hospital. Fatema's driver, Varun, is waiting in the car for us. When he spies us, he pops the trunk and unloads a pile of placards. Murtuza takes one that reads: FGM IS GENDER VIOLENCE! On the reverse it shouts: STOP KHATNA! STOP DR. RUBINA MASTER! Neither Zainab nor I take cardboard signs, but Mom accepts a stack of handbills to distribute to passersby. Most of the group has already begun to walk a picket circle, shouting the slogans written on the signs. Two security guards stand at the doors of the building, looking bewildered. They have lathis — police sticks — but I don't see guns. Still, I catch Nafeesa's eye, gesture for her to leave. She nods, bends down, whispers something in Zee's ear, and points in my direction. Zee scans for Murtuza and me, then she smiles and waves. I watch them walk away.

"Murti, I'm going to stand over there." I point to a spindly copper pod tree that offers shade.

"Sure, Shari. Just text if we get separated?" He hugs me and I nod into his shoulder. He joins the picket circle behind Fatema. Dozens of curious pedestrians stop to observe the show, and, after a time, it's difficult to separate them from the protestors. Mom stands a few feet away, chatting and passing out flyers. Where is Zainab?

The tree provides relief from the sun and the melee. I remember Banu's words, which I shared with Murtuza last night after swearing him to secrecy — I had to spill the amazing story to someone. Zehra's and Rumana's — and now Banu Aunty's — strategy is the opposite of this protest. I have to wonder just how many mothers and grandmothers have been complicit in the underground movement to stop khatna.

A few moments later, Zainab joins me. I expect her to provide comic commentary about the crowd, to make a joke of the gawkers, but she is solemn. I mouth the words, shu tayuu? *What's going on?*

"You know, I remember Rubina Master from my school days. She was one year ahead of me. And she attends the Bandra masjid. She seems like a nice person. I would imagine she thinks she is doing a service?"

"I guess." We watch as the two security guards try to shoo the noisy crowd away as though we are a few flies, instead of a swarm.

"Fatema thinks this will only embarrass her so that she will stop. She won't lose her licence. I hope that's true." She fiddles with her rida's hood tie.

Aleesha climbs the hospital's steps, and speaks into her megaphone. She's pulled a rida over her jeans and T-shirt.

"We are here today to expose Dr. Rubina Master, who performs khatna. What is khatna? It is a form of female genital cutting done by our Dawoodi Bohra community to girls at the tender age of seven. Khatna is gender violence and causes emotional, physical, sexual trauma. Khatna must end! Stop Rubina Master!" She exhorts the crowd to join her in a half-dozen rounds of "Khatna must end! Stop Rubina Master!"

"C'mon. Let's go!" Zainab yells into my ear.

"What? Where?" I yell back.

"Follow my lead." She pulls my arm, and I accompany her around the side of the building, and in the side doors. She pauses to consult the directory; gynecology is on the fourth floor.

"What are we doing?" I ask, but she shushes me and pulls me into the elevator. Inside, there are two other ridawalas, and I realize that we look like them; patients on our way to appointments. On the fourth floor, Zainab pauses, as though considering our next move, then takes me by the elbow down a long hallway.

"Zainab! What are you doing?" I ask, but she shakes her head.

"Shhh."

"I'm leaving." I turn to go.

"No, please, I need you! Just pretend you're here for an appointment," she whispers, glancing around fearfully. Again, no one looks at us askance, the ridas our camouflage. She shoots me a look of desperation. "Please, just come with me."

She takes my hand, and worried for her, I follow, her lady-in-waiting in this unfamiliar game of make-believe.

Ahead is a desk where a receptionist in an emerald rida types at a computer. Sitting beside her is our great-great-grandfather, who thumbs a rolodex. He looks up, nods in acknowledgment. I blink, and then he is gone, the index cards abandoned.

"Name, please?" the receptionist asks. Zainab offers her first and her maiden name and says she has an appointment with Dr. Master. The receptionist squints at her computer display, searching for the missing information, and Zainab says, "Sorry, must go to the bathroom." She grabs my hand and we flee down the hall, our ridas like wings flapping around us. I have no idea what we are doing, but I know I can't stop Zainab. And I can't leave her alone to do whatever unhinged thing she's about to do. Can I?

"You gave her your name?" I hiss-whisper.

"I know, it was stupid. I didn't know what to say. I didn't think of that when I was planning this."

"Planning what?"

She places her finger in front of her mouth to silence me and then gestures with her eyebrows to the door in front to us. Its nameplate reads RUBINA MASTER.

"Zainab! No!"

Zainab turns the knob and bursts in. A woman in a white coat, who is standing by a window, turns to look at us.

"Can I help you?"

"Don't you remember me? We went to St. Mary's together, Rubina. I'm Zainab. I was passing by with my cousin and I thought I'd come up and warn you about the protest downstairs."

"I can see it with my own two eyes." Rubina gestures to the window. "These people are such liars."

"Yes, it is so bad the way that women these days are taking up this cause. They are bringing shame to our community." My eyes bug out at Zainab. What is she saying?

"I know, it's just a small thing, and they are making it into a mountain."

"And why are they targeting you? I mean you do khatna under sterile conditions, not like the traditional way, no?"

"Yes, that's right. I wish everyone would come to doctors for it. It becomes a safe, medical procedure. Like with boys."

"Yes, that was what I was telling my cousin here. She's in town until next week with her seven-year-old daughter. Can you squeeze in an appointment for them?"

"Yes, just ask my receptionist out there." She scans the crowd outside. "The procedure is very quick. We can do it before you go."

My brain unscrambles and I ask, "Do you use an anaesthetic cream?" For some reason, I want to confirm Maasi's account of the procedure.

"You can get one if you want, but it's not required," she says distractedly. Perhaps Maasi's report was based on hearsay.

"Very modern, no? When we were kids, it was done in some aunty's flat." Zainab laughs, shakes her head.

Despite her pretend positivity, her words bring back that apartment, the waiting, the fear. I inhale, shake it away.

"We Bohras are very modern, not like they would have people believe." The doctor bites her lip, and continues to look down at the crowd.

"What are you going to do about them?" Zainab asks.

"Nothing. The security will clear them or they will tire themselves out." She sneers out the window. Why is she not afraid of the yelling below?

"It won't bring trouble to you?" Zainab asks.

"They have no proof. I will deny that we do it."

"You'll deny you do khatna?" Zainab repeats.

"Yes. We simply call it a checkup in our records. There is no record whatsoever."

"No record at all of the khatna?" Zainab confirms.

The doctor shakes her head.

"Smart," Zainab says, tapping her forehead.

The receptionist arrives, frowns at our presence, and says, "Doctor, there is a problem downstairs."

"Yes, I know, and these ladies were kind enough to come and tell me. Will you book this lady's daughter in for a checkup as soon as possible? She leaves next week."

"Yes, Doctor."

"Nice to see you again, Rubina. Keep up the good work and don't be bothered by those paagal women out there."

We follow the receptionist out, and once again, Abdoolally is at the desk. His moustache and beard curtsy as his face lifts into a wide grin. I press Zainab's arm, but by the time she turns, the apparition is gone.

"I thought you said you had an appointment?" the receptionist says.

"No, no. I said I needed to make an appointment. How's next Thursday?" When asked my daughter's name, Zainab offers a fake one, and then we head to the elevator, which, thankfully, is empty.

"Oh, Allah, I hope it turned out nice and clear." She pulls her cellphone from a plastic wallet held by a chain around her neck. "I just have to hit stop and save. There. I practised at home before."

"Omigod, why didn't you tell me?"

"Fatema said not to involve you, that all this was too much stress. But then how could I go alone? I was too scared. I was going to go with Nafeesa, but then you asked her to watch Zee."

"You should have explained on the way up!"

"I was all nerves!"

I shake my head at my cousin, but all the same, am elated by our undercover operation. I say a silent prayer for a clear recording.

The elevator doors open and a security guard ushers us out the same doors we came in.

"Ladies, be careful, there are goondas outside." We head out and Zainab and I break into a giggling fit.

We return to the shade of the tree. Zainab holds the phone up to her ear, listening. "It's clear! The recording is clear!"

There are four security guards at the front door now, and the protest wraps up, Aleesha signalling that it is time to go.

"Thank you all for having the courage to come today and speak your minds. This is only the beginning. I urge you to post photos on social media, with the hashtag 'khatnakhatma'!"

"Khatna khatma?" I ask Zainab.

"*Khatma* means ended, finished. Khatna is finished."

"Khatna khatma!" Aleesha yells and caught up in the moment, I clap along with the group's cheers. I think about how I once tut-tutted through the articles about FGM that came my way, assuming the stories were exceptional, not the norm. Not in our community, not in our family. Not me. I ignored what I wasn't able to see, the delusions keeping me safe but also stuck.

I whisper an apology to all the women whose stories I dismissed as not connected to me. I whisper an apology to all the seven-year-old girls who will not be protected from harm. I whisper an apology to myself for not knowing, for not remembering, for not believing.

I say a quick prayer for the souls of Zehra and Rumana. I thank Allah for Banu, who, all these generations later, has continued their legacy.

We parade to the coffee shop to regroup. Checking the time, I see that less than twenty-five minutes have passed since the protest started, yet it feels as though it lasted the whole day. I message Nafeesa and notice that Murtuza texted ten minutes earlier.

are you ok?

"I looked for you under the tree a couple of times, but didn't see you until the end," Murtuza says, his tone miffed, but I know he was worried.

"Yeah, where were you two?" Mom asks.

"Zainab, I think you'd better fill them in." I look to her.

Zainab describes our escapade while Mom and Murtuza listen, mouths agape. "I'm still shaking all over!"

"No way!" Murtuza wraps his arm around me. "You were a spy today!"

"So, how'd it go?" Fatema joins us, cellphone to her ear. Zainab begins her report, but Fatema interrupts her, "Sorry, ek minute. Varun? Yeah, we are finished. Pull up beside the

Café Coffee Day." She ends the call and looks at Zainab expectantly.

"It's all here," she says, passing the phone to Fatema.

"Arre waah!" she says, and types into Zainab's phone. "I'm sending the file to my email. Great job, Zainab!"

"It wasn't just me. We were a duo." She points at me.

"I wish I could have joined you two."

"Next time wear a rida, and you can go undercover with us," I joke, pulling mine off, revealing knee-length jean shorts and a T-shirt.

"Not on your life!" Fatema laughs.

Varun loads the placards into the car, and the group disperses. Nafeesa and Zee return. I wipe the sweat on her brow with my rida.

"Did you have a good time?" I ask her. She describes, in detail, the park they visited: swings, see-saws, slides. She isn't curious about the protest, as I expect her to be, but then sometimes her questions about serious things don't arise until days or even months later, after she's had time to think. For now, I'm satisfied that it's a playground on her mind.

Fatema pulls Zainab and me aside to introduce us to the reporter, Adnand. He's in his thirties, wears skinny jeans, and trails too much cologne.

"So this is the daring duo!" His smile is bright white, his handshake eager. He tells us that he'd like to post Zainab's recording's transcript and the audio clip on his paper's website.

"I need to listen to it before you take it," I reply, and he nods. "I barely remember what we said and I don't want to be identified in the recording."

"Yes, me, too." Zainab and I find a table on our own. We use Nafeesa's headphones, and we lean close, each holding a bud to an ear. Zainab mouths a silent "oh" as she listens. I gasp at the end, at the part when the doctor admits to keeping false records. The entire exchange takes less than three minutes.

"It's just the beginning, where she introduces herself, that you'll need to cut out," I tell Adnand.

"The rest is fine. Actually, it's great. We caught her!" Zainab adds.

"Of course, I won't identify you at all; we'd mute that interaction or just your names. You needn't worry." He bows his head slightly as he says this, and his smile is genuine.

"I appreciate that," I say.

"The same went for your email, as you requested. By the way, it should be online by now. I'll follow up with a report of the protest and your recording. It's a terrific story!" He bobs his head side to side.

"Show us," Zainab says, pointing at Adnand's tablet. He finds the article and then passes it to her. I read over her shoulder.

"Wait. You posted the whole email exchange!" My eyes scan what looks to be our entire thread. My name is gone, and so is Maasi's, except for in the last message. I pass the tablet to Fatema. "Oh my god! You left in Maasi's name! I thought … I thought you'd only report a summary of the email, to support the allegation that Rubina Master is a cutter! You weren't supposed to include the actual word-for-word conversation!" My voice is shrill rebuke. Then I realize: why did I think that? We hadn't actually specified it, did we?

"Oh," Fatema says.

"Let me look," Mom says, and Murtuza crowds around her.

"But I didn't agree to not include the email, I only asked my editors to remove all the names," Adnand says, taking back his tablet and scanning the page. "Oh, shit, my editor took out your aunt's name everywhere, but neglected to remove it at one place in the end. I'll deal with this." Shaking, he grabs his phone, steps away from the table, and makes a call.

"Fatema, you didn't tell me the email itself would be published." I look to her, but she is a deer caught in headlights. I feel misled, a fool.

"He's fixing it now, and it won't be in the paper until tomorrow," she sputters.

"How many people have already seen the online version?" I ask, not wanting to know the answer.

"Well, our social media person posted it a few minutes before the protest began," Fatema says, recovering her calm, "less than an hour ago." She checks the time, walks a few steps away to make a call.

"Why is everyone angry?" Zee asks, and then I realize, that for the last few minutes, I've forgotten to shield my daughter from all this.

"Oh, it's not a big deal," Murtuza says in a light voice. "The reporter made a small mistake, but we caught it and now it will be fixed. Let's go see what cold drinks they have. I'm thirsty." He takes Zee by the hand to the counter. Fatema returns to our table.

"She's pulling it from Facebook, Twitter, and our website. But it's gone out over WhatsApp, to all the Bohra groups." Fatema's face is flushed, perspiration beading her lip.

Zainab checks her WhatsApp account. "Oh, no. One person has shared screen shots with me already. That means Mom is going to know, eventually."

"Look, I'm sorry. I should have read it more carefully. There was just so much going on today, and I only skimmed the article," Fatema says.

"It's not your fault. It's his. That was incredibly unprofessional," Mom says, pointing to Adnand, who is still giving his instructions to someone over the phone.

"No, it *is* her fault. I didn't want this! I didn't want Maasi to know I was involved. She's always been like this. Rushing ahead and so focused on the big ideas, but forgets it's the tiny details that end up hurting people. She's a steamroller!" I don't know where these words come from, but they feel like they've been stored away for a long time.

"Honey, just calm down. It's no use blaming Fatema." Mom holds my wrist and whispers to me, like a mother embarrassed by her child's outburst at a birthday party.

"Worst-case scenario, the most orthodox people will know that Tasnim is in favour of khatna and tried to arrange it. She comes out as a saint to them, right?" Fatema attempts.

"And she finds out that I deceived her."

"Shari, she was going to find that out anyway. This story was going to get around, and she was going to figure out that something of your email exchange was shared, even if the full thing wasn't printed," Fatema says, her words a reasonable-sounding plea. I stare at her. Of course, she's right. I hadn't really thought about it. And I should have. All I'd been focused on was getting the name of the doctor.

"She is going to feel crushed." I can't help it, but tears escape.

"Why are you so concerned about her? She's the one who should be concerned about you! About all three of you!" Mom argues, pointing to me, Fatema, and Zainab.

I feel small, sick to my stomach. I sit down.

"Listen, Shari. The plan all along was to make you the innocent victim. Remember, you shared it with me and I went public with it?" Fatema attempts. "She'll never know your intent, your involvement, Shari. I promise you that. I'll take the fall."

"And me, too," Zainab says, "I'm going to say you sent it to me and I sent it to Fatema. I thought this whole email thing up, remember?"

Some part of me recalls that this was a logical plan, something I consented to, but now that it's all there in a newspaper article, it no longer makes sense. I feel violated. And then I think some people might put two and two together, know it was me who sent the email, and believe I truly wanted khatna for Zee.

"Okay, everyone," Adnand returns to our table, a nervous smile on his face. "The name has been removed. It's all corrected. We sincerely apologize for the error." When he looks around our little circle, he can tell from our faces that the problem is not fixed. I avoid his gaze, wipe away my tears, embarrassed.

"Listen, we can go to her place now and sort it," Zainab says, calmly, but her tight jaw reveals that she's nervous, too. I'll be leaving this city in a week, but Zainab will be left here to deal with her mother, with the community. I tell myself to pull myself together, to grow up.

"No. I've got to go talk to her. I need to do this on my own. I can't let you take the blame, Zainab." I ignore Fatema, and give instructions to Mom to tell Murtuza to go home, and I step out onto the street, signal for a taxi, and direct the driver to Maasi's flat. Mom stares at me, perhaps too caught up in her own emotions, to mount a credible protest.

The taxi lurches forward, only to stall in Mumbai's never-ending rush hour. My thoughts surge like the traffic pushing around us. I count my breaths, and try to focus amidst the chaos inside and around me.

I am protective of Maasi, yet was unprotected by her.

I brought her into this mess, yet she was the one who brought me into it, all three of us, all those years ago.

I feel at fault and yet she wronged me.

----------◆----------

"Ma'am? Ma'am?" The driver interrupts my thoughts. Incredibly, forty minutes have passed. "It's this place, correct?"

373

I look at where he is pointing. It's Maasi's building, her home since the beginning of my memory. How many times have I arrived here, stepping out of a taxi or rickshaw as a child, an adolescent, a grown woman? I collect my bag, bulging with my rida, and pay the driver.

I take the stairs, need to centre myself, move my muscles.

She greets me at the door, a surprised look on her face.

"I was just passing by." My voice trails off, my mouth dry. Her smile tells me she's pleased. She hasn't heard yet about the online piece, the protest.

"I was just going to have some chai," she says, ushering me in. She asks me a half-dozen questions about Zee, Murtuza, and Mom, which I mechanically answer. I follow her to the kitchen, and she sets two cups on a tray with a plate of butter cookies. I carry them to the living room.

I stir my tea, take a cautious sip. As always, Tasnim Maasi pours half of hers into her saucer and slurps it down. I study her papery, liver-spotted hands that remind me of her mother, my nani. And then Nani's kind presence fills the small flat. What would she think of all that has happened?

As I watch Maasi, I think, *It is going to happen today, this afternoon. Our lives are going to change irrevocably. I cannot stop this moving train.* I swat away these dramatic thoughts, remind myself to stick to facts, to describe things chronologically, to keep the explanations honest.

And yet I am afraid, the child in me whispering that I have done wrong, for I have not kept our secret. I've told my mother what happened. More than that, I've made the secret public. Maasi will see me as a betrayer.

The scalding teacup burns my palm like penance.

Before I stepped into the taxi, Fatema poked her head in and reminded me that what we are doing is good, important. That it's not about a personal grudge, but rather, it's for all of us, the non-specific but sprawling number of us, here and across the world. They were grandiose, Fatema's words, but that's Fatema. I met her gaze, nodded, just so she would go away.

Maasi appraises me. She lifts her right eyebrow and looks at my full cup of tea. I shake my head.

"Still too hot."

"You should do it like me." She playfully demonstrates, emptying the rest of her cup into her saucer, but I can't help but imagine she is speaking of bigger things. Why do I have to make an issue of a tiny cut? Things would be simpler, easier if only …

"Really, try it, haven't you ever had your tea this way?" She beams mischief. Of course I have, many, many times, always at her play-urging.

"All right." I tip my teacup to my saucer and chai dribbles onto her coffee table. I pat the spill with a tissue. "Sorry."

"Anything wrong, Sharifa? You are quiet today."

I look into her eyes. They are chestnut-brown and shinier than they used to be. These are my eyes, too, the eyes of my mother, of all my cousin-sisters, our daughters.

"Haa, Maasi. I'm sorry. I'm very sorry. There's something I need to tell you."

The doorbell tangs and the coward I am, I am relieved. I rush to the door. It's Jaya, her servant, returning from an errand, her arms too full to use her key. I let her in, and she drops her packages, and embraces me like an old friend. Jaya has been working for Maasi since she was a teenager, and I a girl. We've witnessed each other growing up. She is now in her early fifties, but still has the vibrant smile of an adolescent. She lets go, and somehow, her touch has left me taller, more solid. When she closes the door behind her, I go back to the living room, calmer.

"Maasi, why did you take me for khatna when my mother made you promise not to?" My voice sounds ordinary to me, unemotional, almost flat. Yet, my eyes are watery, threatening to overflow. I sit across from her.

She straightens her orna, which has slid to her shoulders, tucking it behind her ears. She, too, is calm, as though she has been expecting this question for decades. Her chest heaves as she takes in breath, and then she settles her gaze on me.

"Your mother was lukewarm, and your father was the one against it. She didn't want conflict with him, so I promised her I would not take you. Just like Murtuza, your father was."

"My mother was lukewarm?" She nods, looks down into her lap. The resemblance between her version and my recent, made-up one is uncanny. Did my mother need the lie of a husband's anger, too?

"I was planning to leave you behind that day, but your Nani pushed me so … strongly. She said that if we didn't do it, then we would be personally responsible for any troubles you had later."

The adults are speaking in hushed tones. And something doesn't feel right; Maasi — younger Maasi, a woman about my age — looks tense and wafts a piquant sweat.

I shake the image away, refocus on the present, realize that she is telling me the truth.

"I agreed with her, thought your mother's decision was short-sighted, that she had lost her way after moving to America, but I was torn … in the end I chose my mother's wisdom over my sister's request."

I can't look at her, so I stare down at my bare toes, the polish from last month's pedicure now chipped.

"I made sure your cut was very, very light — I arranged that in advance, without your nani's knowledge. I thought that would be a good compromise between what your mother wanted and what your nani wanted."

I listen and breathe, keeping my gaze on my feet.

"You see, it was only symbolic for you. It was so you'd be included in the community. If we hadn't taken you, you wouldn't be seen as a Dawoodi Bohra woman today. You wouldn't be naik. As we talked about for Zee."

My eyes travels to her toes now, stuffed into her house chappals. Her nails are milky, the skin at the bottom edges of her toes rough. Tough. A part of me knows I need to respond to her, but for now, I'm storing her words away. I will hold them inside, work them through, sort them.

compromise, very light, symbolic, included, naik

"Are you all right, Sharifa? Have you heard me?" I finally look up to see her pained expression, her wet eyes. She passes me a tissue, and I just then notice I've been crying. I wave her offering away.

"I'm sorry if I ... if I upset you." Her words yank at me, demand a reply. They sound too rehearsed. Has she been preparing for decades?

"You did do the wrong thing," I say, reacting to her "if." The couples' therapist Murtuza and I saw years ago harped at me about my "ifs" and "buts," telling me this was not a proper way to apologize, and I want a proper one now. Maasi's shoulders slump under my words, their weight too heavy for her frame.

"But ... but I thought you were in favour of it — for Zee — at least until you talked to Murtuza." She stares at me like she wants to say more but cannot find the words.

I plough ahead. "There's something you should know. I shared your email about the doctor with Fatema so that her group could take action against her. It was all a setup to get Rubina Master's name. At first, I went along with it half-heartedly. I didn't want to lie to you. But I suppose I made a *compromise* of sorts, too. Between wanting to support Fatema's cause, and wanting to keep you out of it. But somewhere along the way, it became my cause, too."

"The email?" She blinks, making sense of my words.

"That email was published online today and will be in tomorrow's paper." I tell her about the mistake in the online version, and its correction. "However, some people will already have seen it. I apologize *if* that causes you stress, but it was not my error. It was the newspaper's. Then —" I hold my hand up to stop her from interrupting.

"Then, today, there was a protest outside of the Shifa. And an audio recording of the doctor admitting that she does khatna was collected. It will be public now, all of this. Your words, her words. The paper will publish the transcript and post the audio file online."

"So you never really wanted khatna for Zee." She is still catching up to me. She blinks twice, looks to the ceiling.

"No."

"You were just trying to get the name of the doctor for Fatema?" She puts her hand over her heart. Closes her eyes. I snort; I have no time for her dramatic body language.

"Yes."

"And ... and what's this about my name in the newspaper?"

"Check WhatsApp." I don't have the energy to repeat myself.

She picks up her phone, opens the app, and she squints at it. "Read it for me, will you? This bloody screen is too small!"

I do as she asks. Someone has shared a screen shot of the article that contains our email exchange. It's the first version. I wince at my own words, glad my name is nowhere in the thread.

It takes her a minute to absorb everything and for her to turn scolding. "I really don't know why you'd participate in this nonsense, Sharifa. Why you'd think this is even a cause! Khatna is harmless. I did what was best for you."

I taste strawberry ice cream then, milky, creamy, sweet.

"Did we go for ice cream after the khatna?" The strawberry flavour grows stronger on my tongue.

"What?"

"After the khatna? Did you take us for ice cream?"

"Yes. To cheer you up. All three of you were upset, especially Fatema. We went to Kwality."

"What flavour did I have?"

"I'm not sure." She looks confused.

"Try to remember."

"I think your favourite was strawberry? Yes, that's right. You had one of those strawberry girl dolls, so you'd only have that flavour."

"I'm allergic to strawberries or, rather, I became allergic to strawberries after that." I swallow, and the fruit disappears from my mouth, replaced with something sour like vomit. "Mom always thought it was about the pesticides, because I used to love them when I was younger. Then they started to give me an upset stomach. After the khatna."

She's now scrutinizing me, as though I've said the sky is purple. "You've been brainwashed by Fatema. I wondered sometimes if maybe you'd have had an easier time of things if I'd allowed them to do a proper khatna. You might have taken more of a straight path, gotten married younger."

Her lips are downturned, her gaze disapproving. I open my mouth to speak, cannot. Is this what she thinks of me? What of all that non-judgmental special-aunty treatment she dolloped on me all those years? What of the loyalty, the secrets shared? I resist the urge to throw my now-cooled tea in her face. I pick up my purse, stand to go.

"Wait, Sharifa, wait." Her expression has neutralized, turns pleasant again, a mask slipping off, or perhaps slipping back on. I can't tell which is the true one.

"Please wait." It's a request, a plea now. Her entreaties follow me all the way to the door.

But I can't. I won't. I burst out of the flat, run down the stairs. Everything is different, everything changed. I speed-walk home.

∽ SIXTY C∼

Ahmedabad, 1922

"I still think it was petty and selfish for them to contest the will," Rumana grumped to her husband, Saifuddin. "They think they are entitled to have a say over his money when he clearly laid out everything in writing."

"It was your brother Husein who led the effort. I feel everyone else was not so sure about going to court." Saifuddin held Rumana's hand, sensing the sadness under her anger.

"Yes, it was Husein. Ever since Papa started favouring Gulamhussein — getting him into Cathedral and John Connon, then putting him in charge of India Stationery Mart — he's held a grudge." Rumana's eyes filled and she dabbed at them. Since Abdoolally's death, she was often close to tears. But why? She hardly saw the man as a child, and even less often as an adult.

"People expected your father to put his eldest son at the helm of his largest enterprise," Saifuddin remarked. "Husein must have felt overlooked, even if he wasn't the most qualified."

"It was simple jealousy. Well, now he has his bigger share of the pie through his inheritance."

"And you, too. "

"Yes, and I want to do something important with it, continue Papa's charitable legacy, since it was intended that way." She dried her eyes and bit her lip.

Later that evening, she mulled over the story Zehra had told her about their divorce. Each time she did, she remembered the two visits to the khatna lady. There had been a jovial mood the first time, when she'd gone with Zehra. The second, it was a stranger who had taken her. She hadn't been afraid until she felt the intense pain that sliced through her being. It might be all in her mind, but sometimes, if Saifuddin went too fast, that phantom pain returned, if only for a few minutes. It left her feeling violated, broken.

And now that her father was gone, she had a new thought: he was such a powerful man. What if he'd stood with his wife instead of against her? What if he and Zehra had remained married, their family intact?

Yes, she thought. *He'd made a mistake.* And she would find a way to correct it. She wouldn't allow her daughters or granddaughters to be broken by khatna.

∽ SIXTY-ONE ᶜ∽

In the dark, just before we fall asleep, I tell Murtuza, "Maasi wanted me to belong, didn't want me outside the bounds of the community. She felt my parents were straying."

Murtuza turns toward me, interrupts, "Why did you leave like that today? Why didn't you tell me you were going to talk to her? I would have come. I could have helped." I've heard this tone before — excluded, frustrated, cloying.

"Sorry." I explain that it wasn't planned, "It was like my legs were telling me to move, that it was time, and that I had to go. And I had to go alone."

He sighs, and I sense the mild movement of his pillow as he nods in weary understanding. Recovering, he returns to where I left off. "How do you feel about her intention, to help you belong, to be a good Dawoodi Bohra girl?"

"Well, that last part is bullshit. But the rest, well, I kind of like being part of the clan. I like knowing who I am, where I belong."

"I know." He kisses my cheek. "And I should be glad for it, too. It's what got me invited to your parents' place that night we met."

"Yes, a good Dawoodi Bohra girl was set up with a good Dawoodi Bohra boy." My tone is light, joking, my second attempt at apology. He rolls toward me, and I shift onto my left hip so that he can hold me.

I stay awake thinking about Maasi, questioning the authenticity of our connection. Was it real? Or was it a way to keep me close, keep me loyal, so that I'd never break my silence, disclose the khatna to my mother? A way to protect the secret? What she didn't realize was that I held no conscious memory of it, so her good-Maasi act, if it was one, wasn't necessary.

Or maybe it was the deal she made with herself after the khatna, when she reckoned with her conscience. She could permit herself to respect my mother's parenting and my individuality, suspend her judgments and morality, all hands-off precisely because she'd overstepped when I was seven.

Late into the night, I also think about Nani. Was she the real culprit, the one Maasi had to obey? Both she and Nana died when I was still a child. My memories of her are simply benign, as the hostess of our Secret Cousins' Society, a kind grandmother. Was she?

I suppose kind aunts and grandmothers can also cause harm.

We stay home the next day. Zee has a bout of diarrhea; she's been fine most of the trip, but this is the third time in the last few weeks. I have to wonder if she's picked up on the tensions roiling in my own belly.

While Zee naps, Murtuza reads the news articles out loud to Mom and me. Every major paper is running a photo of the protest.

You can see Murtuza's profile in one and the back of Mom's head in another. *The Post*, as Adnand promised, carries an edited version of the recording in their online edition and a transcription in the paper. The stories have also spread over social media, with people on both sides adding commentary. Zainab and I are either villains or heroes, as is Rubina Master. I'm relieved to be an anonymous actor in all this. I laugh at the insults directed at us: "they are not real Bohra women"; "heretics"; "should be better controlled by their husbands." These are too ridiculous to matter. What does impact me are the positive comments for Rubina: "I trust this doctor with my health and my children's health"; "Dr. Master delivered my three daughters, the last two were very high-risk pregnancies." I don't doubt these testimonials. Could she lose her licence to practise medicine? It's daunting to think that I may have helped ruin a doctor's career.

As though reading my thoughts, Murtuza mutters, "How could a 'good' doctor practise khatna? Isn't their edict to 'do no harm'?"

"Anybody can rationalize their actions." Mom shakes her head. "Tasnim felt it was right to follow our mother's beliefs rather than mine."

Mom is reflecting on what I shared with her when I returned home yesterday. "I can't believe she told you that I was on the fence about khatna. It's not true." She shakes her head and I think that perhaps it's partly true and she doesn't remember, or maybe it's not true at all and how Maasi remembers things. Memory and truth are not the same.

Zee stumbles into the living room, rubbing her eyes.

"How are you feeling?" I reach for her and she lands in my lap.

"Okay." She rests her head heavily against my chest.

"Your stomach?" Murtuza asks.

"I'm hungry."

"Give her some rice and a banana. Maybe some ginger ale," Mom counsels.

I nudge Zee to her feet and she takes my hand for the short walk to the kitchen; she's a big toddler when unwell. I half-peel a banana, pass it to her, and she chews lethargically. I pour her a glass of a red sports drink, stored in the fridge for just this circumstance. She gulps it down, and within minutes, she goes from sleepy to silly, bouncing from adult to adult, buoyed by electrolytes and sugar. Watching her, I realize that I, too, feel slightly better today. Even the little muscles around my eyes aren't so tired. I know nothing is resolved — how could it be so soon — yet I sense a shift, a micro movement. I tell Murtuza and Mom this.

"A cure by activism?" Murtuza asks.

"Or by confrontation? I'm proud of you for talking to Tasnim."

"Not a cure by any stretch. But it's like ripping off the Band-Aid. Not my usual way, that's for sure."

"You're more of a 'leave it alone, let it heal under there, then peel it slowly away once it's well scabbed over' type of woman." Murtuza laughs, enjoying his wordplay. I roll my eyes.

"True! So true, Murtuza!" Mom claps and Murtuza takes a bow. Zee watches the show, trying to comprehend.

"Zee, your nani and father are teasing me!" I explain to her. "About Band-Aids?"

I look to Murtuza for help.

"About being fiercely independent. Which is a great quality," he replies. "But sometimes it's nice to rely on others, too."

Zainab takes Zee, Mom, and me to a store called Global Desi, one last shopping trip before we fly out in three days.

"You'll like the styles, very modern," Zainab insists.

"So are the prices," Mom mutters. But Zee and I move from rack to rack, pointing out patterns and colours.

"We have to get something matching." At least once a month, Zee's reminded me of the promise I made before we left New York. This is the first store we've visited that sells similar designs for women and girls.

"I told you they'd have something for you both." Zainab shows Zee and me an orange kurta with a red flower print.

The clerk finds our sizes, and we emerge from the changing room to model them.

"You have another one in medium for me?" Mom asks.

"Yes! Everyone has to have one!" Zee insists, and then Zainab and Mom try on tunics. Before the mirrors, we resemble a folksy girl band. Mom pulls out her credit card, insisting that she wants to buy us all gifts.

"Could we pick up one more, in a large size?" Zainab asks the clerk, and then says to us, "For Fatema. I think she should have one too, no?"

"Yeah," I say. "I guess so."

I check my phone, and read the eight texts sent by Fatema, two a day since the demonstration, that I've ignored. I tap her a message.

can Zainab and I come to your office in twenty minutes?

Within ten seconds she replies.

Yes, great.

I ask Mom to take Zee home.

"I have a better idea. Let's go have ice cream, my Zee Nut!"

"I don't feel like it."

"What? When do you ever say no to mint chocolate chip?" Mom asks.

"Is your tummy upset again?" I stroke Zee's head.

"It's a little sore." She leans her head into my waist.

"Best to take her home, then," Mom says.

Zainab and I grab a taxi to the Bombay Press. During the ride, she chatters on about the ongoing news spreading over WhatsApp, and the angry phone messages she's received from Rubina Master who has accused her — both of us, though she doesn't know my name — of harassment.

"She can't do anything to us. She knows it. She was letting off steam."

"You're sure? We didn't do anything illegal?"

"Ya Allah! No way. She is the one who is doing wrong, and she knows it."

"And your business? What if people decide to shun you?"

"Nah, we only get the goras anyway. Tourists." She looks

confident but I know that things could get complicated for her, her husband, her daughters.

The cab drops us across from Fatema's building, and we traverse the busy intersection, me grabbing on to Zainab's sleeve. I consider what to say to Fatema, how I've been holding tight to a shard of resentment, one that makes no logical sense. At this point, it's only cutting into me, releasing nothing.

The doorman smiles, is expecting us, and directs us to the elevator. We ascend three storeys, and are greeted by Fatema's assistant, who escorts us into her office.

"Oh, I see you went to Global Desi." Fatema points to the plastic bag in my hand.

"Mom bought this for you. We all have matching ones." I pull the orange printed tunic out of the bag, present it to her.

"Lovely," she says, holding it before her.

"A team uniform seems the right thing after all of what we've been through together," Zainab says, creating a segue for me and for Fatema to start talking.

"Listen, I'm sorry I pushed too hard, talked you into something you weren't really prepared for. I've been thinking about this khatna stuff my whole damn adult life, you know? I forget that you haven't, that all of this has come to you as a shock. Even Zainab, who was aware, but —"

"— was in the dark," Zainab finishes Fatema's sentence, and I suspect they've already had this conversation.

"Yes, things have happened very quickly. We went to Dholka, you told me everything, then suddenly I was an email spy for your group."

"Yeah, and then a spy again with me at the doctor's office!" Zainab adds.

"It was very fast. All of it." Fatema nods. I meet her gaze, see the regret in it.

"And then I talked to Maasi." They wait, their eyes curious. I ask Zainab, "You haven't spoken to her yet?

"I've been avoiding her this last week. Been a terrible daughter. I made Nafeesa check in on her so I wouldn't have to."

"I've been avoiding her, too. She texted me twice asking me to visit before I go home. I don't think I can talk to her for a while. Definitely not before we leave. Maybe not even for a month or two ..." The idea is a heavy grey stone in my chest.

"But what did she tell you?" Zainab prods.

"So ... she said that it was Nani's idea, Nani's pressure, but that she agreed with it. She intentionally ignored Mom's request, and probably didn't bother getting your mother's permission," I say, looking at Fatema, "because she felt that it was in our best interests."

"She knew best," Fatema says, with a sarcastic edge.

"She was always so good to me. Now, I don't know who she is, who she was all those years." When I picture her face, the ugly, judgmental mask glimmers chimerically just below the accepting, comforting one.

"She does love you, and you really are her favourite," Zainab coos. "But she's very misinformed, very unquestioning, like I was."

"At least you're trying to stop it from happening to others," Fatema adds. "That's being accountable for your actions. I doubt your mother will ever be accountable to us."

"I didn't mean what I said, Fatema," I break in. "I don't blame you for what happened with the newspaper. I was overwhelmed by everything just then."

"Well, sometimes I do steamroll," she admits sheepishly.

Zainab laughs. "Friends again?"

"The SCC again. We'll never stop being that."

In the silence that follows, I remember something. "Hey, I've been meaning to tell you both, I found out why Abdoolally and Zehra divorced!"

As I give them the rundown — keeping my promise to Banu to only reveal the part I'm allowed — their eyes bulge and mouths gape.

"The divorce was because of khatna?" Fatema asks. "Abdoolally was pro-khatna?"

"Well, it was because they weren't happy together. But then on top of it Zehra caused a minor religious scandal. A public embarrassment."

"So Rumana also didn't allow it for her descendants?" Zainab clarifies.

"Yes. The practice ended in that line. The cycle ended there."

———————◆———————

Before we leave, I visit Abbas Kaaka. I bring along my laptop, and show him the draft blog I've created, and we sit side by side, reading.

"Anything to correct?"

"Not yet. This is so interesting, so good," he says, adjusting his glasses and leaning in. He scrolls down to the part about Abdoolally and Zehra's divorce.

"I collected that from Shaheeda's great-granddaughter, Banu Aunty." I relate the story of how I met her.

"Are you sure this is true? About her religious disobedience? It's quite the story. And it reveals much about Abdoolally's beliefs."

"It's the story that was passed down from Zehra to Rumana. And Banu heard it directly from Rumana, who was her daadi," I assert. "So I suspect it is accurate."

"I saw the write-up in *The Post* a few days ago about the protest at Shifa Hospital."

"What did you think?"

"You know, I hadn't really thought about the issue until I read the paper, saw all the arguments against it. It seems like a practice that is unnecessary, outdated. Like iddat. I wish our community would modernize."

I sigh, and tears well up.

"What's wrong?"

"Well … I recently learned that it was Tasnim Maasi who took me and my cousins to have it done. She is … was … my favourite aunt. It's caused a rift between us."

"Give it some time. Like Abdoolally, she was obeying the rules of the day. Now we know better. Now we can change things." He pats my hand. His advice is both true and too simple.

The bags are packed, and we wait in Fortune Enclave's lobby at 5:00 a.m. for Varun to arrive. A van, not his usual vehicle, pulls into the circular driveway. He rushes out to help with our luggage and Fatema and Zainab poke their heads out the windows, surprising us.

"Hey, look!" Murtuza points at them.

We said our goodbyes last night at Zainab's place, and I thought that was the last we'd see of them, at least for a few years. Too long. I'm relieved that they are here now.

Once on the road, Fatema asks Zee, "So, what did you think of this trip?"

"Good, a little long." Zee is still not quite awake.

"Short vacations from now on?" I ask her, but she doesn't reply. She is limp against my side, asleep again.

While the others talk about the highlights of our India stay, I think about how I'd imagined these eight months would be. I only had the tiniest tip of Abdoolally's iceberg before and now

I've probably dived a foot or two below the surface. In contrast, I've plumbed the depths of my own life story.

I wonder what the year ahead will bring. I asked Murtuza to contact our previous couples' therapist for an appointment to help us navigate our sex life. Perhaps I will ask for some individual sessions as well. I will hate it the whole time. But maybe this is what it means to be in a marriage.

I still haven't returned any of Maasi's calls. That will have to wait.

Within a week of being back in Queens, Zee is at school and I've had my first work meeting with Lenore, reviewing her draft questionnaire for home-schooling parents.

I also allow the Abdoolally blog to go live, finally setting it free. I worry what the family will think, if they will have criticisms of my work, for in the end, I've brought more of myself into the story than I'd first intended.

Here is the introduction:

> This blog is about my great-great-grandfather. It is the summation of eight months of research, but I can't help think it is a terribly incomplete account of his life, for we know so little about him and the people who came before: what of his grandmother, his great-great-grandmother? I imagine counting back and back and back. Who were all these ancestors, what were their

stories? Did they live, as I imagine, in more or less the same fashion for generations, all of them in Dholka, villagers expecting predictable lives to unfold in pretty much the same way as their forefathers and mothers?

It was Abdoolally, my great-great-grand-father, who changed everything, or rather, his mother Amtabai, a widow whose story we know even less about, who grew annoyed with village life and the lack of opportunity there. She is the great woman of this story, is she not?

So it was the two of them who took the first steps into the unknown, to venture into the noise and stink and strange ways of the city. They were the first to disperse us, to be the wind that sent seeds floating south across India, and then westward and eastward across oceans. Others followed their path, but it was Abdoolally who had the foresight to learn the colonizer's language, to build businesses, purchase land, to amass wealth that built schools and clinics, wealth that has trickled down and down and down.

We don't know much about his relationships. He married four times. His first two wives, Sharifa and Shaheeda, died in childbirth. He and his third wife, Zehra, divorced. The fourth, Maimuna, outlived him. See the "family" tab for more information. I wish I knew more about each of them.

Abdoolally's wealth and legacy ensured that women, like his first two wives, wouldn't die so frequently in childbirth and that village children, like the boy he once was, would receive education. It also meant that a clergy, who'd lived simply, offering spiritual advice to its followers, would become empowered to operate like a business. Today they are a kind of multinational enterprise, and seek to control nearly every aspect of their congregants' lives in order to maintain power. Yes, Abdoolally was part of that shift, the great man, unwittingly perhaps, helping to move them away from their original and divinely planned spiritual paths.

And he wouldn't have been alone. Other rich men, some devout, and those making donations to stay in their religious leaders' favour, would have lined the clergy's paths with gold coin. Too many. Too many still do.

My research also led me to an unexpected revelation about the family and broader community: the problematic practice of khatna, which this clergy actively promotes. In doing so, it has caused harm to so many of our naik women, to us. Yes, me included.

But there were women in the family who resisted khatna for their girls, including Zehra, who tried to spare Rumana, her stepdaughter (Shaheeda's daughter), and it's believed that this resistance was part of why their marriage ended. Rumana carried forward Zehra's protest and refused khatna for her daughters and granddaughters.

I've learned more about the movement of strong Bohra women who are speaking out against this practice, quietly and loudly, who are labelling it what it is: sexual violence. They are the new heroes, or heroines, of this story.

If Abdoolally's story has taught me anything, it's that we each have the power to be a part of our community's legacy. We have the power to leave archaic practices behind, create new wealth for our women. We can protect future generations of daughters, not allow them to be broken by violence.

I think Abdoolally, if he were with us here today, five generations later, would be pleased.

~Ɔ EPILOGUE Cᴖ

FGM Symposium. April 2026. New York City

The auditorium dims, and the audience stills. The moderator welcomes the crowd and introduces me as the first speaker. *God, why did she have to put me first?* I take a sip of water, clear my throat, and click on a slide that shows a compilation of news headlines from 2016 to 2025.

"Much has changed in the last decade. As you can see, khatna was made illegal in India. There have been dozens of court cases — starting in Australia, then Detroit, and later all across the U.S., Canada, Europe, India — cutters and parents prosecuted. There are now hotlines for victims, specialized therapies for survivors."

I run my thumb down the cool glass of my tablet's screen, and provide the audience with background information and statistics about Bohras and khatna's emotional, physical, and sexual impacts. The energy downgrades in the room. I move on to the next slide, a photo of our high priest posed with a dead lion five times his size. I hear a couple of gasps. Good, I have their attention again.

"Anecdotal evidence suggests that khatna is still being secretly practised amongst those who are most closely aligned with the apex leader of the Bohras. Thankfully, he has fewer acolytes now as more Bohras have shrugged off his control and have formed more democratic communities, including a large alternative masjid here in New York City. There is even talk that the Indian government might seize his funds and properties and redistribute them to these new configurations. Fun fact about this photo: it circulated on WhatsApp and Facebook in 2018 and people say it was a catalyst for change." Finger snaps popcorn through the auditorium as audience members show their support.

I click on the next slide, a photo of me with my mom, her cousins, and my nani, all of us wearing identical orange-and-red tunics. There is a collective "Awww." I feel a sudden light-headedness. I exhale. Time to get personal.

"So, that's me, at seven years old, in India with my family. I'd like to tell you a little about my personal connection to khatna. Like every other khatna story you'll hear, it's about secrets, lies, and shame." This last sentence sounded better when I rehearsed in front of my full-length bedroom mirror. Now it seems cheesy.

I click on a photo of Mom and Dad, smiling for the camera. Dad's holding a placard that reads FGM IS GENDER VIOLENCE!

"My parents were dead-set against the practice, and even attended a rally, the first of its kind in India, while we were there in 2016. Oh, I should give credit to my mom, who provided me with all these old photos." My gaze slides to the left of the auditorium, where my parents and Nani sit. I told myself I wouldn't look their way until the end of the speech.

"One day, I was supposed to be babysat by an older cousin, but I ended up with my grand-aunt, for an hour or so. Now, Maasi was fully aware of my parents' views about khatna." The audience is quiet, as though holding its breath.

"Maasi told me we were going to the market and then we'd go and get ice cream. I remember feeling excited about that." I pause, take another sip of water, the reel playing in my mind: we were supposed to buy vegetables, but we didn't. I remember thinking that the aborted errand was somehow my fault.

"She seemed to be in a rush, and while we were walking, I tripped and skinned my knee." She scolded me for being clumsy, and her unexpected harshness shocked me. Perhaps she saw it in my expression because she softened then.

"She said, 'Don't worry, I know a nurse who lives close by, and I'll phone her and she can take care of your knee.' Soon after, we arrived at this so-called nurse's place."

A century of dust coated the foyer. The lift was that old-timey kind, with a criss-crossing metal grate that protested with a creak and a sigh when Maasi pulled it closed. I liked watching the cement underside of each floor pass as we ascended.

"An older woman answered the door, and Maasi whispered something to her in Gujarati that I couldn't understand."

The air was stuffy with kerosene. I take a breath and continue.

"I was told to lie down. Maasi said, 'We'll clean your knee and put on a bandage.' Then she told me to pull off my shorts so she could check that there weren't any other injuries. I resisted that, told her it was only my knee, but she shushed me. I didn't stop her when she pulled down both my shorts and underwear. A part of me wondered if she knew better, and so I complied."

Later, I'd blame myself for letting her remove my clothing. Mom told me to never let anyone touch me down there.

"Remember, this was a decade ago; I was only seven." An old man in the front row nods earnestly at me. He resembles one of my great-uncles with his long white beard and topi.

"She said the antiseptic might sting for a second, and told me to look out the window so that it would hurt less. I did, and so I didn't see what actually happened."

The sky was smoggy grey. My knee sizzled. At the same time, I felt sharp fingers and a much stronger, searing pain.

"I believe Maasi tended my knee while the other woman cut my clitoral hood, and while I felt pain in both places, I was confused about what was hurting where. And why." My knee and vulva prickle for a second and I shift from one leg to the other. The old woman's fingers were thick at the joints, her nails stained turmeric-yellow.

"Maasi said, 'Look, you are fine now, nothing happened.' The nurse applied a cream and then they dressed me again. Maasi said, 'You'll feel better in a minute and forget all about this.' I wanted to believe her, and so I did. At least for a while.

"All the way to the ice cream shop, Maasi instructed me to never tell my parents about visiting the nurse, that it was our secret. I thought that I was in trouble for something I couldn't name.

"The pain subsided. When we returned to her place, I must have been in shock. I didn't argue when she undressed me, washed my underwear, and then put them back on me, damp."

She told me, "Chee chee, you've dirtied your panties. But that's good, the bleeding stopped." I was supposed to read out this last line, but something about it feels too crude to say aloud to a roomful of strangers.

"And so, in that child's haze of confusion caused by the manipulation of a trusted elder, I kept the secret. It wasn't until a couple of weeks later, when we were back in New York, and looking at our digital photo album, that I asked about the protest and what it was all about." I turn to look up at the projected image of my parents at the rally.

"And that was when I told them what happened. When I was a bit older, Mom and Nani shared their khatna stories with me and I've come to see this as a weird sort of bond we share. A trauma bond, but also now an activism bond." I lock eyes with Mom, but then look down at my page.

"My parents and nani didn't have much to do with Maasi after I told them what happened. She died a few years ago. I don't know how I feel about her, still."

Nani dabs her eyes with a tissue.

"I'm not really sure what the full impact of khatna has been or will be on my life, but I'm glad I can speak to you about it today. I'll end there, because my time is up, but I'm happy to speak more during the Q and A."

The room explodes into applause. Mom, Dad, and Nani rise to their feet.

～ ACKNOWLEDGEMENTS ～

I am grateful to everyone who guided me and offered encouragement along the way:

Alifyah Taqui, Masooma Ranalvi, Zehra Patwa, Nilufer Barucha, Gulu Rangwala, Rashida Tewarson, Savitri Dindial, Sarah Shulman, and Rashi Kilnani for double-checking details or answering questions about very obscure things.

Rachel Letofsky, my agent, for having my back. Also, the entire CookeMcDermid team for your behind-the-scenes work.

Shannon Whibbs, my editor, who suggested new directions, caught mistakes, and who'll find a grammatical error in this sentence.

Vivek Shraya, for being an early draft reader, friend, and social media guru.

Scott Fraser, Elena Radic, Kathryn Lane, Stephanie Ellis, Laura Boyle, Sophie Paas-Lang, Barbara Bower, freelancer Crissy Calhoun, and all the other Dundurnites who welcomed this book and worked to make it a success.

The Ontario Arts Council and Toronto Arts Council for letting me take time off from my other paid work to write, stare at the wall, and go to Dholka.

Jonah Blank for *Mullahs on the Mainframe* and Priya Goswami for *A Pinch of Skin*, both of which are referenced in this book.

All my WeSpeakOut and Sahiyo comrades who are working to end khatna. We are part of a larger tsunami of feminists working to end gender-based violence across the globe. Readers who would like to learn more can check out WeSpeakOut.org and Sahiyo.com.

I offer this novel as a contribution to this important work.

My father, Shamoon Doctor, who urged me to look back. While this is a work of fiction, pieces of Abdoolally's story were inspired by own great-great-grandfather, Hussonally Dholkawala. Thanks also to the many family members who offered memories and information about him. Special thanks to Maimoona Bengali for filling in details. For those curious about the real man, check out hussonally.wordpress.com.

Silvana Bazet, Fariya Doctor, Chloe Montclaire, and Maggie, who listened so well.

Reyan Naim, who held my heart (who always holds my heart) while I untangled the personal and literary strands of this story.